Legion

Legion

The Destroyer of Souls

Phil Nix

authorHOUSE®

AuthorHouse™
1663 Liberty Drive
Bloomington, IN 47403
www.authorhouse.com
Phone: 833-262-8899

Published by AuthorHouse 03/01/2024

ISBN: 979-8-8230-2114-2 (sc)
ISBN: 979-8-8230-2115-9 (hc)
ISBN: 979-8-8230-2113-5 (e)

Library of Congress Control Number: 2024901859

Print information available on the last page.

Any people depicted in stock imagery provided by Getty Images are models, and such images are being used for illustrative purposes only.
Certain stock imagery © Getty Images.

This book is printed on acid-free paper.

Cover credit
Amy Nix

CONTENTS

Introduction

I first saw the three hills of Con Thien in the summer of 1967 while stationed at the marine base at Dong Ha, Vietnam. At the time, I was an artillery surveyor for the US Army's 8th Battalion, 4th Field Artillery. Our large 175-millimeter guns supported the 3rd Marine Division around the DMZ (demilitarized zone). This book retells a heroic battle that occurred there on May 8, 1967. While the setting and storyline were developed around historical military records, the human characters are fictional. The spiritual battle depicted within is one we all deal with daily.

The military personnel who fought and died there knew Con Thien as the Hill of Angels, or simply, the Hill. The marines had another more fitting name for it—the Meat Grinder. The Americans wanted the Hill for an observation post. Charlie (the enemy) couldn't hold the Hill, but he made sure the Americans paid a heavy price to stay there.

Life magazine wrote extensively about the Vietnam War. On the cover of its October 27, 1967, magazine is the face of a battle-hardened marine, hunkered down in a trench, nervously wondering where the next incoming round will land. The caption read, "Inside the cone of fire at Con Thien." The magazine presented eighteen pages of graphic images of daily life on the

Hill. The photographer was so moved by what he witnessed there that he likened the Hill to a "graveyard."

The May 8 attack on Con Thien by the North Vietnamese Army (NVA) was intended to set the wheels in motion to end America's involvement in Southeast Asia. The primary strategist of that battle was one of the greatest generals of the twentieth century, Vo Nguyen Giap. Had it not been for several last-minute developments and the heroics of the 4th Marine Regiment, the casualties inflicted during the Battle of Con Thien would have been much greater.

After the battle, the marines counted 197 dead enemy soldiers inside the wire. Hundreds of additional dead and wounded were removed from the Hill by the withdrawing NVA forces. Although Giap lost the Battle of Con Thien, he would plan and execute a much-larger operation eight months later: the 1968 Tet Offensive. It also failed but succeeded in changing America's opinion of the war. After twenty years of conflict and the loss of over 3 million lives, the Vietnam conflict finally ended in 1975.

Mike Shaffer fought and won two heroic battles on the night of May 8. One was against the NVA, the other against Legion. One battle won Mike the Bronze Star and a third Purple Heart. The other was the blessing of being a man after God's own heart.

After returning home from the war, Mike married his high school sweetheart and had two children, secure in God's promise to protect his family from Legion's vengeance. For the next twenty-five years, Mike enjoyed a happy life. Yet always lurking in his mind, Mike knew Legion was never far away, patiently watching and waiting for him to die. When that day came, Legion unleashed his fury upon Mike's unsaved son, Tim.

There is a cast of characters list at the end of the book.

Part 1

Mike Shaffer Battles Legion on the Hill of Angels

I want to dedicate part 1 of this book to my friend, Sgt. Arkie J. Wright, who died defending our freedoms on March 19, 1968. Like so many others, his sacrifice should never be forgotten or taken for granted. Thank a vet today. They earned it.

I want to thank my wife, Kathleen, for all her help in editing this book.

Thanks to Ann Volz for her comments and suggestions.

Thank you to my good friend, Scott Cowell. He made the final edits that brought this novel into focus.

A special thank-you to my sister-in-law, Col. Marcia Rossie (US Air Force, retired), for her suggestions in outlining my characters in this book.

Chapter 1

The Snipers

In 1967, the United States was heavily involved in defending the South Vietnamese from the Communists. To counter Charlie's aggression—the North Vietnamese Army (NVA) from the north and the Vietcong (VC) in the south—the US Marine Corps intensified its efforts to recruit snipers. Candidates needed to be returning Vietnam veterans who agreed to attend a five-week scout sniper school at Camp Pendleton, California. Graduates would receive a one–pay grade promotion and a two-week leave before returning to Vietnam for another tour of duty.

Two volunteers were buddies from Conway, North Carolina, Bernie Westgate and Joe Diamond. Upon graduation, they received orders to report to the 9th Marine Regiment operating out of Dong Ha, ten miles south of the river that separated the two Vietnams.

After their much-deserved leave, Sergeant Westgate and Corporal Diamond returned to Camp Pendleton to check out their equipment. Per marine regulations, Bernie and Joe would function as a two-person sniper team. Bernie would be the designated sniper, and Joe would be the backup sniper and security team leader.

The Remington M40, fitted with a Redfield 3X-9X scope, was the sniper rifle they would carry into combat. With an effective range of over eight hundred yards, its accuracy was an improvement over previous models. The security weapon assigned to the team was the old dependable M14 with a second-generation starlight nightscope.

Their flight to Da Nang was scheduled to leave the following morning. So Bernie and Joe decided to take the base shuttle to the range to calibrate their weapons. From the dining hall, they walked over to the rifle range. The firing field was quiet and deserted.

Descending the wooden steps down onto the line, Bernie led the way over to the fourth lane. A wind sock was mounted on a tall pole at the top of the stairs. From its shape and angle, Bernie estimated the wind was out of the southeast at fifteen miles an hour.

Bernie lay prone on the ground, sighting through his rifle scope. Joe sat cross-legged beside him, looking through his spotter scope, setting up their next shot. As they refined their new skills, both marines prepared themselves for thirteen more months in hell.

"Next target," Joe commanded. "Stake with a red flag, twenty-five yards right of your last target. Seven hundred eighty yards. Windspeed fifteen, right to left. Call your shot."

"Target acquired." After a few seconds of rifle and scope adjustments, Bernie asked, "Why are we doing this again, Joe?"

"I don't know, Bernie. Re-upping was your idea. I only went along to keep you out of trouble."

"My idea? You were the one who said, 'Think of how cool we will look with that new stripe.'"

"No, you're not blaming me for this one, Bernie. I remember you saying another tour would add to our college fund."

"Promotion. College fund. What kind of idiots would agree to do this again?"

"We're not idiots, Bernie. We're marines. Now shut up and take the shot."

"Center of knothole below the flag." To counter the previous distractions, Bernie lifted his rifle above the target and leisurely lowered it until the scope crosshairs were centered on the target. Beginning with his body posture, Bernie thought through his checkpoints and reached his comfort zone. He slowly squeezed off his shot and then quickly chambered another round and waited for Joe's report.

"Nice shot, Bernie. Now if you don't mind, it's my turn."

As Bernie stood to hand Joe the rifle, he noticed a captain giving instructions to a lieutenant a short distance away. The two officers acknowledged Bernie's shot with nods and continued their conversation.

A restlessness overcame Bernie as he studied the captain, almost like they had met before. As Bernie searched his memory for clues, he was shaken by a graphic mental picture of his dad lying in a coffin when he was fourteen. Then he had a second vision of his high school car wreck that almost killed him. Then a third image came to mind, of Steve Harper bleeding to death after stepping on a mine during his first tour of duty. Bernie's brain continued to conjure up tragic images of his past, all of which dealt with life and death.

After the events of his personal life were exhausted, a rapid succession of people of peace came to mind: Kennedy, King, Lincoln, and Gandhi. They were followed by images of people of war: Hitler, Stalin, and Tojo. It was like watching an old trailer at the movies. When those depictions were exhausted, Bernie heard a mental voice say, *Life is too short, Bernie. Do what makes you happy.*

Although he could not place the face, Bernie knew the voice. It was the one he heard when critical moral decisions needed to be made. While Bernie never had much time for religion, he knew the difference between right and wrong. However, he didn't understand why he felt remorse after certain bad decisions.

Although the captain's conversation with his subordinate went uninterrupted, Bernie was sure the captain was telepathically communicating with him. *Who is that guy?*

Reading his thoughts, both officers turned toward Bernie, and Legion responded mentally, *I'm your conscience, Bernie. The one you hang with when you want to have fun. Not that other voice that tells you to be good all the time.*

Returning to his discussion with his lieutenant, Legion gave Bernie a suggestion, leaving him with no memory of their brief encounter.

Joe noticed the worried look on Bernie's face and turned to see what he was staring at. After a thorough scan of the range and seeing nothing, he turned back and said, "Bernie." With no response, he poked him and repeated more firmly, *"Bernie."*

Troubled by the sudden rush of anxiety, Bernie looked up and gave Joe a soft, animated "What?"

"The range closes in an hour. Do you mind if I take my turn now?"

"Oh. No. You're right." Bernie cleared the weapon and handed it to Joe. Then confusion set in. He was sure something had just happened but couldn't remember what. Maybe something he had forgotten. Frantically, Bernie searched the events of the last half hour. After another few moments of fevered thought, he reluctantly dismissed it as nerves.

Hearing a voice, he and Joe turned and saw two marine officers walking up the range steps.

"Now where did those guys come from, Bernie?"

"I don't know, but I wouldn't waste the next hour worrying about it."

Eager to resume their target practice, the two snipers got down into their firing positions. As Bernie began searching for Joe's first target, he couldn't help but wonder what the officers were doing out here and how they managed to sneak up on him.

When they reached their Jeep, the two officers turned back toward the range. "I want you on a plane to Da Nang in the morning," Legion instructed Eliphaz. "Your new host is Lt. Jon Sackett. You can pick him up at the terminal before the flight. His orders will take you to Dong Ha. Hook up with Bildad and Zophar there and get to Con Thien. The Creator has given us permission to test Mike Shaffer's faith. The Boss wants us to find his greatest weakness and use it to destroy his confidence."

Legion continued. "That sergeant down there is Bernie Westgate. He'll be on the plane with you. He's starting to question his morality. Keep a close eye on him, but stay focused on your mission. Do not draw any unnecessary attention to yourself. Understand?"

Eliphaz had heard Legion's speech a thousand times before. He knew better than to question his orders, so he nodded his agreement.

Legion was the dominant personality of many other spirits who walked the earth, deceiving the weak and inciting fear and disharmony within the church. The strongest of Satan's horde of demons, Legion has the power to possess anything flesh and blood that does not belong to God. Dispatching Eliphaz and his other troops at will, Legion's sole purpose was to disrupt the movement of the Holy Spirit in the world.

As he and Joe policed their brass, Bernie spotted the officers standing beside their Jeep, silently looking down at them. Their icy stare gave him the creeps. With a smile, Legion blanked out all remembrance of their existence. Then suddenly, he, Eliphaz, and the Jeep vanished.

Chapter 2

The Flight to Da Nang

The following day, Bernie and Joe boarded their large C-141 aircraft and officially began their second tour of duty. Onboard were forty officers and noncommissioned officers (NCOs). Most of the other passengers were marine privates right out of combat training. They were all hyped up and full of piss and vinegar, eager to start kicking Charlie's butt.

The atmosphere on the plane resembled more of a high school football locker room than a plane full of grown men going out to meet the enemy on the battlefield. With one hundred twenty excited marines trying to talk above the air conditioner ducts and everyone else, the decibel level in the plane was holding steady at ninety. You could have driven a motorcycle through the aircraft, and no one would have heard it. The more the marines considered the perils they would soon face, the more their nervousness increased.

Bernie looked around the plane and said to Joe, "Thirty days from now, most of these teenagers will be ready to go back home."

"They'll be OK, Bernie, but they'd better drop the attitude and get their heads screwed on straight, or half of them will go home in body bags."

"I've been thinking, Joe. Shooting targets is one thing. How do you feel about killing someone in cold blood?"

"I don't have a problem killing someone who's trying to kill us. Remember how Simms, Larson, and Sanchez died? For me, this is my chance for a little payback. It's a little late for you to question your new job description, don't you think? You're not having second thoughts about killing the enemy, are you?"

"Not really, I guess," Bernie replied halfheartedly. "I'm sure I won't have trouble pulling the trigger when the opportunity presents itself. I don't know how I'll feel about it afterward."

Echoing Bernie's concerns, Joe replied, "Well, we'll both find that out soon enough."

Bernie noticed a young sandy-haired private whose hillbilly voice carried above all the others. Bernie thought about the dangers he would face in combat and felt responsible for his safety. Saving a few like him led him to become a sniper. Reminded again of his purpose, Bernie convinced himself he could live with his conscience—at least he hoped so.

Bernie reached into his carry-on bag and pulled out his cassette player and headphones. Searching his small travel case, he chose a Mamas and Papas tape and with anticipation, inserted it into the player. He then got ready to kick back and relax. Looking over, he noticed Joe was already immersed in a paperback.

"What're you reading there, Joe?"

"It's a story about Audie Murphy called *To Hell and Back*," Joe said as he turned it over to show Bernie the cover.

"Yeah, I saw the movie. Is the book any good?"

"Murphy was the most-decorated soldier of World War II. He won the Medal of Honor, two Silver Stars, the DSC, the Legion of Merit, and three Purple Hearts. Yeah, the book is great."

Always looking for an opportunity to ruffle Joe's feathers, Bernie added, "Well, nobody was better than John Wayne. Certainly not GI Joe," Bernie said with a straight face.

"What are you talking about?" Joe asked, trying his best not to laugh.

"John Wayne was the greatest marine of World War II. Everybody knows that."

Not knowing how to take Bernie's stupid comment, Joe gave him a prolonged stare and started thinking about how he would call him a dumbass. "Bernie, you don't know jack. John Wayne was not a marine."

"What about *Sands of Iwo Jima*?"

"That was a movie, moron," Joe chided. "John Wayne never served a day in the service. You would know that if you read more books and spent less time watching TV."

"All I'm saying—" Bernie started, but Joe cut him off with a raised hand and I-don't-want-to-hear-it frown.

Satisfied he had pulled Joe's chain enough, Bernie added, "Well, at least don't go getting any ideas about taking on the NVA all by yourself."

"No problem there, Bernie. I intend to survive this tour and return home to the safety of Mom's kitchen. Did I ever tell you she makes the best fried chicken in the world?"

"Yeah, Joe, you did. That's what she served the last time I was at your house. Which, as I recall, was last Thursday night."

Both marines gave each other an insecure grin, trying to convince themselves they did the right thing by agreeing to return to the killing fields of Southeast Asia. Then dismissing the thought, they decided to kick back and relax.

No sooner had Bernie started his player than someone tapped him on the shoulder. Annoyed, Bernie pushed the Stop button and lowered his headphones onto his neck. Leaning on the seat in front of him was a lieutenant. His name badge read Sackett. When they made eye contact, Bernie felt something unsettling about him.

"Can I help you, sir?"

"Where're you heading, Sergeant?"

"Up to Dong Ha to join the 9th Marines."

"Isn't that a coincidence? I'm heading up there myself to join the 26th Marines. Dong Ha is a big place, but maybe we'll see each other again." An odd glimmer in his eye caught Bernie's attention. "This is not your first tour, is it, Sergeant?"

Confused and apprehensive, Bernie replied, "No, I was with the 3rd Marines on my first tour." Then reluctantly, he asked, "Do I know you, sir?"

"We've crossed paths several times before, Sergeant, but I doubt you'd remember me." Sackett ended his sentence with a smirk.

Bernie thought about where he might have met Sackett before but was sure he did not want to know. "How did you know I'd been to Vietnam before, sir?"

"Marine regulations, Sergeant."

"Say again, sir."

"Marine snipers can only be Vietnam veterans. You're a sniper, aren't you, Bernie?"

Suddenly, the hair on his neck stood up like the bristles on a brush. Then desperate for an explanation, he turned to Joe for support, only to find him reading his book, unaware of Sackett's presence.

Bernie caught a strong whiff of sulfur. Turning back to Sackett, he was confronted by a shadowy demonic stare. Sackett gave him a faint smile and a wink. Bernie's eyes grew weary, and he nodded off to sleep.

Sackett reached over and pushed the Play button on Bernie's player. "Sweet dreams, Sergeant. You won't remember this conversation, but we'll see you again."

When Bernie awoke, the mood on the airplane had changed entirely. The confidence these young recruits once had was gone, and the uncertainty of tomorrow had set in.

For many of these raw recruits, this was their first time away from home. For most, it was their first time on an airplane. This tour would be the newbies' biggest adventure, and you could see the uneasiness in their eyes. However, they were marines, and when the time came, they would kill without hesitation and with extreme prejudice—or they would die.

After refueling and adding passengers, the plane left Hawaii and headed for Andersen Air Force Base on the island of Guam. They were on the ground long enough to refuel and pick up several staff officers. Then they were airborne again and started the final leg of their flight to Da Nang.

The closer they got to Vietnam, the quieter it became on the plane. Every young marine on board had been up most of the night wondering how they would react to combat and if they would ever see home again. They were nervous and exhausted. It was not a good way to meet Charlie for the first time on the battlefield.

Chapter 3

Welcome to Vietnam, Marines

The Da Nang Air Base was one of the busiest facilities in Southeast Asia. Military aircraft of every kind were taking off and landing 24-7. Helicopters, jets, cargo, and spotter planes were a constant buzz of activity.

Aircraft arrived in the morning with new personnel from the States. Round-the-clock flights brought in everything from toothpaste to toilet paper, aspirin to penicillin, and sergeant stripes to body bags. Two main flights left Da Nang in the afternoon, one loaded with personnel rotating back to the States. Another took the dead and wounded home to their families.

There were currently four hundred twenty-one thousand US military personnel in South Vietnam. With so many military personnel in Vietnam, many back home wondered why it was so hard to defeat the enemy. Only those with boots-on-the-ground experience knew the answer. It was a politician's war fought with a defective military strategy that was destined to fail.

It was 0735 hours when their airplane lined up on the Da Nang runway. It came in low out of the north, allowing a protected approach from the sea. Once on the ground, the plane quickly taxied to the terminal area and parked, facing the runway.

After a few minutes, the aircrew lowered the rear cargo door and allowed the officers and NCOs to disembark and board a bus. The remaining marines collected their bags and assembled behind the plane.

A tall, stern-looking gunnery sergeant trumpeted, "Listen up, Marines. Form up on me in columns of three." The reaction to the gunny's instruction was immediate.

"Welcome to the Republic of Vietnam," he said gruffly. "Some of you will head out to your units in a few hours. Others might be here for a few days. I will march you over to the processing center, where we will check your travel orders and arrange transportation to your destinations. If you don't already have your orders in your hand, do it now. AT EASE!" the gunny shouted. "Smoke 'em if you got 'em. Make sure you fieldstrip those butts. I better not see anything but ashes hit the ground."

The tired marines were overwhelmed by the heat, noise, and commotion. Just as they were lighting up, a Vietcong mortar landed with a loud bang about five blocks across the runway. Surprised, most of the detail hit the ground. The gunny, Bernie, and Joe were the only ones who heard it coming and knew it was not a threat.

"As you were, Marines," the Gunny broadcasted. "It's only Charlie extending his welcome and invitation for you to join him in a game of grab-ass out in the bush. You will learn to listen to incoming rounds and when to take cover.

"Some of you are under the impression this is all a game and there will be no incoming where you're going. I assure you this will not be the case. There is nowhere in this godforsaken country that Charlie cannot find you. This is his country, and he does not want you here. Engage that brain of yours, and do not, under any circumstances, let it fall asleep until you leave Vietnam 395 days from now."

The distant thump of a second incoming round caught the gunny's attention. Instantly, he saw the opportunity to give these combat virgins their first in-country survival lesson.

"Marines, attention," the Gunny bellowed. "The Vietcong just fired another mortar round, heading in our direction. You will not break formation. Steady. Wait for it." Then he screamed in a loud, stern voice, "Look at me!"

Just as each marine made eye contact with the gunny, the mortar round landed with a thunderous explosion about two hundred yards to the formation's left. The gunny was unfazed by the explosion. Reluctantly, every marine flinched but stood his ground, each drawing strength from the gunny's unflappable composure.

The moment's intensity was interrupted by a piece of jagged airfield matting, landing about thirty feet to the gunny's right. Every marine's head snapped around to see the object sliding directly toward the gunny's foot.

In an act that seemed impossible, the gunny casually looked over at the onrushing piece of shrapnel. At the last possible moment, the gunny lifted the toe of his steel-plated jungle boot and turning it ninety degrees, stepped down on the metal as if it were a bug.

The gunny defiantly stared down at the would-be killer for a few seconds. Then he reached into his back pocket and pulled out a handkerchief. He picked up the still-hot metal and held it up to give the formation their second survival lesson.

"This is what happens to metal when it's blown up. If you look closely, you will see that most of this metal is razor-sharp. A piece of shrapnel a quarter of this size will rip an arm or leg right off your body. It is only one of a thousand dangers you will encounter during your tour. Your job as a marine is to kill the enemy before he kills you then go home and tell all your friends and family about how much fun you had in good ol' Vietnam."

As he studied his charge, the gunny wondered how many would survive their next thirteen months. "Now, if you killers are ready, RIGHT FACE ... MARCH!"

The gunny struck up a cadence march and positioned himself to the right of the column. "I love working for Uncle Sam ... lets me know just who I am." As they echoed their part, the young marines were reminded of something they had learned in basic training. They were part of a team that looked out for one another. As such, they would fight through the pain and the unknown together. At least for the moment, their confidence was restored as they marched on with pride.

* * *

Bernie and Joe checked in at the processing center and learned that a 9th Marine truck would leave for Dong Ha the next morning at 0800 hours, so they had the rest of the day to relax. They dropped their gear off at the transfer barracks and headed for some chow. Later, they treated themselves to a few beers, and something all military personnel did whenever possible—listened to the Armed Forces Radio Network. Knowing the next few days would be uncertain, they decided to call it a night at 2100 hours.

Both snipers got up at 0530, showered and shaved, packed, and headed to the mess hall for a plate of creamed chipped beef on toast. After today, it could be C rations most of the time. They grabbed their gear and walked to the convoy staging area to hook up with their assigned transport truck. It was sunny and already seventy-five degrees. Today would be another hot one.

"What do you bet this trip will take all day, Joe?"

"Well, it did the last time we came through here. I count twenty-four trucks with an M48 battle tank, a Quad .50-caliber machine-gun truck, two Dusters, three jeeps with recoilless rifles, and a reinforced rifle squad for protection. I bet we will even have a

Huey umbrella all the way to Dong Ha. Why would Charlie want to mess with all this firepower? If the EOD (explosive ordnance disposal) teams got out early and Charlie didn't blow a bridge last night, we should be there by 1600 hours."

Chapter 4

Ambush on Highway 1

An army military police (MP) gun jeep led the convoy out of the main gate and north onto Highway 1 for the one-hundred-mile drive up to Dong Ha. As soon as they left the compound, Bernie and Joe could feel Charlie's watchful eyes waiting for an opportunity to strike hard and vanish like a ghost back into the bush. Charlie was the master of concealment and was a ferocious opponent when the odds were heavily stacked in his favor.

Forty miles out of Da Nang, the convoy halted when they came upon a team of engineers working to clear a land mine from the side of the road. Many of the enemy's mines and booby traps were unexploded US ordnance. This one was a large 155 mm howitzer shell. It had enough explosives to take out a tank or a couple of five-ton trucks loaded with marines. The two army gunships protecting the convoy moved forward to search the area around the engineer's truck. This left most of the convoy temporarily exposed. Just the opportunity Charlie had been waiting for.

The marines in the lead trucks watched the bomb disposal team with one-eyed curiosity. Their other eye was nervously surveying the jungle for any concealed threats.

While stopped on the road, the convoy took up a defensive position, spreading several truck lengths apart. With a turret-mounted .50-caliber machine gun, the tank was the second vehicle in the column. Its ominous-looking 90 mm cannon pointed to the right. With their twin 40 mm cannons, the Dusters and jeep-mounted recoilless rifles were evenly spaced down the column. They were all more than ready to play Charlie's game of hit-and-run tactics.

For protection from mines, the floor of Bernie's truck was lined with sandbags. It did not, however, offer any protection from sniper fire. Bernie looked down at the sandbags and thought about the five-ton truck he saw mined on his first tour. The blast was strong enough to lift the heavy truck six feet into the air and turn it into a mangled wreck. Two marines died that day, and six others were wounded bad enough to be sent back to the States.

The truck in front of Bernie had a revolving armored turret mounted onto the bed. Its four protruding .50-caliber machine guns had a 360-degree field of fire. The Quad's assignment was to guard the left side of the column. About fifty yards to the left of the road were the old abandoned railroad tracks that ran up to the bombed-out Freedom Bridge north of the city of Gio Linh on the DMZ.

Bernie glanced at the six-foot mound of earth that supported the tracks and thought it was the perfect place for an ambush. Instantly, he sensed something wasn't right and quickly took command of the situation.

"Get down, Marines, and keep a sharp eye on those tracks." All the marines on the truck moved to full alert. Getting as low in the bed as they could, they shoved their rifles through the side railings and waited.

Bernie quickly reached into his sniper bag, pulled out his binoculars, and stood to scan the tracks. He soon spotted the top of a camouflaged NVA pith helmet on the far side of the tracks. Among the foliage, he could see the glimmer of a radio antenna.

In a loud whisper, Joe asked, "What's going on, Bernie?"

"We've got company on the other side of those tracks. Quick, give me your rifle."

Feeling he only had seconds to respond, Bernie dropped the binoculars and took Joe's M14. Releasing the safety as he raised the weapon, he aimed at the still-unseen radio operator. Twenty yards to the right, Bernie noticed some movement. Turning his rifle to face the new threat, he saw the business end of an RPG (rocket-propelled grenade) rising from the far side of the tracks. The target of choice would naturally be the most imposing threat—the Quad.

Surviving an ambush depends on obtaining superior firepower over the enemy at the earliest possible moment. Bernie knew all hell would break out all along the column when he cut loose on his target. He also realized that at fifty yards, the odds of hitting his partially concealed target on his first shot were slim to none. So Bernie aimed at the rocks on the tracks and fired five quick rounds. Debris flew up into the gunner's face immediately before he pulled the trigger. The gunner flinched, and the rocket sailed harmlessly between the two trucks, exploding in the trees behind them.

Suddenly, two dozen automatic weapons opened up from beyond the tracks. The marines returned fire immediately. The damage by the recoilless rifles and Dusters was impressive. The real damage, however, would be done by the Quad .50.

Being on the receiving end of a single .50-caliber machine gun is a terrifying experience if you can live to talk about it. Especially when considering a .50-caliber round is large enough to punch a hole through light armor. Multiply that by four, and people will die if they are not very well protected.

The enemy fire ended as soon as the Quad gunner opened fire. The one-half-inch-diameter rounds hit hard against the heavy iron rails like a jackhammer, peeling them off the railroad ties into twisted, distorted sections. With precision, the gunner traversed down the tracks. The deformed steel disappeared over the embankment's backside in a large dust cloud. Past the berm, trees fell as the large rounds cut through them like a giant axe.

The noise of the Quad was ear-piercing. The marines stopped firing and watched in amazement at the destruction inflicted on Charlie all by itself. When the Quad stopped firing, Bernie glanced over and saw smoke streaming from its four red-hot barrels. Then he realized how exposed he was. *Dumb grunt. Are you trying to get yourself killed on your second day back in-country?*

The two Hueys turned and charged down the tracks as soon as the firing started. Their rockets and machine guns swept the area beyond the berm. After briefly engaging with the helicopters, the attacking forces retreated into the jungle's protection. An RPG round was fired at the helicopters from inside the tree line, narrowly missing the lead gunship. The door gunners turned their fire on the trees, and the surviving enemy quickly vanished.

Lieutenant Sackett was in the cab of Bernie's truck, hitching a ride up to Dong Ha. Bernie was still high on his adrenaline rush when a voice called, "Sergeant, get those men out of the truck. We're going after those VCs."

Prevented from recognizing Sackett from the plane, Bernie looked down at him in disbelief. "Sir, I don't think that's a good idea."

"Sergeant, get those men out of that truck right now. The VCs are getting away."

"Sir, those gooks are already gone," Bernie argued, "and if they're not gone, they want us to follow them into that tree line. You'll get these men killed if you take them out there."

The fourteen young marine privates on Bernie's truck were now painfully aware of how expendable they were. Hearing Bernie and Sackett arguing over whether they lived or died was enough to give them some serious concerns about why they enlisted into the marine corps.

The army MP convoy commander and his radio operator approached Bernie's truck and stopped to check on the commotion. "Lieutenant, I'm Staff Sergeant Lambert." Glancing at Sackett's name badge, he continued. "What's the problem here?"

"I told the sergeant there to get those men off the truck so we can go after the enemy, and he's disobeying my order."

Lambert asked, "What's your name, Sergeant?"

"Sergeant Westgate, staff sergeant."

"Is that right? Are you resisting a direct order from the lieutenant?"

Bernie took a deep breath and realized that his second tour of duty was about to turn into an extended stay in Leavenworth Prison. He hesitantly replied, "That's right, Staff Sergeant, I am."

"That's pretty brassy, Sergeant. Do you mind explaining why we should not chase Charlie into those trees?"

"Staff Sergeant, other than Corporal Diamond and myself, no one on this truck has any combat experience.

"If we take these kids over that embankment," Bernie continued, "there is no way the convoy can cover us from here. Once we enter the trees, the helicopters cannot see us either. I am sure Charlie did not overlook those two details. That mine was probably put there to get us to stop so Charlie could jump us. My guess is that they're baiting us into a trap."

Lambert knew this marine sergeant was no dummy. His carrying an old M14 when everyone in the column had new M16s told him a lot about his combat experience. "Is that all, Sergeant?" Lambert asked with a concealed grin.

"Staff Sergeant, those were not VCs. They were hard-core NVA. They did not come this far south to get their butts kicked this easily. I'm sure that was just a squad. There's at least a battalion waiting for us inside that tree line."

"Sir, I agree with Sergeant Westgate. It is not a good idea to chase Charlie into those trees. Sergeant, you and your men stand down from that order. Will there be anything else, sir?"

Relieved to hear Lambert back his play, Bernie breathed a sigh of relief and shouted, "Thank you, Staff Sergeant!"

Eliphaz realized he had overreacted and was about to do what Legion warned him not to do. He was fortunate that Mike was there to stop him. However, he was not accustomed to taking orders from humans. Pridefully, he replied, "I'm the ranking officer on this convoy, Staff Sergeant. Marines can't just disobey orders when it suits them."

"Yes, sir. You're the only officer on this convoy, but don't confuse your rank with my authority. I'm in command here, and my orders are to get you and these men to your units without getting any of you killed."

Lambert added in a much-softer voice, "If you don't mind, sir, please get back in the truck while I try and get us back on our way." Turning, he softly whispered, "Jesus, please get us safely to Da Nang."

It is not very often an NCO gets away with challenging a superior's order. In this case, however, Lambert was right. Without exception, everyone in this column was subject to his authority. Lambert could not help but wonder why Sackett was so anxious to lead unseasoned troops into an apparent second ambush.

Lambert watched as Sackett's face went from annoyed to furious. Sackett's body language told him to prepare for anything that might follow. Very slowly, Lambert turned to his right and took a step backward. He reached down and pulled his sidearm from its holster. Cocking it, he held it behind him.

Thinking about his two blundering mistakes, getting distracted from Legion's instructions, and showing his hatred for the Creator's Son, Eliphaz knew he needed to excuse himself before things got any worse. With his ego badly damaged, he turned and headed back to the cab. Once inside, Eliphaz received a stern telepathic message from Legion: *Don't ever let that happen again. Understand?*

Relieved it was just a warning, Eliphaz replied meekly, *Yes, my captain.*

Looking up at Bernie, Lambert asked, "Are there any wounded in your truck, Sergeant Westgate?"

"No, Staff Sergeant. We're all good."

"What exactly do you two do for the marines, Sergeant?"

"We are scout snipers, Staff Sergeant," came Joe's proud reply.

"I thought so. That big bag I saw you with this morning was a dead giveaway. It's nice to have you two with us today. Thanks for not letting Sackett get these young marines killed on my watch," he said with a big grin and a slight nod.

"Corporal Wood," Lambert said to his radio operator, "tell Sergeant Berger to take a detail over and check out the far side of those tracks. Tell him to be careful and be quick about it. Then find out how long we'll be stuck out in the open."

"I'm on it, Staff Sergeant." The corporal took off like a jackrabbit to Berger's truck.

Bernie noticed the writing on the corporal's helmet as he rushed by: "Hwy 1—The road through hell." From his past experiences on the Road, Bernie was certainly in agreement.

As Lambert turned to go, Joe asked, "Did we have any casualties, Staff Sergeant?"

"Fortunately, our return fire was so rapid that Charlie did not have enough time to do any real damage. One of the drivers got his helmet knocked off by an AK-47 round. He's lucky. Two inches lower, and his head would have come off with it. Other than being shaken up a bit, he's OK. A private on my truck was winged slightly. Half the vehicles took a few rounds each, but nothing serious.

"Sergeant Westgate, are you the one who fired on that RPG? If you had not reacted when you did, he would have taken out the Quad and trapped us behind it."

"Yes, Staff Sergeant. Just trying to stay alive."

"Well, that was quick thinking on your part. Are you interested in me putting you in for a medal?"

"Thanks, but that won't be necessary. I would rather you make sure that Private gets his Purple Heart."

"I figured you'd say that."

In a salute to the marines, Lambert added, "Oorah, Sergeant Westgate."

Bernie returned the army's compliment, "Hooah, Staff Sergeant Lambert."

Bernie turned and looked into the faces of fourteen very thankful marines. Nothing needed to be said; nods, winks, and smiles were exchanged. This baptism under fire, though brief, was a valuable lesson learned. In five short minutes, their contempt for the enemy had been replaced by respect. Fortunately for them, it was the most valuable lesson about Charlie.

Bernie flipped on the safety and handed the rifle back to Joe. He reached down, picked up his binoculars, and scanned the tracks for any other movement. "Stay alert, Marines. Charlie may have another surprise up his sleeve."

Though Bernie had no memory of his previous conversation with Sackett, he knew something was strange about the lieutenant's behavior. He had heard some lame orders before, but this was the lamest.

*   *   *

A lone NVA commander rose from his underground concealment just inside the tree line beyond the berm. With binoculars, he surveyed the destruction of his failed attempt at baiting the marines into his trap. Yesterday, he would have lamented the loss of his men. Today, he was more interested in the argument between the two marines at Bernie's truck. Adjusting the magnification, he closely studied Bernie's facial expressions as he contended with the marine officer. Knowing he was the one who fired the shots that disrupted his well-conceived plans, the officer smiled in frustrated amusement.

"Tell the men to hold their positions," he told his adjutant. "There will be another convoy tomorrow morning. Have a detail standing by to collect our dead after the Wild Cat has gone."

The aide acknowledged the command and ran back a hundred yards to the well-hidden fortifications they had spent two days building. It would have been so easy if it hadn't been for Bernie.

"Damned Americans," the commander whispered as he turned to go.

As the commander stepped away, an unseen spirit named Amir was left standing in the wake of his vacated host, who walked away unaware of the demon's presence. Amir smiled as he listened to the conversation between Eliphaz and Lambert. Being one of Legion's agents, he knew how close Eliphaz was to being relieved of his command.

Receiving instruction from Legion, Amir vanished and reappeared in less than a heartbeat, standing unseen behind Lambert. Eliphaz knew precisely why Amir was there. Pride is a heavy burden to bear if you're a demon. It is God's curse and occasionally leaves the spirit incapable of reason and self-control, especially if you've backed yourself into a corner with no supple way out.

Amir anticipated Eliphaz's emotions and knew he was about to go postal, jeopardizing their plans. *Calm down, Eliphaz. You're in enough trouble as it is*, Amir implored.

Eliphaz could feel his anger building. It was like a lion that needed to be let out of his cage. He knew if that happened, Amir would be there to replace him. With great effort, he managed to bridle his anger before it got the best of him. In humiliation, Eliphaz returned to the truck cab.

Amir connected with Corporal Wood's brain and quickly discovered that he and Lambert had discussed salvation. After a telepathic message to Legion, he began scanning the minds of the unsaved marines on Bernie's truck.

When the trucks pulled out, Amir's still unseen spirit rose into the air and flew to catch up to the nearest truck. Coming to rest on the truck bed, he studied the five marines on board and selected his next host. Amused at his cloaked movements, he reached over and touched a marine. Instantly, he was assimilated into his new host. After reviewing his mind for any moral tendencies, he moved on to the other marines. With nothing of interest to report to Legion, Amir flew to the next truck to continue his quest to find those who might oppose the darkness he represented.

*   *   *

Berger and six escort soldiers moved quickly to the railroad embankment. Deploying his M60 machine-gun team ten yards to his right and the rest of his detail ten yards to the left, the sergeant slowly crawled onto the embankment until he could see down the far side. Immediately below him lay the RPG gunner's body, crushed beneath a twisted span of railroad iron. His empty weapon lay beside him. An inspection of his camouflaged uniform confirmed he was NVA.

To his left lay three NVA soldiers buried beneath other sections of rail. Their uniforms were perfectly camouflaged with foliage. They had appeared as nothing but bush from the air, making it easy for the Hueys to overlook them.

Thirty yards away from the tracks lay the severely wounded radio operator. He was propped up against a log with his Russian carbine lying across his lap. Around him were six other lifeless bodies killed as they tried to reach the tree line.

When the radio operator spotted Berger, he slowly lifted his weapon in hatred. The M60 gunner cut loose with a short burst of fire, and the soldier went limp without firing a shot. The gunner sprayed the corpse with another prolonged burst to destroy the radio.

With the tree line only forty yards away, Berger knew better than to try and retrieve the RPG, but he could not leave it behind for Charlie to use again. Getting a grenade from his utility harness, he pulled the pin and rolled it down the embankment toward the dead NVA soldier. The ping from the ejected spoon was his reminder to protect himself. Plugging his ears, Berger waited with his face in the dirt until the grenade exploded. After confirming he had destroyed the RPG, Berger and his men quickly returned to the convoy.

"Staff Sergeant, I confirmed eleven NVA killed with one radio and one RPG destroyed. That was a bizarre sight. Four of those guys died when those displaced rails fell on them."

"Thanks, Sergeant. It looks like that sniper was right about them being NVA. It's strange they would be this far south." After further thought, Lambert added, "Load up, Sergeant. We need to get out of here."

Lambert walked to the head of the column. "What's the situation, Corporal Wood?"

"They've removed a howitzer shell from the side of the road and have it rigged with explosives."

Both soldiers moved behind the MP gun jeep and ducked for protection.

"Fire in the hole," came the call moments before the detonation. The EOD team leader gave Lambert the thumbs-up, and his team started loading their equipment back onto their truck.

Lambert looked past the circling Huey gunships and offered a silent prayer for continued travel mercies.

Lambert looked down the column and gave his drivers the forward sign. When the EOD team moved out, he motioned to the MP jeep to fall in behind. The rest of the column moved up quickly.

The last vehicle in the column was the MP command truck. When it stopped, Wood climbed into the back. Lambert, however, stood there and watched the convoy continue down the road. After a moment, the driver said, "We should be going, Staff Sergeant. We do not want to be out here all alone."

When Lambert failed to reply, the driver nervously repeated, "Staff Sergeant, we need to leave now."

Looking at the driver, Lambert said, "Yes. Let's get out of here."

As he climbed into the shotgun seat, Lambert glanced at the jungle with an uneasiness that told him there was more than Charlie lurking in the shadows. Somehow, he suspected Sackett was a part of it.

The convoy continued toward Dong Ha with no further harassment from Charlie. Trucks loaded with men and supplies dropped off as they passed Camp Sally, Camp Evans, Hue (Way), and Quang Tri.

Chapter 5

Bernie's Encounter with Eliphaz

Highway 1 was a vital means of moving men and equipment in Vietnam. Truckers called it Thunder Road, and for good reason. During the day, it was heavily defended by the Americans. After dark, however, Charlie used his time wisely to plant land mines and set up ambushes and booby traps. He could not stop the United States war machine, but he could slow it down whenever it suited him. Though heavily defended, most of the bridges along Highway 1 had been damaged or destroyed at least once.

The firebase of Dong Ha sat at the junction of Highway 1 and 9. North along Highway 1 led to Gio Linh, then to the destroyed Freedom Bridge over the Ben Hai River that separated North and South Vietnam. West along Highway 9 led to firebases at Cam Lo, Camp Carroll, the Rock Pile, Ca Lu, and Khe Sanh. From there, it continued as a dirt road into Laos and intersected the Ho Chi Minh trail—Charlie's primary means of moving men and equipment into South Vietnam.

Dong Ha is the main supply point for men and equipment along the DMZ. It was home to army, navy, air force, and marine personnel. It functioned as the central triage aid station for all units north of Hue. Equipped with a sizable airstrip, it was a thriving metropolis of military movement.

The remaining convoy trucks arrived at the main gate at 1630 hours. Lambert had just handed his convoy paperwork to the marine guard when an enemy mortar round struck his vehicle. It erupted with a deafening explosion. Shrapnel tore into Lambert's lower back, and he fell face down on the road. Amazingly, the guard standing beside him was knocked down but not wounded.

Bernie's vehicle was the fifth truck in the column, only fifty yards from the blast. He knew from experience that whatever goes up will always come down. "Get down, men," he commanded. "Wait for the fallout."

Immediately, debris started falling all around them. Part of a bumper slammed down hard onto the truck hood; rocks and concrete followed. A truck tire landed on the road and bounced into the compound perimeter wire, setting off a trip flare.

Every marine had his eyes closed with one hand on his weapon and one holding tightly to his helmet. When it was over, Bernie stood up and looked around the truck. "Is everybody OK? Anybody hurt?"

"We're all good," replied Joe. "What was that?"

"A mortar just took out Lambert's truck." Glancing at the smoldering mass told Bernie that no one could have survived. He surveyed the area east of the gate and supposed the mortar came from the far side of the town of Dong Ha. *What are the odds of one round scoring a direct hit at that distance?*

It occurred to him he should have heard the incoming round but didn't. He thought it peculiar when he ruled out the possibility of Charlie placing a mine just yards from the gate. Unable to explain the cause of the explosion, Bernie began searching for another explanation.

Several marines were busy helping Lambert, lying on the road at the gate. A minute later, a jeep raced up, and a corpsman jumped out and ran to help. "Out of the way, men. Let me through," screamed the medic.

Five minutes had passed since the blast. Bernie's concern for the unexplained explosion was interrupted by another ominous feeling. Spinning around, he scanned the area for threats. Although he could not see anything, he felt a presence, as if someone, or something, was right in front of him, crowding him, forcing him backward. His breathing increased as apprehension started to overpower him.

Bernie had the sensation of being sprayed in the face with something like rotting flesh. The odor was so pungent it made him gag. Then after a breath or two, it was gone.

Bernie became so convinced something was in front of him that he slowly extended his left hand to see if he could touch whatever was there. He leaned forward with his arm extended until he touched an invisible gooey mass. At first, Bernie thought it was a type of static-charged Jell-O. He paused when he felt a slight movement. After a few seconds, he realized it was alive.

Bernie quickly retracted his hand and stepped back, leaving a faint void in the object. As the opening closed, it created a small translucent ripple effect that resembled moonlight reflecting off waves on the water. The presence gave Bernie a brief look at its five-foot-tall frame and vanished.

Surprised, Bernie struggled to regain his composure. *What was that?*

Look up, Westgate, and I'll show you, came a familiar voice from deep inside his brain.

Come on, Bernie, look up, came the voice again. *I've got something really cool to show you.*

Reluctantly, he slowly looked skyward.

At first, he saw nothing. Then a speck appeared above the truck. As it got larger, Bernie could tell something was falling. Instinct told him to move, but his feet felt encased in a concrete block.

The object raced downward, then stopped about three feet in front of him. The movement ended so abruptly that it caused Bernie's knees to buckle. It took several moments before he realized the object was a helmet. The front was facing him as if it were placed on the head of the invisible presence. Printed on the front of the helmet was the name Wood.

There was a long silence before Bernie heard the voice again. *That's not something you see every day, is it, Bernie? Now watch this.*

Perplexed, Bernie watched the helmet slowly turn to the left, revealing a piece of embedded shrapnel above the ear. Blood began to ooze from the hole, dripping onto the sandbags on the truck bed. A plastic bottle of insect repellant was tucked into the helmet chinstrap on the back. As the helmet continued to turn, Bernie saw the writing on the right side: "Hwy 1—the road through hell."

"That's Corporal Wood's helmet," Bernie whispered. "Why did it take so long to come down? How did it get here?"

Still fixated on the helmet, Bernie watched it slowly roll upside down. It paused and then slammed down hard onto the sandbags as if shot out of a cannon. Bernie gawked at the still-bleeding helmet for some time before he noticed a piece of paper fixed in space above the helmet as though pinned to an unseen bulletin board. Stepping forward, he bent down to examine the article. The writing gave him a start: *We're watching you, Bernie. Stay out of our way.*

A quick reflex and Bernie was vertical again, unable to comprehend what was happening. Something released the note, and it floated down and came to rest inside the helmet. He closed his eyes tightly and thought, *Get a grip, Bernie. This can't be real.*

Bernie had spent thirteen months in-country on his first tour and had seen some strange things. Fighting against a flesh-and-blood enemy with man-made weapons was what he understood. However, being confronted by an invisible entity with supernatural powers was beyond him. Bernie knew this enemy was not flesh and bone.

After some thought, Bernie opened his eyes to study the helmet again. The note had vanished. He rolled the helmet over with his foot and noticed that the shrapnel was gone. The hole and the blood had also disappeared. Confused, Bernie gave it more consideration and dismissing it, kicked the helmet to the back of the truck, striking it hard against the tailgate.

"Watch it, Sergeant!" Sackett shouted from behind the truck. "You almost hit me with that helmet."

Bernie made the connection immediately. Speechless, he stared down at Sackett, wondering what this demon wanted.

Reading Bernie's thoughts, Sackett answered, "I'm one of many spirits known as Legion. I'm called Eliphaz.

"We roam the earth and use you humans to battle against Christianity. When we get tired of possessing one body, we leave it and move on to another unsuspecting wretch. It's our job to keep as many souls as possible from finding their way into heaven. You humans are so gullible and can be easily tricked into believing anything."

Though shaken, Bernie did not feel overly threatened, which surprised him because, up until now, he thought the devil was a religious superstition.

"Did you destroy that truck and the men on it?"

"Yes, we did," he replied arrogantly. "Lambert got in our way, and we needed to teach him a lesson."

"Why kill the men on the truck?" Bernie asked as he took an aggressive step closer to the tailgate.

Eliphaz stared at Bernie, telling him it was unsafe to come any closer.

"Lambert was recruiting Corporal Wood to the other side. We could not let that happen. Regarding the other four men, let's say they are casualties of a different war."

Bernie thought his conversation with the devil or at least one of his demons was odd, but it didn't seem all that unusual for some reason. The bizarre thing was that Bernie felt he had met this spirit before.

"Then why not just kill me? I was the one who would not let you take these marines out after the enemy."

"We don't want you dead, Bernie. At least not now. We've got some things planned for you if you make it back to the States alive. We punished Lambert because he believes in the Creator's Son. The smell of his righteousness is offensive. You, on the other hand, smell like indifference. Something much more to our liking."

"Is that Lambert lying over there?"

"Yes, that's Lambert," Sackett said as he looked toward the front gate. "He'll live but be disabled for the rest of his life."

"Why not just kill him?"

"To be absent from the body is to be present in heaven, so the Book says. Book thumpers like Lambert are loathsome, but we can't kill him. Besides, as long as he's down here, we can still tempt him."

"So all you do is kill people and punish Christians," Bernie replied angrily.

Enjoying Bernie's spirited reply, Eliphaz replied, "Unfortunately, no. We can tempt anyone, but we cannot harm those who belong to the Creator unless we ask his permission first. He lets us test believers only when it suits him, and even that comes with rules."

"What kind of rules?"

"Like your Ten Commandments, the Creator has ten rules that govern the spirit world. The one I hate the most is rule 1—anything spoken in the name of God's Son by a believer with faith has authority over the spirit world. Fortunately, there aren't many like that around anymore. The other nine rules deal with how we can interact with the Creator and humans."

"What happens if you break one of God's rules?"

"Banishment into the abyss before the appointed time."

"What appointed time?"

"I'm proud of you, Bernie," he said mockingly. "You know absolutely nothing about the Book. It's from Revelation 20:10, 'And the devil who deceived them was cast into the lake of fire and brimstone, where the beast and the false prophet are also, and all were tormented day and night forever and ever.'"

Bernie considered Eliphaz's criticism and felt ashamed. He hadn't given the devil or the Bible much thought before. Now that he knew Satan was real, it gave him a whole new perspective on life and death.

"What was your interest in those fourteen young marines this morning? Why did you want to get them killed?"

Eliphaz gave Bernie a pompous stare.

"Christians, right?"

"Two believers, seven who only thought they were believers, one Jew, one Muslim, two atheists, and one agnostic."

"So why are you telling me this?"

"For one thing, pride is the curse the Creator gave us for rebelling against him. For another, you can't do anything to stop me, so why should we worry about what you know? Who would believe you if you told them? Finally, you're on my contact list."

"What contact list?"

"Unlike the Creator, we cannot be in all places at the same time or know everything. So the Boss sends us out to keep an eye on his subjects. It gives us the chance to update our records. We have talked many times before, Bernie. You could say we're old friends."

"You mean earlier today?"

"No, yesterday on the plane. Remember?"

Eliphaz gave Bernie a suggestion, and their conversation came back to him with a jolt. "Remember that lieutenant on the firing range the other day? That was me in another body."

Startled that Eliphaz had control of his mind, he stared back in amazement.

"With telepathic powers, we can read you humans like a book. Every memory you ever had is there for us to find. We can cause you to see things that aren't there or hide things from you that are. What you see can be hidden from those around you. Take those marines behind you and those in the truck behind me. They have no idea we're talking right now. As far as they are concerned, we are not here at all.

"You're right about that mortar round that took out Lambert's truck being fired from the far side of town. Once in the air, it was like playing catch. It took a nudge or two, but it landed exactly where we wanted it to."

Not liking Eliphaz's meaning, Bernie moved on to his more pressing concern. "So you can read my mind?"

"Of course, I can read your mind. We cannot read Lambert's."

"Why not?"

"You're not a believer. Reading your mind is easy. Lambert belongs to the Creator. So his mind is blocked from us. We can give him suggestions, but he must choose to follow them."

"So you can make the lost do anything, but God protects the saved. Right?"

"That's the way it is. Now, you want to know how we could punish Lambert if he is protected." Without waiting for an answer,

Eliphaz continued, "Earth is our domain. We control what happens down here. The Creator could have protected Lamber and the men on that truck if he wanted to. Now, I think you have one more question for me. Right, Bernie?"

"Yes. How did you do that thing with Wood's helmet?"

"What helmet?"

"Right there …" Bernie began as he pointed down to the now-vanished helmet. After looking around the truck bed, he turned quickly to Eliphaz for an answer.

"You humans only think you know what's going on, Bernie. A great spiritual battle rages around you, and you're so focused on your selfish wants and needs that you refuse to accept them. That's good news for us and bad news for you. We know we cannot win the final battle, but we'll take as many of you pathetic humans with us when the Creator's Son throws us all into the lake of fire."

"If you know you will lose the battle, why continue fighting?"

"We made our bed when we followed the Boss into the first battle against the Creator. We lost and were thrown down to earth to wait for the judgment. I cannot change where I'm going any more than how I get there. The way I see it, I might as well have a little fun along the way. After all, isn't that the same way you humans look at life?"

Bernie's conversation with Eliphaz was interrupted when Joe tapped him on the shoulder. "Hey, Bernie. An ambulance is taking that man to the base hospital. I wonder who he is."

Bernie looked over his shoulder and replied, "It's Lambert." Turning back, he found Sackett gone. *I don't believe what just happened.*

You don't have to believe it, Bernie, Eliphaz replied. *You just have to accept it.*

* * *

It was 1715 hours when the convoy passed through the main gate. Five trucks pulled into the supply compound while the empty vehicles continued to the convoy staging area. Bernie's truck pulled up to the headquarters building and stopped. The sign in front read, "9th Marine Regiment, Hell in a Helmet, Headquarters Company, Dong Ha."

Joe looked at Bernie and said, "So these guys call themselves Hell in a Helmet. It looks like we are in good company now."

"If I were you, Joe, I wouldn't be so quick to consider hell as good company."

Joe was so glad to get to Dong Ha he didn't give Bernie's comment much thought. Bernie wasn't ready to tell him about Eliphaz anyway.

Still feeling shaky about knowing the devil could read his mind, Bernie tried hard to guard his thoughts while Eliphaz was still around.

Bernie hopped over the tailgate and let it down. "All right, men. Grab your equipment and dismount the truck. Corporal Diamond, can you hand me my seabag and the rifle then get these marines into formation?"

"Will do, Sergeant. Here you go."

Bernie dropped his bags beside the truck and reluctantly walked to the passenger door. Sackett was in the cab, looking straight ahead as if in a trance. "Do you need us to get your bag, Sir?"

"That won't be necessary, Sergeant. The driver will give me a lift over to the 26th Marine headquarters," the lieutenant said without looking down.

"You have a nice day, sir," Bernie said as he turned to walk away.

"Oh, Sergeant."

Bernie stopped without turning back.

"I enjoyed our little talk. Remember, the Boss gets upset when his subjects try to defect. The Book says 'broad is the path and narrow is the gate.' It's doubtful you will ever find that one doorway into the Kingdom. Think about that before you go looking for something you don't understand."

Bernie stood there, struggling to refrain from any thoughts. He heard the tailgate slam shut and the truck pull away. Cringing, he stood there waiting for a departing comment from Eliphaz that never came. Bernie could feel Eliphaz's presence depart when the truck turned a corner. If he or one of his kind returned, Bernie was sure he would feel it again.

Chapter 6

Dong Ha

Inside the headquarters building, Bernie and Joe handed the clerk their orders. "Welcome to Dong Ha, Marines. We've been expecting you. Have a seat. Captain Wilson will be right with you."

The structure was a ten-foot-wide forty-foot-long wood-framed building surrounded by three feet of sandbags. The roof was corrugated tin, its sides covered with mosquito netting and rolled-up canvas curtains. Thick sandbagged blast walls set four feet from the building protected the front and back screen doors from flying shrapnel. On one side was the battalion command bunker, on the other a sizeable bomb shelter. Both were dug down about eight feet and covered with steel and five feet of sandbags.

While Bernie and Joe waited, incoming mortar rounds could be heard landing around the firebase, muffled only by outgoing howitzer and armor shells. Most of the incoming projectiles were small-caliber mortar rounds. Not much more than nuisance rounds. Just enough to remind you of the dangers inside a large secure firebase. Charlie could set up and fire three quick rounds then relocate a hundred yards away before the marines could locate their position and return fire.

Captain Wilson walked over and introduced himself. "Leave your gear here and follow me."

Wilson led the snipers outside and down into the command bunker. "Marines, this is Major Bryant, the battalion XO (executive officer). Sir, this is our two new snipers, Sergeant Westgate and Corporal Diamond."

"Welcome to the 9th Marine Regiment, men," Bryant began. "I understand you've been here before. I trust you're ready to get back to work."

Bernie nodded and replied stoically, "That's affirmative, sir."

"Good." Leading the snipers over to the map table, he continued. "Our reconnaissance patrols tell us General Giap's 812th Regiment is gearing up for something big up north. The target could be Gio Linh, Con Thien, Camp Carroll, or Dong Ha.

"The 11th Engineers have just cleared a two-hundred-yard-wide strip of jungle between Con Thien and Gio Linh. We call it the Trace. It has hindered the enemy's movements, but that's about all. We've had two search-and-destroy missions up there over the last three months, and the NVA are doing their best to avoid us. We need to know why.

"I want to move you to Con Thien for a few days to gather some intel before Operation Hickory kicks off later this month. Your maps will identify it as A4. The 4th Marines relieved a South Vietnamese Army garrison up there three days ago. They tell me you snipers are surveillance experts. See what you can find out. Are there any questions?"

"No, sir," Bernie replied.

"Good. We will move you to our new sniper platoon when you return. Get some rest tonight. You won't get much up there."

Wilson led the snipers back into the headquarters building and gave them some additional information. "A Huey will pick you up at 0730 hours. We'll have two army gunships to escort you to A4.

You would be well advised to keep your heads down while you're there. It draws a lot of enemy fire.

"Corporal Myers will show you where to bed down for the night. Is there anything you need before you go?"

"We're good for now, sir. We'll wait for the corporal outside." Bernie and Joe picked up their gear and started toward the door. Bernie stopped and turned back to address Wilson again.

"Sir, an army staff sergeant Lambert was wounded at the front gate when we arrived. Can you find out how he's doing?"

"Will do, Sergeant. We'll see you back here in a few days."

Outside, Joe looked up and spotted two jets screaming northward. "Those are probably F-4 Phantoms. I wonder where they're going."

"Wherever it is, I'm sure Charlie won't like it when they get there."

A block away was a sandbagged tree house mounted on top of three forty-foot-tall telephone poles. These observation towers, scattered all over the firebase, were vital to spotting enemy activity outside the wire. The marine operating this outlook was on his field phone, conveying coordinates for a fire mission.

Two marines walked past them to the shower, wearing only a helmet, flak jacket, skivvies, and Ho Chi Minh sandals. Bernie mused at the casual atmosphere surrounding him and marveled at the adaptability of life in a combat zone.

Myers walked out and gave Bernie their orders and more instructions. "Inside is your radio call sign and the frequency you need when checking in. A4 will loan you one of their radios while you're up there. The helicopter will pick you up on the other side of that observation tower at 0730 hours. I'll check on your army friend and tell you something in the morning."

"Thanks, Corporal," Joe said. "We'll check in as soon as we get settled up there."

"Good. If you follow me, I'll take you to your barracks."

It was 1540 hours when the snipers made it to the mess tent. After a hot shower, they stopped by the base exchange to drop off some letters and see if they could hook up with some of their buddies from their first tour. Then after a Coke and some snacks, they both headed to their bunks for a good night's sleep. The temperature was eighty-five degrees, and the moon was full. "Paint It, Black" by the Rolling Stones was playing on radios all over the base.

Chapter 7

Con Thien

Bernie stepped onto the landing skid and hopped aboard the idling Huey with his sniper drag bag and just enough personal items to get by for a week. Joe joined him with his gear. Behind them were the battalion mailbag and five crates of hand grenades. The gunship was armed with two seven-shot rocket launchers and two door gunners operating M60 machine guns.

Myers ran up to the helicopter and handed Bernie a message. "You guys take care of yourselves. I hear it's pretty bad up there."

"Thanks, Corporal."

"What's it say, Bernie?"

After a glance at the note, Bernie replied, "Lambert has extensive injuries to his back. He will be in a wheelchair for the rest of his life." Bernie looked toward the distant mountains northwest of the compound and thought about his conversation with Eliphaz.

Joe took the message from Bernie and read it himself. Then he asked with suspicion, "It doesn't say anything about his injuries or a wheelchair. How do you know that?"

Bernie replied, "Do you believe in ghosts, Joe?"

"We've been fighting ghosts up here for over a year now. I don't always see them, but I know they exist."

"No, the demonic kind."

"If you're asking me if I believe in the devil, I do. I hope to high heaven I never meet him. Why are you asking?"

"Well, I met him yesterday. He told me about Lambert."

The right door gunner interrupted them before Joe could reply, "Get off quickly and head for cover before the shelling starts."

The Huey's engine roared and lifted off, gaining altitude over the compound. They picked up their two Huey escorts at Highway 9 and turned west. When they reached the Cam Lo River Bridge, the three choppers turned and followed a dirt road north toward Con Thien.

Ten minutes later, Bernie spotted a small bridge surrounded by a fortified compound. From last night's review of his map, he knew it must be the C-2 compound. A minute later, a smaller outpost came into view. *There's Yankee Station.* In the distance were the three small hills of A-4.

A barbed wire perimeter protected the firebase. At the base of the hill, forty yards inside the fence were small fighting bunkers spaced every thirty to forty yards around the Hill. No-man's-land was the area between the wire and the shelters. If anyone was caught there after dark, the order was to assume they were unfriendlies and shoot to kill.

From the air, Con Thien resembled a mole-infested trash dump with an interconnecting trench system joining every inhabited area of the Hill. The volcanic landscape had been struck so many times with mortars and long-range artillery that it had turned the ground into small red granular particles. Debris from ammo crates and destroyed equipment were littered all around—a statement of how much damage Charlie had inflicted on the Hill.

On top of each hill was a large heavily sandbagged observation point (OP) bunker. Located on top of the taller western hill was the OP-1 bunker manned by Company A. As the eyes and ears of the Hill, it had a 360-degree field of vision.

Fifty yards south was the Hill's command post (CP). East on the second hill was OP-2, manned by Company D. On the south elevation was OP-3, occupied by a Special Forces–led group of civilian mercenaries trained by the army to defend their villages from the invading forces from the north.

The engineers assigned to clear the Trace were grouped in the valley west of OP-3. The aid station and two landing pads (LZs) were a short distance away. The 105 howitzers, 4.2 inch and 81 mm mortar batteries were in the valley between OP-1 and OP-2. One hundred yards north were three army M48 Patton battle tanks.

Other armaments, including .50-caliber machine guns, Dusters, 106 mm recoilless rifles, and armored personnel carriers (APCs) were scattered around the base to plug any gaps in the defenses. Four-foot-deep sandbagged pits protected the tanks, Dusters, mortars, and howitzers. The Hill's two most significant weaknesses were its rusting perimeter wire and flimsy outdated bunkers. Now that the marines were the new tenants, upgrading the Hill's old fortifications would become a priority.

The jungle had been cleared back one hundred yards on either side of the road leading to the Hill. As they approached the compound, the two gunships climbed higher to discourage any mortar attacks from the tree line. Bernie's helicopter dropped down quickly above the road and made a beeline for the landing pad inside the south gate. Both door gunners were at the ready in case they received enemy fire. The aircraft hit the ground hard, and with it still moving, both snipers bailed out and ran toward the trench about twenty yards away.

The right door gunner pitched the mailbag to the waiting mail clerk, who quickly followed the snipers into the ditch. Five grunts grabbed the grenade crates from the helicopter and ran back to their man caves as fast as possible. Before the door gunner could scream "Clear," the pilot was already revving the engine. The helicopter lifted off and slowly gained altitude.

The chopper had no sooner left the ground than Bernie heard three incoming mortar rounds from somewhere southeast of the gate. Someone screamed, "Incoming!" and the marines crouched deeper into their holes. Three rounds landed within twenty yards of where the helicopter had been just moments before. The impact of the shells sent dirt and shrapnel in all directions.

The two hovering army gunships spotted the mortar tube smoke and opened fire with their rockets and machine guns. As the marine Huey joined the fight, their fire was directed at the enemy's green tracer fire coming from the trees. They pounded the enemy position until the enemy fire had been eliminated. This engagement was costly to Giap. Though he lost valuable equipment and fifteen good men, keeping the marines focused on the area south of the Hill and away from his secret construction project a few hundred yards east was necessary.

The snipers were impressed with the enemy mortar team's accuracy, directed by spotters hidden somewhere outside the wire. Seeing no urgent need to leave the security of the trench, Bernie and Joe decided it would be a good idea to wait until someone came looking for them.

It wasn't long before a corporal came down to find them. "Are you guys the snipers from the 9th?"

"Westgate and Diamond at your service, Corporal. Take us to your leader," Joe replied jokingly.

With a grin, the corporal answered, "Then follow me, ... wise guys."

Using the safety of the trench, the corporal led Bernie and Joe halfway up the hill. They then left the ditch and hurriedly crossed the compound road into another furrow that ran behind the aid station and up to the CP bunker.

"Major Parks, here are the snipers we've been expecting."

"Good morning, gentlemen. Welcome to the 1st Battalion, 4th Marines. You're just in time to sit in on our morning briefing."

Parks was the commanding officer of A-4. His executive officer, Lieutenant Johnston; Special Forces commander, Lieutenant Summers; and First Sergeant Adams were with him. Everyone in the battalion called him Top. After introductions were made, Parks began his briefing.

"Men, as you know, the NVA are massing northeast of our position. Giap is up to something big, and we must assume he will try to push us off the Hill. We have no idea when this might happen. So we need to prepare ourselves for the possibility of a major attack in the next couple of days. Do an immediate inventory of all provisions and ammunition stores then get your lists to Corporal Rios before 1200 hours. Charlie is probing the wire every night, so we are on full alert until further notice."

"Sergeant Westgate, do you have one of those starlight scopes?"

"Yes, sir."

"Good. We're going to put you two up in OP-2. See if you can locate those enemy spotters on the east side of the Hill. Late this afternoon, take as many out as you can. I'm expecting another probe late tonight. Eliminate them as well. By morning, Charlie will know we have a sniper. So try not to give your position away."

"Affirmative, sir."

Returning to his staff, Parks added, "I want every man on the Hill briefed ASAP on the situation. Ensure the perimeter bunkers are suitably fortified and well stocked with ammo, grenades, food, and water. Make sure there's an M60 in at least every other bunker.

"Top, what's the status of the concertina wire?"

"Sir, that razor wire is in high demand. It may be a day or two before we get it."

"That wire out there is so old a strong wind could knock it down. Call supply in Da Nang and get them off their butts. Tell them I want that wire today. Understood?"

"Understood, sir."

"What about the illumination rounds we ordered three days ago?"

"Sir, we have just enough rounds to last two nights. Provided, of course, Charlie doesn't mess with us. Supply told me our shipment should be here tomorrow afternoon."

"Who the hell is running things down there? We need those rounds now. I don't want to fight Charlie in the dark. Have Long and Shaffer arrived yet?"

"I think they're waiting outside now, sir."

Top stepped outside the bunker and found Mike and David hunkered down in the trench, holding their helmets. Before Top could say a word, he heard the rush of an incoming mortar and ducked back inside the bunker. The round landed just yards from the CP. After the dirt stopped falling, Top stepped back outside. "Do you two want to come in here before you get hurt?"

"Are you kidding us, Top?" Mike asked. "It's safer out here. At least we don't have to worry about the bunker falling in on top of us if it gets hit."

Amused but unwilling to show it, Top growled, "You two knuckleheads get your butts in here right now."

Parks smiled when he greeted Mike and David, "How are two of my best squad leaders doing?"

David replied, "We're a little bored, sir. We heard Top canceled this morning's scavenger hunt. What can we do to stir up a little excitement around here?"

Top gave David an icy stare, followed by an ever-so-slight wink.

"If this constant shelling isn't enough excitement for you, you're about to get your wish," Parks said with a tired grin. "As I recall, you two joined the corps at the same time. How long do you have before you rotate back to the world?"

In unison, Mike and David looked at each other and shouted, "Thirty-five days, SIR."

"Well, good for you. I trust you have your replacements already picked out. Before we get down to business, Top has a presentation to make."

In a businesslike manner, Top began, "Corporal Shaffer, how long have you been running 3rd Squad?"

"Ever since Sergeant Miller was killed. About two months now, Top."

"As you know, squad leaders are supposed to be E5 sergeants. And the corps has finally seen fit to give you that promotion before you leave this beautiful R and R center. Congratulations, Sergeant Shaffer. Here are your stripes. I look forward to signing your rotation papers and sending you back home to your momma. So don't screw it up by getting wounded again. You know how I hate paperwork."

"No, Top. I would not dream of causing the first sergeant any extra work." Mike then included a little marine humor, "May I say, sir, it has been an honor to serve with such a great marine."

With a grin, Top replied, "Make sure you don't." Then changing to a frown, he barked, "And if you call me sir again, I will bust you back down to corporal so fast it will make your head swim. I work for a living." Then still scowling at Mike, he added, "No offense intended, Major."

Mike saw Top's tough character as a façade he put up to hide the feelings he had for his men. As pleased as he was about drawing a rebuke from Top, he knew better than to show it by grinning.

"None taken, Top," Parks said with a laugh. "Congratulations, Mike. Your men respect you because you take care of them, but leadership always comes with risk and responsibility. I am going to echo Top's concerns. Under no circumstances do I want you to take any unnecessary chances from here on out. That applies to you too, Sergeant Long. Got that?"

"Yes, sir," both replied.

"OK. Now for that excitement you requested, there's an enemy buildup northeast of here, and we expect an attack in the next few days. It's the 812th NVA Regiment again. I thought we wiped them out last month. Mike, I'm sending you out with the 3rd Squad tomorrow morning to do a recon sweep around the Hill. Here's your grid map. If Charlie is up to anything, it is doubtful they will mess with you, but take every precaution."

Pointing down at the map, Parks continued. "Take your patrol out the south gate at 0600 and proceed clockwise around the Hill. Avoid enemy contact if you can. Should you get hit, disengage as soon as possible, and we will cover your withdrawal. I want you to stay within seven hundred yards of the perimeter and call in anything that looks suspicious. Watch the northeast and southeast side tree lines carefully. If I were Charlie, that's where I would be. Make sure you're back inside the wire by 1700 hours.

"Any questions, Sergeant Shaffer?" Parks asked.

"No, sir."

"Good. This is Sergeant Westgate and Corporal Diamond. They're snipers on loan from the 9th Marines for a few days. I want you and David to take them over and set them up in OP-2. Hopefully, they can thin out some of those spotters for us. Maybe slow down some of this shelling for a while."

Parks had one more piece of bad news to pass on. "Division says these M16s are starting to jam. We haven't even test-fired ours yet. It looks like our new low-maintenance weapon has a big problem. They will all have to be retooled by the battalion armory as soon as we rotate back to Dong Ha in three weeks. However, that does not help us now. They recommend we fire only semiautomatic. Make sure every marine is informed. Any questions?"

"No, sir," came the unified reply.

"OK, men. You have your orders. Get it done. I'll see my staff back here at 1730 hours. Dismissed."

Chapter 8

Whispering Death

David and Mike led the two snipers east through the trench line toward OP-2. The canvas bag Bernie carried did little to hide its contents. As they crossed the compound road, someone called out, "Step aside, boys. Whispering Death has come to town."

Bernie groaned at the suggestive words. Shooting targets was one thing. He was about to find out what it was like to silently kill the enemy.

From the concealment of the zigzagging trench line, the four marines finally made their way to OP-2 undetected. The bunker was ten feet square and dug into the ground about three feet to provide a low profile.

Howitzer ammo canisters filled with dirt lined the inside walls. The outside was covered with several feet of sandbags. The wooden-plank-framed window on the east wall was about one foot high by six feet long. The back door of the bunker opened into the trench.

Like all the Hill's other fortifications, the bunker's biggest weakness was the ceiling. There was no way to support more than two layers of sandbags with timbers alone. What was needed was a steel-covered roof. The wall protection was respectable, but a direct hit from an artillery round would collapse the bunker and turn it into a coffin for anyone inside.

Mike told the two snipers to make themselves comfortable. "You can set your gear over there." He pointed to the four cots that lined the back wall.

Addressing the two marines in the OP, Mike said, "A sniper team will be with us for a few days. Continue your observations and act as if they were not here. Sergeant Long and I need to leave now." Mike then addressed Bernie, "I'll be back later. Is there anything else you need before we go, Sergeant Westgate?"

"Call me Bernie. That's Joe. We understood you would provide us with a radio."

"Roger that. I'm Mike. That's David. One of us will bring a radio by later." Mike nodded, and then he and David left the bunker.

Bernie stepped to the bunker window with his field glasses and began his surveillance. Joe set up his tripod-mounted spotter scope in the shadows, two steps from the window. Looking east into the Trace, Bernie could make out the firebase at Gio Linh six miles away. He could see small puffs of smoke from what he knew were howitzers. The town of Gio Linh was located a short distance away.

Beyond Gio Linh was the South China Sea. Across the horizon, he could see an aircraft carrier, five destroyers, and numerous other task force support ships. All were cruising just outside the range of the NVA gun batteries north of the river. From Bernie's elevated position, the village appeared as an illusion, floating in the water beneath the vessels.

Bernie spotted an old church steeple above the tree line on the south side of the Trace, a reminder of more peaceful times. The French missionaries who settled in this area named Con Thien the Hill of Angels. He wondered if they would still think that if they could see it today.

A movement to his right caught his attention. A four-inch-long scorpion was scurrying across the window ledge—one of several nasties that populated the Hill with the marines. Removing his Ka-Bar knife, he moved it above the creature and allowed it to move a foot before pressing down and cutting it in half. Using the blade, he flipped the two still squirming halves outside.

One of the OP spotters was standing at the window looking through his binoculars. A cross was inked onto his helmet cover with the words, "In God I Trust." Inquisitively, he asked, "Where're you from, Private?"

"Broken Arrow, Oklahoma, Sergeant."

"Do they believe in God in Oklahoma, Private?"

Turning to face Bernie, the private answered, "Of course we do, Sergeant. Don't you?" He then waited for Bernie's response.

Uncomfortable by the private's pervasive stare, Bernie returned to his surveillance without answering. His thoughts returned to his conversation with Eliphaz. *What was it he said, a doorway into the Kingdom? What does that mean?* Standing there, listening to the rounds landing around the Hill, he considered how faraway God seemed.

While Bernie scanned the Trace, Joe was busy taking notes. After an hour, they had compiled a terrain sketch with four target reference points. With their preparations complete, Bernie took the rifle and stood one step from the window.

With his eyes fixed on the Trace, Bernie slowly reached down and flipped up the lens covers on his scope. He laid the rifle on a sandbag placed on the window frame and got into his firing position. Bernie peered into the scope and waited for Joe to call out his first target. The marines manning the bunker stood in anticipation of watching a sniper do his thing.

"Here's your radio, Bernie," Mike said as he entered the bunker. "The CP call sign is Shield 1. Top wants you to use the call sign Night Stalker."

Mike realized he had walked in on something and quickly added, "I'm sorry. Did I interrupt anything?"

Continuing to look through his scope, Bernie replied, "No, we were just getting started. Night Stalker, huh? Your first sergeant does have a sense of humor."

Mike walked to the window and picked up Bernie's binoculars. "What's your plan, Joe?"

"We've located seven targets. One, believe it or not, is a Russian adviser. I will give Bernie their locations from a target reference point. See that dead tree out there at two o'clock?"

"I see it. That's a long way out there."

"That's TRP 2. 'Drop 50' means fifty yards closer to the Hill. 'Add 50' is fifty yards past the TRP—the same goes for left and right. We will walk the targets in from the farthest out. That way, the closer targets will not see what's happening behind them. Got it?"

"Understood." Mike wasn't sure he wanted to watch this execution, but it was a side to combat he hadn't seen before. Besides, he had already seen a river of blood spilled in the last twelve months. How much different could this possibly be?

"What do you have for me, Joe?" Bernie asked.

"Target 1. From TRP 2, right 100, drop 40," came Joe's instruction.

"Roger. Target 1 from TRP 2, right 100, drop 40," was Bernie's reply.

It took Mike a few moments of looking to locate the target. He would have missed him but for the sun shining off the radio antenna, a mistake that an older, more seasoned spotter would not have made.

"Radio operator in a shell crater."

"Roger. Radio operator in a shell crater ... Target identified."

"Dial 740 on the gun."

"Roger, 740 on the gun ... Indexed."

"Wind 7 mph, mill right. Send when ready."

"Roger, wind from the right at seven mph, mill right." There was a long pause before the shot rang out—*BANG*. Bernie immediately rechambered another round and reacquired his target.

Looking through his scope, Joe followed the air displacement of Joe's first round and observed it was too high, passing just inches above the target. The target reacted by putting his face into the dirt. The only thing visible was the top of the operator's pith helmet.

"Shot was one mill high. Resend."

Knowing the target was about to alert others to their presence, Bernie dropped one mill on his scope crosshairs and quickly fired his second shot. The round's impact was so violent the operator's head exploded, sending an eruption of blood and body parts several yards behind the target. There was no time to think about the goriness of the mission, so both snipers moved on.

"Target 2 ..."

In the next twenty minutes, Bernie and Joe eliminated seven targets, six spotters, and a Russian adviser. With no one directing fire on the Hill's east side, the incoming mortar rounds slowly stopped.

"How are you doing, Bernie?" Joe asked.

After reflecting on the faces of the enemy soldiers he had just killed, Bernie's first thought was of their families. Then he was reminded of what they taught him in sniper school: killing the enemy is not personal. This was the moment of truth he had been expecting, and right now, it was worse than he thought it would be.

There was a long silence in the bunker. The two marines in the OP were stunned when they saw the pink spray that followed the bullet as it ripped through the last unsuspecting target—a mere three hundred yards from the Hill. They looked over at Bernie and wondered what went through a sniper's mind when he made a kill. What a strange emotion for a marine to feel empathy for an enemy they knew as ruthless and uncaring and would just as soon cut your throat as look at you.

"Talk to me, Bernie. How're you doing?"

A few moments passed before Bernie replied with a sad heart, "I'm good, Joe."

Bernie's first kill wasn't easy for Mike to watch. So he laid his field glasses on the window ledge and waited for the final report. He stepped into the trench and thought, *I hate this war. There's no way I could be that cold-blooded. Lord, I'm ready to go home now.*

Chapter 9

Mail Call

The sky was streaked with red as the sun settled in the western sky. Temperatures were in the upper eighties, and the humidity was bearable. A westerly breeze from the coast would last another hour before tapering off and turning muggy.

With the loss of six spotters, the two eastern hills would be granted a reprieve from the shelling. For the first time today, the marines were able to relax. Always wearing their flak jacket and helmets, their rifles were never more than an arm's reach away.

Demarco, Grady, and Lamont defended perimeter Bunker 3. Demarco reclined at the bunker window, staring into the Trace, wondering what Charlie would do next. Grady examined an opened case of C rats, trying to decide if he wanted the meatloaf or beefsteak tonight. Lamont was sitting at a table someone had fashioned out of wood from an ammo crate, cleaning his M60 machine gun. He had just closed the cover when they heard the voice of the company mail clerk, Tony Romano.

"Mail call. Any brothers at home?" Tony said as he entered the bunker. Around his neck was a large canvas mailbag.

"Romano … my main man," Demarco jived back. "Welcome back to the hood."

"Nice to see you brothers are still alive. What's the good word?"

"Not much good to say after finding out our M16s are jacked up," Demarco bitched. "I'd like to bend mine around some bureaucrat's neck. How's a brother supposed to kill the enemy if his gun don't work?"

"Chill out, Corporal. Don't get yourself in a twist," Tony countered as he mimicked Demarco's urban slang, teasing him into their daily battle of wits. "If it makes ya feel any better, all us white boys got the same problem."

"That's easy for you to say. You don't have to live down here in the projects."

"No, but I had latrine duty again today, unlike some people I know. That's the same as payin' your rent for you. Anytime you want to change jobs, say the word."

"Calm down, Anthony. Don't go hasslin' a brother now. I forgot you were so sensitive about that silver-spoon job you got up there on the hill. Next time, I promise to be more respectful of your feelings."

Every marine has a part of the day he enjoys more than others. To Demarco, it was waking up this morning knowing he was only three days away from that freedom bird home. To Lamont, it was thinking about his R&R trip to Bangkok in two weeks. With Grady, it was gleaning the news from the *Grand Rapids Press* newspaper his mom sent him daily. Tony just loved talking trash with his buddies.

Tony goaded, "Did anybody ever tell you you're full of crap, Demarco?"

"Yeah, I get that a lot," Demarco said as he glared back at Tony. "What's your point, man?"

"That was the point, dipstick."

Tired of waiting for Tony and Demarco to finish saying hello, Grady extended an open hand and politely asked, "Where's my newspaper, Tony?"

"Oh, I almost forgot, Grady. Here you go. Lamont, you have two letters from your fan club and, Demarco, you have two. One of them looks official. I would open that one last. You boys take care of yourselves tonight. I'll pick up your outgoing mail in the morning."

"We've got a patrol in the morning. We'll leave ours in the mailbox," Demarco said as he pointed to the ammo can nailed to a post inside the door.

Frowning his disapproval, Tony replied, "You know that's not a US government–approved mailbox, don't you, Demarco? The Man is very particular about pickup and delivery protocols. I could lose my stripe if I don't follow regulations."

"That may not be a US government–approved mailbox, boy, but it is for sure a US government–approved ammo can. Why should the Man care about what I put in the box if he approves the box?" Demarco said with a big toothy grin.

"Well, Corporal, rules is rules, and you may or may not get your mail picked up tomorrow if you put it in that ammo can," Tony fired back with attitude.

"Now listen here, you little wimp. If my mail is still here when I return from patrol tomorrow, I will hunt you down and pound you into a fine powder. You got that, PFC Romanoooo?"

"Yeah, I hear you loud and clear, Mr. Short-Timer. However, did you know that Corporal Rios and I are tight? Being the company clerk and all, he can misplace your orders for a week or two. No more than he likes your sorry butt, he probably would pay me for suggesting something like that."

"You wouldn't do that to a brother, would you, Anthony? That's hard-core, man," Demarco whined.

"Well, we gots ta follow da Man's rules, don't ya know. We gots ta give him his due. It's all 'bout respect, bro."

"Now, don't go preachin' respect to the brothers. We could use a little of that ourselves." Changing to a more accommodating tone, Demarco asked, "OK, Tony. Where exactly would you like us to put our mail?"

"Put it in the ammo can for all I care, man. I just don't like you calling it a mailbox when it ain't one," Tony said, grinning as he backed toward the door.

Demarco frowned and quickly leaned forward as if to go after Tony. Tony promptly gave him a wink and said, "I gots ta split, man. I'll see you dudes tomorrow night." Then he stepped outside and headed down the trench toward bunker four.

Lamont and Grady had been watching this comedy exchange with great amusement. Laughing was strong medicine, and all four marines knew it.

"My brothers," Desmond began, "that white boy sure is good with the sass. I'd swear he was half black if I didn't know any better."

"He's got sass, all right, but he is one hundred percent I-talian," replied Grady. "I heard he volunteers for latrine duty every day."

"Why would he do something like that?"

"So we don't have to, fool. You never wondered why we've been here almost a week and not had to pull latrine duty. Tell me again how you got those stripes, Demarco."

"Well, let me rephrase myself," Demarco said with a wide grin. "That white boy sure has style."

Tony stuck his head back inside the bunker and said, "Seriously now, you dudes need to be careful tomorrow. Those snipers took out six spotters and a Russian adviser today. Charlies got to be pissed about that." After making eye contact with each marine, he disappeared again down the trench.

"Six spotters and a Russian," Demarco pondered as he stared at the empty doorway. "I hope I'm out of here when Charlie decides to get even."

*   *   *

After watching Bernie take out the enemy with surgical precision, Mike needed something to cheer him up. When he left OP-2, Mike stopped by his bunker to pick up his mail and fork and spoon from his mess kit. He then met David at the 1st Squad Bunker for evening chow and to discuss the news from home. As was their daily custom, Mike would lead them both in a short Bible study and prayer.

Inside the bunker, David was sitting at a makeshift table, waiting. "You're late, Mike. What kept you?"

"I just watched Bernie kill a spotter. It was a headshot. There were blood and body parts everywhere."

"Yeah, I heard already," David responded with empathy. "Seven kills, as I was told."

"How did you hear about it so soon?" Mike queried. "I just left there ten minutes ago."

"News like that travels fast around here, bro. Have you noticed incoming rounds have tapered off in the last half hour?"

Mike was so busy trying to erase the image of that dead spotter that he hadn't noticed. Turning toward the door, Mike listened momentarily and answered, "You're right. The shelling's stopped." Eager to put the war on hold for a while, he sat down at the table and asked jadedly, "What's for dinner?"

"Lucky for you, it's not leftovers from last night, Mike." David got up and walked over to an opened case of C rations and returned with two boxed meals. Setting them on the table, he added with an indifferent smirk, "Take your pick."

Mike looked down at his choices—boned chicken and meatballs. Suddenly, he had lost his appetite. It had only been a few days, and he was already missing the three hots and a cot back at Dong Ha. "On second thought, I'm not really that hungry. Mind if I have the fruit can out of yours?"

"Not at all."

While David spread the contents of the boned chicken meal out onto the table, Mike reached into his pocket and pulled out two letters. One was from Katie. The other was from his mom. Laying them on the table, he picked up the can of mixed fruit David had set aside and opened it with his P-38 can opener. *Which letter should I open first?*

Halfway through his can of fruit, Mike picked up his mom's four-page letter and began reading about a surprise welcome-home party their girls were planning for them. The last thing in the note was a very intriguing suggestion.

"David, I got a letter from Mom. When we get home, Katie and Linda are planning a surprise party at the church. It will be catered, and Steve Atwell will be the DJ. She thought it would be the perfect time for us to propose to the girls. What do you think?"

"A double proposal, huh? We already have the rings. That'll be cool, but Katie will kill you if she thinks you know about the party beforehand."

The last thing Mike wanted to do was upstage Katie's big surprise, but seeing the excitement on her and Linda's faces when they proposed was worth the risk. Besides, he could always blame it on his mom. "Then I think we should do it."

Mike and David spent a few minutes discussing how to pull it off without raising suspicions. Keeping his mom involved would be a big part of the plan. With the sun down now, Mike opened Katie's letter. Most of it was about her nursing classes and plans when he got back home. There were six pages of commentary on a dozen different subjects but no hint of a surprise party. On the last page, Katie gave Mike some bad news.

"David," Mike said solemnly, "Jimmy Sanders was killed at Khe Sanh in March. He was manning one of their outposts when they were overrun. This will be hard on his mom. His dad was killed in Korea when he was ten."

"Yeah, that's what Linda said. He was set to rotate back to the States in July. That's too bad. He was a nice guy."

* * *

Grady unrolled the *Grand Rapids Press* newspaper and began catching up on all the hometown news. The big headline was about the deadly F3 tornado in south Grand Rapids. Grady's eyes widened when he learned that the path it took was just three blocks from his crib.

Lamont opened the first of his two letters. Last fall, he received messages from six different girls. When Tony first referred to them as his fan club, he was too embarrassed to tell him he didn't know them. Someone gave his name and address to some sorority sisters at Lincoln University, and they took him on as a writing project. As the popularity of the war started to wane, they gradually stopped writing.

It didn't matter to him who wrote or about what. These were the only letters he received from the States, giving him hope. He had two years left on his enlistment. After that, he planned to take his GI Bill, find a black college, and get a degree in engineering or business administration. Nothing good waited for him in the projects he came from.

Demarco looked at his two letters and wondered which he should open first—the one from his wife or the law firm in his hometown.

He knew something was wrong when her letters became less frequent. Her most recent messages lacked any feeling. With hesitation, he opened her letter and began to read.

Dear Desmond,

I'm writing to tell you I won't be here when you get home … Latoya.

As Demarco read the letter, he tried to understand how she could leave when he would be home in less than a week. *How long has she felt this way? Is there another man?* It took every bit of grit he could muster, but he managed to shove most of his pain into the closet of despair he kept hidden from even his closest friends.

"Is everything all right, Demarco?" Lamont asked compassionately.

"Just a little problem I can fix when I get back on the block."

That might have been the official statement, but Lamont and Grady knew better, looking at his downcast face.

"Semper fi, Demarco," said Lamont.

"Always faithful, Demarco," added Grady.

"It don't mean nothin', my brothers."

The silence was interrupted by the increasing roar of an incoming artillery shell from the north. It landed with a loud bang inside the wire and peppered the bunker with shrapnel. Lamont and Grady looked up from the bunker floor and saw Demarco sitting in front of the window, oblivious to how close he came to dying. Slowly, he released both letters, and they fell to the floor.

Chapter 10

Armed Forces Radio Network

The sun was down, and the marines had settled in for the night. The Hill's mortar battery had just started firing illumination rounds every fifteen minutes. Like a Fourth of July rocket, the rounds are fired one thousand five hundred feet straight up. After bursting, they descended back to earth utilizing a parachute. The spooky flickering illumination lasts about sixty seconds.

The illumination's primary benefit was making it easier for the marines to see at night while temporarily disrupting enemy activity. The downside is that the enemy could hear the mortar when fired and had five seconds to conceal themselves. With some well-placed shrubbery, it was impossible to spot Charlie at night until he was in your face.

The mortar crew fired forty-four illumination shells on a typical night. Major Park's problem was that he had only ninety-six rounds in his arsenal to last two nights. If the Hill were hit tonight, the mortar team would need to fire about sixty shells an hour. So the shortage was a big concern to everyone on the Hill.

From Bunker 4, Greene's large boom box could be heard playing the sounds of the Armed Forces Radio Network (AFRN) station. Currently playing was "We Gotta Get Out of This Place" by the Animals. While the radio station was committed to rock and roll, everyone accepted it. To say that Greene's fire team leader, Corporal Smith, a die-hard redneck, enjoyed it was an overstatement, but he did tolerate it well. When he griped about the music, he did so as a matter of redneck pride, not because he hated the music. To him, anything was better than nothing. AFRN music was not only popular, but it was also great for morale.

"Hey, Darrell, why can't they play something good for a change instead of this rock-and-roll crap?"

"Like what, Corporal?"

"How 'bout something by Buck Owens, Sonny James, Eddy Arnold, or George Jones?"

Like an old game replayed every night, Greene teasingly replied, "Didn't Sonny James and Eddy Arnold play with the Zombies, Corporal?"

"Not likely, doofus."

"Come on, Corporal. Don't be such a square. This is groovy music. The Zombies are a cool band."

"Greene, do you have any idea where you are right now? You are a marine, and this is Vietnam. There are bad guys outside the wire tonight who want to kill you in ways you don't even want to think about. Why don't you stop acting like a hippie and get with the program."

"All this war stuff is bumming me out, Corporal. If I went out there and talked to those guys, I could get them to come over to our side."

"Greene, if you want to try recruiting the NVA tonight, I will gladly open the gate for you."

The disk jockey announced his next selection. "Our next record goes out to all our troops on the DMZ tonight, and it's a good one, 'I Can't Get No Satisfaction' by the Rolling Stones. You guys take care of yourselves tonight."

"Now, I can definitely relate to that song, Darrell."

With animated body movements, Greene replied, "Groovy. Rock on, Corporal Smith."

While all this was happening, Greene stood at the bunker window. Smith stood in the doorway at the back of the bunker. The third bunker occupant, Fuller, was in the trench a short distance away, smoking a cigarette, shaking his head, laughing at this silly clash of cultures.

Suddenly, they heard that ominous sound: *thump … thump … thump*. You cannot tell where a mortar round will land by the sound of the thump. Sometimes, however, you know the next ones are heading in your direction.

Immediately, Greene got that feeling and rushed toward the back door, pushed Smith to the bottom of the trench, and fell on top of him. A second later, the first round landed twenty yards directly in front of their bunker. The shrapnel that peppered the bunker window would have wounded or killed both men had it not been for Greene's quick thinking.

The second round landed almost in the trench line between bunkers 3 and 2. The third round landed twenty yards behind Bunker 1. When the dirt stopped falling, Greene pushed himself up and extended his hand to help Smith to his feet. Smith lay there looking up at Greene in total amazement. Aware of what had just happened, he lifted his hand and let Greene pull him up.

Dazed, Smith realized there was more to Greene than meets the eye. Music was just his way of coping with the war. The hippie veneer was all a facade. Greene was a marine who could hold his own when the time came.

The bunker was rocked but not damaged, and Greene's boom box was still playing. As Smith regained his senses, he started laughing when he heard the song now playing, "Land of a Thousand Dances."

"Greene, I was under the impression you did not understand what it means to be a marine, but I was wrong. I think you understand it very well. Probably better than I do. If you let it, this place will get to you, but as long as you have your music, you will dance your way through this war and back home again. Good job adapting and overcoming your environment. Just so you'll know," Smith added with a grin, "I still don't like rock and roll."

With a straight face, Greene replied, "My parents took me to Disneyland last year for graduation. We stopped to take a walk down Hollywood Boulevard. Did you know that Sonny James has a star there? I've even seen him on the Grand Ole Opry before. 'Since I Met You Baby' is one of my favorites."

Greene paused for a moment to let Smith soak it all in. He grinned and returned to the bunker to continue his watch. Seconds later, he returned to hand Smith a three-inch-long piece of shrapnel he found stuck in the wood frame of the bunker window.

"Corporal, I don't think those guys out there care too much for our music. Bummer."

As Smith watched Greene walk back into the bunker, he could not help but think how amazing it was that a nineteen-year-old could remain so calm and unfazed after such a close brush with death.

It had been five minutes since the mortar round landed in front of the bunker, and Smith had still not moved a step. He had never been a religious man, but suddenly, he wondered if he would get off the Hill alive.

Smith had been in Vietnam for seven months now. This was not the first time he had to duck a mortar round. The marine corps trained courageous fighting men, and Smith had learned well. It was not the near miss that had him spellbound; it was his surprise at Greene's maturity level.

Smith considered the marine core values. *What if,* he asked himself, *there is more to life than honor, courage, and commitment?*

Smith leaned inside the bunker and heard Greene quietly praying. He could barely make out his last words: "Lord Jesus, I pray you will protect us all tonight from harm. Let your will be done in my life. Amen."

Backing away from the door, Smith was impressed by the humbleness of Greene's spiritual conviction. There was undoubtedly much more to Greene than just being a marine. The corps had always held God to a high standard but left each marine to find his own religious path. Although this was not the first time he had heard a marine pray, it was the first time he considered it a personal petition for the welfare of others.

The phrase "there are no atheists in foxholes" suddenly came to mind. Smith wondered what he would rather be when the bullets started coming again: an atheist or a Christian. Looking out into the Trace, he realized it would be a long night of prayer and soul-searching.

* * *

Fuller was stooped down in the trench during the shelling, holding on tightly to his helmet. After seeing that Greene and Smith were OK, he went to check on the marines in Bunker 3. Fuller found Grady and Lamont crouched at the bottom of the trench. It was so dark he almost tripped over them. Just then, the mortar team fired off another illumination round. Seconds later, the Hill was lit up again.

Fuller stepped past the two marines and looked into the bunker. "Where's Demarco?" he asked.

"The last time I saw him," Grady returned, "he was down at Bunker 2."

Fuller moved quickly down the trench to a caved-in section and found Wolf and Finch digging at the dirt like madmen. Fuller assumed the worst and started digging from his side. There were only seconds to make a rescue.

Wolf soon found a boot and started pulling. Another boot was found, and with all their strength, he and Finch pulled Adams out of the dirt. "Adams, are you OK?" Wolf shouted.

After spitting and blowing out the dirt, Adams replied, "I'm OK. Have you found Demarco?"

"No," Finch replied.

"He was right here when the round landed. He can't be too far away."

About that time, Grady and Lamont arrived. "Where's Demarco?"

Turning around, Finch answered, "He's buried somewhere close by. Start looking."

Digging quickly, they found a helmet with a head still in it. Finch grabbed one side of Demarco's flak jacket, and Grady took hold of the other. Lifting straight up and back, they managed to drag him free of the dirt and sandbags. He was unconscious when they flipped him over. Finch brushed the dirt off his face and slapped him several times. Finally, Demarco opened his eyes.

"Are you OK, Demarco?" Finch asked as he started checking him for injuries.

"I think so, man. Get a brother on his feet."

Finch stood him up and pinned him to the trench wall to keep him from falling.

"How about now? Any pain?"

"I'm OK. Thanks, man. When we heard someone scream 'incoming,' we both ducked. The next thing I knew, the trench wall collapsed on top of us." After pausing, Demarco continued, "Which of you dudes was standing on me?"

"Sorry," Finch began. "That was probably me. We didn't know where you were until we found Adams."

"That's OK," Demarco began. "Us brothers are used to being stepped on."

"Shut up, Demarco," Grady scolded. Punching him on the shoulder, he continued. "Show some respect yourself. You'd be dead by now if it weren't for Finch."

Demarco slowly looked around at the five frowning marines and realized he should have kept his misplaced humor to himself. "Sorry, Finch," he capitulated.

"Think nothing about it, dude," Finch replied with a smile. The dust flew when he slapped him on the chest. "Your replacement's not due for another two days. We can't afford to let you die until then."

After the letter from his wife, Demarco thought that death might not have been that bad. Without her, life wouldn't be worth living. They got married shortly after dropping out of high school. Both had working-class jobs, struggling with no promise for a future until he got the idea of enlisting to take advantage of the VA's education benefit. Now, his plans had evaporated, leaving him seriously questioning life.

Finch turned to Adams and started brushing the dirt off his uniform. "You two are going to need a shower."

Mike came running down the trench to check on his men. "Is everyone OK here?"

Finch answered, "Everyone is fine, Sergeant. Adams and Lamont were having a smoke when the wall caved in on them."

Mike looked them over closely as the illumination round faded and added, "Have you girls been playing in the dirt again? Tomorrow, I'll have Corporal Rios order us a bunch of kiddy buckets and shovels."

Fatigue delayed their response, but they all started laughing. Once again, the moment had been overcome by those who knew that war can't be taken too seriously. The moment a marine loses his sense of humor, he's lost his fighting edge. It is easy in combat to transition from laughter to aggression. It is difficult to make that change once fear has taken over.

"Now get some sleep, men. I want 3rd Squad assembled outside the 3rd Squad bunker at 0530 sharp."

"Will do, Sergeant," Finch replied.

Relieved that everyone was safe, Mike moved down the trench to Bunker 1 for his final evening inspection. At 2300, he returned to his bunker, hoping to get a few hours of sleep—if possible.

Chapter 11

Sappers in the Wire

Late that afternoon, Bernie and Joe walked down the trench and found a place to set up for the night's surveillance. It was ninety yards above the perimeter wire and offered an unimpaired view of the Hill's east side. A mortar round had blown out the trench. Close by lay a stack of unused sandbags.

"This will do, Joe. A little work, and we'll have a nice hide tonight. Let's go get some chow and come back after dark."

At1900 hours, Bernie and Joe returned to prepare for their night in the trench. Concealed by the darkness, Bernie and Joe used their short entrenching tools to fill enough sandbags to fashion a sloping firing platform they could both lie on. Then they built a wall of sandbags on either side to protect them from flying shrapnel.

With their work complete, Bernie removed the starlight scope from its case and attached it to the M14. Under minimal lighting conditions, they could spot any movement one hundred yards beyond the wire. It was now 2000 hours and still too early for anything to happen, but knowing Charlie, you could never be too sure.

Bernie was processing his feelings concerning the seven men he had just killed. Still trying to justify his actions, he turned to his partner for moral support. "Joe, have you come to any conclusions about killing the enemy like this?"

"Yeah, I think so. I'm Catholic, and we believe it's a sin to commit murder. While home, I talked to a priest about it, and he told me that premeditated murder and justifiable killings are not the same. To rob and kill someone is murder. To execute someone for that crime is justifiable."

"I can see that, Joe. How do we justify what we are doing?"

"The South Vietnamese people invited us here to protect them from the bad communists. Our involvement in that struggle can only be described as justifiable because it is our act of compassion. It helps me to think of it in terms of protecting my family. If a thief breaks into my home, I am justified in killing him. So you can say we are guarding a neighbor's house. Yeah, I think I can live with it."

Bernie continued his scan of the wire as he considered Joe's comments. Several minutes passed before he responded, "My uncle is a Baptist preacher who fought in the Pacific during World War II. He told me about the same thing.

"I asked him how he dealt with killing the enemy. He said it bothered him until he realized this was a sinful world. Sometimes, evil men must be dealt with for our society and religious freedoms to survive. He said the only ghost that still haunted him was a ten-year-old boy from Okinawa who jumped off a cliff because he thought the marines would kill and eat him."

Bernie and Joe continued to search for enemy movement without any further conversation, each one busy exercising their demons of war. The finality of taking a life is a heavy load to bear, but they were marines and willing to accept the consequences of their decisions.

At midnight, Bernie was so tired he asked Joe if he could take over. Joe took the weapon and continued the watch. Bernie tried to stay awake but couldn't. Joe saw him nodding and whispered, "Bernie, I've got this. Grab some z's, and I'll wake you in a couple of hours." Bernie laid the field glasses down and was asleep in seconds.

At 0215 hours, Bernie was sleeping like a log. The incoming rounds had steadily increased. Some landed as close as one hundred yards away. Bernie was so tired that they didn't bother him at all. Then something ran over the back of his leg. He jumped and quietly shouted, "What was that?"

"Relax, Bernie. It was probably a rat. I killed a big one with my Ka-Bar a little bit ago. Now that you're awake, check out what's going on at eleven o'clock."

Bernie took the binoculars and tried to find Joe's target. The night was pitch-black. It wasn't until the next illumination round ignited that Bernie spotted the two enemy sappers slowly sneaking through the wire. Their bodies were camouflaged with perfectly placed vegetation. Their uniforms were stained brownish red to match the color of the Hill's volcanic landscape. From the line bunkers, they appeared as nothing more than shrubs.

"I marked 'em, Joe. I'll call it in."

Bernie picked up the radio handset and called the CP: "Shield 1, this is Night Stalker. Over."

"Night Stalker, this is Shield 1. Over."

"We have two sappers probing the wire. Over."

"Do you have the targets covered? Over."

"Affirmative. Over."

"Wait for assistance. Out."

A few minutes later, a sergeant arrived and knelt behind them. "What do you have?"

Bernie answered quietly, "We have two enemy soldiers in the wire. Both have a satchel charge."

"The perimeter bunkers have been notified. Take out the targets when you're ready."

Without taking his sights off the targets, Joe whispered, "I've been watching these two for an hour. They're not going anywhere quickly. I'll wait until they clear the wire. That will make cleanup a lot easier in the morning."

There is a cold-bloodedness about war that civilians don't understand. To survive in combat, you must be tougher than your enemy. Death is an everyday fact of life, so you learn to reduce life down to its most basic form. If you cannot turn off your feelings of compassion and mercy when fighting the enemy, he will kill you.

The NVA are masters of stealth and patience. It might take the sappers four hours to get through the wire and another hour to find their targets, but they will do it because it's their job. Both sappers know they're trapped once they set off their charges, so they are prepared to die in the explosion. It is hard to humanize someone with that kind of fanaticism, and Joe knew if he didn't neutralize these targets, someone would die tonight.

At 0330, both targets were ten yards inside the wire. They were inching their way to their objectives. The first sapper would take out the Special Forces bunker thirty yards to his left. The second would attack Bunker 1, manned by Magrini, Slayer, and Littlejohn.

Joe had his sights trained on the first sapper. The other was visible in the upper left section of his scope. Both sappers were unarmed except for a satchel charge and two Chinese hand grenades.

The NVA objective for this invasion was twofold. The first was a diversion to conceal the second. While Bernie and Joe were preoccupied with the sappers, Giap had snuck an RPG team within fifty yards of the wire. When they spotted the sniper's muzzle flash, they would fire a rocket-propelled grenade at the sniper position.

Giap, never overly concerned about his men's safety, was willing to sacrifice two soldiers to locate and eliminate the snipers before his troops rushed the Hill.

"Bernie, don't you think it's strange Charlie knows there's a sniper on this side of the Hill, and they sent these two guys in here to get wasted before they can complete their job?"

"Yeah, that's strange to me too. I wonder what Charlie's up to."

"I don't know, but I need to eliminate these two before they get any closer."

"Everyone on the Hill is waiting on you, Joe."

Joe checked both targets and worked out the mechanics in his head. He decided to fire on the nearest target when the next illumination round burst then take out the second target a few seconds later. Should he miss either mark, the sappers would rabbit and become easy targets for the marines on the perimeter.

Joe heard the mortar thump. Seconds later, the sky over the Hill lit up with flickering light. Both sappers froze in place. Joe took in a deep breath and slowly squeezed the trigger. The round hit the first sapper right between his shoulder blades. Immediately, the second target activated his bomb and rose to charge Bunker 1. Before the sapper could take a step, Joe's round hit him in the chest. His final act of defiance was tossing the satchel charge five yards before him. The sapper fell backward to the ground.

No sooner had Joe fired his second round than he and Bernie spotted an RPG round coming straight at them from outside the wire. They had just enough time to push themselves back down into the trench before the grenade hit the front side of their position. The explosion buried them in the rubble.

Slayer was doing a slow left sweep of the wire when he heard the first sniper shot. No sooner had he turned back right than he was confronted by the second sapper standing fifteen yards in front of him. Before he could react, Bernie's second round struck the sapper hard, and he fell. Slayer did not see the satchel charge, so he immediately opened fire on the RPG team outside the wire with his M60.

At the same time, six other machine guns on the perimeter opened fire in the same area. Slayer got off a short burst before the satchel charge exploded, knocking him to the back of the bunker. The next thing he knew, Mike was reviving him with several sharp slaps to the face.

"Are you OK, Sam? Are you hit?"

Slayer thought about it before replying, "I'm all right, Sergeant. I think I'm fine."

Mike did his best in the darkness to see if Slayer was bleeding anywhere. "You lucky jarhead. Now get your butt up and get that M60 operational." With a pat on the shoulder, Mike handed him his helmet. He then headed out the door and down the trench to find Magrini.

Wiping the dirt off his face, Slayer whispered, "Thanks for the concern, Sergeant." Still groggy from the blast, he pushed himself up and inspected the gun. He recocked his weapon and started firing again, unsure he would hit anything.

Magrini had his rifle laid over the trench wall, scanning the wire for activity when Mike arrived. "Are you OK, Paul?"

"I'm good, Mike. Man, I didn't see that guy until he stood up."

The illumination round had faded when Mike looked over the trench toward the wire. He heard two sniper shots and knew there should be two dead sappers in front of him, but he could only make out a couple of obscure shapes. He immediately realized that all the firing was outgoing, and the threat appeared to be over.

"Check fire, check fire!" Mike shouted, waving his hand.

Others repeated his command, and the firing along the line gradually stopped. It got quiet while everyone waited anxiously for what might happen next. Anticipating the worst, Parks ordered the mortar team to fire flares at two-minute intervals. He knew these were rounds the Hill might need tomorrow night.

Mike took a few seconds to size up the situation and told Magrini to get Littlejohn. He went to the bunker and used the field phone to call the CP.

"Sparks, this is Shaffer. Get me the CP. Over."

"This is Johnston."

"Sir, this is Shaffer. We have two dead sappers in front of Bunker 1. Request permission to take a detail out to secure any munitions they might have. Over."

"Permission granted," Johnston replied. "Bring the bodies back with you as well. I will alert the Special Forces you're out there. I don't have to tell you to be very careful, Sergeant. Over."

"No, sir, you don't. Hold those illumination rounds for a few minutes. Out."

"Roger that. Out."

Magrini, Slayer, and Littlejohn waited for Mike outside of the bunker. The four marines headed down the trench until they came to the ramp that led out of the ditch and into no-man's-land. Mike motioned to his men to remain there while he spoke to one of the Special Forces team in the next bunker.

"We need to go out and get those sappers. Can you make sure your troops know we are going out?"

Specialist 5th Class Rutkowski replied, "Give me a minute to check in with our bunkers."

Rutkowski picked up his field phone to check in with his unit. After a brief conversation, he replied, "Lieutenant Summers is on his way down to take personal charge while you extract those bodies. Good luck, Marine."

"Thanks, Army."

Mike returned to brief his men. "We need to get those two bodies and bring them back here. Slayer, you and Littlejohn get the first body we come to. Magrini and I will get the second. Make sure the sapper is dead. Check his hands before you attempt to move him. Keep a low profile and bring back any ordnance you find. Leave your rifles here. We need to move fast. Any questions?"

"No, Sergeant."

"Good. We will go after this illumination round burns out."

As soon as the light faded, Mike looked down the trench and saw Rutkowski give him the go-ahead sign. The marines scrambled up the ramp and knelt in the shadows beyond the ditch. After a few seconds of caution, Mike gave the signal, and the four men dashed out to retrieve the bodies. Each man knew they were exposed, and the longer they were out there, the better their chances of being spotted.

Mike and Magrini reached their sapper and found him dead. They checked his hands to ensure they did not contain any hidden grenades. Mike rolled the body over and saw two Chinese Chicom grenades attached to his utility harness. Mike felt the pins to confirm they were bent correctly. He grabbed the satchel charge with his left hand and the dead sapper's utility harness with his right. Magrini grabbed the other side of the chest strap, and they ran back toward the trench, dragging the sapper between them. Slayer and Littlejohn were a few yards ahead of them with their body.

When Mike and Magrini were fifteen yards from the trench, they started taking small arms fire from outside the wire. Everyone along the line started screaming, "Hold your fire! Hold your fire!"

Slayer and Littlejohn reached the trench first. They dropped their body at the top of the berm and dove in. Mike and Magrini still had another ten yards to go when an AK-47 opened fire. Mike watched the enemy tracers bury themselves into the sandbags and wondered what he was doing.

When they reached the ditch, both marines dropped the dead soldier and jumped in. They hit the bottom like sacks of potatoes.

Seconds later, another illumination round exploded above the Hill.

Mike looked at Magrini and asked, "Are you OK, Paul?"

"I'm good, Mike. How about you?"

"I'm OK, but I'm way too short for this."

The two marines breathed heavily. They gave each other an extended smile, knowing they had cheated death one more time. With a groan, Mike whispered, "Only thirty-four more days to go. I can do this."

The second Mike and Paul were safely in the trench, the command went out to open fire. Every weapon on the east side of the Hill opened fire on the enemy's tracer rounds. After a mad minute of fire, it was as quiet as a grave.

*   *   *

After the RPG round hit the sniper's hide, Bernie and Joe wasted no time digging themselves out and getting back into the fight. Joe was already searching for targets when the small arms opened fire on Mike and his men. The images were grainy in the distance, but he easily made out the muzzle flashes. Joe aimed just behind one. Two shots and the bursts from that rifle stopped.

Joe spotted another flash and fired again. That rifle stopped firing as well. As Joe scanned for additional targets, he saw the muzzle flash of an AK-47. He fired three quick rounds, and it went inactive.

The outgoing orange-and-red tracer rounds racing off into the night were a statement of marine firepower. Bullets ricocheted off the ground and were kicked high into the air like bottle rockets. With no further incoming rounds, Mike gave the command to cease fire, and there was dead silence.

It was 0400 when the excitement ended. No one on the Hill had gotten more than three to four hours of sleep, but at least they managed to survive the night.

Chapter 12

Delta 23 Leaves the Hill

It was 0515 hours when Delta 23 assembled in the trench outside the 3rd Squad bunker. Despite the sleepless night, all seventeen members were anxious to get off the Hill for a few hours. Mike's men had been trained to attack, but they had been holed up on the Hill for six days, taking more than they dished out. So today would be a one-day vacation for 3rd Squad. Every marine on the Hill was envious and would gladly give a month's pay to go out with them.

Mike stepped out of his bunker, glanced down the line at his men, and wondered if he would lose any of them today. As the leader of 3rd Squad, Mike had lost only one man—a rare statistic, all things considered. He had a sixth sense when it came to danger. It was like something inside told him when to exercise caution. Littlejohn referred to it as Mike's guardian angel.

The first man in the column was Wolf. As the point man, he led the patrol. There was not a man in the company they trusted more. A full-blood Sioux Indian, Wolf's all-business and no-nonsense manner made him the perfect pathfinder. Behind Wolf was Finch and then the new replacement, Adams. He joined 3rd Squad two days before the marines moved onto the Hill.

Behind Adams was the first M60 machine-gun team of Magrini, Slayer, and Littlejohn. Littlejohn was Delta 23's radioman. Behind Littlejohn were Mike and Doc Ryan, a navy corpsman. Next in line was the second M60 team of Demarco, Lamont, and Grady. Grady sported his weapon of choice—the M79 grenade launcher. The grunts called it a thumper, and Grady was a master thumper.

Fuller, the slack man, followed Grady. If Wolf went down, Fuller would be the one to take over on point. Behind Fuller were Greene and Smith. Last in the patrol were O'Neal, Russell, and Tucker.

Mike carefully inspected each man's equipment, everything from ammo to the required two full canteens of water. Except for Adams, each man in the patrol had experience running ops in the DMZ. They knew the drill as well as the danger. They also understood the importance of preparedness. Before Mike's inspection, the senior team members had checked each patrol member at least once.

When he had checked Tucker's gear, Mike looked up the trench toward Wolf. He slowly examined each face in the faint light and silently prayed for their safety. Parker's words of caution came to mind as he returned to the front of the column: *Leadership always comes with risk and responsibility.* As the leader of 3rd Squad, Mike knew the risk they were taking today, and his responsibility toward his men was a load that was taking its toll the closer he came to rotating back to the States.

"Men," Mike began, "I need you to be on high alert once we leave the Hill. We are not expecting any enemy contact, but do not let your guard down, even for a second. If we get hit, our orders are to disengage and let the Hill cover our withdrawal. We need intel today, so sing out if you spot anything suspicious. We're taking a Duster with us today. If I were Charlie, I would consider messing with the marines of 3rd Squad a bad idea."

Each man smiled and nodded his approval. They were now pumped and ready to go.

The M42 Duster is an armored tracked vehicle with twin automatic 40 mm cannons mounted in an open revolving turret that will fire 240 rounds per minute. Developed initially as an antiaircraft weapon during World War II, it was used as an antipersonnel weapon during the Korean and Vietnam Wars. Charlie called it the Fire Dragon. The NVA would rather attack a tank than a much more agile Duster.

"Most of you are seasoned veterans, so you know what to do. Adams, you stay focused and alert. If we get hit, you get in Finch's footsteps and stay there. Understand?"

"I understand, Sergeant." This was his first patrol, and his excitement was ramping up.

"Littlejohn, have you done a radio check with Parks and the three OPs?"

"Affirmative, Sergeant."

"Excellent. You men with M16s, make sure your selector switch is set to semiautomatic. Those weapons will jam if you fire them on automatic. Choose your targets well and stay calm. The Hill is going to cover us like a blanket. Is that clear?"

"Crystal," came their unison reply.

"Wolf, take us down to the south gate."

Mike's heart was heavy as he followed his men down the trench line. *God, I ask that you bring us all safely back to the Hill at the end of the day. Amen!*

The trench line ended at the Special Force's first bunker, twenty yards from the south gate. Wolf halted the squad at the intersection, and everyone immediately knelt to conserve the energy they would need later. Looking over the top of the trench, Mike pulled out his map and rechecked the location of their first checkpoint.

David walked up beside Mike and asked, "Do you have everything you need, Mike?"

Mike glanced at David and smiled. "Yeah. I think we're good."

"Well, be careful out there today. Parks wanted to remind you not to get too close to the tree lines on the northeast and southeast corners. He thinks that's where Charlie is massed."

It was 0600 hours, and the sun was breaking in the eastern sky when the guards opened the south gate for the day's traffic. Announcing its presence, the Duster's diesel engine roared as it descended the compound road toward the southern entrance. Every enemy soldier a mile from the Hill could hear it coming.

"If you ever repeat this, David, I will deny it, but I am glad those army guys are going out with us today."

"Your secret is safe with me, Mike. By the way, the Duster's call sign is Roadrunner. He's expecting you to follow him out the gate."

"Littlejohn, contact Roadrunner and give the army our compliments."

"Will do, Sergeant."

The Duster slowed as it approached the gate. The commander spotted the patrol to his left and waved at Mike to follow him out.

Mike gave the command to move out. "OK, Wolf, fall in behind that Duster."

At that moment, all eyes were fixed on Wolf. He gave the forward hand signal, and Delta 23 turned right out of the ditch and toward the gate.

Inside the entrance was a large red sign: "The world's finest fighting men pass through this gate. They wear a green uniform and call themselves marines. THE PLACE OF ANGELS." Each marine voiced an agreeing "oorah" as he passed.

David could not help feeling concerned as Mike and his squad left the trench. After glancing at the tree line, David bowed his head and began to pray.

As the Duster commander drove through the gate, he rotated his turret to train his cannons on the southeast tree line. This was the northwest corner of Leatherneck Square, one of Charlie's most active playgrounds. The Duster's response would be immediate and deadly if there were any enemy fire—and Charlie knew it.

The Duster gunner aimed his M60 machine gun on the trees west of the road. Twenty yards outside the gate, the Duster driver took a hard right turn and moved off the road in a broad sweep to the north. The turret guns adjusted with the change in direction and maintained their coverage of both tree lines.

"Third Squad, recheck your safeties and load your weapons," Mike commanded. In unison, the bolts ran home on thirteen M16s and two M60s. Grady opened the breech of his M79 and inserted a high-explosive round. Flipping up the barrel, he positioned it across his chest. Their orders were to avoid contact, but if Charlie provoked them, they would be more than happy to engage the enemy before Parks ordered their withdrawal.

Half-timing it through the gate, Wolf left the road immediately past the wire and took a path to intercept the Duster about two hundred yards out.

Mike gave the command, and the patrol positioned itself in a wedge formation with each man spaced five yards apart. The Duster slowly maneuvered itself into position within the wedge, forming an arrow. The Duster cannons pointed forward while its M60 covered the column's backside.

There was a smile on each marine's face as they walked out in the Trace. The excitement and anticipation of the moment felt like driving down a highway with the top down. If they had to die today, this would be as good a place as any.

Defending a position was arduous work for a marine. Patrols were part of their training, so the marines were in their element for the first time in weeks. Even Adams was pumped and ready for his first action. His only problem was his one-hundred-beats-per-minute heart rate. By the end of this patrol, Adams will have the butterflies all under control.

Chapter 13

Golden Hammer 2, This Is
Delta 23 Actual, Over

The Hill had survived the night, but Major Parks knew it was only a matter of time before the NVA hit them hard. He could only assume it would be either tonight or the next. His four biggest concerns were the illumination rounds, the defective M16s, shoring up the perimeter with some new concertina wire, and his rickety old bunkers. The wire was due any day, but they desperately needed those mortar rounds. Unfortunately, the Hill had to use those extra ten rounds last night. They would surely need them tonight.

It was 0700, and the entire Hill was already busy repairing the damage from last night's shelling. With a patrol out in the Trace and the NVA hidden within one thousand yards of the Hill, Major Parks and the three OPs would nervously monitor Delta 23's progress as they maneuvered around the Hill.

Four of the ten checkpoints that Mike would use as he circled the Hill had been preregistered by the 81 mm mortar team the day they arrived. Additional coverage from positions around the Hill could be provided from the 105 howitzers, .50-caliber machine guns, and recoilless rifles. If Delta 23 got into any trouble, the reaction time from the Hill would be swift and lethal.

While Mike was on the west side of the Hill, David led a detail out through the wire on the east side to check on any KIAs from last night's firefight. His orders were to stay within five hundred yards of the wire and bring back anything the NVA might have left behind.

After thoroughly searching the area, David found seven dead enemy soldiers. He recovered an RPG rocket launcher with a haversack of five shells, one Russian AK-47 assault rifle, and various other weapons. David knew the bodies would be gone in the morning, so he left the dead where they could be easily found. It crossed his mind to booby-trap the bodies like Charlie would do, but after a year in combat, he had just enough civility to decide against it.

His men, on the other hand, were not always as respectful. While they were searching the dead NVA uniforms, he watched a private pocket a souvenir he had found on one of the bodies. He did not condone the act, but he understood the feeling. The horrors of combat changed a soldier's life forever. David had seen too many marines leave Vietnam and go home to a life that he knew would be filled with sorrow and grief because they could not deal with the atrocities of war.

Two types of warriors returned to the States: those who wanted to forget and those who could not forget. The last thing David wanted to do was interfere with either healing process.

Before David returned to the Hill, he had his men bring out the two sappers to leave them with the other dead enemy soldiers. He remembered losing one of their marines after a skirmish with the NVA during Operation Deckhouse VI several months ago. They found him tied up and mutilated. It was a memory he was sure he would never forget. Twelve months in-country, and he had seen about everything imaginable. He was holding on to the last strand of humanity he had left. He didn't know it, but the next twenty-four hours would test that resolve even further.

The shelling on the Hill continued nonstop. The only thing that varied was the intervals. They would be as little as every five minutes or as much as an hour apart. Charlie would fire three rounds in close proximity or hundreds of yards apart. Nothing on the Hill was off-limits as far as the enemy was concerned, not even the aid station.

Early that morning, two marines needed emergency evacuation from the Hill. The helicopter landed next to the aid station and came under an immediate mortar attack. In the few seconds it took to load the wounded, six rounds landed within one hundred yards of the helicopter. The helicopter received several shrapnel hits but lifted off without significant damage. The aid station, on the other hand, was not so fortunate. One round landed ten feet from the heavy sandbagged walls. The blast was absorbed, but part of the wall collapsed onto two patients and a corpsman, resulting in a broken arm and a mild concussion.

Delta 23 had just arrived at checkpoint 1 when the enemy fired on the aid station. Hearing the rounds pass overhead, Mike commanded everyone to take a knee. "Littlejohn, tell the Duster we'll be here for a few minutes. Then meet me up front."

"All right, Sergeant."

Mike jogged up and knelt next to Wolf. "Where do you think those rounds came from, Wolf?"

"About five hundred yards beyond that tree line, Sergeant."

Mike unfolded his map and quickly found their most likely position. Knowing the enemy was constantly scanning their radio frequencies, he decided against calling in a grid location because it could be used to identify Delta 23 and its location. Taking out his compass, Mike measured an angle. He took the handset from Littlejohn and called Lieutenant Duncan in OP-1.

"Golden Hammer 2. This is Delta 23 Actual. Over."

"Delta 23 Actual. This is Golden Hammer 2. Over."

"Golden Hammer 2, two hundred fifty degrees, eight hundred yards from checkpoint 1. Over."

"Delta 23 Actual. This is Golden Hammer 2. Wait one. Over."

Duncan had spotted the faint smoke from the enemy mortars and was about to call in his fire mission when he got the call from Mike. With two different angles on the target, Duncan now had the opportunity to triangulate their target information. From checkpoint 1, Duncan drew a line two hundred fifty degrees and measured eight hundred yards from there. He found that Mike's target angle intersected his target angle at a specific grid location.

Wanting to minimize Delta 23's radio time, Duncan replied, "Delta 23. This is Golden Hammer 2. Roger your last transmission. Out."

Duncan called for one round of white phosphorus. Mike heard the howitzer fire and waited. Seconds later saw the smoke of the burning phosphorus rising above the trees. It appeared Duncan had received his message.

Duncan called the artillery fire support center with his correction, and a minute later, a second round was fired. He then called in his final instruction, and soon, three high-explosive rounds were screaming toward the target. Seconds later, several secondary explosions were observed. No one would know what damage was inflicted, but it was at least one mortar team and some ammunition stores. It was not a bad day's work, considering no one saw the enemy.

Mike gave the order, and Delta 23 moved on toward checkpoint 2.

At 0730 hours, a squadron of helicopters could be seen approaching the Hill from the south. One by one, the helicopters dropped their concertina pallets near the southern part of the Hill. Offering protection from above, four heavily armed Huey gunships circled the area, waiting for anything that moved in the tree line. At least for the moment, the mortar attack was halted. The supply helicopters left the area and headed back to Dong Ha. The gunships remained on station until the Hill moved their wire around the Hill.

Chapter 14

Leon Spotted Wolf on Point

At 0750 hours, Mike halted the column and told his men to take five. Without being told, every man in the patrol dropped to one knee. It was already humid, so everyone wiped the sweat from their face and reached for a canteen.

The Duster sat idling, hoping the enemy would show himself. With 45 mph speed, the Duster could rush headlong into battle with cannons blazing and retreat before the enemy could respond. With a fire dragon coming after them, the last thing the NVA would do is give their position away by returning fire.

Taking the handset from Littlejohn, Mike checked in with Duncan at OP-1.

"Golden Hammer 2, this is Delta 23 Actual. Over."

"Delta 23 Actual, this is Golden Hammer 2. Over."

"Golden Hammer 2, we have reached checkpoint 2. Nothing to report. Proceeding to checkpoint 3 in five. Over."

"Delta 23 Actual, this is Golden Hammer 2. Roger. Out."

The government's use of Agent Orange had left the Trace a barren landscape. All that remained around the Hill was dead elephant grass and an occasional lifeless tree. In the years that followed, Agent Orange would ravage the health of many of those who fought in Vietnam.

Mike took his binoculars and scanned the north and south tree lines. Pulling out his map, he moved to the front of the patrol and knelt next to Wolf. "How're we doing, Wolf?"

"I spotted some movement in that tree line over there a couple of minutes ago, Sergeant."

Mike took his binoculars and looked in the direction Wolf had pointed. "Wolf, that's four hundred yards away. I can't see a thing, even with these field glasses. How can you see that far?"

"Indians have eyes like eagle's, Sergeant," Wolf said with his usual straight face.

With a bewildering stare, Mike replied, "Wolf, if you can see that far, I wouldn't want you tracking me."

Not much got past Wolf. He was very much aware of Mike's own powers of observation. Like the others in 3rd Squad, he had seen him exercise caution at precisely the right moment too many times. In many ways, Wolf considered Mike part Indian.

"Sergeant, any Indian can smell the enemy from here."

Mike thought about Wolf's comment and chuckled as he continued looking through his binoculars. "Don't tell me you can smell them, Wolf. Not from here." After another few moments of thought, Mike added, "How can you do that?"

When Wolf failed to reply, Mike turned to see Wolf looking back at him with a straight face.

"Wolf, you can't actually …"

A second or two passed before Wolf raised his eyebrows and cocked his head slightly.

"It's not humanly possible to smell them from here, Wolf," Mike argued.

By this time, Mike felt unsure of his reasoning. Up until now, Wolf was not noted for any sense of humor. So Mike did not know how to take Wolf's seemingly ridiculous suggestion.

One final glance at Wolf, and Mike gave up. "Our next checkpoint is eight hundred yards in that direction. Keep watching and smelling that tree line, Wolf.

"Up and at 'em, Marines. Keep your eyes open and watch your spacing. Don't give Charlie an easy target."

The NVA were ruthless fighters. They will intentionally wound a marine to kill those who came to their aid. Thousands died in Vietnam in this manner. One of the codes that made the marine corps special was their loyalty to a fallen comrade. They called it "No Marine Left Behind," and it bordered on the fanatical.

Charlie understood that bond and used it against them whenever they could. The last thing Mike wanted was to run into an ambush and lose some of his men today. He offered the Lord another silent prayer as Delta 23 headed again into the unknown.

The patrol approached a three-foot-deep dry creek bed lined with small dead trees and scrubs—the perfect place for an ambush. Mike now had a decision to make. Should he follow the creek bed or take his chances in the open? Immediately, that internal voice told him to take cover in the creek bed.

Mike checked his map and learned it continued for five hundred yards northeast before turning north toward the Ben Hai River. Checkpoint 3 was a short walk from the turn, due west of the Hill. From the scattered rock, it was obvious Charlie had been using the creek for cover as they moved unseen through the area.

"Littlejohn, call the Duster and have them position themselves twenty yards to our right flank. Tell them our next checkpoint is half a klick ahead."

"Will do, Sergeant."

As Littlejohn made the call, Mike crouched as he moved up to the front of the column. "What do you think, Wolf?"

Wolf pointed to the tree line and replied, "There's a bunker under that stand of bamboo, Sergeant."

Mike checked the bunker with his binoculars and marked the distance at two hundred fifty yards north of his position. "I see it. Good spot, Wolf. There are three firing ports. Heavily fortified too. We need to walk by this one."

"Sergeant, why don't we let the Duster take that bunker out now?" Wolf asked as he motioned back behind him. "From here, it would be a piece of cake."

"I would like nothing more, Wolf. However, our orders are not to provoke the enemy. That bunker is not going anywhere. What do you think about sending these guys a care package when we get back to the Hill?"

With a slight grin, Wolf replied, "Good idea, Sergeant."

After Mike marked the bunker's grid coordinates on a piece of paper, Wolf handed him a spent M60 casing. "Where did you get that?"

Mike followed Wolf's eyes down to a creek bed full of spent ammunition. *I wonder what happened here.*

Sharing his map with Wolf, Mike pointed out their next checkpoint. "Take us down the creek bed and stop where it turns north. I want to look around before we continue."

"Fuller, pass the word back—there is an NVA bunker to the left. Everyone keep a low profile and do not let them know we see it."

Chapter 15

The Booby Trap

Wolf halted the patrol at the bend in the creek bed. They were now about two hundred yards from the tree line, closer than Parks wanted. Mike signaled the squad to take a defensive position and then moved up to speak to Wolf.

"What do you think, Wolf?"

"Sergeant, there's a tripwire right there," Wolf said as he pointed behind him to a small tree a few feet away.

Mike looked past Wolf and searched for the wire. "If there's a wire there, Wolf, I can't see it. We need to disarm it." Looking back toward the patrol, Mike gave a series of hand signals. Moments later, O'Neal joined Wolf and Mike.

"Shawn, we have a booby trap in front of us. Can you disarm it?"

"Let me take a look at it, Mike."

Mike signaled the patrol to move back thirty yards and take cover. He waited until Wolf had shown Shawn the wire then told Wolf to join the patrol.

"You be careful, Sergeant."

"We will, Wolf. Have Littlejohn inform the Duster we are holding here long enough to deal with this little inconvenience."

"Will do, Sergeant."

Looking over Shawn's shoulder, Mike asked, "Can you tell what kind of booby trap it is?"

"The kind that will kill us both if I'm not careful," Shawn growled. After a thorough examination, Shawn continued. "We've got a fishing line stretched across the creek about eighteen inches high. There's probably a grenade hidden on one side of the ditch. I'm amazed Wolf spotted this one."

Mike made a good squad leader because he understood the difference between protecting his men and training them to protect themselves. While he could deal with this situation himself, Shawn was the mortar team leader—an expert with explosives. That made him the right man for disarming this device.

Mike positioned himself several feet behind Shawn so he could assist if needed. Shawn was used to Mike's overly protective manner and knew asking him to back up was useless, so he did his best to ignore him.

After careful visual inspection of the monofilament wire, Shawn withdrew his Ka-Bar knife and ever so carefully, probed the covering at the base of a sapling on the right side of the creek bed. He could see the wire tied off on this side, so the explosive had to be elsewhere.

Shawn then moved his knife about a foot above the line and used it to slowly trace it to another sapling on the left side of the ditch. It was covered with loose branches and leaves. "Mike, if I trip this thing, you better be moving because I'm diving out of this creek," he said softly.

"I hear you, Shawn. Be careful."

Shawn lightly probed the branches with his Ka-Bar to see which could be removed without interfering with the wire. The stem of the first twig was placed over the top of the tripwire, hiding the device. Gently, Shawn reached over and lifted it slowly.

He saw the line move slightly and froze. Setting it back in place, he knew he needed to look at it from a different angle.

"Back up, Mike. I need some room."

Shawn stuck his Ka-Bar in the ground, removed his helmet, and got down onto his back. Cautiously, Shawn inched his way forward until his nose was six inches under the tripwire. From this angle, he saw that the branch was securely wrapped around the wire.

Shawn reached into his fatigue pocket and pulled out a pair of wire cutters. Slowly, he trimmed the branch until it fell away.

"OK, Mike, I know what we are dealing with now. There's a US hand grenade tied to this sapling. The grenade pin is missing, and the safety lever is held in place by a safety pin attached to the tripwire."

"Well, that was thoughtful of Charlie. By any chance, did you remember to bring your spare grenade pin, Shawn?" Mike said with a little humorous sarcasm.

"You know I make it a point to never go anywhere without toilet paper and a spare grenade pin. Now stop bothering me, Mike."

Shawn returned his wire cutters to his pocket, removed a grenade pin, and slipped it onto his left pinky finger. "Mike, I'm gonna need some help here. When I secure the lever and remove the safety pin, I need you to take my Ka-Bar and cut the grenade loose. Do you think you can do that without cutting off my finger?"

"Yeah, I can do that. Only because I don't want the enemy to hear you scream if you get scratched." Mike looked down and noticed the sweat beads on Shawn's face. On his back, Mike knew he had no chance of escape if anything went wrong. Although Mike had seen Shawn disarm booby traps before, he knew a little humor would do a lot to relieve his stress.

Shawn adjusted his position, reached up, and carefully put his left hand around the grenade, securing the spoon with his thumb. With his right hand, he reached up and removed the safety pin.

"OK, Mike. Cut it loose."

Mike slipped the knife behind the sapling and gently cut the binding to free the grenade. "It's all yours, Shawn."

Slowly, Shawn pulled the grenade close and slipped the grenade pin into the keeper. Mike handed him his Ka-Bar and watched as he used it to spread the cotter pin to lock the lever safely in place.

"Here, catch," Shawn said as he tossed Mike the grenade. "You know," Shawn added as he rose to one knee, "I think these NVAs have a very sick sense of humor. They have all the Chinese grenades in Southeast Asia and prefer to kill us with our own grenades."

"Thanks, Shawn. You can rejoin the patrol now. Nice job. Have the men stay put. Tell Wolf to come forward."

Shawn wiped the sweat from his forehead with the arm of his fatigue jacket and smiled. "Anytime, Mike."

Mike wondered how unusual it was for them to encounter a booby trap in this creek bed. He knew Charlie used it for concealment and would not place a pitfall here unless he knew Delta 23 would be coming by soon.

Wolf crouched as he walked up and knelt next to Mike.

"Wolf, I think Charlie set this booby trap here recently. Can you tell me about how long ago?"

Wolf moved over to the sapling and considered all the clues. He picked up the branches that concealed the device and saw the white sap oozing from the tear. Carefully, Wolf inspected the banding that held the grenade and saw it was wet—a trick Charlie used to keep it from drying out. Wolf ran his hand lightly over the ground and noticed the absence of footprints beyond the sapling—something his father taught him to hide his tracks.

Turning to Mike, he said, "Sergeant, I think that grenade has been here no more than an hour. That's about the time we moved into this creek bed. They were expecting us. It's not safe here."

"I think you're right, Wolf."

Turning around, he pointed to Finch and motioned him forward. "Finch," Mike said softly, "I think we are about to walk into an ambush. Have the men quietly move back up the creek bed another twenty yards and wait. Tell everyone to keep a low profile. We'll be along in a minute."

Mike moved to the edge of the ditch and made eye contact with the Duster commander. Hand signals conveyed the message the patrol was relocating to his location. The commander acknowledged with a nod.

As Finch headed back down the line, Mike looked at Wolf. "We've been lucky so far, and other than this, we haven't seen a thing. It's way too quiet for me. I understand Charlie reluctance to provoke that Duster, but we should have received a mortar round or two by now. What do you think?"

"Sergeant, that bunker back there was vacant, but there are a few gooks waiting for us down this creek bed. I think Charlie has moved their other forces to the east side of the Hill. These local yokels are trying to discourage us from continuing this trail. There's something out here they don't want us to find."

"That's what I thought, Wolf. Let's get out of here."

The Duster sat thirty yards southeast of the patrol, facing the tree line. Mike gave the order after one more scan with his binoculars, and Delta 23 scrambled out of the creek and sprinted to the Duster. Mike motioned the patrol to spread out and assume a defensive perimeter around the Duster.

The list of how you could die in Vietnam was endless. Now it was no longer the mines and booby traps that concerned Mike. It was a single NVA soldier in a spider hole. One AK-47 at close range could take out half his squad before they knew what hit them.

From the corner of his eye, Mike saw Wolf slowly kneel to the ground and cautiously crawl away from the patrol. Sensing danger, he told Littlejohn to call the Duster. "Tell them we have a situation behind them. Then follow me."

"All right, Sergeant."

Mike crouched as he raced to the place where Wolf entered the grass. From a kneeling position, he watched as Wolf disappeared into the grass. As much as he wanted to follow, he had to trust Wolf's judgment. Mike's priority was the Duster and the safety of the other fifteen members of his squad.

When the Duster machine gunner was alerted, he quietly turned to cover Wolf's movement. With great patience and stealth, Wolf inched toward something hidden in the grass. About twenty yards out, Wolf froze in place. The gunner was expecting an RPG round or a grenade at any moment.

A minute passed before Wolf continued his search. Moving to his right, he began to circle behind the unseen enemy. From a height of eight feet, the Duster gunner knew that Wolf was too close to his target for him to fire without hitting him. Realizing the same thing, Wolf looked up at the Duster and nodded. The gunner elevated his weapon slightly.

Wolf reached back and removed his Ka-Bar knife from its sheath. Leaving his M16 behind, he crept forward until he saw an antenna sticking slightly out of a four-foot-deep spider hole. After another few feet, Wolf could see the top of the NVA's helmet. A final adjustment and Wolf looked down upon a forward observer with a radio strapped to his back. Beside him was a Russian-made Simonov semiautomatic rifle.

Wolf was about to plunge his knife into the enemy when he realized something unusual about this setting and steadied his hand. His first thought was that the soldier was dead. It then occurred to him that whatever was in the hole was not entirely human and was very much alive.

"Wolf, we've been expecting you," came a voice from deep within the hole. "We heard you sneaking through the grass."

Lance Corporal Leon Spotted Wolf was very good at reading signs and judging things seen and sometimes unseen. As strange as this encounter would have been for most people, he recognized it as something he had witnessed as a youth. "Hello, devil. Who am I talking to this time?"

"The same one you talked to when you went on that vision quest up Devils Tower. Remember?"

"Bildad. How could I ever forget you? You were a talking coyote the last time I saw you. That is, until I killed you."

Not amused but always willing to play his cat-and-mouse game with humans, Bildad replied, "You might have killed the dog, but you didn't kill me. I'm immortal."

Not humored and ready to put the enemy soldier out of his misery, Wolf replied compellingly, "What do you want, devil?"

"Well, as you know, Charlie is going to bring a lot of heat your way very soon. So we thought we should pay our respects to the soon departed." Bildad paused to see how Wolf would react.

When he failed to reply, the enemy soldier's head slowly tilted upward until Wolf saw the sad face of a youth who knew he was about to die. Unmoved by the age of an enemy that would gladly kill him, Wolf raised his knife to strike.

"Before you kill this innocent boy," Bildad said mockingly, "there is something we want you to tell Mike."

Wolf learned from his father that the Great Spirit was the protector of the Indian people. After becoming a Christian, he learned the full extent of that protection and better understood the One who provides it. It was the Spirit who revealed to Wolf the nature of this meeting. *Wolf, this spirit has come to test Mike's faith tonight. You are not to warn him. This is something he must face alone. Be strong in the coming battle. I will be watching over you.*

"What is it you wanted to say, devil?"

"Tell Mike we are coming for him."

With a forceful thrust, Wolf plunged his knife down into the neck of the enemy soldier. Without a sound, he died instantly. Wolf watched as the boyish face changed into an older, more hardened combatant. He knew it was the boy's face that Bildad willed him to see. There was no remorse for killing this enemy.

Wolf used grass to clean his knife. Searching the body, he found a map with markings that seemed to identify critical locations on the Hill. Securing the radio and rifle, he left the body in the hole and returned to join the 3rd Squad.

Mike was relieved to see Wolf walk safely out of the grass. Wolf handed Mike the map, rifle, and radio. "I brought you some souvenirs, Sergeant. The guy I took them from won't need them anymore."

"How the heck did you know he was out there? Sight? Smell? What?"

"The squelch on his radio was set too high. It made so much noise I'm surprised you couldn't hear it, Sergeant."

At this point, Mike didn't know what to think about Wolf's newfound humor, if that's what it was. "Over that Duster's engine? You've got to be kidding me, Wolf," Mike said sharply. "Tell me something. Are all Indians as sneaky as you?"

"To be honest, Sergeant, after four years at Iowa State, I think I've lost some of my edge. My great-grandfather was a real sneaky Indian. He once stole a horse right out from under Custer. That white man was so full of himself, he rode for another mile before figuring it out."

Amused but still searching for an answer, Mike asked, "Wolf, what exactly did you study at Iowa State?"

"Psychology," Wolf said with a big grin and raised eyebrows.

"Well, that figures. I guess I've become one of your test subjects."

Mike looked up at an amazed Duster gunner who mouthed a silent *wow*. He waved the Duster forward, and the patrol rose to their feet and formed two columns, one on either side of the Dragon. Mike handed the radio and rifle to Adams as he passed, and he and Littlejohn took their place in line.

After Delta 23 left the area, a light blue mist rose to hover above the spider hole. It then raced to catch up to the patrol, searching for a new host.

Chapter 16

Arclight

When the patrol reached checkpoint 3, Mike had suspicions about the lack of enemy presence but had nothing definitive to report. Whatever Charlie was up to, he was keeping it well hidden. However, the closer they got to the eastern Trace, the more Mike's anxiety level increased. He felt the patrol was destined for trouble if they crossed the north road toward checkpoint 6.

Mike gave his men an extended break at checkpoint 4 while he slowly scanned the area for anything suspicious. It was clear that Giap had relocated his forces for his attack on the Hill. The most logical location was somewhere in the eastern Trace. The booby trap was intended to maim the patrol so that it could not continue. Then it occurred to Mike that Charlie might have something else up his sleeve for Delta 23.

"Wolf, what are the chances the guys who left that surprise in the ditch back there are tracking us now?"

"Pretty good, Sergeant," Wolf replied. "There's probably a squad somewhere behind us."

"For what purpose? They can't follow us past the north road without being spotted."

"Whatever is out here," Wolf said as he nodded toward the east, "is important enough to waste a few troops to keep us from finding it. If we press Charlie any further, he might strike us from behind and throw a few mortars our way. If Parks sees it that way, he will probably deal with the escaping enemy troops and ignore their mortars entirely."

Mike agreed. "Let's hope Duncan spots them in time. Let's keep moving."

Mike had to assume Charlie was searching for their radio frequency, and if they were not on to them by now, they soon would be. The last thing he wanted to do was start feeding Charlie information that would identify who they were and what they were up to. If Giap knew they were killing his forward observers, he would come after them.

"Littlejohn, contact Golden Hammer 2 and tell them we are proceeding to checkpoint 5. Have them check our six."

"Roger that, Sergeant."

Littlejohn made the call and replied, "Sergeant, Looking Glass acknowledged our request and said to contact Golden Hammer 3 when we get to checkpoint 5."

"Thanks, Calvin," Mike said with enough smile to hide his concerns.

Mike then walked back to the end of the column. "Paul, keep a close eye on our backside until we reach the north road. We may have a tail behind us. If they come, it will be a quick banzai charge to wound as many of us as possible before retreating to the trees. Duncan should be adjusting his mortars on them by now."

"Got it, Mike."

*   *   *

It took Duncan only a few minutes, but he noticed some displacement and color variations in the grass. Picking up his field phone, he reported back to the major.

"Sir, I estimate a squad of NVA is tracking Delta 23 about two hundred yards back."

"Are they closing that distance at all?"

"Not at this time. They are crawling through the tracks left by the Duster. If anything, they are losing ground."

"Where is the patrol right now?"

"About four hundred yards from checkpoint 5. Should we eliminate the enemy now, sir?"

Parks thought about it and came to the same conclusion that Wolf did. If Giap's troops engaged Delta 23 from the rear, a few well-placed enemy mortars would be all it would take to solve Giap's problem. However, it risked drawing heavy artillery fire from Camp Carroll if Duncan spotted the smoke from their mortars.

"How long will it take the patrol to reach checkpoint 5?"

"About twenty minutes, sir."

Now Parks was faced with his own dilemma. His only advantage was knowing about Charlie's plans to attack the Hill. He needed Mike to find out as much as he could before he called the patrol back in.

"No, I don't want to give Giap any idea we are on to him unless we have to. Cover them for now with our mortars. Neutralize them only if they become a threat to the patrol."

"Roger that, sir."

Duncan reviewed his map, picked out coordinates he could use as his most likely target, and called the mortar team. They zeroed in on Duncan's spot in less than a minute, ready for his orders to fire.

Parker had been monitoring an increase in enemy activity south of the Hill and decided to go over to OP-1 and take a look. When the major walked in, Duncan stood at the north bunker window, looking through his binoculars. "How's our patrol doing, James?"

Without looking up, Duncan replied, "Delta 23 has reached the north road, sir. I don't see any more enemy movement. They are probably holding a position two hundred yards west of the patrol.

"Sir, I've been here for three weeks and not seen anything this bad. Take a look at what's going on south of here."

"Yeah, that's what I came over to see."

Parker went to the south wall and scanned the road south of the Hill. As Huey gunships engaged the enemy along the eastern tree line, a convoy of ten supply trucks sped north toward the Hill. "Charlie," Parker began, "is doing his best to keep those supplies from reaching us. That can only mean one thing."

Duncan picked up on Parker's meaning and replied, "Are you thinking tonight, sir?"

"It certainly looks like it, James. Hopefully, we'll know more when our patrol gets back in."

*   *   *

Adams was the newbie. He struggled to take it all in as he knelt in the almost four-foot-tall grass. Mortar rounds struck the Hill every few minutes, sending vertical columns of dirt high into the air. He heard the muffled boom of the army's big 175 mm guns firing from Camp Carroll, followed by loud explosions. The Hill's smaller 105 howitzers pointed southwest, firing into Leatherneck Square. A slight northerly breeze filled the air with the bitter smell of gunpowder.

The helicopters that had dropped off the much-needed concertina wire at the Hill were now running the gauntlet of fire as they fought their way back to Dong Ha to pick up other loads.

From somewhere north of the DMZ, Adams watched three enemy SAM missiles leave the ground to intercept two jets returning from a mission north of the DMZ. Following the contrail and seeing the explosion, Adams considered the pilot's safety. He saw a parachute open seconds later and start drifting toward the coast. *God, I hope we get to him before Charlie does.*

Adams's brief prayer was interrupted by a quick succession of explosions. Startled, he asked, "What's that, Corporal Finch?"

"That's an Arclight strike. It sounded like it's west of here, possibly north of the Rockpile."

"A what?"

"Arclight. The air force just dropped a bunch of one-thousand-pound bombs on the enemy. They call it saturation bombing. If those boys hit their target, there won't be much left of anything. Twenty miles up, three empty B-52 bombers are returning to Guam. Did you feel the ground shake?"

"Man, it felt like an earthquake. I can't see how we could lose this war with that kind of firepower, Corporal Finch."

Finch remembered when he thought the same thing, but that was long ago. In a fatherly voice, he replied, "David, you will be better off spending your time thinking about how you will get out of here alive. Not how we're going to win the war. Now, be quiet and keep your eyes peeled. Remember where you are. Around here, things change in a heartbeat."

*   *   *

Of all combat duties, Ryan had one of the most difficult. He looked at the faces of his squad and wondered who would be his next patient. In combat, it is never a question of if someone gets hit but when. He looked over at Demarco and remembered when he was wounded in the shoulder. A quick bandage, and he was returning fire.

He also remembered when Miller, their previous squad leader, was hit in the stomach. With bullets flying all around him, Ryan knelt bravely in the line of fire to try and save him, only to have him die before they could load him onto the chopper.

The marines called Ryan "Doc," but he was a navy corpsman. Although qualified to assist doctors in an operating room, he was a combat medic. His job was to stop the bleeding and get the wounded to an aid station as soon as possible.

Chapter 17

A Warning from Charlie

It was 1125 hours when Delta 23 arrived at checkpoint 5, three hundred yards from the Hill's north gate. Mike had his men take shelter in several nearby bomb craters and take some chow. He then moved the Duster a hundred yards closer to the Hill.

So far, things had gone well. It was not a typical patrol, but at least they were all safe. Most were halfway through their C rations when they heard three muffled mortar shots from the northeast. Mike knew immediately these were the ones he'd been expecting all morning.

"Incoming!" he screamed as he jumped into a crater. "Heads down!"

Seconds later, three mortars landed thirty yards in front of them. A half minute later, three more rounds landed between them and the Duster. Then nothing further.

When they thought the attack was over, Mike and O'Neal stuck their heads up to quickly look around. "Shawn," Mike offered, "that was some really poor shooting. I think Charlie is sending us a message."

"About what?"

"About not continuing this patrol."

"Then why didn't they just take us out now, Mike?"

"Giap knows this entire sector is in range of those big guns at Camp Carroll. If Parks is correct, and Charlie is massed in those trees over there, the last thing he wants to do is give us an excuse to start shooting in his direction. No, he is hiding something out there and doesn't want us to find it.

"Littlejohn, I need to talk to Golden Hammer 3."

Littlejohn handed Mike the handset. "Here you go, Sergeant."

"Golden Hammer 3, this is Delta 23 Actual. Over."

"Delta 23, this is Golden Hammer 3. Over."

Mike recognized David Long's voice on the radio. Being just yards outside the fence, he knew David could see them from OP-2 and knew they were OK.

"Golden Hammer 3, we are limiting transmissions from this point on. Over."

"Delta 23 Actual, this is Golden Hammer 3. Roger your last transmission. Out."

"Shawn, I need to get something to Parks. I'll be back in a few. You're in charge."

"Roger that, Mike."

Mike made eye contact with the Duster commander as he walked past. The intensity of his sinister gaze told Mike he had something serious on his mind. As much as Mike wanted to stop and ask him about it, he had other pressing business to attend to.

The gate guard was one of David's men. After a brief conversation, he discreetly slipped the guard a message and the map Wolf had taken from the dead forward observer. "Call the CP and have someone pick this up and get it to Major Parks ASAP."

"Will do, Sergeant. Sergeant Long wanted me to tell you to stop provoking the enemy."

"Oh yeah!" Mike glanced up the Hill toward OP-2 and grinned. "Call him back and tell him I don't need a wet nurse."

Mike put his fist to his chest and gave David a thumbs-up and a grin.

Just then, the field phone rang, and the guard answered. "It's Sergeant Long. He wants to talk to you."

Mike took the phone and replied, "What's up, David?"

"You were right about a tail. There's a patrol hidden in the grass about two hundred yards west of your position. Keep your heads down if they attack until Duncan hits them with mortars. Parker will probably call you back in if they do."

"Thanks, David. How are things up there?"

"The snipers took out two more targets early this morning. Other than that, it's the same old thing."

"OK, I'll see you later."

"Take care, bro."

Mike intentionally ignored the Duster commander as he walked by. Instead, he glanced toward the enemy hidden in the grass to his left. Two hundred yards wasn't cause for serious concern. They were only a contingency option for Giap. If they hadn't hit them by now, they probably won't.

When he got back to his men, Mike found one of his men with a bandage around his leg. "What happened to Tucker, Doc?"

"He took a small piece of shrapnel. It's a minor wound, but he refuses to go to the aid station. I removed the metal and bandaged the wound. I gave him some aspirin, but it's going to hurt like hell. He'll be OK to finish the patrol, Mike."

"Is that right, Tucker?"

"Yes, Sergeant. I want to stay with the patrol," Tucker offered quickly.

"OK, but if you can't keep up, I'll let you walk back to the Hill all by yourself," Mike barked. "Make sure you go to the aid station when we return to the Hill."

"Yes, Sergeant. Thanks." Tucker understood Mike's gruff tone for what it was: concern. He knew this gave Mike something else to worry about, but he couldn't leave his brothers out in the sticks.

Mike looked at his watch and realized he was ahead of schedule, so he gave his men another few minutes to relax. If his assessment of the map was correct, Parker should have all the information he needed to terminate the patrol.

With growing concern, Mike finally commanded, "All right, Marines. Up and at 'em. Make sure you police your C-rat cans. Don't leave anything Charlie can use against us. From this point forward, be on high alert. No talking."

The Vietcong in the south and the NVA in the north were masters at finding insidious ways to kill and maim US troops, from punji sticks covered with feces to elaborate nonmetal contraptions triggered by a hidden trip cord, from grenades hidden in cans to pit vipers hanging from trees.

One of the most lethal and feared was called the Bouncing Betty. Invented by the Germans during WWII, it was a land mine that exploded in midair. If they tripped one of those, it would kill or wound most of the patrol.

Before Delta 23 moved out toward checkpoint 6, a marine walked down to the north gate to retrieve Mike's message and map from the guard. After exchanging some pleasantries, he headed back up the hill to the CP. Parks and his staff were at the map table discussing defense strategies when the runner arrived.

"Sir, these are from Sergeant Shaffer," the runner said as he handed the major the map and note.

Parks took the message and read it. "Shaffer has given us the location of a bunker they spotted by checkpoint 3. That's pretty smart of him not to call this in. Call Duncan and have him take it out after Delta 23 gets back inside the wire."

"Will do, sir."

Top went over to the field phone and called Duncan at OP-1. "Shaffer located a bunker northwest of here. The major wants you to take it out when Delta 23 gets back inside the wire. The target is two hundred fifty yards northwest of checkpoint 4. I will send a runner over with the coordinates."

"Roger that, Top."

Parks spread the enemy map on the map table. He, Top, and Lieutenant Johnston were surprised at how detailed it was. "Every position on the Hill is there, even the aid station," Parks said as he pointed to an area east of the Hill. "I wonder what these marks are? Maybe those Special Forces guys will know."

"Lieutenant Summers is on his way over now, sir," Johnson replied. "We'll ask him when he gets here."

"What do you think, Top?"

"Sir, there's too much information here to be anything other than a battle map. Giap wouldn't release it to his troops if he didn't plan something immediately. We must assume we are the target, and tonight's the night."

"I agree. Call Dong Ha and brief them. Be careful what you say. Charlie is listening."

"Will do, sir."

Chapter 18

The Fire Mission

Con Thien was located two miles south of the Ben Hai River and was the northernmost outpost of the DMZ. Its strategic value as an observation post was vital for spotting enemy activity for twenty miles in every direction. As long as the US military controlled the Hill, Giap's plans to win the war would be hindered.

The army had assigned Duncan as the Hill's forward observer three weeks before the marines arrived. Immediately, they nicknamed him Looking Glass. His job was to coordinate air, sea, and land strikes on targets around the DMZ.

After passing Delta 23 off to OP-2, Duncan turned his attention to the area north of the river. He searched for targets for half an hour before spotting a dust cloud forming in the distance. After a few minutes, Duncan identified an NVA convoy of twenty-five supply trucks speeding south down Highway 1 toward the river.

Duncan noticed a destroyer several miles off the coast and contacted the navy's coastal defense group to call in a fire mission. A minute later, the destroyer fired a single white phosphorus round that landed one hundred yards behind the convoy. A correction from Duncan and the ship fired another shot, landing two hundred yards in front of the caravan. Now that he had the range, Duncan called in another adjustment and ordered, "Enemy trucks in the open, fire for effect."

Ten minutes later, twelve smoldering trucks lay scattered along the road. The remaining trucks managed to make it to the protection of the trees along the river. From there, their cargo would be ferried across the river after dark.

When the navy's jets arrived, Duncan watched the aircraft destroy the damaged vehicles. He thought it was strange the NVA would risk losing an entire convoy unless it was critical, so he called Parks and briefed him on the field phone.

Parks now had another piece of the puzzle. Giap had brought in a last-minute shipment of men and equipment for an attack tonight. He just wasn't as confident about where on the line it would happen.

The decision Parks now faced was grave. With only six hours of daylight left, should he continue repairing his line bunkers or start installing concertina wire on the eastern perimeter? The obvious answer was not the one he preferred, but it was the one that made the most sense.

"Top, how are the bunker repairs coming along?"

"Sir, all repairs should be complete in a couple of hours."

"Good. Contact all the commanders and let them know we expect the NVA to hit us tonight. Have everyone complete their work and get as much sleep as possible. I want everyone up and on full alert at 0100 hours."

"What about 3rd Squad, sir?"

"Tell them to abort the mission and return to the Hill immediately."

*   *   *

Delta 23 was almost to checkpoint 6 when Littlejohn got the call from the CP. "Sergeant, Top wants us to fall back to the Hill."

Relieved he did not have to continue any further into the Trace, Mike asked, "Are you sure?"

"Yes, Sergeant. Parks has terminated the patrol."

As much as he liked being off the Hill, Mike was sure there was trouble waiting for them up ahead.

"Listen up, men. The major has ordered us back to the Hill. I know how disappointing that is, but I think it is the right call. Wolf, take us in."

"Will do, Sergeant."

Delta 23 fell in behind Wolf and walked back to the north gate without grumbling. Mike signaled the Duster commander to fall in behind the patrol.

Mike was sure Giap had something important hidden nearby. A final look around told him it was close. Mike had no idea how close he was to finding Giap's little secret—so close that three different mortar teams were ready to fire on his position. This time, it wouldn't be a warning.

Chapter 19

Mike's Report

Wolf led the patrol through the north gate, across no-man's-land, and into the trench line that ran over to their line bunkers. Tucker limped up the hill toward the aid station. Mike stopped halfway up the hill, hoping to speak to the Duster commander.

With its cannons still trained on the tree line, the Duster commander halted and looked somberly down at Mike.

"Thanks for your help today, Army. Let's do this again sometime."

"It was our pleasure, Mike. Take care of yourself tonight."

Before Mike could ask about the commander's odd behavior, the Duster accelerated and continued up the hill. Mike had met some strange ducks before, but this guy took the cake. Then it occurred to him: *How did he know my name?*

Confused, Mike watched the Duster disappear over the hill and wondered if today could be any stranger. Little did he know he had just talked to Bildad's new host.

Mike's train of thought was interrupted by someone shouting at him, "Watch out, Sergeant!"

Turning, Mike noticed three howitzers, barrels elevated and ready to fire across the road. He had just enough time to turn away and cover his ears before the number one gun erupted. The outgoing round whizzed by overhead. Seconds later, he saw a column of smoke twenty-five yards from the northwest tree line. A minute later, a second round landed close to where Mike thought the enemy bunker should be. Knowing that Duncan had found the target, Mike smiled as he watched the ensuing rounds sweep through the area, setting off secondary explosions.

*   *   *

Parks, Johnston, and Top greeted Mike when he arrived at the CP.

"Nice job out there today, Mike."

"Thank you, sir. It looked like we took that bunker out."

"Yes, I was in OP-1 when Duncan called in the fire mission. One of the secondary explosions was large. I think we destroyed some hidden munitions." Anxious to confirm what he already knew, Parks continued. "What did you find out, Mike?"

"Sir, after we spotted that bunker, Wolf found a booby trap in the creek bed we used for cover. It was a hand grenade with a tripwire. O'Neal disarmed it without any trouble. I'm pretty sure they were about to jump us.

"Then Wolf somehow found and killed a forward observer in a spider hole. He retrieved a radio, a carbine, and the map I left at the north gate. Sir, I glanced at that map. It had the location of every bunker and emplacement on the Hill."

"You're right, Mike. I couldn't believe it myself. When Giap hits us, I think the safest place for everyone is in the trenches. Continue."

"Sir, I think the mortar attack outside the north gate was meant to warn us not to venture into the eastern Trace. I am very sure Giap has something big hidden close to checkpoint 6. My guess is it's a bunker."

"Lieutenant Summers said there are twelve bunkers east of OP-2. It's a good thing I called you back in, Mike. Your patrol was almost on top of them.

"Duncan caught an NVA supply column out in the open north of the river. Giap wouldn't do that unless it were essential to his plan to attack the Hill tonight. I'm sure we know where and when Giap will hit us now."

Parks turned to address his executive officer. "Lieutenant Johnston, call Duncan and have him relocate to OP-2. Maybe he and those two snipers can locate some of Charlie's bunkers before dark. I'm sure Giap will not move his troops in until late tonight. So hitting them now will only delay the inevitable. We'll wait for Giap to make his move and then have Camp Carroll's 175 howitzers take them out before they reach the wire. Anything else, Mike?"

"Sir, the western Trace looked deserted. I'm pretty sure Giap has moved most of his forces to the northeast side of the Hill."

"Thanks, Mike. You can rejoin your unit now."

Mike nodded and left the bunker.

"Top, you fought in Korea. What do you think we should do to counter Giap's attack?"

"Well, sir, moving our armor out of their fortifications and into the open to strengthen the east side of the Hill would not be a good idea when the shelling starts. Our best bet is to hunker down and look like an easy target. Giap will hit us in front of 3rd Squad sometime after midnight. He will come in during a mortar attack with his sappers and RPGs to take out anything in his way. When that's done, he will send in his troops, sweep the Hill, and leave before dawn."

"Then you're suggesting we do nothing?"

"No, sir. I think there are several things we can do. More than likely, Giap will breach the wire in one, maybe two locations.

Before he commits his troops, he will take out the perimeter bunkers. Those old fortifications are too weak to take much more than an RPG round or two. I suggest we move 3rd Squad out into the trench tonight.

"We must confine the attack to the lower half of the hill. To do that, we should strengthen the second-line bunkers. Assuming Giap will hit Company D, we must create a reaction force from Company A to plug any break in the line.

"Once Giap's troops get to the wire, our armor will not be effective. So we should switch out our high-explosive rounds to beehive antipersonnel rounds. Flechettes will be much more effective against ground troops."

"If Giap hits us from the north, how quickly can we move the reaction force back to Company A's bunkers?"

"Less than five minutes, sir."

"Does anybody have anything else to add?"

With no response, Parks added, "Top, what's the status of the illumination rounds?"

"Sir, we did everything we could, but the rounds are still on the dock in Da Nang. They won't be here until tomorrow. I have a flare plane on call from Da Nang."

"Can you see if that plane can arrive by 0030 hours?"

"I'll make the call as soon as we are done here, sir."

"Lieutenant Johnston, I need you in the fire support center tonight. Those howitzers and four-deuce mortars are too important to lose to sappers. Do what you need to do to protect them."

"Yes, sir."

"Can anybody think of anything else?"

"Sir, I have another suggestion."

"What's that, Top?"

"When the NVA withdraws from the Hill, they will move quickly to the river. I suggest we position our night patrol northwest of the Hill as planned then quietly move them to a new location north of the Hill after dark. Maybe we can catch them in an ambush early in the morning."

"That's a bold plan, but I like it. Make sure Company A knows the patrol will pass in front of them. We do not want to lose anyone to friendly fire. Make it happen, Top."

"Will do, sir."

"I'm going to postpone the 1800 briefing until 1900. Make your reports brief. Dismissed."

Chapter 20

The Interview

Smith, Fuller, and Greene were surprised to find a civilian standing outside Bunker 4, taking pictures when they returned from their patrol. The man wore a backpack, helmet, and marine flak jacket over a camouflaged fatigue shirt. Around his waist was a utility belt with a canteen and a first aid pouch.

Smith thought he was too old to be in this hostile environment. "Can I help you?" he inquired.

"Yes," the man said, shaking his hand. "My name is Edward Keys. I'm a news correspondent up here gathering information about Con Thien for *Life* magazine. I understand you are members of the 3rd Squad and have just returned from a patrol. Do you mind answering a few questions?"

"Not at all," Smith replied with a grin. "It's not very often we get to talk to a reporter. Let's step inside out of the sun."

The four men entered the bunker. Each found somewhere to sit, and the marines gave Keys their full attention.

"Now, Mr. Keys," Smith added, "how can we help?"

"As you know, there is a lot of interest in the war, and people back home are starting to question why we're here. I'd like to hear what you say about Vietnam and this place you call the Hill of

Angels. If you don't mind, I'd like to tape this conversation. Let's start with you, Corporal."

Keys raised a finger, indicating he wanted Smith to wait while he turned on the recorder.

"This is Edward Keys at the marine compound at Con Thien, on the DMZ of South Vietnam," he spoke into the mic. "It's two fifteen on the afternoon of May 7, 1967. Interview 11." Keys paused and then continued. "We are in Bunker 4 on the perimeter talking to three marines of the 1st Battalion, 4th Marines. They are members of the 3rd Squad and have just come in from a patrol. Let's see what they've got to say about their day. What's your name, and tell us where you're from?"

Keys held the recorder close to Smith and nodded.

"I'm Corporal James Smith from Cody, Wyoming."

"How long have you been in Vietnam, James?"

"Eight months now."

"How long have you been a marine?"

"I joined up the day after I graduated from high school. That was eleven months ago."

"That would make you about nineteen. Why did you decide to become a marine, James?"

"My dad was a marine in World War II. His dad was a marine before him. It was always assumed I would become a third-generation marine," Smith said proudly.

"Do your parents approve of you being here?"

"Dad fought in the Pacific, so he understands. Moms never said a word, but I'm sure she disapproves."

"What were you doing out there today, James?"

"We suspect Charlie is going to attack the Hill, so we did a recon patrol to gather intel on when and where he might do that."

"What did you find out?"

"There are beaucoup bad guys just north and south of here. We are expecting them to hit us tonight or tomorrow night."

"What goes through your mind when you prepare for something like that?"

"The first time, it scared the crap out of me. The second time, not so much. Right now, I'm kinda numb to it. Charlie will try to get through the wire and kill a few of us, and we'll kill a bunch of them. The tough part is dealing with our dead and wounded. The easy part is taking out all the trash in the morning."

"Explain taking out the trash."

"The enemy we'll kill."

"What do you do with the bodies?"

"Out in the bush, we leave them for Charlie to pick up after we leave. The engineers will probably doze a pit somewhere out there, and we'll throw them all in it. That's not much of a burial but is as much as Charlie will do for them."

Keys paused to think about Smith's cold and insensitive words. Staring into his steely eyes, he wondered how well Smith would fit into society back in the States. Provided, of course, he survived his tour.

Through the bunker window came a rapid succession of muffled thumps. Seconds later, six explosions erupted close by. Their impact was enough to cause Keys to flinch. To his amazement, Smith sat there as if nothing had happened. Keys remembered that far-off stare from WWII and the Korean War that he covered and stood in awe at the resilience of the combat spirit.

Being a correspondent of three wars, Keys knew the answer to his next question before asking it. "How do you sleep through this constant shelling?"

"If you're tired enough, it's easier than you think." Smith's smile was gone now. Just thinking about how tired he was rekindled his exhaustion.

"Do you mind, James, telling me how many of your friends have been killed in Vietnam?"

Key's question took Smith by surprise. He could remember the names and faces of each of the thirteen friends he had lost to Charlie. That did not include the dozens of other dead marines he knew casually. Each died violently and represented a collection of memories he hoped he would never forget.

"Far too many, Mr. Keys." After a long pause, Smith continued. "I will tell you what they would all say right now about Vietnam. Our commander in chief thought it important enough to send the best our country has to offer to help a people who cannot defeat communism alone. We might have to do it back home if we don't stop them here.

"We fight for freedom and the American way. Tell that to the hippies protesting our willingness to die to protect their freedom of speech and right to protest. I can understand their refusal to die to defend the rights of people like the Vietnamese. I do not understand why they call us murderers. They haven't been here, so they don't know what they're talking about."

Moved by the forcefulness of Smith's comments, Keys continued. "I'm sorry if I offended you, James. A lot has changed back home in the last year. One more question. You've been in-country for eight months and on the Hill for five days. Do you have any regrets so far?"

"None whatsoever, Mr. Keys. You said you're doing this article for *Life* magazine?"

"Yes, probably the October 27 edition."

"Good. I'll be home before my mom reads it."

"Thank you for your sincerity, James."

Turning to Fuller, Mr. Keys asked, "Tell me your name and where you're from, Private."

"My name is Private First Class Sam Fuller from Cortez, Colorado."

"How long have you been a marine, and how long have you been in Vietnam, Sam?"

"I've been a marine for six months now. Here in Vietnam for three months."

"Do you miss home?"

"Yes, I miss it, but I'm not ready to go home yet."

Shocked by Fuller's reply, Keys asked, "Why not? I thought you would jump at the chance to get out of this place."

"Second Platoon, Delta Company is my home. Third Squad is my family, my brothers. If I left before my thirteen months were up, it would be like running out on them. When my tour is up, I'll be ready to go back to my other family. For now, my place is right here, even if it's on this stinking Hill for another twenty-five days."

"What happens in twenty-five days?"

"We are stationed here for thirty days. After that, we rotate back to Dong Ha, and another battalion will take our place. The Hill gets about three hundred incoming rounds a day. It is infested with rats and scorpions, and the enemy is so close he can hear us talking right now. No, four weeks is all a body can take of this place."

Keys glanced out the window and wondered how close the enemy could be. From what he had been told, it was never that far away. It gave him a cold shiver to think how vulnerable an unarmed correspondent would be if the enemy attacked before he got off the Hill.

Smith, sitting by the bunker window, heard it first. The three marines made eye contact and quickly moved to the floor, pulling Keys down with them. Sounding like an onrushing freight train, the artillery shell whistled overhead and landed with a loud *wham* on the hill behind their bunker. Falling debris peppered the shelter and sent a dust cloud sweeping through the open doorway.

Knowing the danger was over, the marines rose to reclaim their seats. Keys was shaken and in no hurry to join them. "Wow, that was bigger than those other rounds. What was that?"

"That's Charlie's 152 howitzers from those mountains north of the river." Smith glanced out the window toward the highlands and groaned at the thought of what that shell could have done to their flimsy fortification. "It was just a random round, and we should be OK for a while."

Keys picked himself up and found his seat again. After several attempts at dusting himself off, he continued. "Well, that was close." Marveling at the dangers surrounding the Hill, he asked, "Aren't you guys afraid of dying?"

"There's not a moment of the day that we're not afraid, Mr. Keys," Smith replied. Then speaking for himself, he added, "I don't know what the next few months will bring, but if I die, my brothers here will risk life and limb to get my body back to my folks. Do you see that kind of loyalty and character in those draft dodgers back home? Would they put their lives on the line for you? I don't think so."

"I must say I could not think of anyone I would rather have protecting my rights and freedoms than you, Marines. Tell me about your mail from home, Sam."

Like everyone on the Hill, Fuller was exhausted, and two nights of lost sleep had taken its toll. He replied with a deep wearied breath, "The mail runs almost daily up here. Hardly a day goes by I don't get a letter from Mom. Every week or so, Dad slips in a note about guy stuff. My aunt Goldie sends me care packages every two weeks with all kinds of good stuff—food, books, tapes, and newspapers. Last week, I sent a package to my mom to keep for me."

"What was in the package, if you don't mind me asking?"

"Souvenirs and things I bought at a local market. Other things included a piece of shrapnel, an NVA battle flag, some Vietnamese and US military funny money, and a Chinese hand grenade."

"You smuggled a Chinese grenade back home to your mom?" Mr. Keys said with excitement.

"Of course not. I just wanted to know what you would say about it," Sam replied with a shallow smile.

"Well, you sure had me going. You Marines do have a strange sense of humor."

"That's how we cope with all this, Mr. Keys."

Addressing Greene, Keys asked, "What's your name, and where are you from?"

"I'm Private First Class Darrell Greene. I'm from Athens, Georgia."

"What do you do for entertainment, Darrell? How do you keep up your morale?"

"I like listening to the Armed Forces Radio Network as much as possible. It helps me take my mind off the stress of this place. As far as my morale is concerned, that's seldom a problem for me."

"Why not?"

"The Lord is my pilot. If he's flying the plane, why should I care where he takes me?"

"I'm not much on religion, but I respect your conviction. Tell me, what do you miss the most from back home?"

"That's easy. I like spending time with my girl, Mary Ellen, and lunch with family after church on Sundays. As much as I'm looking forward to seeing Mary Ellen when I get back home, she will have to wait until I see Mom first."

"Well, I was about to ask you what you would do when you get home, but I think you just told me. Let me ask you a couple of more questions. What do you think of America's involvement in Southeast Asia?"

"I think the Vietnamese people need us here to protect them from the North Vietnamese. Without us, a very evil government would crush and enslave these people. As Americans, we should not turn a blind eye to that hostility. If we are the most powerful nation in the world, what's wrong with helping the Vietnamese?"

"I think the answer to that question is a little more complicated right now, Darrell, but I see your point. One final question, who do you think will win the World Series this year?"

"Well, the season is still young, Mr. Keys, but I think the St. Louis Cardinals will win the pennant. They should be the hands-down favorite."

"How can you be so sure?"

"Well, I played baseball for the Missouri Tigers for two years before I enlisted in the marines. That made me a fan. Secondly, the Cardinals have Bob Gibson. He can do it all. If it comes down to game 7, Bob will find a way for them to win."

"Thank you for that insider information," Keys said as he turned off the recorder. "When the playoffs get here, I might find myself a bookie and place a bet. It has been a pleasure talking to you, men. I enjoyed your answers, and I'm sure the folks back home will also. You boys, take care of yourselves. I hope you all make it back home safely.

"One final request. I want to take two pictures. The first one I like is of you three smiling. Let's move outside. I want the DMZ in the background."

The three exhausted marines smiled as Mr. Keys snapped their picture. "Now, can you give me your Con Thien face?"

Smith, Fuller, and Greene knew exactly what Mr. Keys meant. They retrieved their weapons and struck a militant pose. Mr. Keys would treasure this one picture for the rest of his life. A month later, he would discover that two of these young marines would die tonight.

Mr. Keys shook hands with all three marines and embraced them. He knew the stats for survival in Vietnam. He also knew that the survival rate at Con Thien was much lower. As Keys headed back up to the CP, he thought about the disrespect the armed forces received from those who had no idea how much these men sacrificed for freedom. Ten feet from the bunker, he stopped and turned to face the three marines again.

"Men, the people back home do not know what you're going through up here. I will do my best to tell them. Thank you for your service and your willingness to defend the rights of others less fortunate. You're living out what it means to be an American. Look me up if you ever get to the Big Apple. I would like to know you made it home safely."

The four men nodded to one another. Mr. Keys gave them a wave and left as a tear started to form.

"Thank you, Mr. Keys," Greene called after him. "Have a blessed life. Make sure you are not here after sundown."

Mr. Keys lifted his hand as he continued down the trench. He paused as he turned up the incline toward the CP. In a quiet moment, he began to weep and pray, neither of which he knew very much about.

Chapter 21

The Night Patrol

It would be a still and moonless night—perfect conditions for an ambush patrol. An hour before sunset, Sergeant Johnson led his men through an opening in the Hill's west perimeter wire. As soon as the patrol left the Hill, two marines from Company A secured the wire back into place.

For the next hour, there would be no noise discipline. Parks had instructed Johnson to make it easy for Charlie to track their movements until dark. After that, the patrol would pick their spot and settle in for the night—just like they would typically do.

While they were focused on their mission, their thoughts were on those left to defend the Hill. If Parks were right about the attack, some of their buddies would die tonight.

Alpha 22 consisted of seventeen marines and a navy corpsman. They were armed with three M60 machine guns, two grenade launchers, eleven M16s, one shotgun, thirty-four grenades, ten LAW rocket launchers, ten claymore mines, and all the ammunition they could carry. One of the M16s had a new starlight scope sent from home. As patrols go, they were packing some heat.

Johnson's orders were to proceed northwest of the Hill and set up a skirmish line in the dry creek bed Delta 23 had used that morning. Charlie would mark their location and assume the patrol would stay in the same position for the rest of the night. Giap would ignore them, knowing he would have fewer marines to fight on the Hill.

Walking around in the dark in enemy territory is unnerving. You never know what you will encounter until you've stepped into it. While the defective M16s posed a handicap, PFC Barclay's rifle's starlight scope gave them an advantage, allowing them to move unhindered through the night.

The patrol reached the creek bed, confident that Charlie knew precisely where they were. Once in the ditch, each marine picked some grass and secured it to their helmet and utility harness to conceal their silhouette. Later that night, Johnson would move his patrol to a new position three thousand yards north of the Hill. This location put Alpha 22 in a perfect place to cut off Charlie's anticipated retreat to the river.

At 2100 hours, Johnson sent out his advance detail of six marines to low-crawl the two hundred yards to the tree line. Ten minutes later, the next six followed suit. Johnson and the remaining marines brought up the rear.

Barclay was one of the first to reach the tree line. Rising to one knee, he slowly scanned the area. After a few minutes, he signaled the all-clear. Once all eighteen men had moved into the tree line, the patrol quietly continued northeast, with Barclay leading the way.

By 2300 hours, Johnson figured they were about five hundred yards from their objective. After taking a short break, the patrol pressed on cautiously. At 0010 hours, Johnson found the dirt road marked as Highway 605 on his map. After Barclay cleared the area, Johnson quickly led his men to the tree line across the way then east until the faint outline of the Hill could be seen through the trees.

Johnson spaced his men out in pairs, fifteen feet apart. The marines quietly dug in and fortified their positions. Although they expected the enemy to approach from the south, they knew Charlie could be anywhere.

Noise discipline was now critical. Except for the crickets and muffled shelling of the Hill, the jungle was deathly silent. At 0210 hours, a twig snapped behind their position. The marines froze in place and silently waited to identify the sound. Seconds later, another twig snapped, and low voices could be heard speaking Vietnamese.

Through the bushes, Johnson could see the silhouettes of a six-man NVA patrol passing between them and the river. Holding his hand in a fist, he alerted his men to hold their fire and movement. The enemy soldiers continued their path, and in a few minutes, the jungle was silent again. Johnson counted himself lucky. Had the NVA known they were there, they would not have heard the enemy at all.

At 0250, Alpha 22's radio operator called the CP to check in. Five minutes later, a green flare rose from somewhere south of A-4, and all hell broke loose on the Hill.

Chapter 22

Mike Checks on His Men

The last rays of sunlight had faded when Mike arrived at Bunker 1 for his routine inspection. Magrini, Slayer, and Littlejohn had completed their preparations and stopped for some chow. Their conversation was soft and jovial as they talked about summer vacations they had taken as kids. Despairingly, Mike listened quietly in the shadows.

He knew the chances were good that some of his men wouldn't survive the coming onslaught. With his emotions carefully guarded, Mike stepped forward and said, "How're you doing, men?"

Magrini responded, "We're good, Sergeant."

"Do you have enough ammo?"

"Yes, Sergeant."

"How about food and water?"

"We've got that too, Mike," Magrini shot back. "Now stop worrying."

Realizing his distress was showing, Mike paused and then changed the subject. "I hear Raquel Welch will be at Bob Hope's Christmas show this year."

"Man, Raquel Welch," Slayer replied. "Now that's a show I would like to see."

After a few minutes of fragmented conversation, Littlejohn asked, "Do you think they're gonna hit us tonight, Sergeant?"

Reluctantly, Mike looked out past the wire and replied, "Yeah. I think Charlie will come sometime after midnight." Turning back, he continued. "I hate to have you sleep in the trench tonight, but the bunkers will be the first thing they'll go after. You'll be safer out here. After they take out the bunkers, they'll think you're all dead. So don't uncover that gun until you're ready to use it. Understand?"

"We understand, Sergeant."

"We are short on illumination rounds tonight so Parks will slow down the rotation. He'll fire the first round at 2000 hours then every thirty minutes afterward. The three of you need to defend this position at all costs. Make sure you watch your flank if Charlie gets into the trench."

"We got ya, Sergeant."

"Good. I will see you all in the morning. Good night, men."

"See ya, Sergeant," Littlejohn replied.

Mike walked away, downhearted. That internal voice he heard so many times before was now silent. Mike paused and offered a silent prayer for all fifteen members of 3rd Squad. He had just said amen when he overheard Finch and Adams talking a few yards away.

"Where's home, Adams?"

"Los Angeles, Corporal Finch. How about you?"

"Pagosa Springs, Colorado."

"What's it like there?"

"Pagosa Springs sits on the San Juan River. Trout fishing is fantastic year-round. In the middle of town are these awesome hot spring pools. Each pool is set to a different temperature. I grew up skiing at Wolf Creek, just thirty minutes down the road. My hometown is perfect. I wouldn't live anywhere else."

"Pagosa Springs sounds nice. I'd like to go there someday." Adams paused to consider his otherwise dull childhood before he replied. "I was a batboy for the Los Angeles Dodgers. So in the summer, baseball was all we ever did."

Mike tried his best to contain his emotions, so he waited until Adams finished talking about all the baseball players he had met over the years.

"Willie Mays was always my favorite," Mike said as he walked in from the darkness.

Startled, Adams turned quickly in response. "Oh, it's you, Sergeant," he said nervously. Embarrassed, he quickly added, "How're you doin' tonight?"

As weary as Mike was, he smiled and responded, "I would prefer to be out with Johnson's patrol tonight, waiting to ambush the enemy instead of the other way around here. However, we know where and when they will hit us so it won't be a total surprise when it happens. Do you have everything you need?"

"We're good, Sergeant," Finch replied.

"I need you two to stay alert tonight. Try to get a few hours' sleep, but you must be awake and alert at 0100. Don't let the enemy get past you if you can help it. Understand?"

"We understand, Sergeant."

"Good. What's with the painted faces?"

"It was Wolf's idea," began Finch. "He said it's big medicine."

"What kind of big medicine?"

"Wolf said it would scare the hell out of Charlie."

Mike managed a half grin. "If Wolf said that, I am sure it's true. Make sure Charlie doesn't get away to warn his buddies of our new secret weapon. I'll see you men in the morning."

"Yes, we'll see you too, Sergeant."

"By the way, where's Wolf?"

"He's getting the last of the ammo out of the bunker."

When Mike walked up to Finch and Adams, it didn't surprise him that Wolf wasn't around, but he knew he wasn't far away. Wolf was a true Sioux warrior, always prepared for anything. Wolf would make his presence known most aggressively when Charlie came for them. Tonight, he would make his people and the Marine Corps very proud.

Wolf walked out of the bunker with his painted face. A single feather was tucked into the band of his helmet. Mike smiled as a Bible verse came to mind: *"They will mount up with wings like eagles; they will run and not get tired; they will walk and not become weary."*

Mike reached up, shook Wolf's hand, and hugged him. From arm's length, both studied the other's face as if for the last time. Neither felt the need to express their feelings. "You take good care of yourself tonight, Wolf. I expect to see you in the morning."

"Sergeant, do you mind if I prayed with you before you go?"

"Of course, Wolf. I would like that."

"Dear Lord, you are a great and compassionate God. Thank you for Mike's leadership and friendship. Please keep him and all of us safe from harm this night. In your Most Holy Name, I pray. Amen."

After a brief silence, Mike added, "Watch after Adams."

Wolf wanted to warn Mike about Bildad coming for him but knew God had it all under control. After a brief pause, he replied, "I'll do that. You watch your scalp tonight, Sergeant. We'll see you in the morning."

When Mike got to Bunker 3, Demarco, Grady, and Lamont were jamming to a Sam & Dave song on Greene's radio. Not wanting to disrupt the harmony, he joined in by snapping his fingers and nodding his head to the beat.

"Come on, Sarge. Get over here and join us," Grady beckoned.

"All right, but I have to warn you. I sang in the boys' choir back home," Mike shouted over the music.

Realizing the moment's importance, Mike put aside his usual shyness, got between the brothers, and gave them everything he had. Together, they treated the Hill to their unique version of "Soul Man." From the CP, Parks got his first laugh in days.

"That was great, men," Mike said. "Thank you for letting me join you. You dudes need to audition for Motown Records when you get back home."

"Thanks, Sergeant," Grady bantered, "but I think we would have more luck as stand-up comics."

The four marines joked about their disjointed harmony for a few minutes before Mike led them in prayer.

"Hold your fire as long as possible then let 'em have it."

"You can count on us, Sergeant."

"Men, I want to see all three of you in the morning. Do you need anything before I go?"

"Thanks, Sergeant," Lamont replied. "We're all good. See you tomorrow."

*   *   *

At 2200 hours, Giap began moving his troops into his twelve fortified bunkers east of the Hill. With discipline and stealth, the enemy silently crept ever closer to their objective.

If Giap had his way, tonight would be a repeat performance of his brilliant defeat of the French at Dien Bien Phu to end the First Indochina War on May 7, 1954. Against a weak South Vietnamese garrison, his plan would have been a massacre. However, when the marines took possession of the Hill a few days earlier, it was a contingency he had not prepared for. Giap was determined to eradicate the Hill's defenders tonight and make a much-needed political statement that the North was preparing to escalate the war in the South.

* * *

Simmons and Carter stood at the 3rd Squad bunker window, slowly surveying the perimeter for enemy activity. While darkness hid Charlie's movements outside the wire, four spirits stood just ten yards in front of them, cloaked in the supernatural realm.

"Have the preparations been made to receive our new acquisitions tonight?"

"Yes, my captain," Zophar replied arrogantly. "Five transportation platoons are in position, ready to claim what is rightfully ours, even before they breathe their last."

"Excellent," Legion gloated. He thought about man's natural tendency to incite his own violence and marveled at how little effort it took to spread discord and strife in the world. It had worked to his advantage for six thousand years, but he knew the good times would soon come to an end.

At the Battle of Armageddon, Legion and his kind would be defeated by the Creator's Son and cast into the pit for a thousand years. Afterward, God will grant them one final effort to corrupt the hearts of mankind before banishing the wicked forever into the fires of hell. An event that concerned him greatly—but not tonight. He was not concerned about who won or lost tonight's battle. Only about how many he could take to the graveyard with him.

"Behold, my children," Legion said as he spread his arms wide at the drama unfolding around the Hill. "For nation shall rise up against nation, and kingdom against kingdom, there will be earthquakes and famines. These things are only the beginning of the end for mankind. Look at how these marines foolishly spend their last few hours. If only they knew that death is not the end of life, but the beginning of something entirely different."

Legion reminded his three associates of the significance of tonight's business. "The Boss has stressed the importance of our challenge to Mike Shaffer's faith and wants us to review our plan carefully." Fixing his gaze on Eliphaz, he continued. "To make sure one of us does not get sidetracked again."

Bildad and Zophar turned toward Eliphaz and smiled, glad that it wasn't them who screwed up on the road up from Da Nang. Eliphaz knew this was a warning. If not for Bernie Westgate, he would be off Legion's A-team tonight. "You have my word. It will not happen again," he insisted.

"Well, for your sake, it better not. There's a long waiting list for your job," Legion said as he bounced his gnarled index finger off his chest.

"Now, about our plan. Bildad, I want you to take the lead this time. Position yourself outside the wire in front of that bunker down there and wait for my signal. Try to gain Mike's confidence by asking permission to come through the wire. If that fails, try tempting him with something trivial. Something that would get him to find a solution to his problem without asking for help from his Advocate.

"After we soften him up, we'll hit him with our superior knowledge of the Book. However, twisting the truth won't be easy with Mike. The Creator has given him several spiritual gifts, one of which is discernment. He will see through most of our tricks. We need to find one that works. Patience and instilling doubt are the keys.

"Mike is moving over to the next bunker now. We will start our little inquisition at Bunker 5. Remember, Bildad, the Advocate will be there. Do not let his presence distract you from our mission to disprove Mike's worthiness to the Creator. State the accusation against Mike first and then move on. Understand?"

"Yes, my captain."

*   *   *

Smith, Fuller, and Greene were spread out between bunkers 3 and 4. When Mike walked up, Donovan's "Mellow Yellow" was now playing on Greene's boom box.

"How're you doing, men?"

"We're all good, Sergeant," replied Smith.

"Do you need anything?"

"Unless you can get us three-day passes and off the Hill for the night, no."

"Well, getting you a pass would be easy. Getting Parks to sign it tonight will be the hard part. He's expecting visitors in a few hours and wants 3rd Squad to serve up the beer and party nuts. When we get them all hammered, we'll let Greene's mellow-yellow music put the zap on them. In the morning, we might be rewriting the SOP on pacification."

"That's right, Sergeant," Greene responded with excitement. "All we need to do is introduce our hippies to their hippies, and we can end this war tonight."

Smith rolled his eyes and looked at Mike. "This is what I put up with every night. If it's not his detestable music, it's his lame attempt at humor. I tell you, Sergeant, if Charlie doesn't come tonight, I'll put myself out of my misery in the morning." Smith tried his best to lay it on thick for Mike.

Mike admired how well Smith and Greene could deal with the stress. Instead of dreading the impending battle or arguing about their differences, both were content to wait for Charlie to bring it on. *Lord, there is nothing like a marine who knows he's going into battle.*

"Well, it sounds like you two need some marriage counseling. Meet me at the command bunker at 0900 hours. I'm sure Parks can spare a few minutes of his valuable time. Meanwhile, you know what to do. Keep your heads down and the enemy in front of you."

"They won't get past us, Sergeant," was Greene's reply.

As Mike studied the faces of his three marine brothers, the Lord's comforting voice spoke to him again. *Don't worry, Mike. I'm in control of everything.*

"Men," Mike said wearily, "I will be praying that God will keep you safe from harm tonight. Good luck, Marines."

"Thanks, Sergeant. Good night."

Bunker 5, manned by O'Neal, Russell, and Tucker, was supposed to be a man short tonight. So Mike was surprised when he saw three men standing in the dark when he walked up.

"What the heck are you doing here, Tucker?"

"Doc Perry gave me some stitches and sent me back down here."

"I don't suppose there's something else you want to tell me about your discharge from the aid station, Tucker," Mike demanded.

Tucker thought better about lying to Mike and corrected himself, "I checked myself out of sick bay, Sergeant."

"You dumb jarhead. Get your butt back up there right now."

"Sergeant O'Neal and Russell need me down here tonight. If you send me to the aid station, I will only come back later."

"Doc Perry is not going to like this one little bit. I would not be surprised if he writes you up as AWOL."

"How can I be AWOL if I'm at my duty station? I promise to go to the aid station in the morning, Sergeant. You need me here tonight," Tucker argued.

Tucker was right. Mike needed him badly but couldn't let him off without a tongue-lashing. Marines were sticklers for discipline. On the other hand, Mike knew that sometimes orders were meant to be broken. In a stern and building voice, Mike did what sergeants do best.

"Tucker, Parks will bust you back to private, and I'll hand you those papers myself. Insubordination in this outfit cannot nor will it be tolerated by you or anyone else. Do you copy that, PFC Tucker?"

Ready to take his medicine, Tucker snapped to full attention and replied, "Yes, Sergeant. I copy."

Mike positioned himself on Tucker's left side with his nose stuck in his ear. "Outstanding, Tucker," Mike said persuasively. "Now listen carefully. If you know what's best, you'll follow my orders to the letter. Do you *comprehendo*, amigo?"

"Yes, Sergeant," Tucker shouted back.

"Good. I want you to stay here and help Sergeant O'Neal and Russell defend this position tonight. At precisely 0600 hours, I want you to surrender yourself to Doc Perry and pray that he and Parks don't put a boot up your worthless butt. You got that, Tucker?"

Tucker was fully expecting Mike to read him the riot act. So it took him a few seconds to realize what Mike had said. Moving nothing but his eyes, he glanced at Mike to ensure he heard him correctly.

"I'll ask you again, Tucker. Do you understand?" Mike said with a softening voice.

"Yes, Sergeant. I understand."

"Sergeant O'Neal, I am placing Tucker under bunker arrest tonight. If he runs off again or is not in the aid station at exactly 0600, I'll put you on report with him. Do you understand, Sergeant?"

O'Neal had been in the marines long enough to know what Mike did and why. "You have my word that Tucker will make it to the aid station by 0600 hours, Sergeant." Then adding his own bit of humor, he continued. "Request permission to shoot him if he resists."

Mike turned and gave O'Neal a hidden smile then answered firmly, "So authorized."

Mike got nose to nose with Tucker and gave him a prolonged frown. Backing away, he winked and lightly slapped him on the cheek. It was a walking-wounded night, and Mike was grateful for all the help he could get.

Gratefully, Mike added, "Thanks, Tucker. We need you tonight, but you'll have to face Doc Perry all by yourself. How's the leg?"

Tucker relaxed but knew he could be in the doghouse in the morning. At least for tonight, he would do what he had been trained for. "It's OK, Sergeant."

"Shawn, do you have everything ready for the night?"

"It's all taken care of, Sergeant. The phone is here, and the claymore wires have been repositioned."

"Good. Men, make sure you keep an eye on the trench. Don't let 'em sneak up on you from the side. Once we know where they hit us, we will get you some help."

"Roger that, Sergeant."

"I'll see you all in the morning." Mike turned to leave then stopped when he got the sudden urge to talk to O'Neal about his salvation.

Speaking to Russell and Tucker, Mike asked, "I need to talk to Shawn. Can you two give us a few minutes?"

"Sure, Sergeant. We'll walk down and talk to Greene and Fuller."

"Thanks." Mike waited a few seconds then asked matter-of-factly, "Shawn, are you saved?"

Shawn started to reply and froze when an illumination round exploded above them. Mike saw Shawn standing there with his mouth open in the artificial light, looking like a cartoon caricature. Several seconds passed before Mike realized something was terribly wrong. All the distant sounds of nightly combat action along the DMZ were gone. Even the music from Greene's boom box had stopped. Cautiously, Mike scanned the perimeter for any sign of the enemy.

Chapter 23

Bildad Tests Mike's Faith

Mike picked up the field phone handset and turned the crank. Several seconds passed without a response. Starting to feel uneasy, he turned it again. There was still no answer. First Squad's first bunker was forty yards to his left, so Mike called out in a loud whisper, "Yo, 1ˢᵗ Squad." He waited and called out louder, "Anybody there?" Still nothing but silence.

The oddity of the illumination round suspended in the air resembled a shimmering streetlamp. Its erratic shifting shadows cast an eeriness onto the battlefield that played tricks on the eyes. As a wave of isolation swept over him, Mike could feel a cold, evil presence lurking nearby.

Mike exchanged his M16 for the bunker M60 sitting on an ammo crate nearby. He laid it over the trench wall and started to scan the wire. It wasn't long before he noticed a faint reflection from a silhouette outside the fence.

Suddenly, the pungent smell of garlic engulfed Mike. Fearing an enemy gas attack, Mike reached for his mask. A familiar voice whispered, *Wait, Mike. It's not gas. Legion is here to test your faith tonight.*

The Lord's soothing voice had a calming effect on Mike. Still, he couldn't help but wonder what kind of demon this might be. Then the voice whispered again, *Do not fear him, Mike. Legion cannot harm you, but be careful. He is very tricky. It will take all I have taught you to defend yourself. As your Advocate, I will be right behind you, but you must face this examination alone. Trust me, and you will get through this trial.*

Mike confidently studied the mysterious shape that stood motionless in the night. Though separated by fifty yards, Mike had little trouble identifying the form as humanlike in appearance but lacking any detail. Patiently, Mike waited for Legion to present himself.

Mike's mystery guest finally spoke. "Bildad."

Confused by the mysterious sound, Mike whispered, "What?"

"Bildad," came the reply. "My name is Bildad."

"What do you want?"

"I'm here to talk to you about your faith, Mike. Do you mind if I come in?"

"Be my guest if you can get through that minefield."

Like his brother, Eliphaz, Bildad was a master deceiver. Misleading the lost was easy for their kind. Believers like Mike were more difficult to fool. Like all Christians, Mike had weaknesses, and Legion was there to find and use them against him tonight.

Except for his will, Bildad was controlling all of Mike's reality. Everything about this encounter was a deceptive illusion designed to trick him into denying his faith in Christos. Though the visual perceptions appeared accurate, Mike must guard himself carefully against this master deceiver. He knew it was a battle for his soul and would be won or lost in his mind.

The double row of rusting barbed wire that circled the Hill had been installed by the Special Forces eight years earlier. It was ten feet wide and filled with thousands of antipersonnel mines. Anyone unfortunate enough to get entangled in the wire would need to be cut loose. Those who panicked would struggle until they set off a land mine or bleed to death.

Mike did not see Bildad take his first step into the wire, but he saw the explosion. Dirt and rocks were thrown high into the air. The debris rained down like a hailstorm. A minute later, the dust settled enough to reveal Bildad standing there. Mike wondered if the explosion was real or part of Legion's trickery. It was so convincing he couldn't tell.

"Well, that was close, Mike. There really are land mines in here. I don't suppose you'd tell me how to get through it."

When Mike failed to reply, Bildad added, "No, I didn't think you would. Come on, Mike. Give me at least a chance. It's dangerous in here."

Not impressed by Bildad's lame theatrics, Mike responded sarcastically, "You don't need my help, devil. Stop your whining, get in here, and do what you came to do."

Refusing to let Mike spoil his grand entrance, Bildad continued his walk through the minefield. Every step brought a bigger explosion than the last. The noise became increasingly loud, and the dust cloud grew. Bildad vanished and reappeared ten yards closer to provoke Mike into firing his weapon. He paused and disappeared again, only to reappear even closer. After a third Houdini act, Bildad appeared on the berm, looking down into the trench at Mike.

Up close, he appeared like a ghost wearing a tight-fitting black nylon suit over a short humanlike frame. Mike knew that firing at Bildad was useless and an act of fear and doubt. His only hope was to remain calm until he understood this spirit's intentions.

Looking out into no-man's-land, Mike could see the hole in the perimeter wire, wide enough to drive a jeep through. It occurred to him that this was how and where Charlie would attack the Hill tonight.

Bildad jumped into the trench, landing six feet in front of Mike. Bildad changed his appearance to that of a fully clothed NVA major to goad him further. He looked on in amazement as the major grew a foot in height. Now standing eye to eye, Mike appreciated how insignificant he would be without God's protection.

The Advocate stood motionless behind Mike, ready to intercede should Legion's actions turn violent. His battle dress was pure white that reached down to midthigh. He wore a plain gold helmet and breastplate engraved with Hebrew letters identifying his rank and position in God's kingdom. His feet were protected by sandals and bronze ankle guards. Around his waist was a leather belt with a Roman-type short sword in a diamond-studded scabbard. The Hebrew lettering on the blade translated as the "Word of God." While his five-foot-ten one-hundred-forty-pound frame did little to suggest any battlefield dominance, his authority tonight would be unchallenged and absolute.

Mike could be tempted at any time, but because Bildad was there to challenge Mike's faith, God's law required a trial with an Advocate to defend the accused. Understanding the formality of this hearing, Bildad stood impatiently waiting for permission to state the charge against Mike. Seconds seemed like minutes. Minutes like hours. Bildad found himself unable to avoid eye contact with the Advocate. The sternness of his gaze was intimidating. Mike noticed Bildad's agitation and knew who was really in control here.

Legion also sensed Bildad's dread and reminded him of their purpose: *Steady. He's not here to judge us tonight.*

"What is your charge against this man, Legion?" finally came a commanding voice from the heavens.

The majesty of God's resounding voice was terrifying and caused Bildad to tremble. After composing himself, he produced a parchment and timidly addressed the Advocate. "We charge the accused, Mike Shaffer, with unfaithfulness toward your throne."

To the Advocate, this trial was pointless. Because of God's law of substitutionary atonement, Legion had the right to challenge those with sanctified faith. While he could contest a believer's standing before God's throne, he could not nullify the salvation of one who had come under the blood. This can only be done once in a believer's lifetime.

"The charge has been noted into the eternal record. Who represents the accused?"

"I represent the defendant, Your Honor," the Advocate answered.

"Then state your evidence, Legion," replied the Most High God.

Bildad silently cursed the Advocate and from nowhere, produced a book with Mike's name embossed on it. Reading from it, Bildad revealed every sin Mike had committed against his fellowmen and God.

Mike listened to the extensive list and lowered his head in shame. He wondered how God could possibly forgive so great an offense.

With his allegation stated, Bildad waited for the verdict concerning Mike's right to be called a child of the King. Like inflating a tire, Legion started directing all the power his collective forces possessed into Bildad to bolster his waning confidence.

Legion, standing invisible close by, let out a menacing laugh. Its baleful sound echoed into the night. Unable to gain a reaction from Mike, Legion realized any further posturing would be wasted.

"Father," the Advocate began, "Mike Shaffer is one of my flock. He has confessed each of these sins, and I have accepted them all as my own. His debt to you has been paid in full by my blood."

"Then let the eternal record state that the Advocate has nullified these sins. I declare Mike Shaffer exonerated from these charges. Unless there is anything else, Legion, this trial is over."

Not surprised by the predictability of the Creator's ruling, Bildad moved on to the real reason for the inquest. "Then we execute our right to question the accused."

"On what grounds?" God demanded.

"We challenge Mike Shaffer's kingdom rights. He is human and unable to understand agape love. Mike has no real appreciation for the blood that covers his sin. He is, therefore, unworthy of his adoption into your kingdom."

"Then make your case, if you have one," came the Father's tolerant reply.

Bildad began his investigation by testing Mike's dependence upon the Advocate. "You want to fire that gun at me right now, don't you, Mike?"

"I don't think it would do any good, devil. Or should I say Legion?" Mike replied with an attitude.

Unwilling to let Mike distract him from their carefully prepared challenge, Bildad responded, "Go ahead and pull that trigger, Mike. Kill me before I kill you."

Mike ignored Bildad's threat. He knew that bullets were wasted on this enemy. What he needed was the Word of God. "I will not sin against the one true God, devil."

"You're a coward, Mike, a disgrace to your faith and the United States Marine Corps. You know you want to pull that trigger. Now do it," Bildad mocked.

"It is written that those who resist the devil will watch him flee in defeat." With that, Mike raised the barrel of his weapon and flipped on the safety switch.

Immediately, Bildad countered with, "It's also written in the Book that where there is no law, there is no sin. Did the Creator say you could not kill a demon? No. He said you should not kill people. By our count, Mike, you've killed thirty-seven enemy soldiers—men and women who will never see their families again. By your code, you killed them without reservation. You're a hypocrite, Mike. You do what the Creator told you not to, and you don't do what's lawful."

Bildad's knowledge of scripture startled Mike. *What happens if this demon defeats me with my only weapon?*

The look in Mike's eyes gave away his feeling of concern. Bildad smirked and waited patiently, knowing he had already planted the first seeds of doubt in Mike's mind.

The longer Mike thought about it, the faster his brain spun. As he looked at Bildad, Mike realized they were discussing the terms of a surrender he was not ready to make. Mike lowered the M60 and placed it back on the ammo crate with renewed confidence. Unarmed, he turned defiantly to face Bildad again.

"As for me, I will trust in the Lord and wait for his deliverance."

Bildad pressed Legion's plan further. "Have you ever seen your god, Mike?" Bildad paused briefly then continued. "If he does exist, tell him to give us a sign as proof of his existence. Otherwise, I'm the closest thing to a god you'll ever see."

Mike understood Bildad was out to find and exploit his weakness. He thought it best he should start doing the same. Searching his memory for a passage that would help defeat Bildad, Mike remembered a verse from Proverbs: *"Pride goes before the fall. Pride was the devil's weakness."*

"You know as well as I do, devil, the Lord is standing right behind me. So he doesn't need to prove his existence to either of us."

Irritated by Mike's impudence, he replied, "You know who I am, don't you, Mike? I am the one with the power to change the outcome of your day and your entire life. Why is the Creator not doing anything to protect you right now?"

"The Lord said he would never leave or forsake me, devil. So you have no power over me. If that's the best you can do, why don't you leave now?"

"It's not time for me to go, Mike, and this examination is over when I say it's over. Your faith is stronger than most we've seen, but you're human, and all humans have a weakness. What could your weakness possibly be, Mike? Let me guess."

Bildad tilted his head in sarcastic animation. Then he added, "The Book says to love your neighbor. Who's your neighbor, Mike? Could it be O'Neal there?" Bildad pointed toward Shawn's frozen body.

Mike's love for God was what fueled his compassion for others. He was ready to lay down his life for his fellowmen, but Mike knew his life was not what Bildad was after. One of the things he learned in basic training was that every man has his breaking point. Would he break faith with God if Bildad threatened one of his men?

"You cannot defeat me, devil," Mike responded with as much poise as he could muster. "I'm wearing the armor of God."

Smiling, Bildad retorted, "The Book also says that all have sinned and fall short of the Creator's glory. I don't see any armor, Mike. Just an unarmed privileged sinner with no spiritual backbone." Each word was full of hate, followed by spittle that sparkled as it fell to the ground.

"You don't honestly think the Creator will let you wear his armor in your sinful condition, do you? David didn't need the king's armor to defeat his enemy. He was a man of real faith. If you were half the man he was, Mike, you wouldn't need any armor to defeat little ol' me."

"I'll not fight you, devil. The victory here today belongs to the Lord. As far as I can tell, you're losing."

Incensed, Bildad continued. "Oh, I beg to differ, Mike. The Book says your battle is not against flesh and blood but against the spiritual forces of evil. So according to the Creator, this is your battle right now. Elsewhere, it says you must fight the good fight to take hold of eternal life. If you want your inheritance, Mike, you must defeat me right now if you can. Pick up that weapon, shoot me, and I'll capitulate this fight."

"You cannot provoke me, devil. My faith is on a solid foundation. To God be glory and honor forever and ever."

With each rejection, a flood of offensive stench flowed over Bildad like a river of righteousness. In the past six thousand years, he had conned all but a handful of believers into doubting God. Sensing defeat, Legion had Bildad play their last card.

Mike watched in amazement as Bildad vanished into a blue mist that began to rotate slowly. Gaining momentum, the cloud rose and passed like a slender javelin down into Shawn's quivering body.

Legion could not read his mind, but he read Mike's expression. Like others of his kind, Legion was an expert in human behavior, skilled in interpreting speech, emotions, habits, and body language. He was the perfect psychologist. Once he became fixated on someone, he studied them until he found their imperfection and attacked it. Most of his victims are entirely unaware they were under siege.

Much like sitting down at a computer and searching the database for useful information, Bildad began to access Shawn's memories for anything beneficial to his cause. What he found was how much Shawn admired Mike's compassion for others. Now,

Legion knew Mike's weakness. It was now only a question of whether he could exploit it. Bildad let Mike think about it before he animated his new host.

Bildad turned Shawn's head to face Mike without changing any facial muscles. The motion was so unnatural it caused Mike to cringe. His mouth still opened, prepared to answer Mike's earlier question about his salvation. Shawn was like a stringed puppet being put into motion.

Speaking through Shawn, Bildad brought Shawn's body back to life. "What was it you asked, Mike? Is Shawn saved? If he were, I wouldn't be in here right now, would I? Shawn's lost, and he's going to hell tonight, and there is nothing you can do about it. You could have told him about salvation many times, but you didn't. Now his blood will be on your hands."

Mike saw the helpless look on Shawn's face and his heart plunged into a sea of despair. How could he have been so thoughtless? He was so busy trying to keep Shawn alive that he forgot to tell him about eternal life.

Mike felt defeated for the first time in his Christian life; his ministry was about to be destroyed, and it did not matter how much good he had done for the Lord. Losing Shawn to Satan would be too heavy a burden for him to bear.

Then a verse came to mind: *"I will not allow you to be tempted beyond what you can endure, but God will always provide a way to escape temptation."* Mike considered his Christian security and thought about how he could use Bildad's pride against him.

Bildad assumed he had gotten the best of Mike, so he waited for him to see the hopelessness of his situation. Then he asked, "What do you say, Mike? Are you ready to admit you're defeated?"

Biding time to formulate a plan, Mike replied, "What do you want from me, devil?"

"Not much. Just one small thing. Do that for me, and I will exorcize myself from Shawn and leave. I promise never to bother you or Shawn ever again. You have my word on it."

"The word of the devil. How binding is that?"

"Do this one thing, and it will be the last time you ever see me again in this life or the next."

"What's the thing you want me to do?"

"It's no big thing. I won't ask you to eat an apple or anything like that."

"What is it, devil?" Mike said forcefully.

"I want you to say, 'Bildad, you are my best friend.'"

"That's all? I don't have to fall down and worship you or curse God?"

"No, nothing like that."

"What if I said no?"

"Maybe this will help make up your mind, Mike." Shawn's body started to convulse and distort itself in a violent seizure. Shawn fell to the bottom of the trench, screaming in pain. "Help me, Mike," he cried out. "He's killing me."

Mike was frantic, trying to think of a way to help Shawn. Then he thought of something Bildad said: *I will exorcize myself from Shawn and leave. That must be my choice. How do I cast out this evil spirit?*

Mike remembered a sermon he once heard his pastor preach about faith being as small as a mustard seed. *A little faith will move mountains and cast out demons, is what he said. God is allowing this testing for a purpose. I don't know what it would be if not for this. Lord, I'm stepping out on faith right now.*

There was no doubt that Mike would survive this test. The only question was how much damage Legion would do to his spiritual self-esteem. Now that Mike had a battle plan, the Advocate looked forward to the next few minutes with great pleasure.

"All right, devil, I've made my decision. Release your hand from Shawn, and I will give you what you deserve."

Immediately, Bildad released Shawn from his seizure, and a different spirit materialized to face Mike. He was eight feet tall with masculine features that spoke of immense power. Naked and with dark-colored skin, he stood dominant over Mike. With eyes that flashed reddish orange, he stood ready to receive his due.

Undaunted, Mike looked intently up at Legion and said with a slight smile, "So that there will be no misunderstanding, Legion, you will exit Shawn's body and leave us forever if I give you what you deserve. Correct?"

"Yes. Do this little thing for me, and I will leave Shawn's body, and neither of you will ever be troubled by us in your lifetime."

"Do I have your word on that?"

"You have my word on it."

"I'm still not sure I can trust you, devil. Will you swear in the name of God's Son?"

The thought of speaking the name was like being punched in the face. Legion had never uttered it before, so he could not know what would happen if he did now.

When God cast Satan and his forces out of heaven, he condemned them to walk the earth shackled to their sin of pride, never to forget it. Now that Legion thought Mike was on the verge of giving him that long-sought-after crown, he agreed to Mike's terms.

"If you give me the glory I deserve, I promise to leave you and Shawn right now, and we will never bother either of you again." There was a hesitation before Legion finished his promise. "I promise that in the name of … Jesus Christ."

To Legion's surprise, speaking the name produced none of the torment he expected. There was no lightning bolt from heaven. No divine sword appeared to drive him into the abyss. A sense of confidence quickly empowered him as he considered how to use the name against other believers. Legion's pride welled up to the level of a narcotic overdose.

"OK, Mike. It's your turn now. Give me what I deserve."

"Then by the power of God Almighty and in the name of Jesus Christ, I command you to leave Shawn's body. Come out, devil, and leave this place."

Realizing Mike had tricked them, Bildad threw Shawn's body into another convulsion.

Mike responded with conviction and divine authority, "Come out quickly, devil. In the name of Jesus Christ, I cast you out."

Mike watched as a translucent hand extended from behind him. It reached into Shawn's body, grabbed Bildad by the neck, and pulled him out, kicking and screaming. The hand secured him until he stopped squirming, then sat him down, kneeling next to Legion.

Amazed by what just happened, Mike broke out in a slow grin.

After the seizures ceased, Shawn's body collapsed in a heap the moment Bildad left him. Though limp as a dishrag, he was completely aware of everything that followed.

"You asked for proof that God existed," Mike said. "Well, devil, there you have it."

Reluctantly, Bildad looked up at a very angry Legion. With his eyes fixed on Mike, he extended his hand downward to Bildad. Eagerly accepting the invitation, he evaporated and rejoined the many other spirits inside of Legion.

Slowly, an evil smile covered Legion's face. "You said you would give me what I deserve. You didn't do that. So I win. Game set and match, Mike."

"Not so, devil. I promised you only what you deserved."

"What do you mean by that!" Legion snarled.

"The Bible says that God gave Jesus a name that is above every other name. Every knee shall bow, and every tongue shall confess that Jesus Christ is Lord. You asked for something you did not deserve. I correctly reminded you that the glory will always go to Jesus Christ. Checkmate, devil. You lose."

Enraged, Legion lunged toward Mike, ignoring the Advocate's power. From behind Mike came an explosion of light and a strong gust of wind. The light was like blinding fireworks. The wind lightly brushed past Mike's hair but was strong enough to stop Legion in his tracks.

Mike then heard the Advocate say, "This one belongs to Me, Legion. You've had your chance and failed. This examination is over. Now go before I let my faithful servant throw you out." The light faded, and the wind stopped, leaving Mike and Legion facing each other. The Advocate was pleased with how well his young steward had withstood this trial. Smiling, he stepped forward to let Legion know he would not tolerate any more lies tonight.

A few moments passed before Mike sternly added, "I told you, devil. The victory belongs to the Lord. Now it's time for you to leave."

Legion stood defiantly, refusing to believe a human had bested him.

Realizing Legion needed some prodding, Mike picked up the M60 machine gun. He released the safety and brought it to his side with the barrel pointing at his opponent.

"I know this won't kill you, devil. However, I believe these bullets will hurt a lot more now. What do you say? Are you ready to go?"

Knowing the Boss would be angry, Legion had no option but to cut his losses and leave. His attempt at destroying Mike's effectiveness as a believer had failed. He had been defeated by God's saints before, but this one was his most humiliating.

"Guard your family well, Mike," Legion threatened. "You won't be there to protect them forever."

Legion levitated his body six feet into the air and hovered briefly. Then without losing eye contact with Mike, he began to float backward toward the hole he had made in the wire. As he moved over the opening, the damaged wire folded back to its original condition. Unable to cope with his shattered ego, Legion began inflating himself to four times his size. His body pulsed once and deflated quickly in a burst of light that vanished into the night.

With Legion defeated, the Hill came back to life. The flare continued to float slowly downward until it extinguished itself.

Mike was unsure how long he stood and stared out into the Trace. His faith in the Lord had given him the power to overcome Legion's inquisition. In his weakened state, Shawn managed to get up and lean against the sandbags beside Mike. They exchanged weary smiles, and Shawn asked, "What just happened, Mike?"

"I'm not sure you would believe me if I told you, Shawn. How do you feel?"

"Like I just rolled down a mountain. My joints are all sore. My brain feels like I've been on a weeklong bender. Was that thing really inside me?"

"Yes, Shawn. It was."

"I only remember bits and pieces. How did you get it to come out?"

"Let's just say I had a lot of help from a close friend. As I asked before, Shawn, are you saved?"

"No, I have no idea what it means to be saved, but I think you should tell me about it right now."

Mike reached into his pocket, pulled out a small Bible, and told Shawn about the Roman road to salvation.

Chapter 24

It's All in God's Hands Now

Dwight David Eisenhower once said of World War II, "There comes a time when you've used your brains, your training, your technical skill, and the die is cast. The events are in the hands of God, and there you have to leave them."

Major Parks had done everything he could to counter the anticipated attack plans of Giap and the North Vietnamese Army. The die was now cast for both opponents. Mike understood that the pending battle's outcome was entirely in God's hands. There, because of his faith, he would leave it.

Mike arrived at the 3rd Squad bunker at 2030 hours. His mind was in overdrive thinking about his encounter with Legion. He found Simmons and Carter still awake, standing at the window, searching the night for any sign of Charlie.

"Why are both of you still up? One of you should be sleeping."

"We got some sleep this afternoon, Sergeant. We're not tired anyway."

"Well, try to get some more."

"OK, Sergeant."

"Good. I need to go to OP-2 for a few minutes. Make sure one of you is in his cot when I get back," Mike said with an animated growl. With much on his mind, he turned to leave the bunker.

"Sergeant, where do you think they will hit us tonight?" Carter asked.

Realizing he had not spent time today with his two nervous bunker mates, Mike returned to the window. "I'm pretty sure their main attack will be somewhere between Bunker 3 and 4, probably sometime after midnight. Parks is holding two platoons from A Company in reserve. They will back us up once he's sure where to send them."

Mike spent a few more minutes easing their anxiety before leading them in prayer.

As he walked over to talk to Bernie, Mike thought about how disappointed he was that Parks ordered him to defend the 3rd Squad bunker tonight. He didn't understand why he couldn't be with his men when the attack started—until now. The Advocate had been there to protect him from Legion. Understandably, God would now put him in a safe place for the upcoming battle.

Inside, Joe was at the window, looking through his nightscope at the perimeter wire below. Bernie stood close by, keeping him company. Duncan was catnapping at a table in the center of the room. Two other men were asleep at the back of the bunker. Their cots were covered with netting to keep out the mosquitoes and other nasty, creepy, crawly things.

Hearing him enter, Bernie turned and greeted Mike.

"Bernie, I think I know where and how the gooks will hit us tonight."

"OK, let's hear it."

Mike stepped to the window and pointed to the area in front of the 3rd Squad bunkers. "I think Charlie will use Bangalore torpedoes to breach the wire in front of Bunker 4."

"Exactly how did you figure that out?"

"Let's just say I had a premonition."

"Isn't that like a strange vision or revelation?"

"Yeah, it is."

Bernie's mental lightbulb came on. He had been dying to talk to someone about his encounter with Eliphaz. However, with him and Joe being so busy with surveillance, there was never any time.

Curiously, Bernie added, "Did it have anything to do with demons?"

Surprised, Mike looked at Bernie, paused, and then said, "What ... makes you say that?"

"Just a lucky guess. Go on."

"What are you two yappin' about?" Joe complained.

"Not a thing, Joe. Keep your eye on that wire. Remember, our goal tonight is to keep them out, not let them back in again."

Bernie motioned to Mike to follow him outside. Quietly, they continued talking in the trench.

"Now, go on."

"You promise not to laugh," Mike requested.

"If this is what I think it is, no, I won't laugh."

"Well, I inspected my line bunkers about half an hour ago, and suddenly, I found myself in the middle of la-la land alone. The marine next to me was turned into a statue. Then I spotted this thing outside the wire that started talking to me. It even knew my name."

"This thing wasn't about five feet tall, was it?"

Puzzled by Bernie's comment, Mike stammered through the first few words of his reply, "Yeah. It was five feet tall, human shaped, and covered in a transparent suit. His name is Legion, but he called himself Bildad."

"What did he want?"

"He knew I was a Christian and tried to get me to renounce my faith. Fortunately, I had a little help to convince him to leave."

"What kind of help?"

"Are you a Christian?"

"I once thought so. Now I'm not so sure."

"Then I doubt you would understand."

"Try me."

"Do you know what an exorcism is?" Mike asked.

"Yes, but isn't that just a Catholic superstition?"

"Oh, it's real, all right, and the Lord just helped me perform one tonight."

"Three days ago, I would have called you crazy, but not now."

"I take it you had a similar encounter. Tell me about that."

"I met my little demon two days ago on the drive up from Da Nang," Bernie began. "He was almost invisible. I stuck my hand right into his body, which felt like cold Jell-O. He took over this lieutenant's body and made all these weird things happen.

"He blew up a truck and injured an army MP. This demon introduced himself as Legion, but he used the name Eliphaz. He told me the MP smelled funny because he was a Christian. What freaked me the most about this demon was that it could read my mind."

"They cannot possess a believer," Mike began, "or read their mind—only those who are lost.

"Wait a minute," Mike said. "Bildad and Eliphaz. Those names are from the Bible. They were two of the three guys who accused Job of being unrighteous. I think the other one's name was Zophar. I'll be darned. Job's self-righteous friends turned out to be demon possessed."

Bernie asked, "Why do you think Charlie will hit us with Bangalore torpedoes in front of that bunker?"

"When Bildad came through the fence, he blew it up. The hole looked like something a torpedo would make. When he went back through the hole, the wire folded itself back together like before.

These demons are prideful and arrogant. They don't fear us, so they don't care what they tell us. God willed that demon to show me exactly how and where Charlie will come through the wire tonight."

"All that's certainly over my head, but you convinced me. Are you going to tell that to Parks?"

"Parks knows Charlie will attack somewhere in front of the 3rd Squad. Bunker 4 is almost in the middle. What do you think?"

"I think Parks has enough to worry about tonight. He won't commit any of his reserves until he knows where to send them. If it were me, I would not bother him with this."

"I think you're right. Besides, you're gonna spot them before they get close to the wire. Then Duncan will call in a fire mission and take them all out. Right?"

"If they get within a hundred yards of that wire, we'll pick them up and call it in so Parks will have plenty of time to react accordingly."

"I'm glad to hear that," Mike said. "Now I need to go get some sleep if I can. See you in the morning."

"Good night, Mike."

As he stood alone in the trench, Bernie considered Eliphaz's warning again about that narrow gate into the Kingdom. *What is this Kingdom, and why does he not want me to find it? I'll ask Mike to explain it to me in the morning.*

Chapter 25

0255 Hours

From its elevated position, OP-2 offered the best vantage point for spotting enemy activity on the east side of the Hill. Duncan had spent the afternoon setting up his anticipated fire missions for the Hill's artillery and mortar batteries. Should he need additional firepower, he had the 105 howitzers at Gio Linh and the 155s at Dong Ha at his disposal. If things turned desperate, the big 175 guns at Camp Carroll were only a radio call away.

Over the previous three nights, Giap had secretly constructed twelve large bunkers five hundred yards in front of 3rd Squad to position his troops closer to the Hill. He would use these bunkers as staging areas for his main attack force. However, Duncan knew about these fortifications. Once the attack started, Duncan was prepared to bring all his resources to bear on Giap's insurgents immediately.

This information should have made him feel good, but Duncan still had one more pressing question.

"Sergeant, something is not right about this. It's too easy. Why would Giap put two battalions this close to the Hill, knowing we could take them out before they reached the wire? When Parks pulled that patrol in today, Giap should have guessed we were on to him."

"I agree, Lieutenant," Bernie replied. "What could he possibly be up to?"

Joe was busy sweeping the perimeter with the nightscope. Without looking up, he answered, "Giap has figured out a way to silence not only our guns but the guns of Gio Linh, Dong Ha, and Camp Carroll all at once."

Bernie looked at Joe and replied doubtingly, "Just how do you think he will do that, Joe?"

Suggesting that Giap could disrupt the surrounding compounds' firepower all at once piqued Duncan's interest as well. He turned to hear Joe's answer.

While continuing his surveillance, Joe added, "Have either of you read the book *The Guns of Navarone*? It's about a team of commandos sent to take out two massive German guns in World War II so the British Navy could rescue one thousand two hundred stranded soldiers. The mission would have been a disaster had the commandos not destroyed those guns."

"Joe, I should know better to question your book smarts by now, but if you know how Giap is going to take our guns out of action, we would like to hear it."

"Simple," Joe began. "We know Giap has every gun emplacement on the Hill targeted. He will pin us down with his mortars so we cannot use our guns, and he'll do the same to any firebase close enough to support us."

Duncan and Bernie stared at Joe in total disbelief. The logistical complications of something that massive seemed impossible.

"Do you two have any idea who Giap is?" Joe asked smugly. "He's the guy who defeated the French at Dien Bien Phu, and he did it by hiding his artillery right under their nose until the last minute. If I'm not mistaken, today is the thirteenth anniversary of the French surrender."

Duncan and Bernie stood pan-faced, offering no response.

"Come on now," Joe quipped. "Giap is a military genius. How do you think he managed to build those twelve bunkers right under our nose?"

Duncan was the first to make the connection while Bernie marveled at Joe's insight into combat tactics.

"The corporal's right," Duncan began. "Giap's ability to surprise the French with all that artillery was genius. I believe he's hiding his troops just a few yards outside the wire where he can strike us hard and fast."

The sound of a single mortar thump caught their attention. Turning toward the window, the three men watched a green NVA flare rise over the jungle canopy on the Hill's south side. The time was 0255 hours.

"It's started," Duncan said in a raised whisper.

Almost immediately, the Hill started receiving a heavy bombardment. One of the first rounds landed twenty yards in front of OP-2. Everyone inside ducked for cover. Seconds later, OP-2 took several hits that caved in the bunker roof. The marines in the dugout scrambled out the back door and into the trench. Duncan, Bernie, and Joe, however, were now trapped inside.

The NVA mortars were deadly accurate. One by one, Dog Company's fortifications started to take hits. Without Duncan to direct any return fire, the Hill was now deaf, dumb, and blind.

One of the marines who escaped from OP-2 ran the fifty yards down to Mike's bunker with a report. Mike immediately got on the field phone and called the switchboard operator.

"Sparks, this is Shaffer. Get me the CP."

There was a brief pause while the switchboard operator transferred the call to the CP.

"This is Parks."

"Sir, this is Shaffer. OP-2 was just hit. Looking Glass and Night Stalker are trapped inside. Their condition is unknown. Over."

"Roger that, Sergeant. Be advised that we'll be out of illumination rounds in twenty minutes. The flare plane ETA is 50. Gio Linh, Dong Ha, and Camp Carroll are all under heavy mortar attack. For now, we have no artillery cover. We're on our own. Good luck. Out."

As Mike hung up the phone, he looked out of the bunker window toward the east and saw the rapid bursts of light at Gio Linh. South, toward Dong Ha, the same thing was happening there. A heavy mortar attack had pinned down both compounds.

For a moment, Mike was caught up in a vision. Before him lay the bodies of all the lost who would die tonight. Their souls tried to escape Legion's transportation forces, screaming as they were dragged down toward the pit. Mike saw three figures standing just outside the fence. Two stood close together. Mike knew it was Bildad and Eliphaz. He assumed the third shadowy figure standing several steps away was Zophar. His vagueness told Mike he would make his appearance sometime in the future.

The bombardment brought Mike back to his senses. After a quick look around to regain his thoughts, he offered God a short prayer as he started checking in with his five bunkers.

At 0315 hours, with NVA shells landing along the eastern slope, six sapper teams quickly approached the fence. They shoved two bamboo Bangalore torpedoes packed with high explosives through the wire. One was placed in front of Bunker 4 and the second in front of Bunker 3. After the sappers retreated to safety, they detonated the torpedoes, clearing two eight-foot-wide paths through the wire and mines.

Immediately, ten RPGs opened fire on Mike's abandoned line bunkers. With the fortifications neutralized, thirty-five NVA soldiers armed only with two satchel charges and four grenades rushed through the wire. Spreading out, they raced toward the trench.

Third Squad opened fire from their concealed positions along the trench when the sappers were halfway through no-man's-land. Raking the enemy with claymore mines, M60, M16, and M79 beehive fire, the first wave of sappers was quickly killed or wounded.

A second barrage of RPG fire took out four of Mike's five makeshift positions. O'Neal's M60 in Bunker 5 was now the only operational 3rd Squad machine gun. Slayer in Bunker 1 and Lamont in Bunker 3 were the first 3rd Squad members to be killed.

Then a second larger wave of sapper and RPG teams flooded through the wire and raced toward the trench system. M60 fire from the marines' secondary bunkers higher up the hill was effective but could not stop twenty-eight of the enemy from reaching the trench. Like a swarm of locusts, the sappers raced past the marines' first line of defenders. They then headed up the hill to destroy anything that could offer any resistance against Giap's main strike force.

"Sparks, this is Shaffer. Give me the CP quick," Mike requested.

"This is Parks."

"Sir, this is Shaffer. The gooks took out all the 3rd Squad bunkers. Only one 60 is still operational. We have approximately twenty-five sappers in the trench advancing up the Hill. Over."

"Roger. Hold your position, Sergeant. I'm sending reinforcements now. Out."

"Corporal Rios, get me the engineers' CO."

There was a short pause before Rios replied, "I've got the engineers on the line now, sir."

"Dozer, this is Parks. We have sappers inside the wire. Take your men and plug the gap between OP-2 and OP-3. I'm sending a reaction force to tie in on your left flank. We're expecting the main attack at any time. Be advised we will be out of illumination rounds in fifteen."

"Yes, sir." With mortars landing everywhere, Lieutenant Mead led his twenty-one engineers out of the trench and raced the two hundred yards up the hill. No sooner had he positioned his men than a mortar landed nearby, killing him instantly. Though they fought like the devil dogs they were, the engineers would lose two more marines and sustain four wounded in heavy fighting, but not one enemy soldier got past them.

Parks turned to address his First Sergeant, "Top, take one platoon of reinforcements over and strengthen OP-2's left flank. Make it quick. We are down to our last few rounds of illumination. I'll hold the 2nd platoon in reserve here. See if you can find out what happened to Duncan."

"Will do, sir."

Two Alpha Company platoons were waiting for orders in the trench behind the CP. Top took the first platoon and raced off into the night. There was no time for caution. He needed to have his men in position before the main NVA attackers rushed through the wire.

In typical marine fashion, Top and fifty marines rushed down a short section of trench and out into the open, completely exposed to the incoming mortar fire. Navigating around several old fence sections, the marines charged down the hill, across the compound road, and then up toward OP-2. The light faded, and the next illumination round was fired. From behind him, Top heard a marine yell, "Last round out!" The marines now had one minute to reach their objective.

As Top jumped a section of the trench, he saw three sappers running through the channel, heading toward the 105 howitzers.

Without missing a beat, he turned his head and yelled, "Sappers!" Two marines behind him dropped out of the column and ran after the sappers, firing into the trench. Unarmed and with no means of returning fire, the enemy soldiers were quickly killed. One final round ensured they were dead, and the two marines raced to catch up to their detachment.

OP-2 was located atop the east hill. Top's contingent reached it just as the last light began to fade. A series of hand signals and the marines fanned out to take positions that overlooked the perimeter wire and trench. Top looked over and confirmed the engineers were positioned to the right.

With his detail now in a position to repel the enemy, Top addressed one of the marines busy trying to dig Duncan out of the collapsed OP-2 bunker. "What's the situation, Marine?"

"Duncan and the two snipers are trapped inside but alive, First Sergeant."

Top shouted into the bunker, "Lieutenant, are you OK?"

"Yes. Three of us are trapped in the front. I've got a broken leg."

"Sir, this is Top. Sappers are in the wire. We are expecting the main attack at any time. We'll get you out as soon as possible."

"Thanks, Top."

Top left three of his remaining detail to help evacuate Duncan, Bernie, and Joe. He then took three men and ran over to support Mike's bunker. Top stepped inside and found Mike and two others at the bunker window.

"We're sure glad to see you, Top."

"Likewise, Mike. Where's your phone?"

Mike pointed to the corner. Top stepped quickly to the phone and called the CP.

"Major, this is Top. We have secured the left flank of OP-2. The engineers are in position on the right. Duncan and the snipers are alive but trapped inside the bunker. We should have them out soon. Sappers are all over the lower hill. Over."

"Good job, Top. Be advised the flare plane ETA is thirty."

"Yes, sir. Out."

"The flare plane will be here in thirty, Mike. Alpha Company is guarding your left flank. The engineers are on your right. I'll be outside with three marines guarding the bunker. Give 'em hell, Marines."

"Same to you, Top."

Mike, Carter, and Simmons readied themselves for the storm that was headed their way.

Chapter 26

The Main Attack

Vo Nguyen Giap was a commoner with no formal military training. He rose through the ranks to become both a politician and North Vietnam's most prominent general. Noted for his victories against the Japanese, French, and Americans, Giap was destined to become the driving force to end America's involvement in Vietnam.

His attack against Con Thien was complicated and involved numerous NVA units positioned all over the DMZ. Giap needed to eliminate artillery fire support from three other firebases to win this battle. The timing was critical and called for a four-hour window of opportunity. However, having Duncan take out half of his convoy set his timetable back an hour.

The North Vietnamese were desperate for a big victory to give them some momentum against the Americans, so this one battle was vital. Giap's insistence that the attack take place on May 8 to coincide with his big defeat of the French thirteen years earlier was rushed and ill-fated. Had the NVA attacked the Hill before the marines arrived, this would have been a slam-dunk victory against a weaker South Vietnamese Army. Had he attacked an hour earlier, the marine losses would have been much higher.

Giap did not know what to think when the Hill stopped firing illumination rounds. It took him several minutes to recognize his good fortune and send in his main force. Like a giant flood, twelve hundred NVA rushed through the wire breaches in the black of night and struck hard at the twelve surviving members of Mike's 3rd Squad.

Three battle tanks atop the Hill immediately opened fire on the invading force with beehive and .30-caliber machine gun fire. Unbeknownst to the tankers, a sapper team had positioned itself behind them. An RPG round struck the nearest tank. It burst into flames, trapping the crew inside. Two satchel charges took out a second tank. Machine-gun fire from the third tank and a nearby bunker killed the four-men-and-one-woman sapper team.

The remaining claymore mines killed the first fifty NVA soldiers through the wire. M60s raked the enemy with devastating fire. M79 and 105 beehive rounds also took their toll, but the onslaught was too much for 3rd Squad to contend with.

Demarco and Grady moved together to consolidate their strength. They fired as quickly as they could pull the trigger. Looking at the onslaught before them, both marines knew it was hopeless.

When Demarco's M16 jammed, he cursed and hurled it at an advancing enemy, knocking him to the ground. Immediately, he pulled his Ka-Bar knife and prepared himself to meet his maker. Grady got off two more beehive rounds before a flamethrower engulfed them both in napalm. Flailing wildly, neither marine died quickly. Looking down from his bunker, Mike screamed in anguish.

Finch was fifty yards from the flamethrower. He managed to drop the operator just seconds before he was struck in the neck by an AK-47 round. Though bleeding badly, he continued to fire his weapon for another minute before collapsing.

The Special Forces and their civilian militia held their own, supporting 3rd Squad's right flank until a group of NVA rushed past Bunker 1, killing Magrini. Now, the enemy was moving in behind them. Ignoring Littlejohn, they ran around the right end and fought their way up the hill until they encountered the engineers, who stopped them cold. Their M14 fire was deadly accurate as the enemy tried desperately to maneuver around them.

After thirty minutes of fighting the engineers, the NVA regrouped their forces and rushed the Special Forces bunkers from the rear. The non-battle-tested civilian militia panicked and fled, leaving the army to hold the line. Though they lost four of their own, they managed to drive off the enemy in fierce hand-to-hand combat.

Back on the line, O'Neal and Tucker were still laying down M60 fire from the area around Bunker 5. Support from David's 1st Squad bunkers on their left kept the enemy contained to a narrow field of advance. With a burst of AK-47 fire, O'Neal went down with a mortal chest wound. Tucker quickly secured the machine gun and continued firing.

With all three marines in Bunker 3 dead, the NVA now had a causeway into the trench that led up the hill. Suddenly, nine hundred enemy soldiers proceeded up the slope toward Mike and Top's small group of defenders.

Being notified of the enemy's advance, Parks committed his remaining reinforcements above the compound road dividing OP-1 and OP-2. This action blocked off the trench system that separated the two hills and forced the NVA to fight the marines above ground on the middle knoll.

Three enemy soldiers worked their way down the trench until they came upon Bunker 4 from the side. A hand grenade killed Smith. Greene died when he charged the enemy with a jammed M16.

In Bunker 2, Adams was the combat virgin, but when the bullets started flying, his actions were that of a seasoned veteran.

Wolf was ready and waiting when the main enemy force rushed through the wire. Like a ghost in the darkness, he attacked the enemy with a vengeance. Wolf was twenty yards away when he saw that Adams's position was about to be overrun. Stepping over dead bodies, he raced to his aid, firing his weapon until he ran out of ammunition.

Two NVA jumped into the trench in front of him. One turned to face Wolf; the other turned toward Adams. Wolf killed the first one with a single bayonet thrust. He quickly drew his knife and threw it after the second. The blade struck the enemy in the back, who fell dead at Adams's feet. Looking behind him, Adams saw that Wolf had his back and continued to fire down the trench at the enemy streaming up the hill.

Third Squad was now down to five marines—Tucker, Fuller, Wolf, Adams, and Littlejohn—all scattered along a one-hundred-and-fifty-yard stretch of the trench.

The flare plane, delayed in Da Nang because of mechanical problems, finally arrived over the Hill at 0425 hours. Once again, there was light above the Hill. Its spooky shadows danced over the battlefield like a slow-moving disco strobe light. With the enemy stalled and daylight fast approaching, the advantage soon shifted to the marines.

David arrived at Bunker 5 with eight members of the 1st Squad to reorganize the perimeter defenses. Knowing the enemy would retreat through the wire in the next hour, he decided to fortify bunkers 1 and 5 and force the enemy through a crossfire.

Over two hundred bodies littered the ground in no-man's-land. Unarmed troops rushed in and out of the wire, carrying the dead and wounded off to field hospitals and predug burial sites thousands of yards away. Not being a threat, the marines let them continue their work.

David instructed his men to wall up the trench between Bunker 5 to fashion a fighting hole. Then cautiously, he made his way down the ditch. The first marine David came to was Tucker, still holding on to his M60. Breathing heavily, he turned when he heard David's voice.

"Tucker, where's O'Neal?"

"He didn't make it, Sergeant. I am glad to see you. I thought I was all alone."

"You're not alone, Marine. You've got me, and I'll get you out of here. First, we need to move your gun down to Bunker 1 and set up a little surprise for Charlie when he comes back through here. Break into those ammo cans so we can take as much ammo as possible."

Although the firing on the line had stopped, the fighting was fierce up on the hill. Marine fire directed downhill kicked up dust everywhere. David and Tucker quickly opened the cans and draped as many M60 bandoliers as they could carry around their necks.

"All right, now follow me. Stay alert and keep your head down."

The two marines started making their way down the ditch. When David came upon Fuller, he was crouched in the trench's bottom, brushing the dirt off Greene's face. He nodded and glanced over at Smith, lying a short distance away.

David crouched beside Fuller with his hand on his shoulder and waited for him to look up. "You doing OK, Marine?"

"I'm good, Sergeant. Greene charged the enemy with a jammed weapon. They almost cut him in half. Man, I am so pissed right now."

"Well, save it for later. We need to get to Bunker 1 quickly. Grab as many M16 bandoliers as you can and follow us."

Halfheartedly, Fuller left Greene's body and fell in behind David and Tucker, and the three continued toward Bunker 3. There, they came upon the smoldering remains of two marines lying at the bottom of the trench. Burned beyond recognition, David knew it had to be two of the Motown Three, as the brothers called themselves.

"That's not a good way for a marine to die. Let's keep movin'."

Fighting the urge to barf from the stench, the three marines stepped over the bodies the best they could and continued down the trench. They found Lamont slumped to his knees ten yards farther, still clinging to his M60. David thought that those two marines back there must be Demarco and Grady.

"Fuller, secure that gun. We will need it."

Now, with a second M60, the three marines moved out again.

Walking over piles of dead NVA gave David the creeps. He kept expecting one to come to life and start shooting at them. *I hope Mike's taking care of himself up there.*

The interconnecting furrow that led up the hill ran behind Bunker 3. It was the path that most of the NVA took when they advanced up the hill. So David approached it with caution. He was sure the enemy would leave several men to guard their exit route.

Holding his hand up to fashion a fist, Fuller and Tucker froze. Bodies littered the intersection, stacked four deep. David proceeded alone. With his back up against the trench wall, he moved to within four feet of the juncture. Taking a deep breath, David took a grenade from his utility harness and pulled the pin. He tossed the grenade about ten feet up the channel as he stepped across the trench. Then with his rifle trained on the trench opening, he waited.

Someone around the corner shouted, "Lu'u dan!" and two NVA rushed out into David's line of fire. After the grenade exploded, David moved quickly past the two dead soldiers and started firing into the trench. The dust settled enough to reveal three more dead NVA. David quickly changed his magazine and signaled the other two marines to follow.

"Tucker, bring up the rear and watch our six."

"Will do, Sergeant."

When David found him, Wolf had just thrown a dead NVA out of the trench. Adams was a few feet away, guarding their position with his M16. Finch was sitting in a pool of blood at the bottom of the ditch. Despite the carnage around them, Adams's painted face caused David to grin.

"Wolf, you didn't scalp any of these guys, did you?"

Wolf had just singlehandedly killed over twenty NVA, yet he was cool as a cucumber. He wore a red bandanna around his head with a single white feather tucked into one side. His face was painted black and white, with one red dot between the eyes. Wolf was an intimidating-looking marine, about six foot one, weighing about one ninety pounds.

"The thought crossed my mind, Sergeant, but I have somehow misplaced my knife."

"I think it's in the back of that guy behind you."

Wolf turned to retrieve his blade. Wiping the blood on his trousers, he put his right hand on Adams's shoulder and smiled.

"Sergeant, my brother here did a good job taking care of Charlie tonight. The enemy is up there trying to figure out how they can get off this Hill without coming back through here."

Wearily, Adams smiled at Wolf's compliment.

"Well, I'm sure you two badass marines can deal with Charlie's retreat alone, but I need you to come with me to Bunker 1. Grab as much ammo as you can."

David glanced at his watch and noted it was 0505. The sun would be up soon, so they were almost out of time before the enemy started flooding back through the wire.

The marines continued for another forty yards until they found Littlejohn. He sat at the bottom of the trench wall, trying to put a bandage on a shoulder wound.

"Littlejohn, where are Magrini and Slayer?"

"They're both dead, Sergeant."

"Adams, help him with that bandage. The rest of you close off the trench as best as you can to give us some protection. Hurry, the midnight showing of *King Kong* is about over, and Charlie will be heading for the exit anytime now."

The marines worked swiftly, and in fifteen minutes, they had fashioned themselves a large foxhole in the middle of the trench. David and Wolf's warped sense of humor was enough to take the edge off a very stressful situation. They would collapse in exhaustion in a couple of hours, but right now, they were wired and ready for the next engagement.

Talking above the muffled battle that raged a hundred yards up the Hill, David set his battle plan into motion. "OK, Marines, listen up. They'll be coming from everywhere when they run back down the hill. Tucker, you and Adams train your two M60s in front of those two breaches in the wire. The rest of you train your rifles up the hill. We need to force Charlie to the right if we can. I will cover the trench with the third 60. How's the arm, Littlejohn?"

"It hurts a bit, but I can still use a rifle."

"Good. We need another first-class marine right now."

When David gave Tucker and Fuller aiming instructions, he was surprised to see how many dead and wounded NVA had been removed from no-man's-land. All but a handful of NVA bodies remained.

With the 1st Squad stationed in Bunker 5 and the 3rd Squad set up at Bunker 1, David had his little surprise ready for the enemy when they tried to leave the Hill. In silence, the six marines

waited for the enemy to retreat. They wouldn't have to wait much
longer.

*   *   *

Mike, Simmons, and Carter had their hands full with three
hundred very determined enemy soldiers opposing their bunker.
Though their shelter had sustained multiple RPG and grenade
hits, thirty yards away was as close as the enemy could get. Four
times, a sapper had rushed forward with satchel charges only to
be cut down before they could throw them.

After Mike had detonated all his claymore mines, he grabbed
the M79 and started firing beehive rounds at the enemy. AK-47
fire raked the bunker window opening, and the M60 fell silent.
Looking over, Mike saw Simmons and Carter lying dead on the
floor. He rushed to the machine gun and started firing again.
Pausing to insert another ammo belt, Mike saw steam rolling off
the weapon. He knew the barrel would melt if he had to fire it
much longer.

Top and his platoon bravely held their position around Mike's
bunker. Though they had lost six men, they had managed to stop
the enemy from getting past them.

Doc Ryan rushed to aid an injured marine lying in the open.
Two NVA appeared out of nowhere and ran toward them. With
AK-47 rounds flying around him, Ryan managed to draw his .45
and kill one before a bullet struck him in the chest. A marine
nearby killed the second NVA before he could bayonet the marine
Ryan tried to save.

At this point, there were about eight hundred NVA still alive
on the Hill, and the marines engaged in the battle were still
outnumbered 10 to 1. Although several hundred other marines
were on the Hill, they held their positions because of orders.

Their discipline and trust in one another helped save the day for the marines.

At 0525, a bugle from outside the wire sounded the retreat. Every enemy soldier knew the skies over the Hill would be swarming with helicopters in less than an hour. If they did not make it through the wire and into the trees by sunup, their chance of survival would be zero.

Small pockets of fire kept the marines pinned down while the invaders' main body rushed down the trench, carrying their dead and wounded with them. Several minutes later, the remaining NVA executed a well-disciplined tactical withdrawal. Retreating in stages, the enemy kept the marines from following until all the enemy forces had reached the bottom.

David's M60s opened fire when the enemy raced out of the trench. Several dozen NVA tried to rush David's position from the rear, but M16 fire forced them back into the ditch and over toward the main force exiting behind Bunker 3. Fifty valiant NVA soldiers fell dead or wounded. Their comrades secured what bodies they could and carried them through the wire with their weapons.

RPG fire hit both of David's placements, causing a temporary disruption in the marine fire. A dozen NVA with AK-47s stopped inside the wire to cover the retreat. Additional AK-47 firepower engaged the marines from outside the fence as well. The fire became so intense that David's two foxholes could do little more than keep their heads down.

The first rays of sunlight brightened the eastern sky when the last able NVA made it through the wire. The stragglers trapped inside the fence found a place to hide and waited for the opportunity to kill one more marine. All enemy shelling stopped when a dozen marine Hueys arrived at 0620.

Chapter 27

A Surprise for Charlie

Johnson's 2nd Squad could hear the battle on the Hill from their concealed position south of the Ben Hai River. The marines knew that when Charlie retreated, he would take the most direct route to the river and then turn east to the protection of his hidden underground bunker system. Alpha 22 was in the perfect position to cut them off.

To beat Charlie at his game, you must think like him—be invisible and do the unexpected. There was no reason for Charlie to suspect Johnson's patrol could have moved almost three miles undetected in the dark, so the enemy was not expecting them to be there.

Ambush patrols were not for the fainthearted: they were surrounded, all alone, and completely self-sufficient. One minor mistake, the slightest noise or smell, could bring disaster. Part of being a good marine is patience, especially when you're in enemy territory, knowing that a much larger enemy force is coming your way.

When the NVA trumpet sounded, Johnson knew it would take Charlie about an hour to reach his position. Once Duncan was freed from his collapsed bunker, he enlisted the Hill's 105 howitzers and drove the enemy north toward the waiting marines. Guns from Gio Linh prevented Charlie from scattering to the east. As the advancing artillery fire got closer, the anticipation among the marines started to mount. Each man knew they had lost friends during the night, and what happened in the next few minutes would go a long way to even the score.

The advanced element of the retreating NVA appeared at the tree line at 0710. The sun had been up for forty minutes, so visibility was perfect. Three enemy soldiers quickly crossed the road fifty yards to the east then returned minutes later.

Johnson quietly made radio contact with the Hill and told them they had the enemy in sight. Responsibilities for directing artillery fire from the Hill were now his responsibility.

Anticipating the enemy would wait for their stragglers to catch up, Alpha 22 quietly held their fire. Any time now, Johnson expected four to five hundred NVA to step out and run to the tree line on his side of the road. They were ready to spring their trap.

Not wanting to be outflanked, Johnson knew the importance of keeping the enemy from crossing the roadway in force. With Charlie confined to the south of their position, the advancing artillery would soon flush them out in small groups, making it easier for the marines to defend their position.

Not aware of Alpha 22's presence and not seeing any helicopters in the area, Charlie thought it was safe to cross the road. A high-pitched whistle sounded at 0730, and the NVA stepped out from among the trees. The nearest enemy soldier was directly across the road from the marine position.

The first three or four steps were cautious. Then they began to run to minimize their exposure time. The marines opened fire when the first soldiers reached the road. Those who continued to cross the divide were cut down by two M60s that had set up a wall of fire directed straight down the road. The third M60 and the balance of 2nd Squad's other weapons quickly drove the enemy back to the far tree line.

With his map in hand, Johnson relayed his artillery commands to his radio operator. Almost immediately, 105 howitzer shells began pressing the enemy from their rear. With approaching artillery fire from the south and east and an unknown force of vengeful marines to the north, the NVA had no choice but to turn west. That meant Charlie would have to travel several miles out of their way, and most of their wounded would die before getting to a hospital.

It only took the enemy seconds to bring their RPG and AK-47 fire to bear on Johnson's position. While the enemy's rear guard kept the marines engaged, the main body of the NVA quickly moved west undetected. Ten minutes later, all enemy fire stopped, and Charlie vanished again back into the thick vegetation.

Johnson called in two more salvos of artillery before ending the fire mission. The last rounds landed a hundred yards south of the road. Johnson waited another ten minutes then notified the Hill they were ready to return to base.

"Shield 1, this is Alpha 22 Actual. Over."

"Alpha 22 Actual, this is Shield 1. Come in."

"Shield 1, we have engaged a force of battalion-strength NVA and have only minor wounds. The enemy has withdrawn. Estimate approximately sixty enemy killed or wounded. Request permission to return to the Hill. Over."

"Alpha 22 Actual, permission granted. Do you want a ride? Over."

"Negative, Shield 1. Over."

"Roger, Alpha 22 Actual. Wait for an escort. Out."

Five minutes later, four helicopters circled high above Johnson's position. He popped a smoke grenade and confirmed the color before the marines stepped out and quickly crossed the road.

Johnson confirmed that fifty-five enemy soldiers were killed. He moved another forty wounded soldiers out of the sun and did what he could to treat their wounds. Johnson was sure the enemy would pick them up shortly after they left the area. He also knew that at least one of these wounded soldiers would live to kill another day.

Johnson had his men collect the weapons and stacked them in a pile. Rigging the munitions with C-4, they moved about one hundred yards away and detonated the explosives.

During his initial area check, Johnson saw a small piece of red material sticking out from under one of the dead NVA soldiers. Bending down, he rolled the body over and discovered an 812th Regiment battle flag attached to a short, thin pole. Removing his Ka-Bar knife, he cut the flag free and shoved it into his flak jacket. *I think we earned this today.*

Looking up at the circling gunships, Johnson wondered what damage Charlie had inflicted on the Hill. With their heads held high, the marines fell in single file and headed back to the Hill.

Chapter 28

Mopping Up the Hill

Today will be the quietest day the Hill has seen in a long time. A dozen Huey gunships circled above the tree line, daring Charlie to give away his position by using his mortars. In a rare act of compassion, Giap decided he had lost enough soldiers for one day and ordered all his troops to stand down.

Wild Weasel jets circling above prevented Giap from switching on his electronics to use his SAM missiles against supporting aircraft. All ground and naval guns within range of the mountains north of the river were busy pounding Charlie's long-range artillery. The Americans were back in business with the bombardment lifted at Gio Linh, Dong Ha, and Camp Carroll.

An armored column left Gio Linh at 0630 and parked in the Trace about a thousand yards east of the Hill. They pulverized the north and south tree lines using their armor and recoilless rifles. Charlie had no choice but to leave the area. Only then was the area around the Hill secure again. The engineers were dispatched to destroy Giap's twelve bunkers and doze the site flat again.

General Taylor from the 3rd Marine Division arrived at 0815 to assess the destruction. Parks and six marines met him at the LZ and escorted him up the compound road toward OP-2.

"What's the damage, Major?"

"Counting all personnel, our losses were 43 killed, 110 wounded, and 1 missing, sir. We also lost two battle tanks, one Duster, and several other vehicles."

"What about the enemy?"

"We're still running the tab, sir, but so far, we've counted 189 killed inside the wire. We captured 6 wounded NVA. I estimate they carried off at least 400 dead or wounded when they left the Hill. We received word that Sergeant Johnson's ambush patrol killed another 55 trying to escape to the river. The helicopters also caught 6 stragglers in the Trace at first light. As soon as the Hill is secure, I'll send out patrols to check for additional KIAs."

"What about weapons?"

"Sir, we've captured thirty-five AK-47s, ten RPGs, two radios, several hundred pounds of explosives, sixty Chinese grenades, and two flamethrowers."

"Flamethrowers, huh? Charlie's using Zippos now?"

"Yes, sir. As far as I know, that's a first."

"Good job, Major. I'm looking forward to reading your report. Now I want to see the perimeter."

"Sir, it's not safe yet," Parks protested. "We are still finding pockets of resistance on the north and east sides of the Hill. It seems Charlie would rather die than surrender."

"Well, if that's how he feels about it, we'll do what we can to accommodate him, Major, but I would still like to inspect the line bunkers."

"Well then, sir, our best vantage point will be this way."

Parks positioned his escort around himself and the General then moved quickly over the ravaged terrain to the 3rd Squad bunker.

The assault on the bunker had left it severely damaged, barely serviceable. Most of the sandbags on the northeastern corner had been blown away from multiple RPG strikes. The shelter had taken so much AK-47 fire that many external sandbags were drained entirely of dirt.

"Major, a new layer of sandbags and the army would think this bunker is good enough, but it would not meet marine standards. We need to replace them all."

"I agree, sir. Our only problem is getting Charlie to stop his shelling long enough for us to do it."

"I can fix that. I am going to give you four gunships for the next four days. That should give you some protection from these mortars. We will drop all the timbers and steel decking you need in the morning."

"Thank you, sir. That is greatly appreciated."

"Don't mention it, Major. I like to take care of my boys."

Still concerned for the general's safety, Parks replied, "Sir, let's step inside the bunker until Sergeant Thompson finishes sweeping this side of the Hill."

General Taylor was a boots-on-the-ground officer. As a young first lieutenant, he commanded a marine company in Korea. It was not his nature to follow his men into battle. He insisted on leading them. MacArthur had personally pinned the Silver Star on his chest for his heroism during the Chosin Reservoir Battle. Hiding in a bunker was not his style, but he would let the major do his job for now.

The general stopped and looked at a streak of blood on the sandbags outside the bunker doorway. Moved, the general knelt, picked up a handful of red dirt, and slowly sprinkled it over the blood. "I wonder whose blood this belonged to."

"That's probably Sergeant Shaffer's blood, sir. He was wounded, but two other marines died defending this bunker last night."

The general made eye contact with the major and replied, "Major Parks, you have some mighty fine marines in your battalion."

"Thank you, sir."

Taylor and Parks stepped inside the bunker. The general got his first good look at the Hill's eastern side from the window. Before them lay the aftermath of Charlie's wrath, destroyed bunkers, the burned-out remains of two smoldering tanks and Duster, shell craters, and NVA bodies scattered everywhere.

The two officers watched as a line of men cautiously proceeded down the hill. Occasionally the detail stopped and carefully checked each body. As the general and Parks surveyed the damage, a grenade exploded in the ditch below them. Seconds later, six marines stood over the trench, ready to fire.

Parks stepped out of the bunker and ordered one of his marines to check on what had happened. Five minutes later, he returned to give his report.

"Sir, one of our men tried to help a wounded enemy who pulled the pin on a hidden grenade. The marine managed to dislodge the grenade and push the enemy down on top of it before it exploded. The marine was not injured, sir."

Parks pulled the marine close and whispered, "Go tell Sergeant Thompson I said to use his best judgment in dealing with any survivors. Do you know what I mean, Private?" Parks looked sternly at the private to make sure he understood his meaning.

"Yes, sir," the marine said softly as he glanced at the general. "I'll be happy to deliver that message, sir."

The marine ran back down the hill and conveyed the message to Thompson. Turning toward the bunker, Thompson nodded to Parks then communicated the major's orders to his men. They continued their search with great caution. Soon, a muffled shot rang out from Thompson's detail.

Parks knew he could be jeopardizing his career, but after the night he had, he would not risk any more lives today. While considering what might happen if caught, he handed the general a pair of binoculars.

"Thanks, Major," he said as he lifted the glasses to his eyes. "Your men are doing a fine job out there. Caution is always the better part of valor. Don't you agree?"

"Yes, sir, I do. Thank you, sir," Major Parks said as he breathed a sigh of relief.

As the general scanned the area below him, he noticed one of Thompson's men stop and shout something. Thompson ran over and looked down at something on the ground. The general adjusted the zoom on his binoculars and could make out a hand sticking out of the dirt. Thompson called another marine over, gave him an order, and rejoined his detail.

One of the marines ran up the hill and returned a minute later with a stretcher. Setting it down, he joined the other marine, reverently brushing the dirt from a body.

"Major, I think they found your missing marine."

The general handed Parks the field glasses. He watched as they rolled the bloodied marine over and carefully lifted him onto the stretcher.

"That's Corporal Mitchell, sir. We are now all accounted for."

The general could hear the sadness in his voice. Putting his hand on the major's shoulder, he offered him some words of comfort.

"Major, before I got my battlefield commission, I was a sergeant with the 28th Marine Regiment that landed on Iwo Jima. After three days of heavy fighting, we finally reached the base of Mount Suribachi. Another marine and I worked our way over to a position, allowing us to take out a machine gun hidden in a cave about fifty yards up the hill. As we stepped around a boulder, a Japanese came out of nowhere and lunged at me with his bayonet. That other marine pushed me out of the way and took the bayonet. Before he died, he killed that enemy soldier. It bothered me for years until I realized how blessed I was that someone thought enough of me to give his life to save mine.

"Major, your marine died defending this hill. He gave his life so that others could live. Mourn the loss, but celebrate the gift."

Parks thought about the general's words and smiled. "Thank you, sir. I know what you mean."

Marines were busy making repairs all over the Hill. Four-wheel motorized mules transported the dead NVA to the north gate for burial. A steady flow of choppers loaded the wounded marines to take them back to Dong Ha for treatment. The severely wounded would then be flown to better-equipped facilities in Da Nang. The dead defenders lay covered in poncho liners behind OP-2. They would be the last to evacuate the Hill.

"Major Parks, how did they breach the wire?"

"With bamboo Bangalore torpedoes, sir."

"Bamboo torpedoes. These Vietnamese are certainly resourceful."

"Yes, sir."

"The report I read this morning said you knew exactly where and when this attack would happen. Is that true, Major?"

"Yes, sir, but I only reported what my men told me. More of us would be dead now if not for Sergeant Shaffer and those two snipers from the 9th."

"Fill out the paperwork, and I'll ensure they get some medals. I'd like to meet those three marines, Major."

"Sergeant Westgate and Corporal Diamond have already returned to Dong Ha, sir, but I think Shaffer is still over with the wounded. He was the one who led that patrol yesterday and found that enemy map. Would you like to see him now? It looks like Sergeant Thompson has completed his sweep."

"Yes, I would. I'm ready to get out of this blasted bunker."

The officers and their escort walked the short distance to where the wounded waited to be evacuated. A loaded medevac helicopter lifted off, with Duncan sitting in the doorway. His leg was wrapped in a splint and extended outward. He and Parks waved to each other. "Sir, that's Lieutenant Duncan, our army forward observer. He broke his leg when the OP-2 bunker took a hit last night. After digging him out, he started directing fire on the retreating enemy."

"Have you notified the division to send you another observer?"

"Yes, sir. He will be here this afternoon."

"Good."

Mike lay on a stretcher, dozing in the sunlight. He had lost a lot of blood and was exhausted from lack of sleep. Still high on a dose of morphine, he drifted in and out of consciousness. David sat close by like a worried parent, thanking God for sparing Mike's life.

When David saw the general and major approach, he wearily rose and stood in a relaxed form of attention.

"At ease, Sergeant. This is General Taylor from the division. General, this is Sergeant Long, one of my squad leaders. This morning, he organized the perimeter defenses and caught the enemy in a crossfire when they retreated through the wire. He and Sergeant Shaffer only have four weeks before their enlistment is up."

"I am very proud to meet you, Sergeant. You look like you're about dead on your feet. A few days of rest will do you some good. Operation Hickory will be kicking off on the eighteenth. Are you up for one final sweep through the DMZ before you head home?"

"Yes, sir, but just one more," David said with a subdued smile.

The general placed his hand on David's shoulder and replied, "That's the spirit, son. Good job."

Blood had saturated the right side of Mike's fatigue jacket and pants. A corpsman had dressed his wound and secured his arm across his chest with surgical gauze. Mike could hear people talking in his semiconscious state, but he was too groggy to care who it was.

Taylor knelt beside Mike, put his hand on his chest, and gently shook him. "Sergeant Shaffer, are you awake?"

Mike stirred a little and tried to open his eyes. The general gave him another gentle shake, and Mike opened his eyes and slowly looked around. Seeing the general and Parks, he then looked up at David.

"Hey, bro. General Taylor would like a word with you," David said with a sly grin.

Mike made eye contact with the general again and said, "General. Am I in any trouble, sir? I can explain about Tucker."

The general grinned and patted Mike's chest. "No, son, you're not in trouble, at least not with me. That was an outstanding job last night, Marine. The corps needs men like you and Sergeant Long.

"Major, I remember signing promotion papers for a Shaffer last week. Is this the same Shaffer?"

"That's him, sir."

"As I recall, he's been wounded before."

"Yes, sir. This will be his third Purple Heart."

"Outstanding recommendation, Major. I could not be prouder of this battalion. You exemplify the fourth marine motto—'Whatever it takes.'"

"Thank you, sir. I will pass on your compliments."

"Sergeant, you rest now. Is there anything I can do for you?"

"Yes, sir," Mike began then paused. "I'm sorry, General. What was the question again?"

"Rest now, son. Get your strength back, and we'll talk about it later."

"Major, if you don't mind, I want to finish my inspection. How about showing me the perimeter without all these bodyguards? I want Sergeant Long to come along and tell me about what happened last night."

The major dismissed the detail and replied to the general, "It would be our pleasure, General."

David wanted to stay until they loaded Mike on the chopper but knew he would be fine now. "Sir, I'll be right there." David thought to say something to Mike but saw that he had gone back to sleep. After momentarily resting his hand on Mike's head, he caught up with Parks and the general and followed them down to the line bunkers.

The three marines stepped into the trench at Bunker 1, where men hurriedly made temporary repairs. Half the detail was busy filling sandbags. The other half was busy replacing roof timbers. There was a lot to do before sundown.

David explained to the general how he set up the crossfire and his encounter with the NVA at the intersecting trench. The general listened attentively and occasionally asked questions. Slowly, the three marines made their way down the channel.

The general stopped when he came to the charred remains of a marine combat boot. He reached into his pocket and withdrew a small camera. The general bent down, took a picture, then stood and bowed his head. After a minute of quiet meditation, he continued his inspection.

Parks turned to David for an explanation.

"It belonged to Demarco or Grady, sir."

Feeling his pain, the major replied, "David, the tough part of being an officer is not what happened last night. It's explaining to the parents how bravely their sons died in combat. This is not the type of detail I include in my letters."

The three marines shared a silent moment, reflecting on the death of their two brothers. As Parks continued with the general, David struggled to keep up.

Taylor stopped at Bunker 3 to view the temporary repairs on the perimeter wire. "Major, I'll see you have time to repair that wire properly. Did you receive your concertina wire?"

"Yes, sir. It was delivered yesterday."

After the officers satisfied their curiosity and moved on, David stepped inside the damaged bunker. Looking around, a piece of paper half buried on the floor caught his eye. Exhausted, the last thing he wanted to do was to bend over and pick up a worthless piece of paper, but something compelled him to do so.

Stepping closer, David stooped down and wiped the red dirt off several sheets of paper. Picking them up, he began to read, "Dear Desmond, I'm writing to tell you I won't be here when you get home ... Latoya." With a glance at the unopened legal document, David's heart broke. Tears filled his eyes, his knees buckled, and he collapsed in a sobbing heap.

It took him several minutes to regain his composure. He glanced at the letter again and noticed it was dated two weeks ago. *Dear Lord, why, Demarco? He was supposed to rotate back to the States tomorrow. Then he could have tried to salvage his marriage. I commit his soul to your care.*

Just past Bunker 5, Taylor found two marines from David's 1st Squad sitting in the trench. The first marine had his face buried in his hands with his rifle between his legs. The second marine had one elbow on his knee, reading to the first marine from a small Bible. Oblivious to his presence, Taylor snapped their picture and spent another minute watching and listening.

Taylor turned to Parks. "These pictures are for my journal. Everywhere I go, I take two or three pictures as keepsakes, and when I have time, I enter what they are about. This picture is one of my favorites because that marine is reading from the Word of God. Has the division chaplain arrived yet?"

"Yes, sir. He got here before 0700. I believe he is at the hospital now."

"He's a good man of God, Major. A first-rate counselor. If any of your boys need counseling, he's the one to see."

"I will certainly pass that on, sir."

Lieutenant Johnston had been assigned to clean up the aftermath. He had ordered the engineers to dig out a burial pit about six hundred yards north of the Hill. At 0900 hours, a convoy moved out of the north gate. It consisted of a dozer, a Duster, an Ontos recoilless rifle, an APC, and a rifle squad from Alpha Company. An hour later, a sizeable six-foot-deep pit was ready to be filled.

The APC escorted the dozer back to the north gate. A second dozer joined it, and twenty NVA bodies were loaded into the scoops and taken to the pit to be dumped. After several trips, 197 brave NVA soldiers were laid to rest. The dozers covered the hole, and everyone returned to the Hill escorted by Alpha 22, returning from its patrol.

Taylor finished his inspection at 1100, and Parks escorted him to the LZ and waited for the battalion helicopter to arrive. As the general's chopper lifted off, Parks looked to the south and spotted a dozen Hueys heading his way with replacements from Company C. By 1700 hours, the Hill was patched up again and ready for combat. At 2100 hours, the enemy continued their mortar bombardment of the Hill. Things were now back to normal, with Charlie ruling the night.

Part 2

The Battle for Tim Shaffer's Soul

The second part of this book is dedicated to Jesus Christ. He paid the debt that secured our spiritual freedom.

Chapter 1

Hello, Devil

Marine Sgt. Mike Shaffer was mesmerized, looking out the 3rd Squad bunker window. He was exhausted from lack of sleep and five days of nonstop mortar attacks. His brain was now on overload, refusing to accept the nightmare he had just endured. Mike's only awareness was a deafening silence. Although his gaze was fixed on the battlefield, he did not see the thirty-four brave NVA soldiers before him who died trying to take his position.

Mike did not hear the bugle that sounded the enemy's retreat, but he saw their movements as they scurried back down the hill. In desperation, they needed to reach the safety of the jungle before the marine gunships arrived at first light. An RPG round fired by a retreating soldier struck the front of Mike's bunker. The explosion sent a shock wave through his body like a defibrillator jump-starting his heart. The rocket's accuracy would have been perfect had it not been for the unseen force that had already saved his life several times tonight.

Mike looked down at the smoke rolling off the barrel of his M60 machine gun. His right finger was frozen in place, depressing the trigger on an empty weapon. Instinct told him to reload, but his energy was now spent. A cool breeze blew through the bunker window and teased his senses as he tried to overcome the numbness in his body.

A flare dropped from a spotter plane circling above the Hill illuminated the area enough to reveal the scattered carnage around him. Mike's heart sank when he saw the destruction of the 1st Squad bunker eighty yards away. He prayed his best friend, David Long, was not there when it happened.

It took some effort, but Mike finally relieved the cramp in his trigger finger and released the gun. As his mind broke through the fog, Mike's thoughts turned to the 3rd Squad at the bottom of the hill. The enemy had fought their way past them to reach his position and was now flooding back down the hill to engage them again from the rear. Mike knew it would be too late by the time he reached his men, but he had to try anyway.

Turning to leave the bunker, Mike noticed the bodies of his bunker mates, Simmons and Carter, lying dead on the floor. The memory of how they died came back to him like a hammer hitting an anvil. *I was standing right next to them when it happened. Why them, Lord, and not me?*

His left arm hung limp at his side, unaware of the pain and blood loss. The concern for his men was the only thing keeping him going. Although his mind was willing, Mike's body gave out just outside the back door of the bunker. To keep from falling, he backed up against the sandbagged wall. Looking down, Mike spotted blood covering the left side of his fatigue pants. Its wetness glistened in the semidarkness and told him he was about to pass out. Slowly, he eased himself down into a sitting position, leaving a streak of blood on the sandbags.

Mike had spent the last twelve months fighting Charlie all over the DMZ. He was sure this was it for him with only thirty-three days left on his enlistment. As he was about to fall unconscious,

Mike heard a voice say, "Wake up, Mike. I'm back to collect on what you owe me."

Mike knew before he opened his eyes it was Legion. He watched as an NVA soldier calmly walked through the trench and stopped just a few feet away. Slowly, he lowered his AK-47 assault rifle and pointed it down at Mike's chest.

Undaunted by the gesture, Mike greeted his tormentor, "Hello, devil. Are Eliphaz, Bildad, and Zophar in there with you?"

"Yes, they all say hello." Savoring the moment, Legion added, "How are you doing, Mike? You look like death warmed over."

Ignoring Legion's sarcasm, Mike replied, "What are you doing here? I thought we got rid of you last night. You know there is absolutely nothing you can do to me now. Remember the rules?"

"Oh yes. God's rules. Well, it seems I have found a way around them."

Completely unconcerned by Legion's suggestion of circumventing God's law, Mike waited for an answer.

"It's simple, really. Let me introduce you to my new assistant, Nguyen Van Lam. He hates Americans with a passion. I might not be able to kill you, but he can. Right now, I am in complete control of his mind. However, he will pull the trigger the moment I leave his body. If you have any last words, Mike, you need to say them quickly. I have other pressing matters to attend to tonight."

Mike studied the enemy soldier's face and figured he was no more than seventeen, conscripted into service by the Communists. The one thing they both had in common was a strong sense of survival. The difference between them was that while Mike could go home in a few weeks, his enemy could not leave until the war ended or he died, whichever came first.

The fact that Legion was confronting him again was a surprise until he heard the Advocate whisper, *Mike, it is not your time to die. Your purpose in life has not yet been fulfilled. Take heart. I will get you home to your family and Kate.*

A weak smile crossed Mike's face as he replied to Legion's arrogance, "You do not know when to quit, do you, devil? The Lord defeated you once tonight, and he is about to do it again."

Legion should have known that killing Mike without God's permission was impossible. However, the Lord was using Legion's wounded pride against him. Anxious to be done with him, Legion replied, "Goodbye, Mike. I'd like to say it has been a pleasure, but it wasn't."

Still maintaining his tenuous smile, Mike returned Legion's stare and whispered, "Goodbye, devil. Give my regards to your daddy when you see him."

The next few seconds would have tormented lesser men, but Mike did not falter in his faith. "Though I walk through the valley of the shadow of death, I will fear no evil; for thou art with me …"

Sensing another presence, Legion looked up just in time to see the first muzzle flash, quickly followed by another five. The body of the NVA soldier reacted to the bullet impacts and collapsed in a heap beside Mike. First Sergeant "Top" Adams and two marines rushed in from the shadows. Kneeling beside him, Top grabbed Mike by his bloody flak jacket and gently slapped him on the cheek. "Stay awake, Mike. You'll be OK."

"Top. Where did you come from?" Mike asked with the voice of a drunk man.

"I had the strangest feeling you were in trouble again, Mike." Top cut open Mike's flak jacket and fatigue shirt with his Ka-Bar knife and inspected the wound. "You've lost a lot of blood, but you will not die on me. That's an order, Marine."

While Top worked to stop the bleeding, Mike turned his attention back to the dead NVA soldier. As he watched, a fluorescent blue vapor began to seep from his body and lifted itself to a position a few feet above the bunker. Holding on to his last few moments of consciousness, Mike pointed behind Top and asked wearily, "Top, look at that."

Top turned toward the enemy soldier. "I don't see anything, Mike. What are you talking about?"

"The blue vapor that just left that guy's body. It's up there. Don't you see it?"

Unable to see anything, Top turned to the two marines guarding the position and shrugged his shoulders. They shook their heads in confirmation.

"You're hallucinating, Mike," Top said as he administered a dose of morphine, "and about to go into shock. Now, lie still. A corpsman will be here in a minute."

As Legion prepared to rush off to find his next host, he left Mike with an ominous warning: *See you later, Mike. Guard your family well. Zophar will pay them a visit one day soon.*

The Advocate appeared atop the bunker, invisible to all but Mike and Legion's passing ghost. *Legion, you are to keep your distance from Mike and his family. As long as he lives, they are under my protection.*

Without a reply, Legion flew off into the night, convinced this would not be his last word with Mike.

Hearing the Lord's blessing, Mike closed his eyes and blacked out.

Chapter 2

The Hospital Ship Repose

Because of Legion's vendetta against Mike, Christos assigned the angel Poyel to watch over Mike. His assignment was to guard Mike against any physical threat from Legion's wrath. Together with the Spirit of the Lord, who protected his soul, both would become Mike's lifelong unseen companions.

Poyel was a mighty warrior, one not to be taken lightly by the opposition. In his battle dress, Poyel stood his post beside Mike's bed. Around his waist was a wide leather belt with an empty scabbard. In his hand was a long sword that radiated the holiness of God.

Poyel studied Mike carefully, marveling at God's love for such frail and disappointing creatures. Grateful to be in the service of the King, Poyel had overcome his envy and accepted this task joyfully. However, others of his order were not so accepting. When faced with the prospect of being subservient to God's newest creation, one-third of his angels rebelled, were defeated, and were forced to leave heaven forever.

Slowly, Mike opened his eyes and looked around. The clock on the wall read 1416 hours. Other than the shallowness of someone snoring, there was silence. A second scan of the dimly lit room told

Mike he was not at Dong Ha. If he wasn't there, then where was he? More importantly, what day was it?

Still groggy and in some discomfort, Mike smiled when he noticed David sleeping in the chair beside him. Reaching over, he felt the bandage on his arm and wondered why it was there. Then the memory of the battle revealed itself. To counter his sorrow and grief, Mike's thoughts turned to the Lord.

The whispered sound of Mike praying was what roused David. Grateful that Mike was finally awake, David waited for him to finish. Emotional and afraid he would start crying, David stood and quietly turned to leave the room.

"Where're you going, David?" Mike said softly.

Choking back his feelings, David answered with a sniffle, "To let the doctor know you're awake."

"Can you get me something to drink first? I'm spittin' cotton."

David walked over to the bedside table, poured Mike a glass of water, then helped him drink it.

"How are you doing, Mike?" David asked with great concern.

"The pain is not too bad," Mike said weakly. "How long have I been out?"

"Two days. It's May 10."

"Where are we?"

"The hospital ship *Repose* in Da Nang harbor."

"Why are you here? Shouldn't you be back on the Hill?"

"Almost a quarter of our men were killed or wounded. General Taylor pulled the company back to Dong Ha and replaced us with Charlie Company. Our next mission is Operation Hickory. Believe it or not, we will support the 1st Battalion, 9th Marines."

"Not the Walking Dead," Mike said wearily.

"That's them. Giap has at least one massive tunnel complex just south of the Ben Hai River, and we need to find and destroy them. Kickoff is set for the eighteenth. The general gave me a three-day pass to come sit with you."

Suspiciously, Mike asked, "Why would he do that?"

"Because he wants to personally hand you that third Purple Heart when you get back to Dong Ha. He sent me down here to see when that would be convenient for you. He also said you're confined to the base for the rest of your tour."

"What about my men?"

Reluctantly, David broke the news to Mike. "Tucker, Fuller, Wolf, Adams, and Littlejohn were the only ones who made it." Knowing how his friend would take the news, David quickly added, "You would have been proud of them, Mike. They took out the first rush of sappers. Then while you had them pinned down at the bunker, they moved over to the right flank and together with 1st Squad, caught Charlie in a crossfire when they left the Hill." David intentionally omitted the part about him leading the rest of Mike's squad to safety and organizing the perimeter defenses. This action would earn David a Bronze Star.

Despondent over losing his men, Mike fell silent and drifted off into a daze. Understanding he needed time to process the news, David sat close by and waited for his next opportunity to learn more about Mike's mental state. For the next hour, Mike lay motionless and transfixed in thought.

A knock on the door broke his concentration. The door opened, and a doctor walked into the room and stood beside the bed. Mike turned to face him without a greeting.

"Good afternoon, Mike. I'm Dr. Yamada. I see you're awake now. How are you feeling today?"

Mike held eye contact with the doctor but did not reply.

"Very well. There's no rush, Mike. We can talk about it when you're ready."

The doctor reviewed the chart at the end of the bed and then turned his attention to Mike's bandage. "How do you think our patient is doing today, David? I understand this is his third Purple Heart."

"He seems fine, Doctor, considering he just found out he lost most of his men at Con Thien."

"Con Thien. Half of my ward is full of marines from up there."

After the doctor completed his examination, David followed him out into the hallway. "What do you think, Doc?"

"The wound will heal, but I think Mike has posttraumatic stress disorder."

"We are both scheduled to rotate back to the States next month. How long do you need to keep him here?"

"General Taylor has contacted me about Mike. I'll tell you what I told him. We will keep him for another three days of observation. If there is an improvement, I will let him return to Dong Ha for a few weeks of bed rest. If not, we will ship him stateside for extended counseling. I'll order you both something to eat and have one of our counselors drop by to see Mike later."

The doctor paused and asked, "Why is the general so interested in Mike?"

"Because he wants to give Mike the Bronze Star for his actions at Con Thien. He saved a lot of lives up there."

"Well, Bronze Star or not, Mike needs to show me he has things under control before I discharge him."

Mike had that far-off look in his eye when David walked back into the room. Suppressing his concerns, David walked over and sat down.

Without turning, Mike asked, "What did the doctor say?"

"He said your wound would heal just fine, but he thinks you have PTSD. He is going to keep you here for another three days.

If you're not better by then, he will ship you to a hospital in the States, probably San Diego."

Without responding, Mike continued staring a hole into the ceiling.

"Did you hear me, Mike? If they send you to a stateside hospital, it could be months before they complete their examination. You'll be lucky to get home by Christmas."

Mike had put himself on a guilt trip over the loss of his men, and David knew the sooner he started talking about it, the quicker his recovery time would be. Coddling him was not the answer. So he took a chance and did the unexpected.

"Mike," he said firmly, "do you want your mom to see you like this? You need to stop feeling sorry for yourself and be grateful that God thought it was important enough to get you off the Hill alive. I lost two guys there myself, but there is nothing I could have done about it.

"In a week, I will be back in the DMZ looking for Charlie, and I don't want the distraction of worrying about you. Now snap out of it, Marine, or I swear I will drag you upstairs and throw your worthless jarhead butt overboard." Jumping up, David gave Mike his best Cagney impersonation. "You dirty, double-crossing rat."

Mike turned toward David during his comical rant. He held his somber expression until David had finished then managed a shallow laugh. "Man. That has got to be the worst Bogart ever."

"Cagney, you dork. It was Cagney."

"Whatever. Can a guy get anything to eat around here?"

"The orderly will bring you something in a few minutes."

David was glad to see Mike talking like his old self, but he knew the sudden mood swing was not a good sign.

David reached into his pocket, pulled out six letters, and handed them to Mike. "One is from your mom. The other five are from Katie," he said as he gave Mike a wink. "No one back home knows anything about you being wounded."

Mike laid them on his lap and said, "These can wait. I need to tell you something important. Can you prop this bed up a little?"

David fidgeted with the bed and finally got Mike into a reclining position. David sat down, and Mike told him about Legion.

"The night of the battle, I encountered a spirit named Bildad. He had permission from God to challenge my faith. Shawn and I were down on the perimeter talking when suddenly, he turned into a statue. I was the only marine left on the Hill. When Bildad took possession of Shawn's body, he threatened to kill him if I didn't deny my Christian faith.

"David, the Lord helped me trick Bildad into leaving Shawn's body. He turned into this larger demon named Legion. He was outraged when the Lord made him leave the Hill. He said another spirit named Zophar would return for my family when I die.

"Later that night, Bernie Westgate told me about a run-in he had with another spirit named Eliphaz on his drive up from Da Nang. Bernie said he took possession of a lieutenant's body and tried to get a squad of marines killed."

"Eliphaz, Bildad, and Zophar. Where do I know those names from?"

"The Bible. They were Job's accusers."

"Well, isn't that interesting."

David considered Mike's far-fetched story and was a little apprehensive. He knew that whatever happened that night, Mike believed it.

"The Lord said he will protect my family while I am alive. However, if they are not saved by then, Zophar will go after them with a vengeance. What am I going to do, David?"

"Stop it, Mike. Don't invite any trouble here. All you need to do is lead your kids to the Lord before you die. Then what can Zophar do?"

Mike knew David was right. Although he did not relish looking over his shoulder for the rest of his life, he knew that whatever the future held, the Lord would lead him through it.

Chapter 3

Home at Last

Their plane landed in Dallas at 4:05 p.m. As Mike and David walked across the tarmac, both marines felt the urge to kneel and kiss the ground. They had proudly served their country for three years. However, while they were away, many Americans wanted to end the war in Vietnam. Service members were no longer seen as heroes but as baby killers, so Mike and David wisely chose to wear their civvies on the plane.

Mike had been sweet on Katie Summerset since the sixth grade. David was in seventh grade when Linda Thomas moved in across the street. Both couples had attended different junior high schools but became best friends during their sophomore year at Garland High.

The gridiron had been a common interest for Mike and David. In junior high, they had played against each other for several years. David was the stud quarterback, and Mike was the speedy wide receiver with flypaper hands. Garland High did not win many games, but David and Mike did what they could to excite the fans on Friday nights. Both had college-level potential and received scholarships from several universities during their senior year.

Katie met Linda in the eighth grade, but their friendship took off at youth camp the following summer. Both girls were cheerleaders and members of the Mighty Owl High School Band. They both ran track, Linda on the relay team and Katie finishing second in the all-district cross-country meet her senior year.

After graduation, Mike and David joined the marines, just as their fathers had done during World War II. Being second-generation marines meant a lot to them at the time. However, they were more than ready for civilian life when their enlistment was up. The marine corps was an experience they would not have missed, but it was not something they wanted for their children.

The guys had been away for thirteen months, and the anticipation of their return had grown in the last few months. The girls were so excited that they arrived at the airport two hours early.

"Katie, there's Mike and David. They're finally home." The girls hugged each other and squealed with delight.

"Linda, I didn't think this day would ever come. Oh, thank you, Lord. Thank you."

Mike thought their parents would pick them up at the airport, so he was surprised to see the girls waving to them.

"David, it's the girls," Mike said just before he broke out in a dead run for the gate, with David following close behind.

Mike dropped his travel bag the moment Katie launched herself into his arms. Still favoring his wound, he managed to hold her up almost entirely with one arm. Letting her momentum spin them around, they kissed and clung to each other tightly. Time stood still while the two quietly enjoyed this long-anticipated moment. Ending the kiss, Katie took Mike's head between her hands and said softly, "Mike, I missed you so much. I can't tell you how happy I am you're home now."

Mike had no sooner said "me too" than Katie kissed him again. Many of those walking from the plane stopped and applauded.

Katie was an attractive, petite brunette, about five foot three tall, and weighed one hundred twenty pounds with blue eyes. As his elbow began to fail, Katie noticed the grimacing look on his face. "What's wrong, Mike? Put me down," she demanded.

Backing up a step, Katie began to look Mike over closely. She was so glad to see him; she didn't have time to notice the bandage below his short-sleeved shirt. Reaching over, she gently lifted his shirt sleeve and asked with great concern, "What's this, Mike? What happened?"

For all Katie knew, Mike never left the safety of Dong Ha. She would have worried if she knew he had been fighting the enemy in the jungle, so he and David decided to spare their families all the details of their combat experiences until they got home.

Downplaying its severity, Mike replied, "It's nothing, Katie. Just an injury I received a month ago. It's almost healed."

David and Linda stood a few feet away, still clinging to each other, watching the worried look on Katie's face build. David knew Mike had to do some explaining to do and was curious about how Katie would take it.

Like other Americans, Katie had followed the newspaper and television reports on Vietnam. Almost overnight, the news media villainized the war and incited protests nationwide. Their graphic editorials of 1967 and '68 alone were enough to convince the public it was a war that was not worth fighting.

Katie had her suspicions but refused to think that Mike was ever in any real danger. She looked him in the eye and sternly asked, "Mike, what else have you not told me?"

It was time for Mike to fess up, but how could he begin to explain his past year in combat? How could he tell her about Con

Thien in the middle of the airport? What would she say when she found out this was not the first time he had been wounded?

"Katie, I didn't want you to worry, so I left a few things out of my letters. The important thing is that I am home now, and we can get on with our lives. I need a little time to explain a lot of things to you. I promise to tell you everything, but not right now. Not here." Mike's eyes were pleading with Katie to give him time to figure things out.

Katie's joy weakened at the possibility that Mike had lied to her about the dangers he faced. She loved Mike dearly, but distrust was raising its ugly head. Her dad told her it would take time for Mike to settle in when he got back home. *Dad's right*, she thought. *He's been through hell, and I need to give him some time to adjust.*

"Mike," she began. "I'm glad you're home safe. You can tell me about the war another time, but I want to know about this wound tomorrow."

"I promise to tell you about the wound tomorrow, but explaining everything that happened that day will be hard." Sensing her feelings, Mike added, "Katie, I have never lied to you and never will. There are things about combat you cannot put in a letter. You understand that, don't you?"

Katie thought about the sincerity of his motives and snuggled up close to Mike, secure in the fact that he was now home safe. Feeling guilty about thinking he had deceived her, Katie replied with a satisfied smile, "I'm sorry for doubting you, Mike. It was thoughtful of you to spare me the pain of worry and fear. Now, if you two guys are ready, let's get your bags."

"Yes, let's go before Mike gets into any more trouble," David joked.

Katie gave David a playful smirk as she and Linda led them through the terminal. At the baggage claim area, Linda called to tell her mom they were on their way. Arm in arm, the two couples made their way to the parking lot. The girls were excited about the surprise party at the church. The guys were excited about surprising the girls with wedding proposals.

Mike spotted his parents' red 1965 Buick Sport Wagon and chuckled. "Dad trusts you enough to let you drive his car? What have you not been telling me, Katie?"

Katie batted her eyes and opened the tailgate. "OK, Marine. Stow that bag, and get your butt into the car," she said with a straight face that quickly turned into a laugh hidden by both hands. "Your dad told me to say that." She giggled. "He also told me your driver's license has probably expired and not let you drive."

"Anything you say, … sweetie," he replied playfully.

Mike reached for the door handle and glancing across the top of the car, spotted a man staring at them in the middle of the exit lane. He felt an uneasiness but dismissed it and opened the car door.

No sooner had Mike settled into the shotgun seat than he jumped slightly, shaken by a sudden graphic mental image of the flamethrower engulfing Demarco and Grady. This "flash-bang," as he came to call it, would be the first of many such disturbing visions of combat. While David would deal with his posttraumatic stress well, Mike would need six months of VA counseling to get his under control.

Mike quickly looked over at Katie, who was busy checking her mirrors. He was relieved to know she missed his little incident. Now, filled with doubts, Mike did not hear Katie ask him if he was glad to be home.

Putting her hand on his, she asked, "Mike, are you all right?"

Slowly, Mike looked down at her tiny hand and smiled. Without looking up, he replied, "I'll be fine, Katie. I guess I'm a little tired."

"Well, snap out of it. We have things to do."

As quickly as he fell into his mood swing, Mike sprang back to life. "Well, what are we waiting for? Let's stop by McDonald's. I've had a craving for a Big Mac for months."

"Maybe later," Katie said as she eased the car into reverse.

David was worried about how Mike would reacclimate to civilian life after Con Thien. Seeing Mike jump and his brief distraction gave him even more cause for concern.

"How am I back there, Linda? Are there any cars coming?"

"You're good, Katie. Let's go. We're going to be late."

Knowing the evening's agenda, David couldn't help but ask, "Late for what?"

Thinking she had almost let the cat out of the bag, Linda looked up and saw Katie glaring at her in the mirror. In a panic, she replied, "Ah, … Katie, we might have time to stop at the McDonald's over by the church, but we need to get there before six or the line will be crazy long. You know how good their burgers are."

Through the mirror, Katie gave Linda an "I'll take care of you later" look.

"Good. I can almost taste those french fries now," David said as he chuckled. *They'll kill us if they find out we know about the party.*

As Katie backed the car out of the parking space and turned into the exit lane, Mike looked up and saw the man standing a short distance away, pointing his finger at him. Then Mike felt Zophar's presence and realized he had foolishly let his guard down. Katie accelerated the car and before he could react, drove the car right through the man as if he were a vapor. Startled, Mike took a deep breath and was grateful that Katie didn't see his tormentor.

Zophar reappeared behind the car and smiled as he watched it leave the parking lot, content with his first encounter with Mike. However, he failed to consider what happened next.

From behind him, Zophar heard someone say, "Ahem." The voice was familiar—one he had once called a friend eons ago. His first thought was why he had not expected this visit. His second was worry that this might be his last spiritual breath.

Knowing the danger of any sudden movements, Zophar slowly turned to face Poyel. He was not surprised to see the sword at his throat an inch away. From that distance, a quick flip of the wrist and his head would fall to the ground, sending him to the pit to await the Judgment. Unable to retreat, Zophar waited to learn his fate. His smile was now gone.

Sternly, Poyel glared back and waited to ensure Zophar got his situation's full impact. "Do you know why I'm here?"

It was only then that Zophar realized that he had been tricked. With Christos's help, he had forgotten the warning about keeping his distance from Mike and his family.

In a plea for mercy, Zophar replied, "To remind me not to get too close to Mike or his family?" A nervous smile crossed his face.

"That's right. The Lord is giving you a warning this time. Keep your distance. Do you understand?"

Relieved to know he was granted a pardon, he replied, "Yes, I understand fully."

Poyel was no fool. He had heard Zophar's empty promises before. He needed to let his enemy off lightly, but not too lightly. With a movement that was over before Zophar saw it coming, Poyel put a short gash on the side of his face. The sting was great, but the wound had already started to heal.

Poyel lowered his sword and waited to see if this would end the lesson. "You can leave now."

Foolishly seeing Poyel's clemency as a weakness, Zophar struggled with the urge to respond in anger. Just as he reached for his sword, Legion sent him a message. *You idiot. The Creator has fooled you again. Now leave before I replace you.*

With his pride severely damaged, Zophar gave Poyel his most contemptuous smile and vanished.

Satisfied he had won this confrontation so easily, Poyel was glad he did not have to cross swords with Zophar. Although he was more than a match for Legion's flunky, he knew God's will was being fulfilled in Mike's life, and Zophar had a major part to play.

Chapter 4

The Proposal

The drive to Garland was all about the girls. Their conversation was animated and giddy, talking all the way about things the guys read in their letters weeks ago. Mike and David just smiled in expectation of the catered dinner they were supposed to know nothing about.

Katie entered the church parking lot and pulled up in front of the gymnasium. The church parking lot was deserted except for Pastor Beckman's 1955 Chevy. The guys, however, knew everyone would be parked in the back.

Mike waited until they were out of the car before making things difficult for Katie. "What are we doing here, Katie? I thought we were going for burgers."

"I promised the pastor we would stop by briefly to say hello before we did anything else. He's excited about you boys coming home."

Mike pointed to the McDonald's across the street and said, "This can't wait until we've had some dinner, Katie? I haven't tasted real fast food for thirteen months."

"Yeah, Katie," David added. "We haven't eaten all day. Let's have a burger first. The pastor won't mind if we are a few minutes late."

Katie started to panic. She had forgotten how difficult these two could be when it came to food.

"Come on, David. Let's run across the street and grab some burgers and fries. You girls wait there. We'll be back in a couple of minutes. I'll get something for the pastor too."

Mike and David turned and started walking toward the street when Katie decided she'd had enough.

"Stop right there, you two." She stood with arms folded. "We are going inside to see Pastor Beckman first. You'll have to wait a little longer for your burgers. Now get your butts inside before I lose my temper," she growled.

Katie could not believe what had just come out of her mouth. She'd never said anything like that before. Even Linda looked at her in amazement.

Surprised, Mike turned and replied with a pitiful expression, "I'm sorry, Katie. I guess we aren't that hungry anyway."

Enjoying her new sense of power, Katie gave Mike a stern look and pointed toward the door. "Move it, Marines."

Mike studied the determined look on Katie's face closely and wasn't sure what to think. She was only trying to get them into the gym so the party could start, and he was fearful he'd made her mad. Suddenly, the excitement of being home began to fade as sadness started to invade his reason. As a feeling of displacement engulfed him, Mike's doubt and fear began to take over.

Reading the confused look on Mike's face, David took his arm, pulled him toward the gym door, and jokingly said, "Come on, Mike, I think she means business."

Unaware of Mike's roller-coaster ride of emotions, Katie thought about what Mrs. Shaffer told her about how she managed to keep Mike's dad in line. *Wow, she was right. This attitude stuff really works.*

Inside, the gym was full of people, all gathered around four sets of beaming parents. Seeing his mom and dad calmed Mike's anxiety. He and David played their part by acting surprised. Thrilled to have their men home, the girls proudly led them to the center of the room while the crowd shouted, "WELCOME HOME!"

As everyone began to clap, Katie and Linda held tightly to their guy's arms, their faces beaming with pride.

Mike leaned down and whispered, "You know, Katie, you're pretty cute when you're bossy."

When the Supremes began singing "Back in My Arms Again," Mike looked past the crowd and spotted Steve Atwell waving to them from the DJ table.

Speaking into the mic, Steve said, "Welcome home, boys. It's nice to have you back." Then he added, "Let's hear it again for Mike and David."

Once more, the crowd applauded and cheered.

The gratefulness Mike felt in his heart was almost tearful. Holding her close, Mike whispered, "I love you, Katie. I am happy to finally be home."

Katie broke out in a massive smile as she and Linda placed their guys between them to form a reception line. Sticking two fingers in her mouth, Katie let out an ear-piercing whistle and waved everyone over.

Grinning, Mike looked down and asked, "You got that from Mom, didn't you?"

Blushing, Katie scrunched her shoulders and gave him a playful wink. Pastor Beckman squeezed in between Mike and David and offered a thankful welcome-home prayer.

After half an hour of hugs, kisses, handshakes, and back slaps, the two couples finally made it to the buffet. The food was all they needed to convince them they were really home. David and Mike were eager to reacquaint themselves with their friends and family. Never letting go of their hands, Linda and Katie were content to follow and let their guys be the center of attention.

While the mothers distracted the girls, their dads discreetly handed Mike and David a small white box. David walked over to Steve and made a request then found Linda and led her to the short DJ platform. Everyone in the room knew what would happen next—all except Linda and Katie.

"Can I have your attention, please," Steve said. "David has something he would like to say."

David waited for Mike and Katie to join them on the stand.

"Mom, Dad," David began as he spoke into the microphone, "you raised me to be the man I am today. You taught me to stand on my own two feet, blaze my own trail in life, and trust in the Lord. For that, I will always be thankful. My life changed greatly when I met Linda—it was all for good."

David turned to face Linda. He looked deep into her eyes and continued. "She wrote me every day I was gone. In those letters, she reminded me about all the important things in life, one of which is her. For all her encouragement and love, I would like to say ..." David knelt to one knee, opened the box, and offered it to her. "Linda, will you marry me?"

The hush that fell over the room was electric as everyone waited for her answer.

Instantly, Linda's hands went to her face in shock. She thought they would talk about marriage sometime before school started, but tonight was not the day she would have guessed. It was a huge surprise. Linda was so fixated on the ring that she had trouble responding to David's question. Everyone knew the answer would be yes, but she couldn't get it out. Linda's face glowed with delight. Looking at David, all she could manage was a slow nod.

"Then I'll take that as a yes."

The crowd erupted in excitement. David stood and placed the engagement ring on her finger. He took Linda in his arms and kissed her then whispered, "Surprised?"

"Nothing could have surprised me more," Linda replied breathlessly.

After another extended kiss, David looked at Mike and asked into the mic, "I'm going to need a best man, Mike. Are you interested?"

Mike smiled and nodded. "I'd be honored to do it, David."

"Linda," David continued, "I know this is sudden, but have you thought about who your maid of honor will be?"

Linda spun around and threw her arms around Katie. The girls shrieked and started bouncing up and down together on the small stage. David grinned when he found himself going up on the platform every time the girls went down.

Playing to the crowd, David added, "Why am I not surprised?" Seeing the delight on his mom's face, standing about ten feet away, he gave her a contented grin.

Mike stepped over, shook David's hand, and discreetly took the microphone. He then casually stepped over behind Katie.

Kneeling to one knee, he opened his box and waited for the girls to calm themselves. Expecting what would happen next, the room quickly fell silent again. Confused by the sudden stillness, the girls looked around for an explanation. Linda spotted Mike kneeling behind Katie and raised both hands to hide her joy.

A completely unsuspecting Katie saw Linda's reaction and realized that something was happening behind her. Before she could turn, Mike's voice boomed through the microphone, "Katie, will you marry me?"

Katie was caught entirely off guard. After exchanging a long stare with Linda, she asked in a whisper, "Did he say what I think he said, Linda?"

Beaming, Linda replied, "It sure sounded like it to me, Katie."

It was exciting when David proposed to Linda. Having Mike propose to her, all in the same night, was a fairy tale come true. She slowly turned and found herself staring into the microphone while Mike patiently waited for her reply. With an expanding smile, Katie shouted, "You bet I will!"

While the crowd applauded, Mike placed the ring on her finger. "Katie, I promise I will love you forever."

He then embraced Katie and gave her a quick smooch, enjoying another extended hug. Content with the thought that years of hopes and dreams were about to come true, a hundred things raced through her mind. As she struggled to take as many mental notes as possible, she stopped at the one thing that meant the most to her—the ring.

This double proposal in the middle of her surprise party seemed too coincidental and rehearsed. So she pulled Mike close and softly asked, "When did you and David have time to buy these rings, and who told you about the party?"

David and Linda overheard Katie's question and leaned forward to hear Mike's reply. He knew his mom had been giving Katie marriage advice, so now was not the time to rub a gotcha in her face.

Mike lowered the mic and quietly answered, "David and I bought the rings last summer when we were home on leave. Our parents kept them while we were away and handed them to us just a few minutes ago. Mom told us about the party a month ago and suggested we propose to you girls tonight."

Katie just looked at Mike. Knowing he knew about the party was one thing. Knowing he managed to keep his proposal plans secret for a year was another. Having lost sight of her joy again, she thought about what to say next.

From Katie's silence, Mike knew he was in trouble. Returning the mic to the stand, he turned to explain. "Katie, I did not mean to spoil your surprise. It was a great surprise even if I already knew about it."

Mrs. Shaffer had what many people call perfect timing. She always knew the right thing to say at precisely the right moment. Seeing that Mike and Katie were sharing a serious moment, she quickly walked onto the stage and whispered something into Katie's ear. Katie paused and gave her a nod. Now, with a huge smile, she gave Mike a big hug.

Mike looked at his mom and wondered, *Wow, Mom. What did you say to her?*

With a look of satisfaction, Mrs. Shaffer took her son's hand and led the two couples off the stage to form a second reception line. The parents assembled behind the two couples to lend their support.

Later, Mike asked Katie what his mom had told her. Giving him a sly grin, she replied, "Your mom said she was the one who suggested you should propose tonight. She said the prospect of a double proposal was just too priceless to pass up. Which, by the way, was awfully sweet. She also said that I should warn you about keeping secrets."

"Secrets, Katie? Really? I think this party was your little secret," Mike retorted with a grin.

Katie smiled and nuzzled her head into his chest, thanking the Lord again for his safe return.

It was eight o'clock and time for the parents to say their good night. That is, after one final ceremony.

Steve took the microphone and announced, "Let's thank the four families for sponsoring this awesome party." After a round of applause, he continued, "If any of you would like to stay, I'm going to play music until Pastor Beckman tells us to leave. Our next song is a slow one by Percy Sledge, 'When a Man Loves a Woman.' This dance is reserved just for Mike and Katie, David and Linda."

Pastor Beckman thoughtfully walked over and turned off most of the gym lights. The atmosphere was now just right. The parents stood close by and thought about a similar moment they too once shared. When the song ended, eight parents were tearful yet joyful in believing God had ordained these two unions.

"Now for our next song," Steve offered, "'Gimme Some Lovin'" by the Spencer Davis Group." Instantly, fifty young couples rushed to the floor to start gyrations that made no sense to anyone but themselves.

With the increased volume, Mr. Shaffer shouted to his wife, "I think it is time to go, Sarah."

"Oh look, George. The kids are still slow dancing to whatever this is they're playing."

After a few moments of reflection and thankful prayer, Sarah said, "Come on, folks, let's go to Ashburn's for ice cream. George is buying."

At the door, Sarah thought about how some things had not changed over the years. She remembered when George asked her dad for her hand in marriage. She glanced at her son, still slow dancing with Katie, and thought, *He's such a romantic, just like his father.*

Chapter 5

Thanksgiving 1968

It was eleven o'clock, and the family had gathered at the Shaffers' for Thanksgiving dinner. Grandpa Shaffer, Grandpa Roberts, Uncle Johnny, Aunt Lisa, and Mike's dad, George, were in the living room watching the Macy's Thanksgiving Day Parade. Mike's brother Jason and sister Mary stood at the bottom of the stairs, trying their best not to look too interested.

Jason was in his freshman year at Baylor. Mary was a sophomore at Garland High. It wasn't the excitement of the day's activities they were looking forward to. It was spending time with Mike before he headed over to Katie's house. As far as they were concerned, Mike was their hero.

Seeing them waiting, Mike tiptoed down the stairs and managed to sneak up behind them. Smiling and with arms extended, he embraced them both, pulling them tightly to himself. "How are my favorite brother and sister today?"

After several minutes of doting, Mike grinned and whispered, "Watch this. Hey, Dad. What time is the Texas, Texas A&M game on today?"

"The game starts at two o'clock, Mike. Texas is going to kick A&M's butt."

Johnny, George's younger brother, and his wife, Lisa, who lived in Waco, were avid A&M fans. "I don't think so, George. This is A&M's year."

"Texas beat A&M last year, and they'll do it again this year."

"A&M is better this year and on a five-game winning streak."

"Yeah well, Johnny, Texas won six in a row this year too."

"Yeah, George, but Texas lost to TCU last week."

It had been twenty years since George and Johnny agreed on anything, and nobody could remember what that was. The bantering was always harmless, and no one ever got offended. Mike wrote it off as competitiveness until his mom told him the real reason: "Those two love to hear themselves talk." The only thing Mike knew the two had in common was the Dallas Cowboys.

"Hey, Dad," Mike said, winking at Jason and Mary. "Who are the Cowboys playing tonight?"

"Saint Louis. Meredith, Rentzel, and Hayes are having a great year. The Cardinals don't have a chance."

"I couldn't agree more, George," added Johnny. "The Cardinals are going to get trounced."

Sitting with his back to Mike, Grandpa Shaffer slowly stuck his right thumb up and pumped his fist to signal his approval.

Still smiling, Mike said softly to his two siblings, "Promise me you won't grow up to be like those two old farts." The two teenagers giggled.

"Don't be like me either," he added with a wink. "I'll see you two later."

Walking into the kitchen, he found his mom and two grandmas busy fixing dinner. Mike picked a cracker off the appetizer plate and shoved it into the cheese ball. When it broke, Mike felt confused, wondering what to do next.

Mike's mom was aware of his struggles with PTSD. Seeing his countenance drop, she handed him the cheese knife. Sheepishly, he looked up and saw her smiling. Turning, he hugged her and said, "Thanks, Mom. You're the best. What time is dinner?"

"Two o'clock. Can Katie be here by then?"

"No, Katie's aunt and uncle from Louisiana are in town this year," Mike said as he leaned up against the counter. Mike winked at his two grandmothers and continued. "They moved their dinner plans up to one o'clock so she could be here by two thirty. She said not to wait for her. If I'm back by two, do you mind if I go over there for a while?"

"You're a grown man now, Michael. Of course, you can go. Tell Katie to bring her wedding planner. I have a suggestion for the flowers. Why don't you wait and walk her over when she's ready? We'll wait for dinner for you."

"Thanks, Mom. I love you." Mike kissed her. He walked around the counter, hugged each of his grandmothers, and headed out the back door to walk the two blocks to Katie's house.

"OK, Grams. Work a little slower. Dinner is now at two thirty."

Sarah's mother-in-law grinned and replied, "Now, Sarah, you know George is not going to like having to wait on his drumstick."

"We've been married for twenty-five years now, Helen. George knows dinner will always be ready when I say it's ready and not a minute sooner."

Laughter broke out in the kitchen as the three mothers thought about how grateful they were that everyone was home for the holidays this year.

The day was sunny, and the temperature was in the midsixties.

On the way to Katie's, Mike had time to reflect on his summer. He and Katie had spent most of their time at the lake running up the hours on Mr. Summerset's boat. If they were not at the drive-in on Friday and Saturday nights, they cruised the strip with David and Linda in the 1965 Bel Air Mike's dad bought him for school.

Katie and Linda were now in their senior year at the Texas Women's University in Dallas. They each had part-time jobs, trying to save every penny they could. Mike and David were enrolled at SMU, spending their freshman year on campus. Campus life was tranquil and relaxing, quite a contrast from the trenches of Con Thien.

At his dad's insistence, Mike joined the VA the week after he got home. Two weeks later, he saw a counselor about his posttraumatic stress. After months of sessions, the doctor suggested Mike talk to his dad about his mixed-up emotions. That summer, they spent many hours talking about life, death, and the future—everything but Legion.

Mike felt pretty good about the progress he had made in therapy. Now that he had a better handle on his feelings, he decided that today would be the day he talked to Katie about losing his squad.

Mike knocked on Katie's door and waited. Mr. Summerset answered and said, "Mike, how are you doing? Come on in. Katie's in the kitchen getting another cooking lesson from her mom."

"Thank you, Mr. Summerset," Mike said as he stepped inside. The smell of turkey filled the house. "Man, it smells good in here."

"Make sure you say something to Katie about the dressing. She made it this year."

"Yes, sir. I'll do that."

Mr. Summerset led him into the den, where Katie's ten-year-old cousin, Gracie, and several other younger family members sat in front of the TV watching the parade. "Make yourself comfortable, Mike. I'll let Katie know you're here."

Mike settled into one of the folding chairs set up for the evening's activities: a What I'm Thankful For game and a Hallmark movie.

Lorne Greene and Betty White hosted this year's parade. As they introduced each float, balloon, and marching band, Mike looked at

Gracie and remembered how he loved watching the parade when he was her age. "What's your favorite balloon so far, Gracie?"

Without turning, she replied, "Dino the Dinosaur and Bullwinkle."

Trying his best to get her attention, he asked, "What is your favorite float?"

Again, without turning, she answered, "Cinderella's carriage." Not wanting to be bothered, Gracie added, "I think Katie will be out in a few minutes, Mike."

Amused that he was being ignored, Mike resisted the urge to interrupt her again. Before he knew it, he was ten years old again, captivated by the pageantry that still held his attention for all these years.

Katie walked up behind Mike, put her arms around him, and playfully nibbled on his ear. Softly, he said, "If that's not you, Katie, I'm in a lot of trouble right now."

Straightening up, she spiritedly popped Mike on the head and replied, "Well, who else would it be?"

"I thought it might be your cousin Cathy. You know she's always been sweet on me."

Popping him a little harder, Katie walked around and sat on Mike's lap. Moving her head to within inches of his, she teasingly said, "Well, she will just have to get over it. You belong to me, mister. Don't forget that. Besides, Cathy is way too young for you." Friskily, she inched closer and gave him a lengthy kiss. There were seven people in the room watching all this unfold. Katie did her best to make Mike as uncomfortable as she could.

Mike noticed Gracie grinning. *Great, now I've got her attention.*

Katie saw the panic on his face and smiled sweetly. To make things worse, Gracie started singing, "Mike and Katie sitting in a tree. K-i-s-s-i-n-g. First came love, then came marriage, then came Katie with a baby carriage."

Katie was too old to worry about Gracie's teasing but could see Mike's discomfort. "What do you think about kids, Mike?" After a long pause, she added, "One? Two? Ten?"

Embarrassed, Mike turned a deep shade of red. Softly, he whispered, "Katie, we have a choice right now. We can either go for a walk. Or I'll have to go home and take a cold shower."

After having her fun, Katie got up and said, "Well, come on, Marine. Let's go for a walk." To Gracie's amusement, she pulled Mike out of his chair and led him to the door like a little puppy.

Mike was surprised at Katie's behavior. They had set their wedding for June 15. *Lord, give me strength.*

Mr. Summerset and several other family members were in the living room watching football. "Dad, Mike and I are going for a walk. We'll be back in time for dinner."

"Go have fun, kids," her dad said with a grin. "Mike, are you feeling all right? You look a little flushed."

The look on his face told Mike he was somehow aware of Katie's little joke. "Mr. Summerset, do you know your daughter has an evil side to her?"

"Yes, I do. Katie gets it from her mom, and the way I hear it, your mom's not helping the situation either. They're creating a monster, Mike. Get used to it."

Everyone in the room grinned. Mike got the odd feeling there was more to the joke than he understood.

"Mike, remember, you've got seven months to change your mind. After that, you're stuck with her. I'm not taking her back."

"Thank you, sir." Drawing a deep breath, he concluded, "I'll keep that in mind."

"Bye, Dad. We'll see you in a bit."

Still holding Mike's hand, she led him through the front door, down the steps, and onto the front yard. Stopping, Mike said,

"Katie, that wasn't funny. We can't keep our commitment to the Lord with you acting like that."

"I'm sorry, Mike," she said with a restrained smile. "You're right. I promise not to do that to you again. Our moms assumed I would wait until we were married before I pulled that one on you." Then Katie put on her best-embarrassed look.

Mike thought about how grown-up Katie had become. She was certainly not the young girl he knew in high school. Beginning with her hair, he carefully studied every feature of her face. Lifting her hand high above her head, he twirled her around and noticed how petite she still was. Overcome with joy, Mike considered how blessed he was to have someone so wonderful to share his future with. A tear ran down his face, and Katie knew he was ready to tell her about Vietnam.

"Mike," she began slowly, "you said you had something to tell me." She knew that Mike had a big hole in his heart about something. He had been hiding that pain for months now. "Whatever it is, Mike, you can tell me."

Mike led Katie across the street to a small park, and they sat on a bench. Solemnly, he leaned over and put his elbows on his knees. He looked down at the multicolored river rock at his feet and hoped he could get it all out without crying.

Katie could feel his sorrow but patiently waited until Mike was ready to talk. She scooted close and put her arm around his broad shoulders.

With a deep breath, Mike began. "Have you seen last month's copy of *Life* magazine? It was the one about Con Thien."

"Yes," she said hesitantly. "I cried for an hour when I read it. It was dreadful there. Why?" A worried look came over Katie as she anticipated Mike's next words.

"Well, there was a terrible battle fought there on the morning of May 8. David and I were there when it happened." Mike paused to gather his thoughts. With a soft gasp, Katie put her hand to her heart and waited.

"We moved onto the Hill a few days before the attack. I didn't tell you, but they made me squad leader after Sergeant Miller was killed. There were fifteen in my squad. Ten of them died that night defending the Hill."

Mike sat up and stared at the old gnarled elm tree nearby, hoping to draw strength and wisdom from its wizened branches. Katie sat there in shock. Now, she was very grateful for what she didn't know about Mike's life as a combat marine. She laid her head on his shoulder and asked, "Is that where you got the Bronze Star?"

"Yes. My squad was on the perimeter when the enemy blew two holes in the wire and got inside the compound. They didn't have a chance, Katie. The other five could have also been killed if it wasn't for David. I was ordered to man our squad bunker farther up the hill." By now, Mike was numb but intent on telling her everything about that night.

"It was about four in the morning when they reached our second line of defense. Two guys died helping me defend our bunker. I don't remember how it happened, but that was when I was wounded. Katie, that was my third Purple Heart." After a pause, he continued. "Our company lost forty-four men that night, another one hundred ten wounded. I spent my last four weeks recovering at Dong Ha while David and the rest of the company went out on another sweep of the DMZ."

He had already told her about being shot and spending five days on a hospital ship. Now, hearing the rest of the story, Katie was speechless. Part of her wanted to cry, but she knew it was vital to be strong for Mike's sake.

"I need to tell you about something else that happened that night. It's a little bizarre, but I swear it happened." Katie sat silently as Mike spent the next thirty minutes explaining his encounter with Legion.

"I don't know about guardian angels, but I honestly believe the Lord has been protecting me, keeping me safe for a purpose. I need to find out what that purpose is. I'm certain it is something we must do together."

Mike had just finished telling Katie about Zophar and Legion when Mr. Summerset called from across the street. "Hey, you two. It's time for dinner."

"OK, Dad. We'll be there in a minute," she called back. Turning to Mike, she said, "I'm so sorry you had to go through all that. I want you to know you can talk to me anytime about anything. Thank you for sharing this with me." Standing up and taking him by the hand, she gently tugged on his left arm. "How's the old wing doing these days, Marine?"

Mike looked deep into Katie's eyes and smiled. "Good. Now let's go stuff ourselves and think happy thoughts for the rest of the day."

Relieved to have finally confided in Katie, Mike got up and added, "Come on. I'll race you to the house." Like a couple of giddy teenagers, they ran across the street, laughing as they went.

Arriving at the porch one step behind Katie, Mike took her hand and thought how perfect the day was, especially now that he had that monkey off his back. Glancing back at the park bench, he turned and said, "I've seen Mom and Dad do crazy stuff like that for years. Until now, I had no idea why. Now I think I get it. Don't you, Kate?"

Thrilled, her face lit up like a Christmas tree. Kate was her nickname before they moved to Garland. Although she preferred it, everyone called her by her given name. Looking deep into Mike's eyes, Kate replied, "As a matter of fact, that was the first thing your mom taught me. She said it kept your dad on his toes for all those years. Yes, I think it will work for us too."

Chapter 6

The Rehearsal Dinner

The night before the wedding, the Shaffers hosted the rehearsal dinner at Dunston's Steakhouse in Dallas. Sarah might have planned the evening, but George picked the restaurant. The head table was occupied by Mike, Kate, David, Linda and the pastor. The four parents sat together to the right, with the grandparents to the left. The remainder of the wedding party sat at three large tables in the middle.

After the guests had ordered their meals, George and Sarah stood up. Tapping his glass with a knife, George took his wife's hand and began. "Thank you all for joining us on this very happy occasion. As you know, this weekend is all about Mike and Katie." Acknowledging his mistake, George grinned and quickly corrected himself, "Oh, I'm sorry. It's Mike and Kate now."

Kate pointed her finger at George and proudly nodded her approval. Mike placed his hand on top of Kate's hand. Turning to face him, she quietly mouthed, "I love you." Mike squeezed her hand and gave her a confirming wink.

Seeing their intimate exchange, George glanced at Sarah and continued with a lump in his throat. "Sarah and I are thrilled that Mike chose Kate as his wife. We both feel this was the Lord's doing, and if they trust him, he will richly bless them for the rest of their lives. Before the food arrives, I would like to ask Pastor Beckman to say a few words."

"Thank you, George," began the pastor. "I have known the Shaffer family for over twenty years and the Summerset family for about eight now. It has been a blessing to watch these two families mature, not only in the Lord but also in the community. I want to thank both families for what they mean to so many people, especially our church. To the Shaffer and Summerset families, may the Lord bless and keep you in his will." The pastor raised his glass and sipped his iced tea.

Addressing Mike and Kate, the pastor continued. "What is marriage? Marriage is a vow, a commitment you must take seriously to survive. A healthy marriage is when two people get up every morning to sing their favorite song together and not worry about who is out of key for the day. What is love? Love is fragile, a glass that shatters if you hold it too tightly. Don't smother each other by worrying about who's right or wrong. Learn to admit your mistakes before they fester into something ugly.

"Happiness is not about having what you want but being content with what you have. Learn to find your happiness in each other. On the other hand, patience is being still before the Lord and waiting on him to show you the way."

Lifting his glass to the bride and groom, Pastor Beckman concluded his toast. "To Mike and Kate, may your days together be many and your disagreements few." He and all those present lifted their glasses in agreement.

"I see our meal is ready, so let us thank the Lord for this wonderful food that he has provided."

After finishing their meals, the two couples started working the room to greet their guests. The parents soon joined them. After the servers cleared the tables, Kate asked the waiter to bring in the groom's cake. Keeping it light, she decided on an SMU-themed cake with red and blue icing and a figurine of the bride dragging the groom by the back of the collar.

After dessert, David stood and announced, "It's time for Linda and I to toast the bride and groom." Linda stood and joined him.

"I first met Mike at a ninth-grade football game. He intercepted one of my passes and returned it for a touchdown. Later in the game, it was fourth and five at the twenty-five-yard line. We were behind by six points. I took the ball on a quarterback sweep. Just as I turned upfield, I saw Mike coming at me hard and fast, ready to take my head off. I gave him my best move and left him lying there like a cow patty. When I crossed the goal line, I remember thinking that boy can run but can't tackle worth spit."

David held up a sign, and everyone responded, "Poor Mike."

"I first met Kate at cheer camp," Linda began. "I was this shy, introverted little girl who couldn't do half of what she could. If there were an award for the most popular, Kate would have won it. Everyone oohed and aahed every time she did anything. I remember thinking Little Miss Perfect was full of herself.

"One of our daily exercises was to do a round-off back handspring. Everyone did theirs correctly. I started running to do mine, slipped, and landed flat on my rear end. Humiliated, I sat there in tears. Kate was the only one who came over to help me up. We've been best friends ever since."

Linda held up a sign, and in unison, everyone said their oohs and aahs.

"The hard part about being a marine in Vietnam," David continued, "is that everyone wants to shoot you, especially the girls. It must be some strange courtship thing they do over there." David picked up a small four-inch-diameter bull's-eye and stuck it to his shirt. "This was my target of opportunity. This was Mike's target." Picking up another target, David leaned over and tied it around Mike's neck.

"Notice that my target is much smaller than Mike's. That's because I kept my head down and played it safe. Mike, on the other hand, was always rushing into danger, daring the enemy to shoot him. Most of you don't know it, but Mike was wounded three times in Vietnam. Tell us, Mike, where were you wounded."

"Yeah, Mike, tell us where you were wounded," Kate prodded.

Embarrassed, Mike looked at Kate's devious smile.

"If you don't tell them, I will," she said softly. Mike looked at the surprised look on his mom's face and knew his secret was about to be exposed. As far as she knew, Mike had only been wounded once.

Looking up at David and then over at his mom again, Mike quietly said, "My arm, my leg, and my ... butt."

"Mike, you'll have to speak up. I don't think anyone heard you."

"My arm, leg, and butt," Mike repeated louder. Everyone erupted in laughter, and Mike's reddish facial color deepened. The last person he wanted to know about his derriere wound was his mom, who sat there with both hands on her cheeks, trying her best not to laugh.

Waiting for the laughter to die down, David continued. "The butt seems an odd place to be shot, Mike. Tell us how you managed to get shot there."

"I was withdrawing from the enemy."

"Mike would never admit this, but he retreated because a girl was coming at him with an AK-47." David paused again and let the laughter die down. "Which brings us back to Mike's bull's-eye. A rather large target, wouldn't you say? Three wounds in Vietnam and not one on the target. Mike was wounded again the day he met Kate." David picked up a cutout of Kate's name and stuck it to the center of Mike's target. "Congratulations, Kate. You succeeded where so many other girls have failed."

Linda held up her sign again, and everyone said their oohs and aahs.

Mike put his head in his hands in embarrassment. Kate put her arm around his shoulder and speaking to the audience, shouted, "It's OK, Mike. I'll leave my six-shooters with Dad for the first year."

David cued the guests, and everyone shouted, "Poor Mike."

"Now," David announced, "we would like to offer some words of wisdom to the bride and groom."

"Mike, Mae West said that marriage is a great institution. Kate may have gotten her man, but you got the ball and chain. Which reminds me of another institution—prison."

Completely engaged now, the guests countered with, "Poor Mike."

"Kate," Linda added, "remember that marriage is a relationship in which one person is always right, and the other is the husband."

George shouted, much to everyone's approval, "Amen, sister!"

"Mike, remember that you will be the head of the family, but you will only have as much authority as Kate gives you."

"Poor Mike," came the cooing reply from the guests.

Enjoying the roasting of her son, Mrs. Shaffer let out an additional "Poor Mike."

"Mike, learn how to compromise your differences. Admit you're wrong so Kate can agree with you."

"Poor Mike."

"Mike, remember that marriage is all about happiness. If Kate is not happy, neither are you."

"Poor Mike."

"Mike, they say that marriages are made in heaven, but then so are thunder, lightning, and five-foot-three-tall Texas tornadoes."

"Ooh."

"Aah."

He and Kate laughed so hard they were in tears. Mike said, "David, you know the shoe will be on the other foot next week? We will get even."

David grinned and looked over at George and Sarah, who were still rolling in laughter. Nodding her approval, Sarah stood and happily applauded David and Linda's entertaining performance.

David held his glass high. "As your best man, Mike, I would like to toast the bride. To Kate, a great marriage is not when the perfect couple comes together. It is when an imperfect couple learns to enjoy their differences. May those differences be few and far between." In unison, everyone lifted and sipped their drinks.

"To Mike," Linda began, "love doesn't make the world go round. Love is what makes the ride worthwhile. May the love run smooth and the ride less bumpy."

George and Sarah stood to offer their toast. "I think it would be appropriate for Sarah to toast the bride and groom."

"Thank you, George."

Sarah looked across the room to her mom and dad. Their smiles confirmed their approval of this marriage. Mike and Kate would have their moment tomorrow, but Sarah was having hers now.

"Over the years," Sarah began, "George and I have discovered some essential truths about marriage. First, laughter is an ointment that heals a lot of pain. Find the humor in both the good and bad times. Second, regardless of who did what, never go to bed mad. Third, love is another word for forgiveness. I cannot promise you will be as happy as George and I have been, but if you put the Lord first, the other second, and yourself last, you will do well in life." Extending her glass, Sarah added, "To Mike and Kate, may you give us lots of grandbabies."

"Well said, Sarah," said George. "Amen."

Mike and Kate stood to toast his parents. "Mom, Dad, I cannot thank you enough for all you've done for me over the years. It's a debt I can never repay. I am here today because you showed me how to love. I promise to honor my commitment to Kate for as long as I live. Hopefully, there will be a grandbaby or two for you to spoil along the way. To the best mom and dad a guy could ever have."

"Mom, Dad," Kate added, "you raised me in a house full of love. You provided for all my needs, even when I knew you couldn't afford it. It's time for me to start a new life with Mike. I promise to build that new life in a way that will honor all you taught me. To the best mom and dad a girl could ever hope for.

"Mike and I would like to toast our guests." Lifting her glass, Kate continued. "May the joys we share today bring us great happiness tomorrow."

As the final dinner formality, Mike and Kate passed out gifts to their wedding party. Kate gave Linda a pearl necklace. Mike handed David a box wrapped in plain brown paper.

"Thanks, Mike."

"David, I spent a lot of time trying to find you the ideal gift. I hope you like it."

Picking up on Mike's sincerity, David unwrapped the box with great interest. Once the paper was gone, he held a beautifully handcrafted box with the word *Browning* on the cover. David looked at Mike and then back at the box, too surprised to offer any reply. Using his thumb, he released the latch and slowly opened the case. Astonished, David looked at Mike and said, "This is incredible. Where did you find it?"

"Well, Dad knows a friend of a friend who knows this guy whose brother owns a gun shop in Houston."

"Well, thank you again. I didn't buy you anything this nice."

"This is something I really wanted you to have."

David held the gun up for everyone to see, "It's a Browning 1911 issue .45 pistol ... in mint condition."

George thanked everyone again and reminded them that the wedding was promptly at two. Pastor Beckman closed the dinner in prayer, and the guests slowly filtered out. The family said their good night, and soon, the four of them were left.

"Mike, that's an awesome gun you bought me. I don't deserve it."

"David, you saved five of my squad. I don't know how I would have handled losing them all. Thank you."

Chapter 7

Mike and Kate's Wedding

David expected Mike to be anxious when he picked him up to drive him to the church. Instead, Mike was overflowing with confidence, ready to put a hectic week behind him and take that limo ride to a hotel in Dallas for a weekend honeymoon.

"Mike, are you OK? I thought you would be a nervous wreck by now."

"This is my wedding day, David. In two hours, I'm getting married to the most wonderful girl in the world, and I will enjoy every minute of it."

"Well, couldn't you just look a little nervous? I'm getting married next week and already have the jitters."

Smiling, Mike responded, "We'll both be fine when we leave for Acapulco next week. Can you believe the girls paid for a week in Mexico?"

"Don't forget our parents bought the plane tickets."

When they arrived at the church, neither was surprised by the number of cars in the parking lot. "Well, David, the girls are already here with half my family," Mike joked. "So technically, I'm late. Nice going, Mr. Touchdown."

"Stop your whining, Mr. Cow Patty. It's ten after twelve, not ten till two. Nothing is going to happen until the pastor gets here. Now chill out."

David slapped Mike on the shoulder, and they started toward the gym door, laughing. Mike got a shiver and stopped. Turning, he saw a woman staring at him from the McDonald's parking lot.

"David," Mike said as he grabbed his arm and pointed across the street. "Do you see that woman over there, next to the curb?"

David looked and replied, "I don't see anyone, Mike."

"You may not see her, but she's there. It's Zophar."

David and Mike had talked several times about Zophar. At first, David dismissed it as Mike's struggle with posttraumatic stress. However, because of Mike's success with counseling, he was inclined to believe him now.

David looked across the street again and asked, "How can you be so sure?"

"I can feel him."

"What's that like, Mike? I don't feel a thing."

"It's that anxiousness we had that last night on the Hill, waiting for Charlie to hit us. We knew he was close, patiently waiting for that right moment."

Mike paused to consider God's protection and added confidently, "Zophar has become my thorn in the flesh. He's there to remind me how much I need the Lord. I always know when he comes around, but the Lord keeps him at bay."

"Mike, we've been home for over a year now. How many times have you seen him?"

"A couple of dozen times, I guess."

"Oh my gosh. He's taunting you."

"Actually, I'm taunting him by living. I attacked his pride, and he will not rest until he gets his pound of flesh. He can't do anything to me now but will go after my family when I'm gone."

After another glance across the street, David said, "Come on, Mike. We have a wedding to go to. Don't let him spoil your day."

Mike gave Zophar a defiant look and whispered, "Nothing can spoil today, devil. Not even you."

The door closed behind Mike, leaving Poyel on guard to ensure Zophar kept his distance. After a minute of visual engagement, Zophar assumed his natural unseen form and started across the street, right between a dozen unsuspecting motorists. Knowing his intent, Poyel took a few steps to intercept him.

Separated by a few short yards, the two sworn enemies glared at each other. Though unseen by human eyes, the age-old tension mounted as Zophar confronted God's messenger.

"Why do you protect and serve these pathetic humans, Poyel? They mean nothing to you," Zophar growled.

"They are like you in many ways, Zophar—prideful, self-centered, and devoid of any natural love for God. However, they are the Lord's prized creations and worthy of life. It is enough for me that he loves them. Your pride has so embittered you that you've forgotten what real love is like."

Zophar's pride was his downfall, but being compared to a human was an insult that demanded satisfaction. Slowly, Zophar removed his sword and readied himself for battle.

Unfazed by the threat, Poyel withdrew his sword and assumed a defensive position, preferring to let his opponent make the first move.

Zophar's lunge was swift, but Poyel had little trouble countering it. A rapid succession of thrusts and parries gave no advantage to either adversary. Small bolts of lightning jumped between them each time their swords touched. As the frenzied combat continued, the lightning flashes engulfed them both. The thunder it generated was like a continuous low-pitched boom. In worldly terms, the battle continued for an hour. In the spiritual realm, however, it lasted less than a human heartbeat.

Realizing the futility of his efforts, Zophar summoned some help. Immediately, Bildad and Eliphaz appeared to join the fight. Spreading out, they were prepared to come at Poyel from three sides.

Confident his sword was more than a match for all three, Poyel angered them further by making sure each saw the word *Justice* engraved on his blade.

"Are you three sure you want to do this? You will be banished to the pit if I remove your head with this blade." With a smile, Poyel lowered his sword, daring them to attack. This time, he wouldn't be as tolerant as their last encounter.

There were now three very agitated spirits, ready to fall on their swords to appease their lacerated pride. Before things got out of hand, Legion appeared behind them—all eight feet of him.

"What are you three idiots doing?" he reprimanded. "This is not what I told each of you to do. I suggest you get to it."

Without hesitation, all three vanished in puffs of blue vapor. Each hoped that Legion was not half as mad as he sounded.

Legion stepped toward the angel and respecting the power of Poyel's weapon, stopped a safe distance away. "You'll have to excuse my mischievous friends, Poyel," he said. "Sometimes they can be a handful." After a stare that would melt steel, he flippantly added, "You wouldn't want a job, would you?"

Amused by the offer, Poyel just grinned.

"Well, I had to ask," Legion added.

Feeling the presence of another spirit, he nervously looked around and vanished.

Satisfied with the outcome, Poyel returned to the church to resume his post.

Good job, Poyel. I knew you could handle it.
Thank you, Lord.

*   *   *

Inside the gym, six church members were busy putting the final touches on the reception decorations. After admiring the wedding cake, Mike and David proceeded to their assigned room to dress.

Later, Pastor Beckman came by to get them. "Mike, are you and your party ready to go in?"

"Yes, sir." Then Mike added, "Saddle up, boys. It's time to ride."

David rolled his eyes as the pastor chuckled, leading the men into the sanctuary and onto the stage.

David thought Mike's comment was cornball, so he asked, "Mike, are you sure you're OK?"

Mike looked out at three hundred visitors and swallowed hard. "I was fine until we came in here. Now I'm not so sure."

"Mike, I will seriously hurt you if you pass out on me. Breathe deep and relax your knees. You'll be fine."

The back door of the worship center opened, and the music started. The flower girl and young boy bearing the rings walked in together, followed by the two bridesmaids and the maid of honor, Linda. All stood reverently when the wedding march began.

Mike felt a bead of sweat drip down his forehead and then off the end of his nose. With all eyes facing the rear, waiting for Kate to enter, Mike slipped his handkerchief out of his pocket and wiped his face. His brain and heart were racing to see which one could flatline first. Mike thought how funny it was that he could stare down the devil one minute and have so much trouble now. "Lord, if You're not too busy, I could use some help right now," Mike whispered.

David and Pastor Beckman heard the murmur and did their best not to laugh.

Mike's anxiety and fears melted away when Kate and her dad stood in the back doorway. He looked at Kate, and everything was right with the world. While every eye in the room was on Kate, David leaned forward and asked, "How are you doing, Mike?"

"Everything's good now. Have you ever seen anyone look so beautiful?"

David saw that deer-in-the-headlight stare and whispered, "Mike, I hope I do half this good next week."

Kate's dad walked her onto the stage. Kissing her cheek, he gave her hand to her new husband and then went to sit with his wife. Mike might have been at peace with the world, but most of what the pastor would say next was a blur. Kate had to nudge him to get the "I do" out, and David poked him to take the ring.

George held Sarah's hand as it rested on his knee. Mike's brother and sister sat on the other side of their mom, content that their brother was happy.

Sarah thought about how calm and collected Kate looked and how lovestruck her son was. She felt herself becoming tearful. Anticipating the moment, George handed her his handkerchief.

"Mike, you can kiss the bride now," the pastor instructed.

Smiling, Kate waited for Mike to come out of his trance.

Softly, as if holding an exquisite rose, he kissed Kate and thanked the Lord for his great blessing. The couple turned and faced the audience.

"Ladies and gentlemen, I introduce to you for the first time Mr. and Mrs. Mike Shaffer."

Mike managed to survive the service but was drenched in sweat. He realized he now had a problem—both knees were locked. "David," he whispered over his shoulder. "I need some help. I can't move."

Calmly, David walked over and gave Mike a big bear hug. "Lift both knees, Mike," he whispered. "You'll be OK now. By the way, I need a holster for that .45 you gave me."

Unseen by everyone, Poyel held his position above the wedding party. A soft smile replaced his otherwise somber expression. Raising his sword as a salute toward heaven, he lowered it and gently anointed Mike's and Kate's heads. *Lord, bless and lead this union in your will. May this couple bring you honor and glory. Amen.*

Unseen from the back of the sanctuary, the Lord smiled his approval.

Chapter 8

Kate's Announcement

After their brief honeymoon in Dallas, Mike and Kate moved into a small apartment close to SMU. The following weekend, David and Linda were married, and the two couples left for their combined honeymoon in Mexico.

When Kate graduated from college, she found a job as a nurse at a local hospital while Mike found a part-time job to make ends meet.

His freshman year had been a little distracting for Mike. With school, work, a social life, and Kate, time was hard to manage. Now that it was his sophomore year, he had settled into a routine and became very serious about his business administration degree. After the start of his last semester, most of their conversations turned to kids.

One afternoon, Mike sat at the dining room table doing his homework. Kate walked in, sat across from him, and placed a calendar on the table. Mike highlighted a sentence in his book and looked up. "Hi, sweetie. How was your day?"

"Mike, graduation is only a couple of months away. Mr. Palmer has already offered you that management job, and I got a promotion last month. We've put back enough money to get a better place in Garland. Don't you think it's time we started thinking about a baby?"

Mike leaned back in his chair and smiled. She had been hinting for weeks, so he had already thought about it. They both were twenty-five now, and he knew they needed to start making plans.

"Do you think we can afford it?"

"I think so."

"What about maternity leave and the doctor bills?"

"I have three months of paid leave, and my insurance will cover 80 percent of the expenses. We can pay installments on what's left."

"Who will take care of the baby after that?"

"Mike, both our moms will jump at the chance to care for her after that."

"Wait, you said 'her.' I naturally assumed we would have a boy first."

"It could be twins, and it wouldn't change a thing."

"A baby does sound nice, as long as I don't have to change any dirty diapers," Mike said with an upturned nose.

Kate looked sweetly at him and fluttered her eyes. "If we started tonight, Mike, I think little Timmy could be here by the end of October." Pointing to the calendar, Kate added, "Tonight would be the perfect time to make a baby."

It took a few seconds for him to pick up on her meaning. "You mean ..."

"Yes, Mike," she said, pointing to today's date. "Tonight would be a perfect time to make a baby. That is, of course, if you can spare the time."

"Aren't we supposed to go out with David and Linda tonight?"

"I canceled it." Kate gave Mike more eye flutters.

"What if someone calls?"

"The phone is already off the hook."

"Well then, it appears I have run out of excuses." Mike put a marker in his book and closed it. Then giving Kate a playful frown, Mike added, "This will not take too long, will it, sweetie?"

With a sexy smile, she replied, "Well, that all depends on you, doesn't it, … honey?"

Mike enjoyed Kate's playfulness. However, just when he thought he had her figured out, she always gave him something new to consider.

"Are you going to wear that red nightie I bought you for Christmas?"

"Well, I thought about wearing something a little less."

Shocked once again, Mike blushed and replied, "Then I'll race you to the bedroom."

* * *

The following day, Mike immersed himself back into his studies, not giving much thought to the prospects of fatherhood until one night in April.

Mike got home from his part-time job at about four and went to the living room to study for a business law exam. After he settled into his chair, Jake, Mike's tabby cat, jumped into his lap and after a little loving, climbed up and found his spot on the chair's headrest.

Kate arrived home an hour later and quietly went right to the kitchen. The apartment was small, barely big enough for the two of them. Hopefully, with the news she had for Mike tonight, they would be out shopping for a new home in Garland this weekend.

"Mike, dinner is almost ready."

Mike washed up and went to the kitchen. Kate stood at the stove, dishing up tonight's dinner—hamburger helper. He walked up behind her, put his arms around her slender waist, and kissed her neck. "I love you, Kate. I see you made my favorite meal again tonight. That's sooooo sweet."

"Mike, everything I make is your favorite. Well, everything but the tuna helper."

"Yeah, I'm sorry I'm so finicky."

"Mike, I could put cat food on a dog biscuit, and you would eat it."

"Well, only if you put cheese on it too."

Smiling, Kate looked over her shoulder at him and grinned. "What was really in those C rations you told me about?"

"Nothing I care to discuss."

Taking his chin in her hand, she pulled him down and kissed him again. "Now park it, Marine."

You would have thought the hamburger helper was steak the way Mike went after it. Kate marveled at how satisfied he could be with the simplest of meals, which was good because that was all they could afford on the tight budget she had them on.

After finishing his meal, Mike helped Kate wash the dishes. Mike read scripture after dinner and discussed its meaning and application as was their custom. They then held hands and prayed for the names on their prayer lists.

With a serious look, Kate began to tell him she was pregnant. "Mike, you know how I've been sick a lot lately?"

Concern swept over Mike. "Yeah …"

"Well, I went to Dr. Beller today, and he said it wasn't the flu." Kate paused to let him think about it.

"Well, if it's not the flu, what is it?" he demanded.

A big grin crossed her face, and she replied, "I'm pregnant, Mike. We are going to have a baby."

Surprise and relief hit Mike like a brick. "You mean … I'm going to be a father?"

"Yes, Mike. You will be a daddy, and I will be a mommy. Is that awesome or what?"

A thousand questions raced through Mike's mind. "Are you OK? How are you feeling right now? When is it due? Is it going to be a boy or a girl?"

"Slow down, Mike. It's only morning sickness, and the baby and I are fine. The due date is October 22, so it's too early to know if it is a boy or a girl. Dr. Beller assured me everything is normal."

Mike reached out and took Kate's hand. Then with his other hand, he softly touched her cheek. "Is there anything I can do for you?"

"Well, Daddy, I think you already did it." Kate looked into his eyes and gave him a flirtatious wink. "What you can do is hit those books and ace that test. We need to go shopping for a new house. Our lease is up at the end of next month."

Mike graduated with honors from SMU in the spring of 1971. He then started a new job in the electronics industry in Dallas. He and Kate bought a house in Garland's latest subdivision, just two miles from their parents. A week later, David and Linda moved in across the street.

Timothy Allen Shaffer was born on October 23. Linda gave birth to Brad on December 3. Three years later, the Shaffers had a daughter named Rebecca.

Chapter 9

Sunday, October 23, 1983

It was nine thirty when the Shaffers arrived at church. They met the Longs in the foyer, and the four adults walked to Mike's Sunday school classroom. Brad and Tim escorted Rebecca to her room and continued to the sixth-grade room. Already seated was Tim's latest distraction, Mary Jones. Tim gave her a warm smile as he walked past.

Tim dropped his Bible on the boys' table and returned to speak to Mary. "Are you going skating next Saturday afternoon?"

Tim was a flirt, the heartthrob of every girl in school. So Mary nervously answered, "Yeah, I'll be there. What about you and Jenny? Did you break up?"

"Jenny didn't want to have any fun, so I broke it off. I'll see you there, OK?"

"Sure," Mary said with a blushed smile.

When their new teacher entered the room, Tim sat next to Brad. "Good morning, class. My name is Mrs. Stevens. Today is promotion Sunday, so several of you may not know me. Let's go around the room and introduce ourselves."

After several minutes of sharing, Mrs. Stevens made some announcements before introducing her message. "Our lesson today is on the great tribulation. You have an outline of the lesson on your table. I encourage you to take notes. Now, turn in your bibles to Matthew 24:21. Kim, can you read that verse for us?"

Tim and the rest of the class opened their bibles and followed along as Kim read the scripture. Mrs. Stevens was a good storyteller. In her midthirties, she taught seventh-grade history at a local junior high, so she was the perfect fit for this restless age group. However, Tim's mind had wandered off five minutes into her lesson. Aware that she had lost him, Mrs. Stevens continued her instruction while closely monitoring Tim's behavior.

Mrs. Stevens concluded her lesson in Matthew 24 by reading verses 45 and 46.

"Who then is the faithful and sensible servant whom his master put in charge of his household to give them their food at the proper time? Blessed is that servant whom his master finds so doing when he comes."

She paused to see if she could regain Tim's attention, who was busy doodling on a church bulletin.

Tim's lack of interest in spiritual things was no surprise to Brad. He thought it was a phase he would one day grow out of. With Mrs. Stevens waiting, Brad poked Tim back to reality.

"Tim, perhaps you can tell us what verse 46 means."

Without looking at the scripture, Tim replied, "It means fortunate is the servant who faithfully waits on the Lord's return."

Astonished by Tim's reply, Mrs. Stevens said, "Why, that's right, Tim. Blessed is the one who remains faithful until the end."

Tim's reply shocked even Brad, who was sure Tim had not heard a word of the lesson.

Mrs. Stevens glanced at the clock and said, "It's time to go, class. Please take your worksheets with you. I will see you all next week. Tim, can you stay for a minute, please?"

Brad slapped Tim on the shoulder and smiled as he raised his eyebrows. "I'll wait for you outside, buddy."

"Tim, you seemed a little distracted today. Is there anything wrong?"

Tim paused to consider his reply. "Well, Mrs. Stevens, Mom's been on my case about my grades lately. She doesn't understand how much harder the sixth grade is from last year."

Her initial impression of Tim was much different from his response, so she knew she had to talk to Pastor Beckman to get the real story of Tim's character. "You can go now, Tim. Try working a little harder at school. You do not want to fall behind. OK?"

"All right, Mrs. Stevens. See you next week," Tim replied with his most convincing smile. He then joined Brad in the hallway.

"What did the teacher want, Tim?"

"She told me how much she enjoyed my answer. She said it was exactly what she was looking for."

Tim smiled as he and Brad joined their parents in the worship center, feeling cocky about how easy it was to con his new Sunday school teacher.

*   *   *

After his sermon on the Second Coming, Pastor Beckman read the announcements. "As you know," he began, "the Billy Graham Crusade starts today in Oklahoma City. It will run through next Sunday night. Our chartered bus will leave the parking lot at 8:00 a.m. on Friday. We will spend Friday night there and drive back on Saturday after the service. The Myriad Center will hold fifteen thousand, so it will be crowded. I have two tickets left if anyone is interested in going."

Tim knew his parents would not miss the opportunity to see Billy Graham preach, so he was not surprised when his dad flashed him their tickets. "You're going to love it, Tim," he whispered. "Brad and his parents are going as well."

As much as he loved pleasing his dad, Tim would have preferred to be at the skating rink with Mary next Saturday.

Tim looked for Mary to break the bad news when the worship service ended. "I'm sorry, Mary," Tim said dejectedly, "but I cannot go skating on Saturday. We are going to the crusade next Friday."

"That's OK, Tim. Dad said we're going too. Maybe we can sit together on the bus."

"Yes, we can." Tim's disappointment turned to excitement. Immediately, he started planning his first move on a very innocent and unsuspecting Mary Jones.

* * *

The bus left the church parking lot on Friday morning and headed north toward Oklahoma City. All but Tim eagerly anticipated an inspiring sermon by one of the greatest evangelists who ever lived. Brad expected to sit with Tim on the bus. Instead, he sat by himself across the aisle from Tim and Mary. Until this point, they had been inseparable. Now, Brad felt like he had been replaced. This was the first of a long list of disappointments regarding Tim.

* * *

"Kate, did you notice Tim sitting with Mary Jones?"

"Yes, but a little too close and friendly to my liking," she said with a whisper. "This is not normal behavior for a twelve-year-old boy. The girls are usually the pursuers at this age. Not the other way around. Besides, did you see how lonesome Brad looked sitting there by himself? Mike, you should talk to Tim about girls and his friendship with Brad."

"Why me?"

"You're his father, Mike. You deal with Tim. I will tend to Becca."

Mike gave it some thought and got up to walk to the back of the bus. As he passed, he noticed Tim and Mary cuddling up close, holding hands. A glance at Brad confirmed Kate's apprehensions. *Kate's right. I need to talk to Tim.*

*   *   *

It took almost an hour for everyone to get checked into the hotel. "We're on the third floor, Kate. Where's Tim?"

Aggravated, Kate replied, "I saw him walking down that hallway about ten minutes ago with Mary. It would be best if you found them. Becca and I will wait for you at the elevator."

"Where's that?"

"Down this hallway."

Mike picked up his overnight bag and went to find Tim and Mary. The hallway was vacant, but something told Mike to proceed quietly. The first open area he came to was the dimly lit dining room. Peeking around the corner, Mike spotted the two in a corner kissing. Backing up a few steps, Mike thought about his reaction. Not wanting to embarrass Mary, Mike called out, "Tim, are you down there?"

"We're in here, Dad." Hurriedly, Tim led an embarrassed Mary to the hallway. "I was just showing Mary where we will have breakfast in the morning."

Mike did his best to hide the fact that he knew better. "We have our room key now, son, so we need to go to our room until dinner. Your parents are waiting for you in the lobby, Mary. We will see you later."

"All right, Mr. Shaffer. Bye, Tim."

"Bye, Mary."

Mike waited for Mary to reach the end of the hall then put his hand on Tim's shoulder and said, "Mary is a nice girl, son. I would hate to see her get hurt, wouldn't you?"

Knowing his dad was on to him, Tim quickly fabricated an excuse. "That's nothing, Dad. Just a little kiss. It was her idea, anyway. I won't let it happen again."

After a pause, Tim added, "You believe me. Don't you, Dad?"

Reluctantly, Mike answered, "Sure I do, Tim. I believe you." With a forced smile, he continued. "Now, let's get the girls and go to our room."

Standing at the far end of the lobby was a man looking at him. Though he had never seen the man before, Mike felt the coldness of Zophar's icy stare. Concerned for the welfare of his family, Mike's protective nature took over as he told his son, "Tim, I need to talk to that man over there. Stay here for a minute."

Mike fearlessly started up the hall to challenge Zophar's presence. Surprised at Mike's aggressiveness, he realized he had, once again, overplayed his hand. Knowing that God had limits on how close he could come to Mike and his family, Zophar smiled and headed through the vacant lobby. Mike ran to catch Zophar before he reached the door. Tim heard his dad's anxious voice and followed him into the foyer.

Mike grabbed the man's arm and spun him around at the lobby door. The confused look on his face told Mike that Zophar had already vacated the man's body. Scanning the room, Mike quickly found him. Hovering on the ceiling was a pale-blue cloud that only he could see. Mike's anger increased as he stared at the demonic wizard.

"Hello, Mike," the demon taunted. "How's the family?"

Zophar had pushed the boundary when he entered the small hotel lobby. When Mike rushed him, the allowable proximity was breached. Before Zophar could think about leaving, the flat side of Poyel's invisible sword struck him hard. The force was strong enough to drive Zophar's apparition through the wall, slamming him hard against the building next door. Embedded into the wall, he hung there in severe pain. The angel's warning was clear: stay away from Mike and his family.

Removing Mike's hand from his arm, the man asked, "What's up with you, pal?"

It took Mike a few seconds to reply. Turning to face the man, Mike replied, "I'm sorry, sir. I thought you were someone else."

"Well, next time, just say something." With no idea why he was in the hotel, the man opened the door, slowly walked across the parking lot, and got into his car. In confusion, he sat there briefly before driving off.

"Who was that man, Dad?"

"Someone I hope you will never meet, son." Regaining his composure, Mike added, "Now let's go find your mom and Rebecca."

"What took you so long, Mike?"

"I'll explain later, Kate."

*   *   *

The church bus arrived at the convention center early, so they were pleased to have sixth-row seats. Tim didn't like that his dad insisted that he and Mary sit with him during the service. Tim thought of it as punishment for sneaking off with Mary. While that was part of it, the real reason was that Mike knew Zophar would not be that far away. He could not let his guard down until he was sure Tim was saved.

"Thank you for coming tonight," began Dr. Graham. "Please turn in your Bible to Daniel chapter 2."

After waiting for the audience to find the verse, he continued. "Daniel is a prophetic book. Its importance is most relevant to today's society. Now, at this time, Nebuchadnezzar was the king of Babylon. When he conquered Jerusalem, he took many Jewish captives back to Babylon, including four Jewish men, Daniel, Shadrach, Meshach, and Abednego. The king trained these young men in the ways of the Babylonians to help him build his rapidly expanding empire.

"One day, the king had a dream that no one in his kingdom could interpret. Hearing of this dream, Daniel went to the king and gave him a good interpretation. The king was pleased and acknowledged Daniel's God as Lord of all. As a reward for his report, the king put Daniel in charge of his kingdom.

"Now, our story continues several years later in chapter 3. One day, the king built a great golden statue of himself and commanded all the people to bow down and worship his image. Knowing they could not serve God and man, Shadrach, Meshach, and Abednego refused to bow to the king's image. Enraged, the king cast them into a furnace. Yet to the king's amazement, he saw four men dancing around in the fire. He said one looked like the 'son of the gods.' The king commanded the three Hebrew youths to come out. When they left the fire, not even the hair on their heads was singed. The king was so astonished by this miracle that he blessed the Most High God.

"Nebuchadnezzar had another dream in chapter 4 that spoke of the downfall of his kingdom. The Bible says that pride goes before the fall and the king's problem was his pride. He acknowledged God as Lord of all, yet instead of serving God, he chose to serve himself, costing him his kingdom. The king discovered too late that he could not serve two masters, for he would either hate one or love the other. You cannot serve God and the world."[1]

Tim and Mary looked interested as they sat through the service. Mike had talked to Tim several times about his salvation,

---

[1]   Paraphrased from Billy Graham's archive sermon on Daniel 3.

but Tim always managed to let his dad know he was not ready. When the speaker gave the invitation, Mike nudged Tim and said, "That was a great sermon, Tim. What did you think?"

"Yeah, that was great, Dad. Mary and I want to go down and give our hearts to the Lord. Is that OK with you?"

Amazed, Mike replied, "Of course, son. Do you need me to go down with you?"

"No, Dad. We got this."

Tim and Mary stood and made their way to the field to find a counselor.

Kate saw them leave and asked, "Where are they going, Mike?"

Mike was so shocked that he could only point to the crowd forming near the stage.

All Christians hope their kids will one day make that crucial confession of faith. Mike and Kate were no different. A lot of prayers were offered in hopes of this day. One down and one to go was all they could think of. Surely, this is one Zophar will not get his hands on.

Besides Tim and Mary, five others from their church went forward to be saved.

Half an hour later, Tim and Mary joined their delighted parents. Everyone was excited that seven of their own had found the Lord.

"Son, your mother and I are so proud of you. There will probably be a baptism service next Sunday." Mike hugged his son and put Tim's earlier mischief aside. Now, he and Kate could focus all their energies on helping Rebecca find the Lord.

Legion, Bildad, and Eliphaz sat twenty rows behind them with Zophar, who was still sore from his encounter with Poyel's sword. Each shared the same thought: *Mike's son is a great liar.*

Chapter 10

John Zophar

In the fall of 1992, Mike went to the doctor for a swollen lymph node in his armpit. By the following March, civilian doctors had ruled out most of the apparent diagnoses. Fatigue, weight loss, and decreased appetite all pointed to something serious. Fearing cancer from exposure to Agent Orange, Mike made an appointment with the VA hospital for a specific test. He was sure the results would not be good.

That Sunday, Mike found the sermon of particular interest. Afterward, he met the pastor at the front of the church. "That was a great sermon, Pastor. Your analogy of Satan as the angel of light was spot on point. I never looked at it that way before, but it reminded me of something that happened to me in Vietnam. I want to talk to you about it this week if you have the time."

"I've always got time for you, Mike. Can you meet me here tomorrow about four?"

"Yes, sir. I'll see you then." With some difficulty, Mike raised his arm and coughed into his sleeve. "Sorry, Pastor. I can't seem to shake this cough."

Pastor Beckman had noticed the change in Mike's health and extracurricular activities. He had given up everything he loved to do: golf, running, and bowling. According to Kate, all Mike did was sit around the house and read his Bible when not working.

"Mike, have the doctors diagnosed that swelling under your arm?"

"I'm scheduled for a new test on Tuesday at the VA. Hopefully, I'll find out something by next Friday. See you tomorrow at four."

"By the way, Mike, how's Tim doing at SMU this year?"

"Grade-wise, he's doing very well. It's strange, though. Tim had this passion for football in high school, but now there's no desire. He turned down their football scholarship to focus on academics. After a year, he still hasn't decided on a major. I don't know what to think."

"Well, I'll continue to pray for him, Mike."

"Thanks, Pastor."

Kate and Rebecca waited for Mike in the car. "Where are you taking us for lunch, Mike?"

"How about Peggy Sue's BBQ?"

Kate looked at Rebecca and smiled. "Why are we not surprised?"

Mike slowly backed the car out of the parking space and made his way to the exit. At the curb was an indigent man holding a sign that read, "Ex-Marine needs help." Still lost in thought, Mike reached into his coat pocket and pulled out the twenty-dollar bill he kept for just such occasions. Rolling down his window, he handed the man the bill and said, "I hope this will help. We want to pray for you. What's your name?"

Kate looked over at the man and smiled. The man nodded to her and said politely, "Good afternoon, ma'am."

Addressing Mike, he replied, "John."

"Church service starts at six o'clock tonight, John. Come join us, and I'll take you for a burger afterward."

The man smiled and said, "Thanks, Mike."

Puzzled, Mike looked at the man more closely and asked, "Do I know you, John?"

"It's been over twenty years since we last talked, but you should remember me."

Mike studied the man and tried to remember him. "I'm sorry. What's your last name, John?"

"Zophar … John Zophar."

Just then, the overpowering smell of garlic got Mike's attention. At once, he thought of his encounter with Bildad on the Hill. Startled, Mike stared at the man and wondered why he was now standing here talking to him after all these years of keeping his distance. He had seen him, or at least the people he possessed, countless times, but at no time this close. Something had changed.

Alarmed, Mike looked over at Kate and Rebecca, sitting behind her in the back seat. They watched the traffic, expecting Mike to pull out any second. Both were unaware of the evil threat standing just a few feet away.

Zophar knew he had made his point by the look on Mike's face. "On second thought, Mike, tonight is not good for me. Thanks again for the donation."

Zophar looked at Mike's unsolicited generosity, and his contempt grew, knowing their day of revenge was rapidly approaching. With a sneer, he turned to Poyel, sitting beside Rebecca in the backseat, and nodded. *The day is almost here, Poyel, when we get our full compensation.*

With threatening eyes that flashed as lightning, the angel offered his proclamation. *Yes, but there are two sealed in the promise that you cannot have. Christos had granted you this encounter. Now leave.*

Zophar understood the severity of his situation and quickly backed away from the car. Turning, he walked away, leaving Mike confused.

The car behind him honked. Kate looked at Mike and asked, "Are you OK, honey?"

Shaken, Mike gave her a nervous smile and turned toward Dallas. Mike saw the man standing beside the curb, muddled over the twenty-dollar bill he was holding, unaware that Zophar had just paid him a visit.

After church that evening, Mike sat down with Rebecca and discussed her salvation. Once convinced she was saved, Mike called and spoke to Tim.

Their conversation did not go as Mike had hoped. Tim was as elusive as always and downplayed Mike's concern for his spiritual well-being. Troubled, he sat there, almost in tears. Poyel watched him closely, considering what could be done to ease his pain. He reached over and gently touched the long-healed wound on Mike's arm. The fears vanished as Mike's indwelling Spirit broke the mood: *Your purpose is almost complete, Mike. I am with you to the end. Everything is in my hands.*

When Rebecca went to her room, Mike took Kate by the hand and led her into his study. "Do you remember that homeless man in the parking lot after church?"

"Yes," she said cautiously.

"That was Zophar."

Gripped with sudden worry, she asked, "I thought you said he would not come around while you are alive. Are you sure it was him?"

"I'm positive. Kate, I didn't feel his presence this time. That has never happened before."

Mike took a deep breath before continuing. "Kate, I wasn't going to tell you until I knew something, but the VA is testing me for Hodgkin's lymphoma on Tuesday. The doctors have ruled out everything else it could be."

Kate was a nurse. She had spent over twenty years studying the diseases generated from exposure to Agent Orange. Mike had all the symptoms: fever, fatigue, night sweats, lymph node swelling, and she feared it was cancer. Fighting back a tear, she took Mike's hand and kissed it.

"Mike, the Lord said that whatever we ask in his name, he will give it to us. We need to pray and have faith."

Mike considered how faithful God had been all these years, but something told him prayers would not change the direction he was now being led. He loved his family but loved the Lord more because of his faith. For that reason alone, Mike knew God would provide for his family until he saw them again in heaven.

That night, Mike and Kate spent several hours praying for God's will and grace. Whatever his plan was for their future, they were ready to accept it unselfishly.

When Mike got up the next day, he felt better than he had in months. He even managed to drive to the gym and work out for a few minutes without too much pain. That afternoon, he met with Pastor Beckman and told him about his encounters with Legion.

"Pastor, Zophar would not have come around yesterday unless he knew I was dying. If this is stage 3 or 4 cancer, as I think it is, I probably don't have much longer to live. My faith has protected us so far. After I'm gone, Legion will come after anyone in my family who is not saved. I am very sure Kate and Rebecca are saved. It has got to be Tim. Why else would Zophar hang around all these years?"

Pastor Beckman was in his early sixties. He had seen some strange things during his ministry and even witnessed a demonic possession once. "Mike, you are the spiritual leader of your family, but you're not responsible for their sin or redemption. Over the years, you and Kate have done a great job raising your kids. Both have confessed their faith. If that confession was sincere, they are God's children now. If not, they belong to Satan. You've done everything you could do.

"My advice is to spend as much time with them as possible. Keep something in mind, Mike. You can offer Tim the living water, but you cannot make him drink it."

"Yes, you're right, Pastor. However, that's not a lot of comfort when it concerns your family, especially one of your kids."

The two men talked and prayed for another hour before Mike excused himself to go home. He pulled into the driveway, turned off the engine, and silently prayed before going in to talk to Kate and Rebecca.

Chapter 11

The Diagnosis

On Friday, Kate drove Mike to the VA Clinic for his consultation. They both expected bad news, but you would have never known it from Mike's countenance.

Dr. Stone was sitting at his desk when the nurse brought them in. The doctor rose and walked around the desk to greet Mike and then extended his hand to Kate. Mike was the doctor's sixth patient this month with the same diagnosis. Although their diseases were different, the cause was all the same: Agent Orange.

"Have a seat."

Mike and Kate sat down and watched the doctor return to his chair. The slight smile on his face gave Kate the idea that his report was better than she expected.

"I'm not going to keep you in suspense, Mike. You tested positive for Hodgkin's lymphoma. It's stage 4 and has likely metastasized to the liver, maybe even the bones. With treatment, you might live for another year. Without treatment, you may only have six months left."

Just as her balloon of hope started to leave the ground, the doctor's report brought her back to earth. Stone's bluntness in delivering the news seemed very unprofessional to Kate. Wondering how a doctor could be so matter-of-fact about it and still maintain a smile was beyond her.

Though shaken, Kate regathered her thoughts and asked, "Are you sure it's stage 4, Doctor?"

"Yes, we ran this test twice, Mrs. Shaffer."

After a long pause, she asked, "What are our options? What would you recommend?"

"I cannot tell you what to do, of course, but it comes down to the quality of life and how Mike wants to live out his last days. If he chooses not to endure the treatments, he can probably have three or four good months before he needs hospital care. If Mike decides to do the treatments, we must start aggressive treatments immediately. It will make him sick and weak. As his white cell count drops, his immune system will be compromised. Being a nurse, I think you know the rest."

Not ready to consider life without Mike, Kate replied selfishly, "How soon can we check him into the hospital?"

Mike was not surprised by the diagnosis. It was what he expected. Mike had stared death down before and would do it again, even if the result would be different this time. Unless the Lord had a miracle up his sleeve, he was ready to be called home. His only regret was that his family would have to face Zophar alone.

"Kate, the treatment will not do anything more than make me sick. I would rather spend my last days enjoying my family. I'm sorry, but I think that's what the Lord wants me to do."

"It's not fair, Mike," Kate whispered despairingly.

"I know, Kate, but the Lord knows what's best for both of us."

"Doctor, can we give you our final answer on Monday? Kate and I need to pray about it this weekend."

"That will be fine, Mike."

"Thank you, Doctor, for your time."

Mike opened the door, and Kate left the room. As he was about to go, Mike caught a whiff of that same pungent odor Zophar marked him with on Sunday. Stopping, he heard Legion's sinister voice: "Have you figured it out yet, Mike?"

Calmly, Mike said, "I'll be out in a moment, Kate. I need to have a private word with the doctor." Mike closed the door and turned to face a smiling Dr. Stone.

"It's been fun, Mike, but our little game is just about over. You'll get your reward, and we will get ours."

Now that Mike's end was near, Legion expected to see fearfulness. However, Mike showed him what he was still made of. Mike returned to the desk and replied assertively, "You are so pathetic, devil. Do you think your pitiful efforts to intimidate me will somehow gain you something or change anything? I am dying, but that does not permit you to come here before your appointed hour. Begone. Do not come back again until I'm in the ground."

At that moment, Poyel appeared beside Mike wearing jeans and a white T-shirt. The intrusion was expected but not welcomed on Zophar's part. The smile on the doctor's face quickly vaporized when he read the words on Poyel's shirt: "He Is Risen."

Zophar cursed the Lord in a rage and left the doctor quivering in his chair. Mike watched his quick exodus and thought it was strange. Was it something he said that would have caused such a response?

Legion and his associates had been dogging Mike for twenty-five years, using hundreds of visitations to keep him engaged in their little feud. Each time, Poyel was there to keep Mike safe. He always felt his presence but had never seen him—until today.

Feeling the presence next to him, Mike turned to see a fair-skinned man weighing about one hundred and forty pounds. Poyel's appearance would have fooled everyone, but Mike knew him immediately. The message on his shirt was incredibly satisfying.

"I wish I'd thought of that twenty years ago."

Appreciating the humor, the angel smiled and replied, "Mike, my name is Poyel. I'm here to escort you to the Lord's throne room when you're ready. You have run your race well and fulfilled your purpose. It's time to say your goodbyes to your family."

It was a bittersweet moment for Mike. He had served the Lord faithfully for years with one goal: to see the King in glory one day. With his reward in sight, Mike felt guilty for doubting the Lord's ability to take care of his family.

Aware of his emotions, Poyel told Mike what he needed to hear. "I will continue to watch over Kate and Rebecca when you are gone, Mike. You will see them soon. There is no time where you are going, so it will seem like only a day before they join you.

"You did everything you could to show Tim the truth, but he refused to believe it. He's made his choice. Now, he must face the consequences of his actions." Poyel put his hand on Mike's shoulder, granting him the strength to overcome his parental concerns.

"What's it like there, Poyel? Is it as lovely as they say?"

"More so than human words can express."

Poyel studied the tired look on Mike's face and remembered all the times he courageously held his own against Legion's horde of demons. His faithfulness made him special to the Lord, and he was grateful for the task of watching over Mike. With admiration, he added, "Kate is waiting, Mike. You should go now. Enjoy the time you have left with your family. I will see that Legion does not bother you or your family anymore."

Confused by the loss of time and unaware of Poyel's presence, Dr. Stone looked at Mike and asked, "What did you say, Mike?"

With a smile, Mike replied, "I said thank you for your time, Doctor."

With Zophar gone and no memory of his visit, Dr. Stone sat in confusion as Mike closed the door.

Outside the VA Medical Center was a Vietnam memorial park bench shaded by a large oak tree. Thinking back to another park bench years ago, Mike led Kate by the hand, and they sat down to consider what needed to be done next. He handed her a handkerchief and said, "Go ahead, Kate. Get it out."

Kate took it and began to cry. Putting his arm around her, he laid his head against hers. He lovingly continued, "Kate, you've always been the strong one I could count on to pull me through any situation. Now, it's my turn to comfort you. We've had a good life together, but I'm not dead yet.

"How about the three of us meet Tim for a nice dinner tonight so we can give them the news? Let's have our folks over for burgers tomorrow afternoon and meet David and Linda for dinner tomorrow night. We can take the pastor and his wife to lunch on Sunday and tell them. Does that sound OK to you?"

Kate wiped her eyes and wondered how Mike could be so rational.

Mike smiled warmly and handed her an envelope with the words "To my best girl, Kate" on it.

She looked at Mike and asked, "What's this?"

"Open it and see," he replied with a tired smile.

Kate loved surprises, especially ones that came from Mike. Opening the envelope, she saw a letter from Norwegian Cruise Lines. The message began, "Thank you for choosing Norwegian. We are looking forward to serving you during your 7-day cruise to Alaska. Please let us know if there is anything we can do to make your stay with us more enjoyable. We are including your itinerary with this letter."

Kate read the itinerary and said, "Mike, you know I've always wanted to go to Alaska, but this cruise leaves next weekend. We've got so many other things to do and not enough time to do it all."

"Kate, this might be our last chance to take a trip together. I want it to be about the two of us. Let's go have some fun while I still can. We can worry about everything else when we get back." Mike then produced a second envelope and handed it to her.

"What's this?"

"It's the plane tickets. We leave next Friday. I want to spend some time in Seattle."

"Is there anything else you want to tell me, Mike?"

"Yes, I'm taking the next two weeks off. You and I have some funeral business to take care of Monday morning, and then we need to go shopping for our trip."

Kate looked at Mike with admiration in her heart. She gave him another questioning look, and Mike countered. "We've got to go, Kate. I've already paid for the trip."

Smiling, Kate stood up and pulled on Mike's hand to lift him off the bench. Hugging him, she kissed his cheek and said, "Mike, I always thought we would grow old together, but how could I complain if the Lord calls you home? I will love you for the rest of my life."

Hand in hand, Mike and Kate walked to the car, both heavyhearted but secure in the thought the Lord would direct this last pathway together.

Mike stopped about twenty feet from their car. He turned to Kate and said, "How 'bout I race you to the car? The winner buys dinner tonight."

Kate considered the distance to the car and smiled. "Mike, you have never beat me in a race. What makes you think you can do it now?"

"Let's just say I have a plan."

"OK, Marine. Show me what you've got. We'll go on three. One ... two ..."

"Wait, Kate, your shoes untied."

When Kate knelt to inspect her shoes, Mike said, "Three." Placing his hand on her head, he pushed off and started a slow sprint to the car. Kate could have easily won but decided to humor him instead. Pacing herself to arrive at the vehicle just behind him, Kate pinned Mike up against the car, just in case he got shaky.

"So that's how it's going to be for the next few months," Kate said with a big grin.

Mike was winded but broke out in a laugh. "Kate, you know I'm a much better runner than you are."

Kate's attitude toward Mike's death changed entirely after that little race. It reminded her of what they promised each other the day they were married: take the good and the bad and smile as they faced it together.

Chapter 12

The Alaskan Cruise

Their plane landed in Seattle Friday afternoon. It was early June, and the temperature was in the upper seventies. The sun was shining with no rain in the forecast. Mike wanted this trip to be memorable for Kate, so he worked with a travel agent for a week until he was satisfied with the itinerary.

They rented a car at the airport, drove north, and crossed the bridge into the historic district of Ballard. Kate was speechless when Mike pulled up in front of their hotel. The four-story flaxen stone building with alternating wrought iron balconies and walk-out windows. The grand entranceway was covered with a protruding pale blue marquee with *Hotel Ballard* in scripted letters.

Always practical, Kate asked, "Mike, this is incredible. Can we afford this?"

"Please don't worry about money on this trip, Kate. We're on vacation. Let's go check in."

Inside, the lobby was spacious and decorated in light colors and beautiful tile. The furnishings were modern, with a fireplace and a stunning glass chandelier.

The bellboy led them to the elevator and up to the third floor. Mike tipped him as Kate entered the room and opened the balcony doors overlooking Salmon Bay. Mike dropped their overnight bag on the bed and joined her. Putting his arms on the railing on either side of her, he snuggled up close, nuzzling his nose deep into her silky hair. They spent a few peaceful minutes watching the boats and activity on the street below.

"Mike, this is so lovely. Thank you for this week. Let's not talk about anything negative. Only the positive."

"I agree, Kate. Now I'm hungry. Let's go have lunch over there," Mike said as he pointed across the street.

Kate laughed as she noticed the sign on the corner: Bitterroot BBQ. "Mike, you are so predictable."

Turning, she wrapped her arms around Mike's neck and nuzzled her face into his chest. Fighting back the tears and the thought of life without him, Kate quickly composed herself, took him by the hand, and led him toward the door. "After lunch, I want to go shopping."

Mike and Kate spent the afternoon shopping at the trendy boutiques along Ballard Avenue. Kate's amusing antics as she tried on a floppy, wide-brimmed hat and a pair of chunky platform shoes were therapy for Mike's failing body. They both savored every moment together.

Arriving back at the hotel, Mike informed Kate they had just enough time to clean up before their dinner reservations. "It will only take me a few minutes to get ready." Like a giddy schoolgirl, Kate grabbed her makeup bag and rushed to the bathroom.

Seafood was Kate's favorite food, so she was thrilled when Mike pulled into the Seattle Fish Company parking lot. After an extensive review of the menu, Kate ordered scallops and roasted potatoes. While Mike knew he couldn't eat it all, he ordered the crab cake and fries. As the sun began to set, the waiter lit the table candle and asked if they needed anything else.

"No thanks. Dinner was delicious," Kate replied.

Enjoying the moment, Mike tried his best to keep the conversation going. "You know, this is one of the oldest fish markets in Seattle. My travel agent highly recommended it."

Kate's eyes sparkled as she stared back at him.

After a short pause, Mike asked, "Did you hear me, Kate? This restaurant is quite popular with the locals.'

"I heard you, Mike."

"Then what are you thinking about?"

"Do you remember that ski trip we took to Breckenridge with the kids?"

Pleased to be reminded of something he had not thought of in a while, Mike replied, "That was our first family ski trip. As I recall, you three had no trouble picking it up. I didn't catch on until we went back the next year."

"We called you the big pie that year. Remember?" Kate smiled lovingly and extended her hand to Mike.

Cupping it in both hands, Mike replied, "I remember. I could only point those ski tips together to keep from killing myself." The thought of that trip together flowed back into Mike's memory like a gentle breeze. Kate smiled and gave Mike time to reflect on their fun times they shared with the kids.

The next day, Kate let Mike sleep in while she readied herself for whatever Mike had planned for the day. Softly, she brushed his hair and cooed into his ear, "Mike, darling, are you going to sleep all day?"

"What time is it?"

"It's eight o'clock."

Mike opened his eyes and slowly sat up on the edge of the bed. "Man, that was the best night's sleep I've had in weeks. Give me a few minutes, and we will go downstairs for breakfast. What do you want to do today, Kate?"

"I want to go sightseeing."

As he showered, Mike could tell his pain was steadily increasing. He was determined, however, not to let it slow him down this week. The doctor told Mike to increase his medication if his pain worsened. He looked in the mirror and told himself he could put it off until they got back home.

After the Space Needle, Discovery Park, and the Aquarium, it was time to head back to the hotel. Instead of going out, they decided to call room service and let Mike have another good night's sleep.

The drive to Vancouver would take two and a half hours. In the parking garage, Mike tossed Kate the keys and said, "How about you drive?"

Kate gladly accepted the invitation and replied, "Then get your butt into the car, Marine. Just tell me how to get there."

Mike smiled as he thought about her playfulness and humor. When his meditative and structured side got the best of him, Kate was always there to snap him out of it. She was more than a wife. She was his best friend.

After checking in the rental and taking a short cab ride, they arrived at the terminal at eleven thirty on Sunday morning. Kate had never seen a cruise ship up close, and this one was huge. It was the seventy-thousand-ton *Regal Princess*. Once they checked in, they went up to deck 10 to find their stateroom.

"Mr. Shaff," the cabin steward began, "there is a newsletter and everything you need to know about the ship in the welcome packet on your bed. If you're hungry, there is a buffet on the top deck. The dining halls open at six. Is there anything else I can do for you?"

"No, not right now. Thanks."

Kate laid her purse on the bed and stopped to smell the dozen yellow roses on the dresser. She opened the card and read, "To Kate, my best girl." Mike placed his arm around her waist, kissing her hair just above her right ear. Turning, Kate wrapped her arms around him, nuzzled up close, and softly whispered, "Mike, you are the most thoughtful person I've ever known. Thank you again for this special time together."

Feeling a little emotional, Mike smiled and pointed to the far side of the room. "Let's check out the balcony."

Kate walked over and opened the balcony door. Outside, she was treated to a lovely view of Vancouver Harbor. Mike picked the ship newsletter and the cruise itinerary off the bed and joined her.

"Mike, it is so beautiful. Remind me again, where are we going?"

Mike sat in one of the lounge chairs and began looking through the newsletter. Kate moved the other chair close to Mike and sat down, eager to have him tell her all about their trip. With her hand resting on his arm, she waited for his reply.

"Well, the ship leaves here at five thirty. We cruise the Inside Passage tonight and arrive in Juneau tomorrow. On Tuesday, we are in Skagway and Glacier Bay on Wednesday. We spend Thursday in Sitka and sail all day Friday, arriving back in Vancouver next Sunday morning."

Turning the page on the newsletter, Mike added, "There are ship activities every day, a twenty-four-hour pizzeria, two pools, and four whirlpools. We have reservations in the Palm Court Dining Room tonight at six fifteen. After that, we can take in the show. Tomorrow, we can choose our shore excursions for the week. Somehow, I don't think we will be bored. Now, we've got a big ship to explore. Let's go do it."

* * *

The hallway was crowded when they stepped off the elevator next to the restaurant. As they waited in line, Kate was captivated by the size and elegance of the room. It wasn't the fanciest place she had ever been. Still, the number of attentive servants bustling about was more than impressive. She slipped her arm around Mike's and moved as close to him as she could.

Reflecting again on all those things that made Kate so precious to him, he whispered, "I love you, Kate."

The hostess was Australian, possibly in her early twenties. Mike had been watching her for several minutes, fascinated at how efficiently she could seat her guests.

"May I help you, sir?"

"Yes, reservation for Mike and Kate Shaffer," he said proudly.

"Good evening, Mr. and Mrs. Shaffer. It is nice to have you with us tonight. Reyna will show you to your table."

The greeter led Mike and Kate down some steps to a table next to a window. After getting them settled, she handed them a menu. "Your waiter's name is Aroon. He will be with you in a moment. Enjoy your meal."

Kate slowly surveyed the room, people watching. Honeymooners and those celebrating golden anniversaries alike were all enjoying themselves. One couple caught her attention. They looked to be in their sixties, about the same age as her parents. While the room was alive with laughter and conversation, the two just held hands and smiled at each other. She watched them for several minutes, and they never said a word.

Mike followed Kate's eyes to the couple seated a short distance away and knew exactly what she was thinking. That could have been them twenty years from now. Fighting off his sorrow, he patiently waited for her to finish her reflection.

"Mike, this is so lovely," she said gently.

Mike took her hand and replied, "And you are the loveliest person in the room, Kate."

Catching her in the middle of a blush, the waiter stepped forward and introduced himself. "Hello, my name is Aroon. I'll be your waiter tonight. May I take your drink order?"

"I'll have water."

"I'll have iced tea," Kate added.

Aroon recited the evening specials and left to get their drinks. Kate and Mike turned their attention to the window. A pilot boat was positioned alongside, escorting the ship to the deep waters beyond the harbor. The protection of the surrounding land gave the sea a picturesque smoothness.

Aroon returned a few minutes later with drinks and fresh bread then took their orders—roasted tenderloin for Mike and shrimp scampi for Kate.

A uniformed ship's officer stood at the top of the stairway that led down into the restaurant. His presence caught Mike's attention immediately. The officer studied the room and then entered the busy dining area. It soon became apparent the officer was heading to their table. Mike feared it was another visit from Zophar. However, Mike's anxieties began to fade as the man got closer.

Stepping to the table, the officer quickly glanced at the top page of his clipboard and introduced himself. "Good evening, Mr. and Mrs. Shaffer. My name is Christos."

Mike confirmed the man's name with his badge and noticed his position—destination manager. The man's smile calmed the last of Mike's fears.

"It's a pleasure to have you dine with us tonight. We hope the food will be to your satisfaction. If not, please let Aroon know, and he will be glad to bring you something different."

With a reserved smile, Kate responded, "Thank you, Christos. I'm sure it will be wonderful."

Seeing the strain on Kate's face, the man asked, "Mrs. Shaffer, are you feeling all right tonight?"

Christos's soft voice had a soothing effect on Kate's sadness. It was as if his voice was the only one in the room. Intending to say it was only a mild headache, she was surprised when something more private came out. "Mike has cancer and only has a few months to live."

As soon as she said it, the tears began to flow. Christos gently touched Mike's and Kate's clasped hands. Kate's weeping stopped, and she was dry-eyed again. Released from her gloom, Kate broke out in a beaming smile directed entirely at Mike.

Their reverie was broken by the waiter. "Here are your salads. Your food will be out in a few minutes."

"Aroon, the man who was just here, do you know where he went? Christos. The destination manager."

"I'm sorry, sir, but I didn't see someone standing at your table. Our hotel manager's name is Bjorn Falkner. I don't think we have a destination manager or staff member named Christos on this cruise."

Aroon refilled their glasses and excused himself to check on another table.

Astonished, Kate and Mike looked at each other in wonder. "Are you thinking the same thing I am, Mike?"

"Yeah, I think I am, Kate. Hebrews 13:2—'angels unawares.'"

*   *   *

The ship docked in Juneau at one o'clock. Mike and Kate disembarked and boarded a helicopter to fly out to a glacier. Arriving back in Juneau, they spent the day exploring the town. That afternoon, they took the Mount Roberts Tramway to the top of the mountain above the city. The view of the surrounding fjords from one thousand eight hundred feet was breathtaking.

It was eight thirty when Mike and Kate boarded the ship. After the buffet, they headed to their room to spend some time on the balcony. The wake from the boat sparkled as it reflected the moonlit night. Kate spotted a lighthouse in the distance and thought about the Lord. Without Mike, she knew the Lord would guide her through this life-changing event.

"Mike, this is Becca's senior year. She wants to attend Richland College in Garland next fall. What do you think?"

"They have a full range of classes if she changes her mind about being a teacher."

"Right now, teaching is all she wants to do."

"Did she include Richland in all that grant paperwork she filled out last spring?"

"Yes, Richland is still her first choice."

"Then I think that's a good idea," Mike added, saddened that he would not be there for Rebecca's high school graduation. "Now we need to get to bed. The ship docks at Skagway tomorrow, and we have more fun things to do."

*   *   *

It was nine o'clock when they boarded the bus for the short ride to Liarsville, USA, to pan for gold and enjoy a tasty smoked salmon luncheon. As they dipped their pans into the trough, Mike noticed Kate's tiny hands and marveled at how blessed he was to share his last days with her.

"Mike," Kate shouted. "I found some gold!" As she continued to swirl her pan, her excitement grew. "One, two, three flakes. We're rich."

"Let me see." Mike used his finger to push the remaining sand away. "Kate, I think you've struck the mother lode. Maybe I should take this more seriously." For now, Mike forgot about the pain and the dreaded hospital stay waiting for him back home. While they didn't strike it rich, they both had fun acting the same part.

The evening show was a pirate adventure that Mike found hysterical. After visiting the dessert bar, Mike and Kate found a couple of chairs in a remote section of the deck to enjoy an hour of sharing more memories.

On Thursday morning, the ship slowed as it pulled into Glacier Bay. The sounds of hundreds of growling harbor seals filled the air as the captain silently inched deeper into the bay. Small pieces of ice floated by that once belonged to the shifting ice mass looming in the distance. Its mysterious groaning and creaking sounds were a testament to God's creative wonder.

Pointing out to sea, Kate shouted delightfully, "Mike, look at those three water spouts over there. I bet those are whales." After a panoramic scan, Kate added, "This is so wonderful."

"Yes, you're right, Kate. We should have done this years ago."

The ship left Glacier Bay at four o'clock and headed south toward Sitka. Mike and Kate lingered on deck for another half hour until Mike got chilled.

"Mike, you're freezing. Why didn't you say something?"

"I'm OK, Kate. We can go if you're ready."

"Of course, I'm ready," she said firmly.

Kate canceled their planned excursion in Sitka, electing to spend the day on board relaxing in the shade of the promenade deck. A steward brought Mike a blanket, and soon, he was napping in a deck chair. Kate sat with him for an hour, thanking God for the time he had given them together.

"Kate," came a soft voice from someone standing beside her.

Looking up, Kate found herself looking into the compassionate eyes of Christos. Immediately, her heart soared as she felt his tender spiritual embrace.

He extended his hand and added, "Walk with me."

Kate stood and took his hand. Christos walked her down the deserted deck. Without speaking a word, he stilled all her heartache. Kate felt the oneness of their spiritual bond. She was reminded again that there would be a good life for her after Mike was gone.

As they looked down upon Mike's slumbering body, Christos asked, "Do you know why I chose you for Mike, Kate?"

With anticipation, she answered, "No. Why?"

"Because Mike needed someone to give him balance. I gave him purpose, but he required your stability to succeed. You see, Kate, I needed both of you to do some things in life, and you did them very well together. Thank you for your faithfulness."

Christos led Kate to the railing, where he reminded her of those special times when she and Mike unselfishly met the needs of so many others.

In the distance, Kate could see St. Michael's Cathedral. Its brass dome and cross extended a warm welcome to its visitors. Dozens of bald eagles circled above. Others perched on building tops, trees, and the many totem poles scattered throughout the town.

Knowing Kate was fine now, Christos quietly took his leave.

Smiling now, Kate softly offered, "Thank you, Lord."

Chapter 13

Mike Passes Away

Kate pulled into the hospital parking lot at five in the afternoon. Taking a much-needed break, she had gone home to clean up and grab a bite to eat. While she walked up to Mike's room, she thought about how much fun they had on their cruise. Just the two of them, it was like a second honeymoon to her.

Before school started, they took Rebecca to Galveston for a week's vacation. Tim said he had a job interview, but Kate suspected he was pouting about his dad's illness. Despite his pain and fatigue, Mike squeezed out three months with his family before checking himself into the hospital. That was two weeks ago.

Rebecca and Kate handled Mike's dying as well as Christians should, allowing the sovereignty of God to buffer their emotions. Around Mike, they were both upbeat and encouraging. Tim, on the other hand, was reserved and somber. The sicker Mike got, the less he came around.

Whenever Kate tried to talk to him about it, the more he withdrew. Tim told her he blamed God for his dad's illness. "Why would a caring God allow this to happen to my dad?" he would say.

Efforts to reason with him were brushed aside. Her last attempt to convince him Mike would not want him to feel this way turned into an argument. Saddened that Tim could not see past his selfishness, she knew Tim would be defenseless when Zophar came calling.

Poyel was standing guard outside Mike's room when Kate arrived. The brilliance of his battle dress would have blinded her if her human eyes could have seen him..His shield was royal blue, engraved with a fierce crimson-colored lion. As Kate approached, Poyel lifted his sword in salute. A smile crossed his face as she passed.

Kate saw the doctor writing something on Mike's chart while a nurse put some medication into his IV tube. Kate glanced at Mike and noticed that he slept peacefully.

The doctor finished his notation. He took Kate by the arm and led her to a corner of the room. "Mrs. Shaffer," he said respectfully. "There has been a change in Mike's condition. You should call in the family. He probably will not last the night."

The doctor's words cut Kate like a knife. She had been dreading this day for months. With the end near, she would have to gather her strength and say goodbye.

"Is he coherent? Can he understand anything?"

"No. Mike was in a lot of pain, so we sedated him." Emphasizing the urgency, the doctor added, "He doesn't have much time left."

"Thank you, Doctor."

Poyel appeared and stood beside the bed, his sword tucked away in its scabbard. It was a special moment for him, and he wanted to experience every detail of Mike's transition from this life to the next.

Kate got on the phone and called her mom, who then called Mike's mom. Within an hour, the waiting room was full of friends and family. Kate sat by Mike's bed, holding his hand when Pastor Beckman entered the room. She glanced over and gave him a composed look. As much as she did not want Mike to go, she knew he would be in a better place where there would be no more suffering.

Without a word, the pastor walked to the other side of the bed from Kate, knelt, and prayed for Mike's safe passage into the kingdom of God. "Dear Lord, receive Mike's spirit into your presence and comfort these two God-fearing families. If it is your will, Lord, I pray that you banish Zophar from Kate's family and keep him from exacting his revenge. In your holy name, I ask it. Amen."

Puzzled, Kate looked at the pastor and asked, "How long have you known?"

"Mike told me last spring, the day after Zophar approached him in the church parking lot. Do you know which one of the kids he will go after?"

"It's Tim." She sighed. "He blames God for his father's illness. Now he's not listening to anything I say."

"I'm sorry, Kate. Would you like to start sending family back in small groups?"

"Yes, that would be best."

"Can I do anything else?"

"Not now. Start with Mike's parents and Tim and Rebecca. Then send in his grandparents and brother and sister. My parents and David and Linda can wait until last."

"Thank you, Pastor."

Pastor Beckman gave Kate an encouraging smile and a nod. He then left the room with a sad heart. Mike wasn't just a member of his church; he was a friend, one of his deacons, and an excellent Bible study teacher. Mike served on the Garland school board and volunteered time at the local homeless shelter. He touched a lot of people in the community. His death would be felt by many.

As Kate sat with Mike, she sensed a presence in the room with her. Searching the room, she saw nothing, but the feeling intensified. Instead of fear, Kate felt a reassuring calmness. Then a voice told her, "Kate, it is time to tell Mike goodbye. He needs to take his place of honor at my table tonight. His work on earth is complete, but yours must continue for a while longer. Lean on me, and I will be your strength. The evil one cannot harm you or Rebecca."

"Is there nothing you can do for Tim, Lord?"

"Tim fell in with the wrong crowd years ago. He chose a different path and rejected me. Attend to Mike for now. Tomorrow, you will feel differently."

"Lord ..."

Knowing what she was about to ask, the Lord interrupted her and added, "Kate, I know it is hard to understand why I called Mike home. My kingdom has expanded through his life. You will see it increase by one more through his death.

"As far as Tim is concerned, his confession of faith was false, and the devil has filled his heart with pride and anger. As much as it breaks my heart, he does not love me. The choice was his to make. Know that you are my child, Kate. Continue to walk in my truth, and I will lead you home."

Kate considered the Lord's words and smiled gently. "Lord, the thing I'll miss the most about Mike is our runs together." looking at Mike, she continued. "Will there be places for us to run in heaven?"

"My child, you can take a trail every day for all eternity and never see the same tree twice. Perhaps the three of us could find a nice path one day soon."

Kate's eyes sparkled at the thought of sharing a trail with Mike and the Lord. "Can you give Mike a message for me?"

"I would be delighted, Kate."

"The last time we raced, he beat me, but only because he cheated. Tell him I forgive him," Kate said with a chuckle.

The Lord laughed and replied, "I'll tell him, Kate, but I think you let him win. Just like he's been letting you win all these years."

Kate laughed silently. "All this time, he let me think I was the runner in the family. I guess he got the last laugh."

"Kate, the fun you two have shared has brought Me great joy and amusement. It's a laugh the three of us will share for a long time to come. I could not be more pleased with how you both have unselfishly lived your lives. You did all I asked of you and then some. Thank you again for your faithfulness. Mike and I will be expecting you one day soon."

The Lord laid his hand on Kate's shoulder. She pressed her cheek against it contentedly. The warmth of his touch was comforting and uplifting. Kate knew she and Rebecca would be fine without Mike. She released his hand, and the Lord departed.

The door opened, and Mike's mom and dad walked in with Rebecca.

"Where's Tim?"

"He's not here yet, Mom," Rebecca snapped.

"Has anyone called him?"

"We left several messages on his phone," Sarah replied. "I don't think he's coming."

Rebecca walked over to her mother and hugged her warmly. Kate patted her arm and said, "Thanks, Becca. It's his loss, and I will not worry about it."

George and Sarah made their way around the bed and surrounded the girls for an extended hug. Both were heartbroken over Mike's pending death, but their faith was strong and would get them by. It comforted them, knowing that Mike would soon stand healed in the presence of the Lord.

"Is there anything we can do?" Sarah asked.

Still holding Mike's hand, Kate answered, "Yes, there is something you can do that would be very helpful." She reached into her purse with her free hand, removed a business card, and handed it to her mother-in-law. "Can you call the funeral director tonight and tell them I will be in tomorrow morning? We made all the arrangements last spring. All I need to do is set the funeral date and sign a few papers."

"I'll be glad to, honey."

The family turned their attention back to Mike and silently reflected on individual memories they each held dear. After several minutes, George led them in prayer. Sarah ran her hand through Mike's hair and kissed him on the forehead. Pausing at the door, Sarah looked over her shoulder and gave him a parting tearful smile. "Goodbye, son. I'll see you by and by."

"Mom, after everyone has been in, can you and Dad come back and sit awhile with Becca and me?"

Sarah's heart went into her throat. "Thank you, Kate," she stammered. "We would love that."

Over the next hour, small groups came in to say their goodbyes. With his family gathered around, Mike died peacefully. After kissing Mike goodbye, Kate went to the waiting room to console those who remained.

With strength and confidence, Kate announced, "Mike passed away a few minutes ago. Now he's in a better place, so do not mourn his death but rejoice in his new glorified body. Thank you for coming. David, would you honor us with a prayer?"

*   *   *

Across town, Tim sat drinking beer, forcing himself to have a good time with his friends, Kain, Candy, and Ginger. Between flirts and smooches with Candy, Tim checked his voicemail, hoping his mom would call to say God had healed his dad. He was too busy thinking of himself to accept that his dad's suffering would end.

He didn't know it, but Tim stood at the edge of a cliff, ready to cross a threshold from which there would be no return. If his dad survived, he would go back to playing the religion game, envisioning himself as the prodigal son. If his dad died, he would take the final step that led away from the path his dad laid out for him years ago. It was his fleece to test God. It was also his way of telling God, "If you love me, then heal my dad."

Chapter 14

Mike's Funeral

The church was packed with people paying Mike their last respects. His closed coffin lay in the shadow of a cross-shaped pulpit. Upon it was a portrait of Mike wearing his marine dress uniform, taken during the 1987 Grapevine Veterans' Day Parade. At the last minute, Kate decided on a closed-casket service. Mike had lost so much weight, and she wanted everyone to remember him the way he was before the cancer ravaged his body. The pallbearers that day were David and the five surviving members of Mike's 3rd Squad: Littlejohn, Wolf, Adams, Fuller, and Tucker.

Throughout the service, Kate held up like a rock. The songs were upbeat and inspiring. The sermon was all about Mike's unwavering Christian faith. At Kate's request, Pastor Beckman ended with an altar call. As the congregation ended the first verse of "Just as I Am," a middle-aged man stepped out of the back pew and walked to the front carrying his Bible. A hush fell over the flock when the man took Pastor Beckman's hand. The choir director motioned to the pianist to keep playing softly.

"It's Jon Kelly," Kate whispered to her mom. "We've been praying for his salvation for years."

Jon's wife, Helen, joined them. Quietly, Jon spoke to the pastor for several minutes. The three joined hands, and the pastor led them in prayer.

Addressing the congregation, the pastor said, "Please have a seat. I have an announcement to make. Our brother Jon has given his life to the Lord."

Most of those present knew the significance of Jon's long-anticipated declaration of faith and applauded. A rapid succession of amens and halleluiahs could be heard throughout the sanctuary.

Quieting the congregation, the pastor continued. "Jon would like to share something with you. I think it is truly incredible." The pastor handed him the microphone, saying, "Tell them what you told me, Jon."

Jon slowly looked over the parishioners and began. "I've been coming to worship service here for twenty years now." Looking at Kate, he continued. "As you know, Kate, Mike was Helen's deacon. Six weeks ago, Mike came to visit us. I could tell he was sick. After he and I talked for about an hour, I had this uncontrollable urge to get my life straight with the Lord. Mike led me through the plan of salvation. We got down on our knees and thanked God for his grace."

The room broke out in another round of approval. Kate remembered what the Lord said about his kingdom expanding by one through Mike's death. She reached for a tissue just as the tears started to fall.

"Before he left that night, Mike went out to his car and returned with a box wrapped in wrinkled red paper. Inside was this Bible." Jon held it up and continued. "I would like to read what Mike and Kate wrote in the front."

With the pastor peeking over his shoulder, Jon opened his Bible to the front page and began to read, "Dear Jon, Isaiah 1:18 says that though your sins are as scarlet, they are made white as snow. The promise of that verse was realized when God's perfect sacrificial lamb died for your sins. Kate and I pray that one day you will surrender to his authority. Signed, Mike and Kate Shaffer. June 19, 1979."

Kate remembered the night she and Mike signed that Bible and the many times they prayed for Jon's deliverance. *Thank you, Lord, for Mike's life and now Jon's.*

"The incredible thing about this Bible," Jon added, "is that Mike carried it around in his car for over fourteen years. When Mike went into the hospital, I decided to wait until today to come forward and join the church. Mike was truly one of a kind, Kate. Thank you."

With gladness, Kate stepped out of her pew and embraced Jon and his wife. "Jon, I am sure Mike is leading the heavenly host in praise right now. This means more to me than you know."

When he thought it couldn't get any better, Pastor Beckman felt a tug on his coat. Looking down, he saw five-year-old Amy using her finger to tell him to come down to her. Kneeling, he asked, "Can I help you, Amy?"

"I want Jesus to save me too."

Smiling, he looked to the ceiling and thought, *Thank you, Lord. Today is truly an incredible day.*

Chapter 15
Tim Meets Zophar

The lengthy funeral procession pulled into the Garland cemetery at three o'clock and slowly made its way to the gravesite. Greeting the mourners was a large black marble tombstone with the name "Shaffer" etched in gold lettering. Below was a shroud-draped cross and a rose. To the left were "Mike Shaffer" and "October 14, 1993." To the right was "Kate Shaffer."

Tim sat in Kain's car a hundred yards away—angry with God for taking his dad. Unaware of the spiritual battle raging within for his soul, he sat there in defiance of everything his dad held dear. The reflection from Mike's tombstone seemed almost supernatural. Tim could feel it reaching out to him.

"Man, there are a lot of people over there, Tim. Was your dad that important?"

"He was to me." His dad's loss had crushed Tim. Blinded by bitterness and deep sorrow, he could only think of his needs and wants.

After Pastor Beckman completed his brief message, three members of a marine honor guard took positions at the head and foot of Mike's casket. After a long silence, a fourth member raised her bugle and began to play taps. The sound sent a cold shiver down Tim's spine. The three marines stood at attention and saluted Mike's flag-draped coffin.

When the music stopped, two of the guards began folding the flag with high military precision. Several minutes later, a captain knelt before Kate and handed her a smooth triangle-shaped burial flag.

"Mrs. Shaffer, on behalf of the President of the United States, the United States Marine Corps, and a grateful nation, please accept this flag as a symbol of our appreciation for Mike's honorable and faithful service." The captain stood and slowly saluted Mike's flag. Then he turned smartly and walked away.

A three-person firing team delivered Mike's final military honor. Kate jumped at each of the three volleys. Each one reminded her of how proud she was of Mike's service to God and country. With her eyes fixed on the casket, Kate rubbed her hand across the flag. She smiled in admiration at the honorable life Mike had led as a marine and a Christian.

With Rebecca on one side, her mother on the other, and an unseen Poyel standing beside the coffin, Kate was sure she would never be alone.

Slowly, the mourners got back in their cars and drove away. Soon, only David, Linda, Brad, Rebecca, and Kate remained at the gravesite. Tim stared at them with his emotions clouding his thinking and wondered why they took so long to leave. His plans for the evening were fast approaching, and he didn't want to be late. Glancing at his watch, he thought, *Come on, Mom. The cemetery will close in thirty minutes.*

Finally, only Kate remained at the grave. After another few thoughts of goodbye, she turned and went to join her parents and Rebecca in the limo. The air was crisp, so Kate smiled and pulled her sweater up around her neck. The trees decked out in their fall colors caught her attention, and she began to examine their beauty. Kate glanced in the direction of Kain's car. At first, she didn't notice it. Then she stopped and looked back at the car. Instinctively, Kate knew Tim was there.

Tim sat there defiantly, not caring if she knew or not. *Get in the car, Mom. You're going to make me late.*

Kate reached out her hand and motioned for Tim to join her. When he did not respond, she got into the car crying. The limo drove away, leaving only the caretakers in the area.

"Dude, that was weird. How did she know you were here?"

"I don't care," Tim snapped back. He regretted his words immediately. He was mad at her for defending God but didn't hate her. As much as anything else, Tim wanted her to play the part of the grieving widow. He had seen her smiling as she walked from the grave. Tim did not understand her joy that Mike was now present with the Lord—no longer suffering. *How did she know?*

"You're cold, man," Kain said with a frown. "If that were my mom, I would be down there with her."

Kain's comment was aggravating, but he ignored it. All he wanted was for her to leave so he could say his goodbye alone.

Kain and Tim waited for several minutes and then drove to the grave. After looking around to ensure everyone was gone, Tim got out of the car and walked quickly to his dad's resting place. The caretakers had already lowered Tim's casket into the grave. They stopped their work and moved a short distance away, allowing Tim some privacy.

Tim stood there in silence, looking down into the grave. He came today for two reasons. The first was to honor his dad. The second was to decide what he should do with the rest of his life. Going home would be the same as admitting to his mom he was wrong about God. Then who could he blame for his dad's death?

As Tim stood on the edge of decision, he thought about something his dad told him years ago: *Son, God is a mystery. His*

ways are higher than ours. Don't blame him if he does not give you
everything you ask for in life.

Tim wondered why that bit of fatherly advice came to mind, but he discarded it. Although he no longer wanted anything else to do with God, he could not see that the Lord was still pulling at his heartstrings to get him to turn from his chosen path of destruction.

Rebelliously, he bent down and picked up a handful of dirt. After a few seconds of thought, he tossed it onto the coffin. Anticipating the loneliness that would follow, he felt his emotions starting to well up. He promised himself he wouldn't shed any tears for anyone else as long as he lived.

"Sorry to hear about your dad, Tim," came a voice beside him. "I will miss him greatly."

Irritated by this intrusion, Tim asked angrily, "Who are you?"

"My name is Zophar. Mike and I go way back. We fought in Vietnam together."

Tim had heard his dad talk about Zophar before, but Zophar blocked his mind, keeping him from remembering who he was and why he was there. "You knew my dad in Vietnam?" he asked inquisitively.

"Yes, I was with Mike the night the enemy got inside the wire at Con Thien. He led me safely through a minefield and kept this crazy man from beating me to death. I owe your dad big-time, Tim. He is one of only a few people I've ever respected. He will always be a hero in my book."

Zophar surveyed the peacefulness around him and smiled at the many lost souls Legion had plucked from this cemetery. Tim followed Zophar's eyes as they descended into the grave. Speaking quietly, he paid Mike his last respects. "Our adventure together has finally ended, Mike. Now, we must go our separate ways. I know we did not see eye to eye on many things, but I'm glad you found the place you were looking for. I'm sure Kate and Rebecca can get along fine without you. I promise to take good care of Tim."

Tim struggled to understand Zophar's words, but he was sure it was a language he was not familiar with.

"Do you consider yourself a religious man, Tim?"

Confused, Tim stopped to consider the question. "Yeah, I was saved and baptized. Until a few months ago, I was active in church."

"I didn't ask you if you went to church, Tim. I asked you if you were a religious man. Think about it. How much faith does it take to be saved, and in whom must your faith be placed? Take your dad, for instance. He was a mountain of faith. He believed in the Creator and was considered righteous. Are you sure you're saved, Tim?"

Tim thought about his salvation in terms of once saved, always saved, and never really considered the true meaning of faith. He confessed faith in Jesus, but other than that, it didn't mean anything to him. He never really believed in all that church stuff anyway. It was always something he tolerated for his dad's sake.

Reading his thoughts, Zophar continued. "Tim, I've traveled the world and talked to thousands of people about their faith. You could say I've looked deep into their souls. The thing I have discovered is that everyone believes in a god. To some, he is Muhammad. To others, he is Buddha. He is Christ in the Christian faith. The Creator can be whoever you need him to be, Tim.

"The Creator is not partial to any one religion. There might be some minor differences in theology, but faith in the Creator is the only thing that matters at the end of the day. You do believe in the Creator, don't you, Tim?"

Zophar grinned at how easily Tim could be deceived—not at all like his dad.

Beguiled by the logic and treachery in Zophar's words, Tim replied, "Of course, I believe in God."

"Then you believe that only those who believe in the name of the Creator will be saved. You do believe that, don't you, Tim?"

Zophar had gained Tim's confidence and was now in complete control of Tim's reasoning. Hypnotized by Zophar's cunning delivery, he quickly replied with a spirited, "Yes. I do."

"That's good, Tim. Your dad would be glad to hear you say that." Zophar's words fell off his lips like a hissing snake.

Taking full advantage of Tim's submissive state, Zophar continued. "Tim, do you believe in miracles?"

"Yes, I believe in miracles. I've just never seen one. Why?"

"The Creator gave me special powers to perform miracles, things people cannot do today. I make it a point never to use them unless it is essential. In your case, I think this is one of those occasions. What would you say if I granted you a short visit with your dad?"

Tim's imagination sprang to life. "You mean talk to him face to face?"

"Yes, that's what I mean. The conversation must be short and limited to just a few questions. If you agree to do me a small favor, I can make that happen for you. What do you say, Tim?"

Tim was so focused on the prospect of talking to his dad one last time that he ignored the notion that Zophar's favor might not be in his best interest. "Yes, I'll do anything." Tim had no idea that with this statement, he had just sold his soul to the devil.

This was the moment Legion had waited for. However, it was time for some fun with his new convert. "Good. We can talk about the debt details later," Zophar replied with a smile.

The miracle Zophar was about to perform for Tim was only an illusion created in Tim's mind. Zophar would give Tim a mental hologram of his dad, queue him questions, and let him fill in the answers with things he wanted Tim to hear.

"Tim, your dad is transitioning to the other side, and this communication may be too weak to work. The connection may be lost if you raise your voice or attempt to touch your dad. Do you understand?"

With excitement, Tim replied, "Yes, I understand."

"Good. It's been a long time since I've done this. I hope I can remember how to do it," Zophar added to heighten Tim's expectations.

Zophar closed his eyes and started to mumble. He watched as Zophar extended his hand, pointed down into the grave, and said, "Mike Shaffer, your son wants to talk to you. Speak if you are there."

After a long silence, Zophar gave Tim his first suggestion. "Tim, is that you?"

Mike's voice seemed real but was created entirely from Tim's imagination. Quickly, Tim's mind constructed a hologram of his dad. For effect, Zophar willed him to imagine Mike hovering above the grave.

"Yes, Dad. It's me."

Like directing a scripted play, Zophar cued Tim's mind again. "I'm moving toward the light with others in my group. It's beautiful down here, son. I can't wait to show it to you."

"What should I do now? Should I stay in school?"

"Son, you've learned as much as you can from school and church. It's time for you to find your own path in life."

"Dad, why did God let you die? He could have saved you if he wanted. Mom didn't understand when I told her it was his fault you're gone."

"Don't blame the Creator, Tim. He did what he thought was best for all of us. As I told you before, he's a mystery. His ways are different than ours, but I don't think he will mind giving you the freedom to make your own choices now that you're older and wiser. Don't blame your mother either. Give her a little time, son, and I'm sure she will come to see it your way."

"Dad, how much faith do I need to be saved?"

"Faith is what you want it to be, Son. It doesn't matter what you believe as long as you believe in the Creator. Follow your heart, Tim, and you will reach your final reward."

"What about the things you taught me about Jesus?"

"He was a great man of faith, Tim, a perfect example of how one should live a good life. However, don't put too much stock in all those old Bible stories about him being the Creator. There is only one god alive on the earth today, and his name is Apollyon."

Tim's head spun at Zophar's rampage through his brain. He thought his dad would not mislead him, so he bought Legion's lie hook, line, and sinker.

"Tim, I need to go now. Take care of yourself. Goodbye. I'll see you soon."

"Goodbye, Dad. I love you."

Like a dimmer switch, Zophar slowly faded Mike's image until he was gone, leaving Tim with the mistaken idea his salvation was now in his own hands.

"Tim, I owe your dad a lot and would like to help you get started in life. Here's my card. Come by the office late tomorrow afternoon, and we'll discuss the favor you owe me. I might find a job for you to do. Afterward, I'll treat us to dinner." Motioning to the car, he added, "You can bring your friend if you like."

"Thank you for allowing me to talk to my dad again. I'll see you tomorrow, Mr. Zophar."

"Zophar will do, Tim. Mr. Zophar is too formal for us to be such good friends now, don't you think? Tim, I've been admiring your cologne. What is it?"

"It's called Innocence."

Zophar leaned forward and took a deep breath. "I like that. It reminds me of the sweet smell of ignorance." With Tim's mind still in a cloud, Tim only heard "the sweet smell of youth."

Zophar smiled as he drove away in a brand-new black Cadillac.

A man of style and sophistication, Tim thought. *Any friend of Dad is a friend of mine.*

A parting glance into the grave, and Tim returned to Kain's car.

"Who was that guy, Tim?"

"He was an old friend of my dad. I might have a job for us. Do you want to go for an interview tomorrow? If nothing else, it's a free dinner."

"Yeah, as long as it does not include manual labor," Kain replied with a smirk.

As Kain drove his car through the cemetery gate, Tim left the memory of his dad behind, thankful for the prospects of a new benefactor.

Chapter 16

The Warehouse

Tim and Kain pulled up in front of Zophar's warehouse just before five. The sky was overcast with light rain. The temperature was in the midfifties. Tim rechecked the address and said doubtingly, "Surely this can't be the place."

Tim stepped out of the car and stared at the numbers on the building, suspicious but hoping this was not the correct address.

"This building has been deserted for years, Tim." Looking around at the other derelict buildings nearby gave Kain some concern. "What did you say this guy does for a living?"

"All I know is what's on his card—'Vice President of Product Acquisitions, Abaddon Industries.'"

"Abaddon," Kain replied. "That means the place of the dead. Look at where we are, Tim. There's not another person within half a mile. Why would anyone choose such an out-of-the-way location for a business? Where's his car? I don't like this, man. We should split."

Curious now, Tim looked around for clues to explain why Zophar would pick this strange location for his enterprise.

Fronting the warehouse was a four-foot-high loading dock. Centered on the pier was a concrete stairway leading up to a business entrance. With hesitation, Kain followed Tim up the stairs to the door. Beside the door was a button with an old rusted sign that read Ring for Service. Tim pushed the button and waited. A buzzer sounded, and the door lock tripped, allowing the door to spring open slightly. The door creaked as Tim pushed it farther. Cautiously, he entered. Kain stopped at the threshold and surveyed the interior carefully before following, leaving the door open in case they needed to make a fast getaway.

The building skylights let in enough light to provide limited visibility. A single light shone above a large roll-up door at the back of the warehouse. Zophar's Cady was parked inside thirty feet away. Besides a couple of dozen large unopened crates sitting to one side, the spacious warehouse was empty. Close by was a rusted forklift that looked like it belonged in the sixties.

Along the wall to Tim's right were several offices with glass windows. A staircase led up to a catwalk that abutted another set of offices. Zophar called down to them from the top of the stairway. "Nice to see you made it, Tim. Come on up."

Tim's eyes followed the eerie echo of Zophar's voice as he chased it through the warehouse. Turning to Kain, he said, "Remember, he does not like to be called Mr. Zophar. He prefers Zophar."

"Man, I don't like this one little bit," Kain protested. "Let's get out of here."

"Let's hear what the man has to say first."

Kain glanced back at the now-closed front door and reluctantly followed Tim to the staircase and climbed to the top.

Zophar greeted Tim with a handshake. "Hello, Tim. Who's your friend?"

"Kain, I want you to meet Zophar. Zophar, this is William Kain. Everyone calls him Kain."

Taking Kain's hand, he replied, "It's good to meet you, Kain. Both of you come inside, and we'll talk business before dinner. I hope you like barbecue. There is a perfect place across town I've been dying to try. It's called Peggy Sue's BBQ. Do you know it?"

Tim's eyes lit up like a billboard. "Yes, that's my dad's favorite restaurant. The food is awesome." Tim's countenance fell when he realized he referred to his dad in the present tense.

Pleased at Tim's slip, Zophar covered it with, "Yes, he's the one who recommended it." Zophar withdrew two beers from the old rusted refrigerator next to the door and handed them to Tim and Kain. "Why don't you boys have a seat?"

Tim and Kain walked past Zophar and sat at a large old wooden desk. Then Zophar began his age-old game of suggestion and illusion.

"Thanks. You're not having one?" Tim asked.

"No, I prefer something much ... stronger."

Zophar's office was clean. The furniture was wood, dating at least to the fifties. A dozen antique filing cabinets lined the wall to Tim's right. The table behind Zophar's desk was bare except for an empty file holder marked Progressing.

The desk furnishings were relics of a bygone era: a stapler, tape dispenser, pencil sharpener, and a sizeable daily planner. On one side of the planner were two stained white coffee cups; one held several pencils and an ink pen. The other was half full of rusted paperclips. Sitting on the desk was an old black AT&T office phone. A genuine leather chair that looked like it came right out of the box stood in sharp contrast to the other furnishings.

A single folder lay on the right side of the desk with Tim's picture paper clipped to it. Tim assumed it was his new personnel folder.

The thing that caught Tim's eye was the planner. It was for the year 1967. The top sheet was May, with the eighth circled in bold red ink. He would have dismissed it if Zophar had not tapped the date with his finger. Tim focused on it with a strange fixation as if it were the only thing in the room.

Still reading his thoughts, Zophar asked, "Do you know the significance of May 8, 1967, Tim?"

"No, sir."

"That was the day of the Battle of Con Thien. Your dad was wounded and given the Bronze Star for bravery. Did he tell you about losing ten of his squad in that battle?" Not waiting for Tim to reply, he continued. "I remember one man in particular named Shawn O'Neal. I took his loss very personally. Too bad. He and I would have become such good friends."

Tim noticed Zophar's far-away stare and wondered about his meaning.

Zophar had patiently waited for the opportunity to destroy Mike's firstborn child. Now that he was about to do it, the excitement he expected was not there. Tim was a spiritual wimp compared to his dad and not worthy of his efforts. Still, he enjoyed the cat-and-mouse game he played with all of his victims.

"You're wondering about the chair, Tim? It's one of my few indulgences. I spend half my time here and want to be comfortable. At my age, those wooden chairs don't sit very well."

Just then, the desk phone rang. "Excuse me for a minute." Zophar picked up the phone and listened to the caller's short message. "OK, bring it in."

"Excuse me for a moment, boys." Zophar stepped out onto the landing and looked toward the back of the warehouse. He waved to someone, closed the door, and returned to his desk.

Tim heard the rear door open, and a car pulled in. Tim could tell it was a high-performance car as it drove across the warehouse floor. It stopped just below Zophar's office. The driver slowly revved the engine to a loud pitch and then turned it off just as the office windows started to vibrate.

Tim grinned at Kain, and together, they took the first sip of their beer. A little suggestion from Zophar and their heads began to spin. Now that Zophar had Tim and Kain's impaired attention and curiosity, he started his little sales pitch.

"Business may look slow around here to you, boys, but I'm so busy I need to add some part-time help. How would you two like a job? The work's not hard, pickups and deliveries mostly."

Zophar reached into his desk and laid two bulky Motorola cell phones on his desk. "You will need to be on call 24-7. These are strictly for business use only, you know." He then produced two credit cards and laid them on each phone. "Some of my associates are out of town, so I need you to travel occasionally. Your title will be an executive courier for Abaddon Industries. So what do you think? Does that sound like something you would be interested in?"

Tim and Kain sat there in total disbelief. The opportunity of a lifetime had just landed in their lap, and they were speechless.

Tim spoke first. "I don't know what to say, Zophar. Thank you. Yes, of course, I'll take the job."

"What about you, Kain? What do you say?"

With growing suspicion, Kain gave Zophar a long stare and replied, "All this seems too good to believe. How do we know this is legit?"

Tim turned quickly to challenge Kain's question. "What do you mean by that? Zophar is an old friend of my dad. Of course, his business is legit." Turning to Zophar, Tim added, "I'm sorry, Zophar. Maybe I shouldn't have brought Kain along."

"No, it's all right, Tim. I understand Kain's reluctance. He knows that opportunities like this don't come around very often. It's OK if he doesn't want to take the job. Unfortunately, I need both of you. Tell you what. I need to go downstairs and talk to my two associates. You two talk it over, and I'll be back in five minutes."

Zophar stood and left the room. Tim turned to face Kain. "What are you doing, man? Do you want to blow this deal for us? We can have it all—money, traveling the world chasing women."

"Tim, this deal sounds highly suspicious. I can't put my finger on it, but this setup is not right. Do you have any idea what we will be transporting?"

"Well, obviously, the man trusts us. For all we know, it will be money, diamonds, or something else of value. What do we care? Come on, Kain. At least try it for a week and see what you think. What could that hurt? I need this job, man. Do it for me," Tim said desperately.

Kain thought about it and replied, "OK, I'll try it for a week. However, I'll be gone if this turns out to be illegal. I have no interest in going back to jail."

"Great."

Zophar came back in and stood behind his chair. "Well, do I have two new employees or not?"

"Yes, sir," Tim said. "We've decided to come on board. When do we start?"

"Good. I've got a special pickup for you to make tomorrow evening, say, around five. You can start then. Here's a key to the back door. Always park inside and keep the door locked. Now let's go have some dinner."

Zophar picked up Tim's file and dropped it in the Progressing bin then led Tim and Kain downstairs to another surprise. "A black 1993 Dodge Charger. What do you think?"

"It's awesome," Tim answered. "Are you into fast cars?"

"No, I wouldn't be caught dead in that thing," Zophar replied. "This is your signing bonus, boys. You can take it with you tomorrow night. I'll meet you out front, and you can follow me to the restaurant."

Zophar got into his car and drove toward the rear door. Halfway through the warehouse, the door mysteriously opened and closed after he went through it.

"How do you suppose he did that?" Kain asked.

"Beats me. I wonder where his two associates are."

As Tim followed Kain to the front door, two ghostlike figures stepped out of the shadows and stood beside the Charger. When Kain had left the warehouse, Tim heard someone whisper his name. The soft sound increased in volume and faded as it rushed at him from various parts of the old warehouse. Tim felt someone watching him, so he quickly turned and scanned the area around the car and saw nothing.

One of the unseen forces gave Tim a suggestion, and he glanced down at the BRN2DY personalized tag on the front of the Charger. Its meaning was clear, and Tim got his first twinge of concern that maybe this undertaking was not such a good idea.

Now thoroughly spooked, Tim stepped quickly through the door and held the knob with both hands as if expecting something would follow him out. Nervously, he glanced over his shoulder to judge the distance to Kain's car. He then bailed, jumping from the dock platform to the ground. Once in the car, Tim's panic attack ended, giving way to a serenity that left him thinking of nothing but dinner at Peggy Sue's Barbecue.

Chapter 17

The Package

It was ten to five when Tim and Kain arrived at the warehouse's back door. Once inside, Kain pulled his car up next to their shiny new set of Hot Wheels. Slowly, they walked around the Charger, running their hands down its sleek lines. Zophar's light was on, so they quickly scaled the stairway and knocked on his office door.

"Now, that's what I like, punctuality. Come on in, boys. Are you ready to go to work?"

Tim replied, "Yes, we are, Zophar." Kain, still a little suspicious, offered only a forced smile.

With a beaming grin, Zophar answered, "Then welcome to the Abaddon family." Kain's doubtful expression did not escape Zophar's attention. He knew he would have to deal with his attitude at some point, but for now, Tim was his only assignment.

Kain cringed at the word *Abaddon*. He saw right through Zophar's façade and hoped Tim would recognize it before it was too late. They did not belong there, but Kain couldn't leave without Tim. He was older and felt responsible for Tim, who was just now beginning to understand the ropes.

There was a map of Dallas spread out on the desk. Zophar began to explain the details to his new associates. "I need you to

drive to Richardson, pick up a package, and bring it back here."
He handed Tim a slip of paper. "Here's the address. Do not draw
any attention to yourselves, so don't try and see how fast that
Charger will go. This trip will be a trial run to see how well you
do. It should not take you more than an hour and a half. Any
questions?"

"Just one," Tim asked. "How do we identify ourselves?"

"That's easy," Zophar said with an expanding grin. "They'll
recognize the car. Anything else?"

Tim and Kain both shook their heads no.

"Good. There's just one more thing." Zophar opened the desk
drawer, removed two loaded handguns, and laid them on the desk.

Stunned by this new development, Kain took a step backward.
Slowly, he raised his eyes to meet Zophar's taunting grin. After
an extended stare, he turned to Tim and said, "I told you I'm not
going back to jail."

Tim extended an open hand to tell Kain to wait. Then he
asked Zophar, "What do you want us to do with those?"

"You're transporting my valuables. Should someone try to take
them away from you, I expect you to stop them. If it helps, consider
yourselves my private security guards." After briefly pausing, he
added, "Either you take the guns, or I will get someone else to do
the job."

Zophar could have given Kain the necessary suggestions to
gain his cooperation. He was pleased to watch Tim squirm around
on his hook, and it was satisfying to watch Tim take Kain down
with him.

Tim took both guns off the desk and turned to face Kain.
Tim pleaded with Kain, offering him one. "You promised me you
would do this job for a week. You can do this, man."

A hundred things raced through Kain's mind as he weighed
the pros and cons of joining Zophar's shady enterprise. The job of

a lifetime was within his grasp, and all he had to do was take the gun. As concerned as he was about being caught and sent back to jail, Kain could not help but wonder how much money Zophar would pay him for this hour-and-a-half service.

With inspiration from Zophar, Tim added, "Kain, think about the money. Credit cards, travel, short hours, a cool car to drive. What more could you want?"

Kain looked at Zophar with distrust for a few seconds. Unfazed by the hesitation, Zophar smiled and patiently waited for Kain to make up his mind. Tim was praying that Kain would not let him down.

Finally, Kain took the gun from Tim and glaring at Zophar, replied, "This is not what I signed on for, but I told Tim I would give it a try. So I guess I'm in."

"That's good," Zophar said. "You won't be sorry when you get your first paycheck. Remember to be back here by six thirty. I'm expecting another call, so there might be another run tonight. Now off you go and be careful."

Reassuring Kain he had made the right decision, Tim put his arm around his shoulder as they left the office. "How about you drive? I'll navigate."

Still stewing over the terms of his employment, Kain didn't say a word as they walked down to the car. He fired up the engine and gave it a brief acceleration then drove to the back of the warehouse. Tim got out and pushed the button to open the door. He closed it after Kain went through.

Driving a car with so much horsepower seemed to calm Kain's despondency. When they pulled out onto Highway 75, both men felt cocky.

It took them thirty minutes to find the address in Richardson. Tim exited the car and knocked on the front door. From inside came the sounds of country music and laughter.

An attractive, slender blond answered the door, wearing a black tight-fitting jumpsuit zipped midway up in the front. Tim estimated she was about the same age as his mom.

"Is there anything I can do for you, young man?" came her seductive query.

Blushing, Tim stammered, "Yes, I'm here to pick up a package."

Looking past him and seeing the Charger, she replied, "Wait here a minute." Leaving the door open, she turned and strolled to the other side of the room, ensuring that Tim got an eyeful of her backside. Returning, she handed him a small brown paper package.

Reaching over to straighten his collar, she added, "You tell Zophar that Kitty approves of his new runner. Stop by if you're not doing anything later tonight. I promise to make it worth your while." Pulling him close, she lightly kissed and released him. Tim's slow-forming grin exposed his inexperience. Kitty gave him a wink as her eyes disappeared behind the slowly closing door.

Tim got in the car and buckled his seat belt. Turning to Kain, he said, "From now on, man, you're the designated driver."

"What is this place?"

"I'm pretty sure it's a cathouse, dude, and the madam here is drop-dead gorgeous." Tim said goodbye to the last of his inhibitions, saying, "She invited us to come back after work tonight."

Kain was about to voice his approval when he spotted a police cruiser turn the corner and slowly approach them from the front. "Tim, it's the cops."

"Well, play it cool, man. We haven't done anything wrong." Kain's gun lay on the seat between them. Tim quickly put both weapons in the glove box and shut it just as the police car pulled up and stopped beside them. Slowly, the driver's window opened. Reluctantly, Kain rolled his window down.

Tim couldn't count on how Kain would handle the situation, so he leaned forward and asked, "Is there anything wrong, Officer?"

"That's a nice car, boys. A little out of place for this neighborhood, though," said the driver. "What are you two doing on this side of town?"

Tim held up a map he had retrieved from the glove box and replied, "We must have missed a turn somewhere, Officer. We need to get back to our dorm. Can you help us find US-75 South?"

The two officers looked them over carefully. Kain acted so nervously Tim thought he would give them away.

The cruiser driver asked Kain, "Can I see your license and registration?"

While Kain removed his wallet and handed the officer his license, Tim partially opened the glove box and removed the registration under the guns. He handed it to Kain, who gave it to the officer.

"I see this car belongs to Abaddon Industries. Do you work for Zophar?"

Kain could already feel the handcuffs. There was no doubt in his mind they were going to jail. He thought about the guns and started to panic.

"Yes, sir, we work for Zophar," Tim replied.

The officer began to study Kain more closely. When the two officers started talking, Tim was sure one recognized Kain from somewhere.

The officer returned the papers to Kain, saying, "US-75 is about a half mile from here. Follow us. By the way, tell Zophar he needs to get rid of that personalized plate. It's against the law in Texas. The next time, we'll give him a ticket. Understand?"

Tim replied, "Yes, sir, we'll tell him."

Surprised but grateful, Kain turned the car around and followed the police cruiser to the highway. He flashed his lights at the officers, took the on-ramp, and headed back toward Dallas.

Kain pulled the Charger back into the warehouse at six twenty-five. Feeling good about their run, he and Tim walked up the stairs and knocked on Zophar's door. Zophar looked up and waved them in. Inside, they walked over and stood in front of the desk. Tim handed him the package and waited for him to inspect it.

"Nice job, boys. You're right on time. Have a seat. Were there any problems?"

With their memories blocked of their encounter with the cops, Tim replied proudly, "No, there were no problems."

Zophar unwrapped the package and produced six stacks of twenty-dollar bills. "Here's a little advancement on your paycheck, boys." Sitting the money on the desk, he slid two stacks across to Tim and Kain, who sat there reveling in their good fortune.

Both men acknowledged their appreciation, and Zophar continued. "I assume you met Kitty. She's one of my best associates. You'll need to watch out for her, though. She knows things most women never heard of."

"She sent her regards," blushing, Tim replied.

"I'm sure she did," Zophar said with a sly grin. "I need you, boys, to make two deliveries to some other associates tonight. Their names and addresses are in this envelope. Try to be back here by nine. Are there any questions?"

"No, sir. We can handle it," Tim responded.

Zophar turned his attention to Kain and waited to see how he would reply.

Kain looked at the three stacks of bills in front of him. Each is wrapped in a white banding with $2,000 printed on it. Now that he could put a dollar value on the risks he would be taking, his involvement in Zophar's little scam was a little more palatable.

Kain studied Zophar's face carefully and wondered how much he could be trusted. If he knew people on the police force, maybe he knew a judge or two that could keep them out of trouble.

Tim squirmed in his chair at Kain's prolonged hesitation. When he couldn't stand it any longer, Tim asked pleadingly, "Kain?"

Without expression, Kain turned to face him. After another few moments of silence, he answered, "Tim, this setup is as illegal as it gets. If we get caught, they will put us away for a long time." Kain pointed to the money before them and added, "That's a lot of temptation, Tim. Are you sure you want to do this?"

Tim's first impulse was to say yes, but something deep inside warned him of the consequences of his answer. He looked at the money and then up at Zophar. So sure of what Tim would say, Zophar released his mental hold on him and allowed Tim to make a freewill choice.

Kain was right. Zophar was a shady character, certainly not someone his dad would call a friend. While the money, friends, and free-spirited lifestyle were all nice perks, it was not what drove him to this decision. When his dad was alive, he was content to play the part of a Christian. Now that Mike was gone, Tim felt like an orphan and alone in the world.

Knowing this decision would determine how he would live the rest of his life, Tim considered the two roads he could travel. The rough road would be admitting to himself, his mom, and his church that he had been wrong about God. The smooth path would be continuing with a lifestyle that gave him the freedom to be his own man.

With his decision made, Tim gave Kain and Zophar his final answer. "Yes, I do."

Kain turned to Zophar in a businesslike manner and said, "Then I think we're both in."

"Good," Zophar said as he handed Tim a plain-looking briefcase. "There are two packages inside this case, each marked with the name of whom you will give them to and the directions. Tell the recipients that everything is on for tonight. Any questions?"

"No, sir."

"Good. Where are your guns?"

"They're in the car," Tim replied.

"It is company policy to carry them whenever you're on the clock. Understand?"

"Yes, sir. It won't happen again," Tim replied.

"Make sure it doesn't. Now get going," Zophar said with a snarl.

Tim thought something was unusual in Zophar's instructions as they walked down to the car. It was almost like he gave him a mystery to solve. *What is on for tonight?*

Inside the car, Tim opened the envelope and read the contents. "Our first delivery is in Farmers Branch. Take Singleton Boulevard through West Dallas, then north at Highway 12."

"The interstate will be faster," Kain replied.

"What, ten minutes? We're not in that much of a hurry."

Kain acknowledged his approval with a simple "Bueno."

As Kain drove to the back of the warehouse, Tim felt something wasn't right. A quick review of his most likely oversights produced no clues. Kain stopped at the door, and Tim got out to open the door. Still unsettled, he inspected the backseat closely as the car pulled through. Tim pushed the button again and stepped outside to wait for the door to close. He then got back into the car, and they were on their way.

Kain was quiet as they drove to the first delivery point. This gave Tim time to think about what Zophar said about everything being on for tonight. *What does that mean? What are we transporting?* Anxiety had given way to curiosity, but Zophar kept him from maintaining a steady thought.

Tim studied the map with increasing anticipation and guided them to a one-story office complex on Josey Lane. Kain parked in front of the building next to a shiny new black Audi. Through a well-lit window, Tim could see a man wearing a western-fitted shirt and a cowboy hat sitting at a desk just inside the door.

"Well, this is quite different from the warehouse," Tim whispered. He got out of the car and walked over to the door. Suddenly, the apprehensions he felt in the warehouse were back. Needing reassurance, Tim glanced around and made eye contact with Kain, who waved him onward. Hesitantly, Tim knocked on the door.

"Come in," the man shouted in a deep, gruff Texas twang.

Tim opened the door and stepped inside just enough so the door could not be closed behind him. He waited patiently as the man continued to hammer at his computer keyboard.

"I'll be with you in a moment," came a second voice in a distinct Yankee accent. Tim noticed the different voices but dismissed them as his imagination.

Tim noticed a box on the desk with a business card taped to the top: Joseph Eliphaz, Vice President of Product Transportation, Abaddon & Associates. Tim questioned why someone in transportation would work in a small remote office like this.

Finally, the man stopped his work and began to proofread his entry. Growing more concerned by the second, Tim lifted his right hand behind his back and checked the handgun he had tucked inside of his belt.

The man finally looked up and demanded, "Who the hell are you, and what do you want?" Tim was sure he heard yet another voice.

The man's tone was enough to tell Tim he was in trouble if this was the wrong address. "Zophar sent me to deliver a package," he said nervously.

"Zophar, huh? My name's Eliphaz. You wouldn't be Tim, would you, amigo?"

"Yes, sir," Tim stammered.

"Well, that's good," the man said as he lifted a newspaper to reveal a .45 Colt lying on the desk. "Well, where is it?"

Shaken by the gun, Tim replied weakly, "Where's what, sir?"

"The package, you dummkopf. Give me the package."

Freaked by a sixth voice, this one a German female, Tim hurriedly opened the briefcase and handed him the package with his name on it. Uninterested, Eliphaz took the parcel and flipped it onto the desk. Surprised by the gesture, the mystery of its contents intensified.

Tim wanted to leave as quickly as he could. "Zophar wanted me to tell you everything is on for tonight."

"So tonight's the night. Did Zophar remember to invite you?"

Hearing yet another voice, this one very friendly, Tim was ready to run, but curiosity now held him by the nose. "No. Invite me to what?"

"Why, the big party, of course. Zophar just made another acquisition. So it's time for all of us Abaddon employees to celebrate. Don't worry, you and your friend outside can go as my guests. I'm sure it was an oversight. As new associates, the Boss would insist on you being there."

Eliphaz broke out with a big smile. Standing, he walked around the desk, vigorously shook Tim's hand, and backed him out the door. "Tell Zophar that I'll be there. See you later. G'day, mate."

The door closed, leaving Tim on the sidewalk, wondering what had just happened. Seconds later, the light shining through the window went off. Tim inched his way to the window and peeked inside. To his surprise, the furnishings were all gone. Instead, all the signs of an office under renovation were scattered about the room. Turning, Tim noticed that the black Audi was also gone. It was as if everything associated with Eliphaz had vanished.

Tim replayed it in his mind to reassure himself that his conversation with Eliphaz had really happened. The one thing that stood out to him was the man's speech. He counted at least nine different voices, each with its own tone and personality. Mean, friendly, threatening, then happy. It was almost like he was schizophrenic or something.

Back in the car, Kain asked, "Well, I guess the dude wasn't home. Too bad. Where are we heading next, Tim?"

Unable to explain this bizarre encounter, Tim franticly searched for an explanation to two mysteries: was Eliphaz real, and why did Kain not see him? *I know that he was real. I know I talked to him. I touched him. Why did Kain not see him?* Then the package came to mind.

Quickly, Tim opened the briefcase and discovered one package was missing. At least partially relieved, Tim had to figure out why Kain didn't see Eliphaz. Or did he?

They had known each other for two years. Kain was three years older and in many ways, was Tim's mentor. Until now, there had been no indication that Kain couldn't be trusted. What would motivate him to start now? The more Tim thought about it, the more suspicious he became. Leaning far back in his seat, Tim looked at Kain and wondered what he was up to.

Hiding his feelings, Tim replied, "Irving. Back down Highway 12."

Suddenly, Tim heard someone whisper his name. The sound rapidly pulsated through the car. He turned quickly to inspect an empty backseat. "Did you hear that, man?"

"Hear what?"

"Someone whispered my name."

"I didn't hear anything, Tim. Relax. This is your first job. It's only the jitters."

"Yeah. That's it—the jitters," Tim said apprehensively. His emotions had now moved from suspicions back to fear. "I think

I'm losing my mind, man. Let's get out of here," he whispered as he looked at the vacant building.

When Kain pulled out onto Josey Lane, Tim's worries melted away. His thoughts were now focused on Kitty and the good time she had promised him tonight.

* * *

Kain exited the highway and turned west onto E. Irving Boulevard. Following Tim's instructions, he turned onto South Main Street toward Heritage Park.

Tim pointed and said, "That's the building on the left. Turn around and park in front."

"The lights are off, Tim. It looks like this dude's not home either."

"Yeah. It looks that way."

Kain made a U-turn and parked in front of the building.

A dozen teenagers were quietly assembled at two picnic benches across the street, all staring at the building as if waiting for someone. The park was well-lit, but Tim's side of the road was dark and deserted.

"Doesn't that scene look strange to you, Tim?" Kain said as he nodded toward the teen assembly.

"Yeah, almost like something is about to go down."

"Who are we supposed to meet here again?"

"The man's name is Bildad."

From the car, Tim could see the bustle of patrons frequenting three restaurants in the next block. Their laughter and actions indicated that more than one had too much to drink. Tim glanced at his watch: 8:15.

They sat in the car, waiting for Bildad to show up. Quickly, their patience started to wear thin.

"This guy's not going to show either, Tim. We need to leave. These kids across the street are starting to bug me. I think they're waiting on this Bildad too."

"Zophar will not like it if we leave without delivering this package. Let's give it another few minutes. Bildad knows to meet us here."

Tim realized he had been staring at the traffic light at the corner, counting its cycle of changes: green, yellow, red. Five times, it had advanced. Curious about how much time had passed, Tim glanced at his watch again—still 8:15.

Once again, Tim's fretfulness hit him with a gigantic thud. Tim was now in panic mode again, feeling like he couldn't breathe. "I'm gonna knock on the door, man. Then we'll get out of here."

Tim got out of the car and quickly stepped to the door. Throwing his usual timidity aside, Tim pounded on the entryway. "Bildad, are you in there?" Waiting only a few seconds, Tim beat the door again. After a third desperate attempt, he slowly backed away until he bumped into the car.

While he was at home, Tim always had a sheltered and pampered life. Mike had been a doting father, smoothing out the rough edges for him. Now that his dad was gone, there was no one to help him with decisions. It wasn't until he met Kain that he had to start weighing the consequences against his choices.

For the first time in his life, Tim faced a new emotion—regret. The strange events of the last few hours had made him seriously reconsider his involvement with Zophar and Kain. Tim now felt hopelessly alone. Instead of looking to God for help, his only thought was of his mother.

Now that Zophar had broken Tim's spirit, it was time for the final scene of a life without God.

Sensing something to his left, Tim gradually turned his head toward the intersection. A tall, well-built man stood at the far light, waiting to cross over. Dressed in black, he cast the image of a modern-day version of the Grim Reaper. When it cycled to green, the man stepped into the street. Slowly, he walked toward Tim. Each step brought a heightened sense of trepidation.

The teenagers in the park all stood in expectancy. Turning to face them, Bildad sent them a message to be patient. In unison, they all sat back down.

The man stopped a few steps away and with penetrating eyes, stared deep into Tim's soul. This intrusion gave him the feeling he was on an operating table, having his last bit of goodness surgically removed. Each extraction brought Tim a more profound awareness of his shame. Purified of his feelings toward God, Tim was now ready to meet the Caretaker.

The man released Tim from his mental hold and waited for him to regain his thoughts. "You wouldn't be Tim, would you?" The man's nefarious tone made Tim's blood run cold.

Terrified, Tim replied, "Yes, I'm looking for the man who lives here. His name is Bildad."

"My name is Bildad. Do you have a package for me?" With a mental proposal, Bildad removed all of Tim's fears.

Calmly, Tim replied, "Yes, sir, I do." Tim opened the case and handed him his package.

"Thank you, Tim. I understand that everything is on for tonight. Correct?"

"Yes, sir," Tim said confidently.

"Good. Make sure you're there on time. We could not start the party until our newest acquisition is present."

Oblivious to Bildad's true meaning, Tim thanked him and got into the car.

"Who was that creepy guy, Tim?"

"That was Bildad. He has his package. Now we are free to go." Tim spotted the teenagers across the street standing, and added, "Pull up to the light and stop. Let's see what happens next."

Bildad walked to his door, unlocked it, and turned on the lights. He then motioned to the crowd it was time to assemble. "Come, my children. It's time for fun and games." Tim and Kain watched twelve drug-starved adolescents rush across the street and into the building. Casting a final glance at Tim, Bildad entered the building and turned off the lights.

"Well, I'll be damned, Tim. Bildad is nothing but a drug dealer. Now let's get out of here."

"That sounds good to me. We have a company party back at the warehouse, and I'm sure Zophar will not mind us leaving early to go to Kitty's."

*   *   *

It was nine thirty when they pulled into the warehouse. Tim was expecting to see some signs of a party. Instead, the warehouse was dark. Even the light in Zophar's office was off. Maybe he misunderstood, and the party was elsewhere.

Kain pulled up and parked next to his car. He then shut the engine off but left the headlights on. Getting out of the car, Tim took the briefcase and stood in front of the Charger. "That's strange. Zophar's car isn't here. He's not here."

Kain got out of the car and walked around behind Tim. "He's up there, Tim. He'll be down in a minute."

The bullet hit Tim in the back and lodged in his liver. He went down hard; blood immediately started to flow. The impact of his fall jarred Tim's gun loose from his belt, and it lay beside him.

Tim was still alive and conscious when Kain rolled him onto his back. He displayed no emotion as he looked Tim in the eye and took his phone, credit card, and money. Kain placed both phones and credit cards in the briefcase. Closing it, he laid it on the hood of the Charger. Pocketing the money, he walked back and stood next to Tim.

At the top of the stairs, three spirits appeared to witness the final chapter of their twenty-five-year vendetta against Tim's family. Resembling jackals, Zophar, Bildad, and Eliphaz stared down at him with contempt. In an instant, the three disappeared and reappeared to join Kain around the body lying before them. They snickered as they watched Tim labor to take his final breaths.

"Tim, can you hear me? Are you still alive?" Zophar asked scoffingly.

Tim looked at his three dispatchers in pain and asked, "Why? What did I do to you?"

"Oh, it wasn't you, dear boy," Zophar said. "It was your dad. He stole something from us twenty-five years ago, and we swore we would pay him back one day. Unfortunately for you, today was that day."

Tim knew he was dying, getting weaker with every drop of blood that flowed from his body.

"You're bleeding out, Tim. You'll be dead in a minute. However, before you go, we have one more thing for you to do."

In unison, the unholy threesome combined their energies into a single telepathic thought and gave Tim his final instruction.

Tim reached for the gun lying beside him. With the last of his strength, he lifted it toward Kain and pulled the trigger. Kain had little time to react before the bullet struck him in the chest, killing him instantly. Tim's arm fell to the floor with the gun still in his hand. Tim glanced at the body beside him and turned back to face Zophar.

"Do you have any last words, Tim?"

Tim whispered, "God, I'm sorry for all I have done." Convinced he had settled his debt with God, he closed his eyes and died, thinking only about being with his dad in heaven.

When Tim had breathed his last, the passenger side door of the Charger opened. The front seat was pushed forward, and a fourth spirit stepped out of the backseat and closed the door. With the pride of a protective father, Legion stepped forward and joined his three favorite assassins. "Well done, my devils. The old wound has now been healed. The Boss will be pleased to have this one finally cleaned up."

Legion looked down at Tim and thought about his dad. "Mike Shaffer was a worthy opponent. A great man of faith. His son, however, was not much of a challenge. At least he is one less soul that will see the Creator's Kingdom.

"Tim, later tonight, an anonymous tip will lead the police to this warehouse and find your body. Investigators will find the money, Kain's car, and the drugs we will leave behind. They will decide it was a gang-related argument. Your mom will have to live with this little scandal you left her. Sleep tight, my son. When you wake up, we have one final surprise for you."

Legion waited while his associates arranged the crime scene perfectly—every detail put in place—so that no one would ever suspect they were there.

"Zophar, you and Eliphaz meet Bildad and me at Kitty's place to discuss your next assignments. We'll take the Charger. I've always wanted to drive one of these fast cars."

Zophar uncloaked his Caddy parked a few feet away. Laughing, the four evil spirits stepped into their cars, pulled out the back door, and drove off into the night—ready for their next conquest.

Chapter 18

Tim Meets the Caretaker

Tim sat with his eyes closed. His mind was alert but not seeking clues to explain his surroundings. Occasionally, he could hear a noise or sense a movement. However, the disconnect with his mind had shut down all his physical responses and motor skills.

While his body sat there unresponsively, Tim's soul was trying to communicate with his brain, telling it to wake up and prepare for the approaching danger. His carnal nature had been the controlling factor in all of Tim's actions. He had limited his soul to that of a moral compass, continually reminding him of right and wrong but possessing no spiritual conviction. In death, his soul waited to assume responsibility for all the crimes his body had committed against God.

Most religious people go through life thinking the road to heaven is dependent upon good deeds and behaviors. Tim's soul knew that assumption was false, but years of explaining that to his brain had failed. Now, all that remained of his wasted life was the punishment that goes with telling a benevolent God no.

Tim's spiritual coma ended with his first thought in a millennium: *Where am I?*

Instantly, his eyes shot open in worry. Surrounding him was a softly lit expanse that appeared to exist within a cloud. Tim considered the possibility he was inside a sphere or containment facility. The only word that came to mind was separation—from what he did not yet know.

Turning his attention to the floor, Tim saw something resembling a conveyor belt. His next discovery was that he sat on what was like an old movie theater seat, his being one of fifty other connected chairs in his row. There was one row in front and an endless number of rows behind him—bodies as far as the eye could see. Each body wore an orange uniform with a white name tag engraved in an unknown language. Tim tried to convince himself this place was heaven, but if it was, it was not what he had expected.

Tim watched the empty row in front of him move forward and fall into a trap door. He felt his row move forward a short distance and stop, leaving him now seated in the last seat of the first row. A door appeared at the far end of his row and opened. The body in the first seat stood up and walked through, with the door closing behind it. There was a pause before the door moved and opened to receive the next body. It also disappeared through the door.

At first, the movement of the door down his row was rapid. Then as the door got closer to Tim's body, the slower it seemed to move. This gave Tim time to search for answers about this most unusual place. Slowly, bits and pieces of memory began to break through the veil.

The first thing that came to mind was his name. *My name is Tim Shaffer. I graduated from Garland High School and am a sophomore at SMU. I have a sister named Rebecca. My parents are Mike and Kate Shaffer.*

Tim paused as he remembered his dad's death. There were no emotions to evoke any feelings of loss. A self-centered lifestyle had isolated him from the true meaning of love, so Tim broke off his relationships with friends and family as his heart hardened toward God. In the end, his dad was the only one he cared anything about.

In comparison, Tim and his dad were polarized opposites. Mike was the personification of love. On the other hand, Tim was so obsessed with his self-worth that he never had time for anything other than what best fit his humanistic lifestyle.

There was a dark side to Tim that he kept carefully hidden. To those who knew him, he appeared to be a good person who attended church occasionally and feared God. However, he always held church commitments and responsibilities at arm's length. Ministry and sacrificial giving weren't part of his thinking process. Therefore, he avoided charity and goodwill like the plague.

Tim was not a patient person. Like many of his generation, he wanted the things in life to be given to him without having to work for them. From his first impression, Tim guessed that time and possessions in this strange place had no tangible meaning. He did not know that love and grace were alien to this place.

While the room was at a pleasant ambient temperature, Tim felt a warm breeze brush across his face. Its foul odor gave him a hint of sulfur and burning flesh.

In front of him, Tim noticed a previously unseen curtain gently moving. A faint red-and-white light glimmered as it moved behind it. A different curtain moved from another side of the room as another soft glow danced across its far side. Then other subtle movements could be seen everywhere: walls, ceiling, and floor. How odd, Tim thought, that the curtains on the ceiling and floor were all hanging horizontally. The glimmering light and odor were now part of Tim's growing list of questions.

Looking back over his shoulder, he noticed someone he recognized two rows back. In all, Tim counted five other people from his past. Then he spotted Kain sitting in the row behind him. As they made eye contact, Tim remembered Kain as the one who killed him. However, instead of thinking about revenge, he accepted it as nothing meaningful now.

Perhaps the most unusual thing about Tim's surroundings was the occasional vacant seat. In the row behind him, he counted two. In the row behind that, there were three.

With his brain fully engaged with his soul, Tim tried to sort through all the questions that raced through his brain. His fear of the door began to mount as he watched it draw closer. Tim's mind dared to ask its first significant question: *Is this place heaven?*

Sarcastically, Tim's soul gave the brain the bad news. *Does this place look like heaven to you? If it weren't for you, we wouldn't be here.*

Tim's brain refused to accept his counterpart's suggestion. *Maybe heaven is through that door.*

Are you serious? screamed the soul. *You don't get it, do you?*

Ignoring the question, the brain asked its second question. *Who are all these people?*

These are the lost souls of earth, the soul replied. *Once they die and are judged by God, they come here to receive their punishment. I warned you a thousand times about this place. You were too stupid to listen.*

The brain assumed his body was dead or somehow immobilized, but refused to admit this place could be hell.

The door moved to the seat next to him and opened. The body rose and entered. Then the door closed. Tim could see that the door was nothing but a frame with no depth.

Tim's brain asked a final question: *What about the vacant chairs? Where are those bodies?*

Before his soul could answer, the door opened in front of Tim. Deep inside, an ominous voice beckoned, "Tim Shaffer, the Caretaker will see you now."

Until now, the only movement Tim had was his head. So he had no awareness of any feeling below the neck. When his body stood and stepped toward the door, Tim realized he had no control over it.

The body paused at the threshold to reveal a blackness that Tim could not grasp. He glanced over his shoulder and watched the now-empty first row of seats descend into the floor. Then the next row of bodies moved forward to replace it.

As his body stepped through the door, it was in total darkness. There was no light seeping in through the still-open door. It was as if Tim had stepped into the back of a cave. The darkness was so dense that Tim could feel its weight pressing on his face. His first sensation was mild suffocation. He knew this was his last breath of freedom if he could call it that. Tim had been clinging to a thread of hope, but when he heard the door slam behind him, he knew all hope was gone.

The body walked a short distance into the blackness and stopped. Tim faced two dimly lit gray stone pillars supporting an overhead plank. Carved into the plank were the words "The Graveyard of Pride." Tim's eyes were drawn to the writing like a magnet, making it impossible for him to look away. Tim's head was forced backward as the body moved under the plank. His eyes felt like they were being pulled from their sockets. Once the words were no longer visible, Tim's head slammed down hard onto his chest.

After his eyes had adjusted to the dimness, Tim realized he was on a narrow bridge. The lighting along the bridge gave the effect of a hole through the darkness. Lacking side barriers, Tim considered that a fall from this bridge would be into a bottomless pit.

The bridge emptied onto a landing where a man sat at a desk. In front of the desk was a single chair. Standing to the right of the desk was a tall creature Tim perceived as a fallen angel. His two charred wing stubs symbolized his high rank in the underworld. His function at this reception was that of a bailiff. Behind the bailiff was a massive red metal door with a large deadbolt lock.

Tim could only watch as his body continued to walk across the bridge. Each step he took brought on an increased sense of dread. Glances toward the man at the desk told Tim he would not be the bearer of any good news.

Before he reached the end of the bridge, the body stopped to face a mirror that suddenly appeared. On Tim's forehead was branded the number 666. Tim's worst nightmare had come true. He had the mark of the beast, and he was in hell. Tim wanted to run and hide, but even if he could, where would he go?

"Take a good look, Tim," called the man. "Your whole life has been a lie, and now you must pay for your sins."

The body walked to the chair and plopped down. The man in front of him wore a black uniform. On his chest was a name tag that read "Head Caretaker." Tim understood instantly it was Legion. Sitting on the desk was a file with Tim's picture and name scripted on it. It was the same file that was in Zophar's office.

Expressionless, Legion stared back at Tim for a long minute. When he finally spoke, it was with a deep, authoritative voice.

"Welcome to the Graveyard of Pride, Tim. This is what you can call your orientation meeting. Out here, we like to keep things relaxed." Without turning, Legion's thumb pointed to the door behind the bailiff and added, "In there, things are quite different. I assure you that hell is not what you think it is. There are no little men in red suits and pitchforks sitting on your shoulder, tempting you to do things you know you shouldn't. You are here because Christos refused you access to his kingdom. Our job is to make sure you never forget why.

"The purpose of this meeting is to allow you to ask questions about why you're here and not in that other place. Before we get to that, let me introduce you to those who helped orchestrate your transition to our little shop of horrors."

Three spirits randomly materialized behind Legion. "I think you've already met Zophar, Eliphaz, and Bildad. They were instrumental in guiding you through your failed attempt at life. Normally, I send them out on our most difficult cases. Your dad was up to their challenge. You, however, were hardly worth their time. I don't mind telling you, Tim. For them, getting you here was all about revenge."

Legion picked up Tim's dossier and asked, "Do you know what this is, Tim? This book is a record of everything you've done in life. Let me read you the first entry: 'My son, Tim, was born today.' God made that entry, Tim, and he was proud of you for the first few years of your life. However, things changed as you got older. His next-to-last entry was this: 'My son, Tim, rejected me today for the last time. He does not love me anymore.'

"Do you know what day that was, Tim? It was the day they buried your dad. I'll get to God's final entry in a minute. Now, Tim, what question would you like to ask first?"

Tim had always called himself a Christian. However, as far as faith-producing works were concerned, there was none to offer in his defense. In terror, Tim glanced at the door and worried about what awaited him on the other side.

"You should be worried, Tim. Your meaningless life has led you to this moment, and you're about to get everything you deserve." Legion smirked as he remembered that these were the exact words Mike said to him that night at Con Thien.

"It says in your book that you lied to that nice Sunday school teacher, Mrs. Stevens, and your best friend, Brad. It also records that your intentions toward Mary Jones were anything but honorable. Of course, you lied to your dad about that too. He knew better, and it crushed him, but he never said a word to you about it.

"You didn't just lie to your dad, Tim. You lied to God. If you've got something to say in your defense, now is your last chance to say it."

As Tim fretfully searched his mind for that one reason why he should not be there, the four demons followed his mental efforts like they were watching it on a computer screen. The harder he thought, the more they leaned forward in anticipation of Tim's predictable response.

"Tim, surely there is something you can offer in your defense. A single act of kindness, maybe. Possibly offering a glass of water to someone parched or giving some crumbs to a starving man. Perhaps you once bought some Girl Scout cookies or something," Legion added mockingly. "Think harder, Tim. Time's running out."

Tim saw himself fast approaching that moment of truth he had avoided his entire life. Unable to find anything that would keep him from the fate he had brought upon himself, he finally gave up and asked the only question available to him. With a humbled and defeated spirit, he asked, "Why am I here?"

"Well, Tim," Legion replied, slamming the palm of his hand down hard on the desk, "that's a great question. I'm glad you asked that one first. It's simple, really. You were born in sin, and by your own choices, you're still wearing it like an anvil around your neck. You had a chance to have that yoke taken from you, but you said no. You thumbed your nose at Christos, and now you must pay the piper.

"I bet you're wondering about your so-called profession of faith. We were there the night you made it, Tim, sitting just a few rows behind you. You fooled everyone, but we knew better. Do you know how we could tell? It was your body odor. You went down there smelling like sin and came back smelling like sin. Nothing changed, Tim. It was all empty words. No commitment.

No sincerity. Your attempt at fooling God was so pitiful you didn't believe it yourself. So you went right on sinning.

"You see, Tim, God made this place for both of us. After the final battle, he put us in here as overseers. Now, because of your unpardoned sin, he sent you down here as well. As it turns out, Tim, our two punishments are the same. I bet you did not know that. Did you, Tim?" Legion laughed at how easily it had been to keep that truth secret from so many.

"We see many like you come through here thinking their insincere profession of faith was good enough to save them from God's wrath. This brings me to a question, Tim. Do you remember standing before God at the Judgment?"

Tim's first thought was no; then it came flooding back to him.

"Remember what God said to you when he did not find your name in the Book of Life? It was his final entry into your book, Tim. GUILTY!" Legion screamed.

"Now you're down here with the rest of us—FOREVER.

"Your pride kept you from accepting God's offer of salvation, Tim. You thought you could get to heaven on your terms, and now look where you are."

Tim's fear of hell was great, but his fear of God was now so overwhelming it felt like he was holding up a mountain. Now, for the first time in his life, Tim could see how worthless his life truly was.

Tim became aware of a vile stench emanating from his body. Looking down, he saw rottenness festering on his arms. In moments, his entire body was covered in painful boils.

"Tim, you've spent your entire life thinking your pitiful excuse for faith would save you. Your dad believed in a Savior who died on a cross and rose from the grave. All you cared about was your self-righteousness. Even I know how pathetic that is.

"You wanted to know about those empty seats, Tim. Those are the only ones who made it to heaven. Do you know why there were so few? Unlike you, they took their faith seriously. Your dad believed in divine purpose, and he fulfilled his. You were called and never surrendered to yours. Think about it, Tim. God offered you a free pardon from this place, and you turned him down. How do you explain that, Tim?" Legion laughed and added, "Just as I thought. No answer.

"We are just about finished here, Tim. However, I do have something I want to show you."

Legion pointed to the expanse above them. "Look at your family, Tim. Notice how happy they are. I don't have to tell you who is standing there with them."

Tim looked up and saw an image of what he knew was heaven. There was his family talking to the Lord. They were all dressed in white robes and crowns of glory. Tears streamed down his face as regret began to engulf him. He tried to open his mouth and shout to them, but Legion cut him off.

"Don't bother, Tim. They can't hear or see you. Because they are not capable of regret, you're nothing more than a long-forgotten memory. It's like you never existed."

The anguish of a life wasted was devastating to Tim. So he hung his head in shame.

Legion closed Tim's book and handed it to the bailiff, who, in turn, handed Legion the book for his next appointment.

"Tim, because you have been convicted of treason by the High Court, it is my pleasure to administer your punishment. Bailiff, execute the verdict."

The bailiff motioned for Tim to come. Obediently, his body stood and walked to the door.

"You won't need that uniform where you're going, Tim."

Tim's body unbuttoned the uniform and let it fall to the floor. His exposed nakedness was his final humiliation.

"There are only three rules down here, Tim. First, you can weep and wail all you want to, but talking is strictly forbidden. Second, gnashing teeth is optional, but I think you will find it unavoidable in time. Third, once you reach your assigned plot, you are required to kneel in honor of Christos for all eternity."

Tim watched anxiously as the deadbolt moved and the door slowly opened. Flames rushed into the room. To his surprise, the fire burned but did not consume him. The smell of sulfur saturated the air. The sensation that struck him first was dehydration.

"Get used to the thirst, Tim. There's not a drop of water down here."

Tim turned his head and saw small stands of flame dancing around the room, reflecting off gently moving curtains. With his last question now answered, it was time for him to enter his eternal home. Tim stared into the flames and waited.

After the body passed through the door, it closed with a loud echoing boom. There was a creaking sound as the deadbolt slid back into place. From every direction came the sound of a dull, low-pitched hum, as if sung by a large choir singing the same lamenting note.

Far below him was an endless flaming landscape that radiated a slow-pulsating orange glow. From a distance, two foreboding spirits approached him. Taking his arms, they flew Tim to a small plot reserved especially for him. As the spirits released him, he gently floated down to the ground. The two demons waited for him to assume his required kneeling position. Tim realized his mind had regained control over his body as he prostrated himself. Reaching down, he touched the earth and felt its searing heat.

"Get used to it, stupid," said his soul. "If you had listened to me, we would be with your family now."

Around him were thousands of spirits escorting new arrivals to their place of internment. Glancing around, Tim saw 65 billion other flaming bodies kneeling, weeping, and gnashing their teeth in misery.

In agony, Tim bowed his head and cried, "Lord, I am genuinely sorry for everything I have done."

"It's too late for second chances, Tim," Legion broadcasted. "God has disowned you. He is no longer listening to your pitiful prayers."

Tim looked down and saw what looked like roots coming out of the ground and attaching themselves around his feet and knees, securing him in place. Tim was not just a prisoner in confinement; he was now permanently attached to this horrible dungeon he unwittingly chose for himself.

The inmate's body to his right was ablaze and riddled with painful boils. His macabre face was like something out of a Hitchcock episode.

With deep sorrow and regret, Tim realized he was now eternally separated from God's love. He would have been in heaven with his family if he had only submitted to the Lord. Yielding to the woes he had brought upon himself, Tim released a loud wail and started beating his chest with his hand.

Seconds later, the laughter of Legion and his host of evil spirits echoed throughout the abyss.

When the last lost human soul had humbled himself in the Graveyard, the host of the underworld assembled to rejoice over their great accomplishment one last time. "Well done, my children," Satan announced mournfully. "Now, we must join them."

Defeated, the Prince of the Power of the Air and his followers assumed kneeling positions among the other condemned bodies in the Graveyard of Pride, never to rise again.

From his Throne, Christos lifted his hand and announced, "All those who opposed me have been defeated. The old earth has passed away. A new earth has begun." A pulse resembling a giant tidal wave of light left the Throne and raced throughout the universe he created. The pride that caused Satan and mankind to fall had been destroyed. Those in the graveyard finally understood that all their vain attempts to dethrone God had failed. The sacrificial Lamb of God now reigns victorious over his kingdom.

Chapter 19

Kate's Journey Home

The path Kate walked was paved with shiny gold bricks. Each one was placed and leveled with precision and care. To her left was a short stone wall that separated the path from an endless patch of stunning flowers. Although she could name each plant, she had never seen them before. As she breathed in their soothing fragrance, Kate felt at peace. There were no worrisome thoughts of her past life, no anguish over losing Tim to Legion, only the fond memories of the good times she shared with those who made it to the place she was headed. She remembered she was in her eighties when she passed. Now Kate was young again, about thirty—never to age again.

To the right of the path was a narrow stream filled with river rock; their colors were unique to the world she came from. Its gentle flow was relaxing. Kate knew this water flowed from the throne of God. As the water passed by larger exposed rocks, the rippled sound was amplified to that of a small waterfall.

Kate felt no urgency to reach her new home, so she stopped to admire this extraordinary setting. A short distance beyond the brook was a forest full of beautifully shaped trees. Throughout the woods were patches of fall colors intermingled with areas of varying shades of green, pink, yellow, and red. All appeared to have been brushed on by a giant paintbrush. The landscaper of this forestland must have had the four seasons in mind when he planted each sapling.

Above her was an infinite blue sky that held no sun. The oddity of the thought never crossed Kate's mind. Her knowledge of this one-of-a-kind place and its Curator were revealed to her the moment she set foot on the path. The needs of her past existence were replaced by a strong desire to praise the One who called her to this exquisite place.

A family of geese swimming in the brook slowly made their way toward Kate. Stepping from the path onto an immaculately manicured lawn, she felt its softness under her feet and remembered those innocent barefoot days she enjoyed as a child. In the distance, deer, bison, lions, and other land creatures roamed leisurely and without fear.

Before her was a pool of crystal-clear waters filled with fish that gathered as she approached. Frogs along the banks croaked out their still-familiar tune while birds of every kind cheerfully sang their melodious praises to Christos. To Kate's delight, all of nature was in complete harmony, offering their tributes to the enthroned King of kings.

Beside her appeared a mighty angel dressed in a pale-blue robe. Upon his bronze belt was an engraved tribute to the Lamb of God. The glory of his presence pleased her greatly. "Welcome, Kate. We have been expecting you. What do you think of your new home so far?"

"This is so wonderful. It is even more beautiful than I expected."

The angel handed Kate a crystal bowl of small pellets. "You can feed them if you like."

"Oh, thank you very much. I would love to."

Kate scattered a handful upon the waters and watched delightfully as the fish playfully consumed their meal. Kneeling, she extended her hand and giggled as the geese assembled to take the food fearlessly from her hand.

The angel added, "Taste the living water, Kate."

The fish and geese seemed to understand and slowly swam away. He handed her a wooden carpenter's cup. Kate took the goblet and filled it half full. She then lifted it to examine it more closely. The engraving that circled the cup was in the ancient Hebrew dialect. Reading it for the first time, Kate had no difficulty deciphering the accolades ascribed to its owner.

Her first sip was filled with expectation, and it did not disappoint. It was the purest water she had ever tasted, laced with a sweetness that suggested honey. She took a second sip, and it tasted like strawberries. After a third sip that turned out to be citrus, Kate realized she could change the taste of the water as she pleased—one of the perks of her inheritance.

"He is waiting for you down the path, Kate. There is no rush, so take your time."

With his wings extended, the angel ascended into the sky and moved back down the path she came from to encourage other travelers.

As she walked along the trail, the landscape changed, sometimes dramatically, but the way remained flat and straight. Up ahead, Kate noticed a sign. As she got closer, she saw it was also written in Hebrew, with an arrow that pointed down the trail toward her new home.

Kate had no idea when she started her journey or how long she had traveled. The path was like walking on a cloud. The mountains to her left and right looked like they had been placed there for her personal enjoyment. The trail continued through the meadow between them. Kate was so taken with their splendor that she felt compelled to stop again.

Another angel appeared and suggested, "Why don't you stop and rest, Kate?"

Sitting conveniently beside the path was a park bench. Kate thought about when she and Mike sat on a bench much like this one outside the VA hospital the day they got the news of his illness. Now, however, there were no feelings of sadness or regret. Just the joy of knowing that Mike was waiting for her arrival, and as much as she had missed him, he was not the reason she was on this journey. Just a little farther down the path, Christos waited for her with arms opened wide. The thought stirred her with a passion she had never felt before. She knew it as the agape love that was recorded in the Bible.

A woman traveler stopped to pass the time. Like all the other travelers, she wore a full-length white robe with a crimson sash. "Hello, Kate. How are you today?"

"I am filled with joy on this gorgeous day, Sally. How are you?"

Their conversation started small, talking about the loved ones they expected to see again very soon. It moved from there to the earthly journey that led them to this path then to the excitement of finally arriving home. While this was the first time Kate and Sally had met, they were blessed with a common bond that united them as if they had been lifelong friends.

Others stopped to greet Kate. Each had a story about the wonderful things they had seen along the way. Like Sally, these were people she had not known before, but she now knew them as family.

Only one path led to the eternal home Kate journeyed to, and only a few faithful followers of Christos would find it. Those who failed to find the path suffered the same fate as Tim, eternally lost in a sea of misery and regret. Those who travel this road must walk it alone. Their backgrounds are varied, but their testimonies are always the same. They discovered the path by putting their heartfelt trust in the One who prepared it for them.

A voice softly said, "You are almost home, Kate. It's time for you to join us." With a quickened spirit, Kate rose and continued her journey. Behind her was an endless line of saints, just as eager to see the Lord.

Up ahead, Kate saw a beam of light radiating from the ground, shining into the sky. Its random upward flow of energy was the only source of illumination here. With her joy building, Kate knew she had arrived at her destination.

The traveler in front of her stopped briefly at the light before continuing the path. As she got closer, Kate realized the light emanated from a man standing beside the way.

The man hugged the traveler and pointed down the road just as she arrived. The traveler was given a gold crown and continued down the path toward the eternal city.

When Christos turned to greet Kate, she was taken by his gentle, yet piercing eyes. He was of average height and slender build. Extending his hands to take hers, Kate couldn't help but notice the nail-scarred hole in each wrist. It was the Lord, the One who took away the sins that would have damned her to hell.

Christos welcomed his child with compassion and authority. "Hello, Kate. I've been waiting for you. Did you enjoy the path?"

"Yes, Lord. Thank you for inviting me."

"It was my pleasure, Kate," the Lord said as he took her in his arms and hugged her. "Welcome home, my child. Your reward is just down the road." The Lord pointed to the vast city now visible beyond him. "Mike is waiting for you at the gate, and Rebecca will be along shortly."

"Lord," Kate protested. "Thank you for this beautiful mansion, but you have always been my purpose in life. Without you, I would not be here to enjoy it."

The Lord's reply was tearful. "Thank you, Kate. That was a lovely thing to say." Then a puzzled look crossed his face that concerned Kate.

"What is it, Lord? Did I say something wrong?"

"No, not at all, my child. I just thought that maybe your room should have been a little bigger."

Concerned that the Lord had misread her meaning, Kate inhaled to offer a quick retraction. Before she could respond, the Lord stopped her and gave her a wink. "Just kidding, Kate." With a big grin, the Lord added, "Go find Mike. He has much to tell you. I will be along after the last traveler has made their way here. Then the three of us can find that trail we discussed."

After receiving her new crown, Kate waved goodbye to the Lord and headed down the road toward the New Jerusalem. Kate looked over her shoulder at the Lord and marveled at how God could love her so much He died to bring her here.

Kate's heart surged as she beheld the splendor of this remarkable palace the Lord had prepared for the redeemed. It was like a never-ending jasper wall that extended into the expanse above her. Its walls stretched as far as the eye could see to the left and right. The path ended at a large opulent gate with doors open wide.

An honor guard of twelve angels formed a double-row reception line. Their shields and swords had been returned to the armory, never to be used again. Their wings were outstretched high above them in a welcoming salute.

From the outer court, Kate saw Mike and several others greeting new arrivals at the pearly gates. He ran out to greet her. Kate was not allowed to remember how Mike looked when cancer had destroyed his body, but seeing him now young and healthy again was joyful.

The hope of this reunion was the last thing they discussed before he died, so they were prepared for it. Mike and Kate had shared a human type of love in the world. However, in their new eternal home, their feelings for each other had changed to a heavenly love. They were no longer united as husband and wife but unified in the body of Christos.

"Shalom, Kate. I am so glad you have arrived. How long was I gone before you started your journey?"

"Greetings, Mike. It's been almost thirty years. I missed you so much, but the Lord took good care of us."

"Yes, I know," Mike replied. "He kept me posted on how you and Becca were doing. I understand the three of us have a jogging date."

A silent yet meaningful moment passed between them before Kate asked, "Where are Mom and Dad?"

"They are waiting for you with a multitude of others."

"Good. Becca is on the path. She will be here soon."

Kate stopped to greet each angel as Mike led her between the honor guards. Standing seven feet tall, each dressed in brilliant white robes with crimson sashes and stoles, a tribute to Christos's purity and sacrifice, each knelt, took her hand, and pressed it to their bowed forehead, symbolizing their pledge of devotion and service. She responded to each greeting with an extended hug. The angels reacted joyfully with wing flutters expressing their admiration and affection.

George and Sarah stood just inside the gate at the fountain in the city square with many friends and family, waiting for Kate's arrival. Their spiritual reunion was quite different from the human excitement of having a loved one return from a long trip. After this reunion, the partiality of family ties would be overshadowed by the unity of eternal fellowship with Christos and the redeemed.

Also waiting on Kate was Poyel. The security she felt after Mike's death only suggested his presence. Now aware of all he had done to protect her and Becca, Kate ran to him with open arms. Poyel extended his wings upward and embraced her. She had eternity to reacquaint herself with others, but meeting Poyel for the first time was a special welcome-home moment.

"Thank you for all you did for my family, Poyel. I am so glad to finally meet you."

"You are welcome, Kate. It was my pleasure." Over the years, Poyel had developed a special fondness for Kate. The sincerity of her prayers and testimony spoke volumes to him about her love for Christos. This was a common bond they would continue to share through the ages.

"I'm here, Mom," came a voice behind her. Kate turned to see Becca's smiling face. Although her love for her daughter had changed to that of a sister, she still remembered their close bond after Mike's departure.

"Yes, you are, Becca. Welcome to paradise."

"Yes, it is so breathtaking. Everything I hoped it would be and more."

Mike smiled as he embraced them both. He was grateful his family had made it safely through the storms of life.

"Dad, let me introduce you to my family, those who came after you."

Slowly, a small crowd of people began to surround them: children, grandchildren, and great-grandchildren. They were all there because of the faith that Mike passed on to his family and the faith Becca shared with her family.

One by one, Kate's friends and family came by to say hello. David, Linda, Jon Kelly, and many more were all there, each with a special thank-you for all the kindness she and Mike had extended to them in life.

"Look," Poyel proclaimed as he pointed toward the gate. "The King has arrived."

With the last of the redeemed now present, Gabriel blew the trumpet, and the heavenly host shouted so loud the gates to the abyss shook violently. Tim and his cellmates trembled in fear, regretting the day they were born. Satan and his horde grudgingly bowed their heads in submission and acknowledged their long-overdue tribute: "Christos is Lord. He is risen." Their pledge brought a tidal wave of regret, and sorrow echoed throughout the graveyard.

Christos walked through the crowd and welcomed the saints. Then he thanked the angels for their faithful service, and a sudden hush fell over the city.

Remembering her comment on the path, Christos walked over to Kate and smiled. All eyes in heaven were now fixed on her. With Mike, Becca, and Poyel at her side, Kate led out singing the first verse of "How Great Thou Art." The other redeemed in Christ quickly joined in. Poyel, the other angels, and the heavenly orchestra waited respectfully then joined in on the chorus.

Afterward, Christos stilled the fellowship and made an announcement. "Come, my friends. Our banquet table awaits. Let us be thankful for all our Father has provided."

3rd Squad Cast of Characters (Delta 23)

Name/Nickname, Rank, Corps	Description
Mike Shaffer, Sgt., USMC (Delta 23 Actual)	squad leader
Paul Magrini, Cpl., USMC	Bunker 1
Sam Slayer, LCpl. USMC	Bunker 1
Calvin Littlejohn, PFC, USMC	Bunker 1 radioman
Jack Finch, Cpl., USMC	Bunker 2
Leon "Wolf" Spotted Wolf, LCpl., USMC	Bunker 2 point man
David Adams, Pvt., USMC	Bunker 2
Desmond Demarco, Cpl., USMC	Bunker 3
Tyrone Lamont, PFC, USMC	Bunker 3
Gerald Grady, LCpl., USMC	Bunker 3
James Smith, Cpl., USMC	Bunker 4
Sam Fuller, PFC, USMC	Bunker 4
Darrell Greene, PFC, USMC	Bunker 4
Shawn O'Neal, Sgt., USMC	Bunker 5
Robert Russell, LCpl., USMC	Bunker 5
Bruce Tucker, PFC, USMC	Bunker 5
Larry "Doc" Ryan, HM, USN	Medic

Main Supporting Characters

Bill Lambert, SSgt., MP USA	convoy commander
Larry Parks, Maj., USMC (Shield 1)	commanding officer (CO)
Phillip Johnston, 1st Lt., USMC (Shield 2)	executive officer (XO)
Rod "Top" Adams, 1st Sgt., USMC (Shield 3)	first sergeant
James Duncan, 2nd Lt., USA (Looking Glass 1)	forward observer (FO)
Lonny Summers, 1st Lt., USA	Special Forces CO
Preston Stiles, 2nd Lt., USMC	Company A CO
Steve Lester, 2nd Lt., USMC	Company D CO
Steve Winslow, SSgt., USMC	2nd Platoon sergeant
Henry Johnson, Sgt., USMC (Delta 22 Actual)	2nd Squad leader
David Long, Sgt., USMC	1st Squad leader
Bernie Westgate, Sgt., USMC (Night Stalker)	2/9 Marines sniper
Joe Diamond, Cpl., USMC	2/9 Marines sniper
Jose Rios, Cpl., USMC	battalion clerk
Edward Keys, civilian	news correspondent
Jon Sackett, 2nd Lt., USMC (Eliphaz)	2/26 Marines
Vo Nguyen Giap, Gen.	North Vietnamese Army
Legion, "the Caretaker"	Satan's horde of demons
Eliphaz	Legion character no. 1
Bildad	Legion character no. 2
Zophar	Legion character no. 3
Katie "Kate" Summerset	Mike Shaffer's wife
Linda Thomas Long	David Long's wife
Tim Shaffer	Mike Shaffer's son
Rebecca Shaffer	Mike Shafer's daughter
William Kain	Tim's friend